IMPACT

The air rushing around us is louder now. We must be getting closer to the ground. The pod gives a sickening lurch, and the side I'm on drops, sending my stomach into my throat. I'm looking up at the people strapped in opposite me, all of them tilted forwards.

The parachute. It's all too easy to imagine a hole in it, the air rushing through, our drag decreasing as we plummet towards the ground, the hole getting wider with every second. And there's nothing I can do. Nothing *any* of us can do.

Through the cockpit window, I see the ground. We're close enough to pick out every rock, every crack in the terrain. It's rushing towards us, way too fast.

"Everybody hang on!" Syria says. We're skimming over the ground now – it's moving too fast, the texture of the dirt blurring as I look at it. I try to picture Carver and Prakesh, holding them uppermost in my mind.

There's a grinding, wrenching crash. The pod flips over, and then everything goes away.

By Rob Boffard

Tracer
Zero-G
Impact

IMPACT

ROB BOFFARD

www.orbitbooks.net

ORBIT

First published in Great Britain in 2016 by Orbit

1 3 5 7 9 10 8 6 4 2

A CIP catalogue record for this book
is available from the British Library.

ISBN 978-0-356-50517-6

Typeset in Palatino by Palimpsest Book Production Limited
Falkirk, Stirlingshire
Printed and bound in Great Britain by Clays Ltd, St Ives plc

Papers used by Orbit are from well-managed forests
and other responsible sources.

MIX
Paper from
responsible sources
FSC® C104740

Orbit
An imprint of
Little, Brown Book Group
Carmelite House
50 Victoria Embankment
London EC4Y 0DZ

An Hachette UK Company
www.hachette.co.uk

www.orbitbooks.net

For Nix

Prologue

The meteor tears a hole in the sky.

The low-hanging clouds glow gold, as if the sun itself has dropped into the atmosphere. Then the white-hot rock rips them in two.

There's a shape behind the flames, just visible past the corona. A long cylinder, black against the clouds, attached to the meteor by a shimmering cord. The cord breaks, and the crack is loud enough to knock frost off the trees below.

The man on the ground throws himself to the dirt, hands over his ears, as if the pieces were passing right above the tree line. Icy mud soaks his skin, but he barely notices.

His cheek is pressed to the ground, the world turned sideways, but he can still see the pieces. Their white heat has faded to a dark red. Most of them are vanishing over the eastern horizon, but at least one seems to be plummeting right towards him, screaming down through the air.

He scrambles to his feet, trying to run. But the piece is nowhere near him – how could he have thought it was? It's going down in the east, the red metal fading to scorched black.

His heart is pounding, and in the split second before it vanishes over the horizon, its shape leaps out at him.

That's not just a meteor.

It's a ship.

Slowly, ever so slowly, the roar begins to fade. There's a final crackle, like fading thunder, and then it's gone.

His legs are shaking, but none of his companions notice. They're as stunned as he is, staring up at the sky.

One of them is moving, pushing through the brush, yelling at them to follow him.

"Think there'll be survivors?" someone shouts.

"No one survives a crash like that," comes the reply.

But the man isn't so sure. A long time ago, he was in one just like it.

1

Riley

The alarm starts blaring a split second before the shaking starts.

Aaron Carver is floating in the centre of the ship's medical bay, and Prakesh Kumar and I get thrown right into him. Everything else in the room is strapped down, but I can see the instruments and the bottles shaking, threatening to tear loose.

"What the hell?" Carver rolls away from us, putting his arms out to stop himself from crashing into the wall. The ship is rattling hard now, the metal bending and creaking, caught in the fist of an angry giant.

"It's re-entry," Prakesh says. He's holding onto the ceiling, and his body is swinging back and forth as the pull of gravity increases.

"Can't be," I say, my words almost swallowed by the noise. "It's too soon!"

But it isn't. We've been in Earth orbit for a week. Normally the ship would be spinning to generate gravity, but we've spent the past day in zero-G as we prepare to plunge through the atmosphere. There was supposed to be plenty of warning before

3

we actually started re-entry – enough time for everyone to get into the escape pods. It shouldn't be happening this fast. The G-forces were supposed to come back gradually.

My stomach is doing sickening barrel rolls, and my hands feel *heavy*, like my fingers are weighed down with rings. "I thought this was supposed to be a smooth ride," I say, trying to keep my voice calm. "The asteroid—"

"No good," Carver says. He grabs hold of a strut on the ceiling, the muscles standing out on his powerful upper arms. His hair is almost as long as mine now, although he doesn't bother to tie it back, letting the blond strands float freely.

"I *told* them," he says. "You can shape the damn asteroid as much as you want but if you're using it as a heat shield, things are going to get – *shit!*"

He spins sideways as the ship jerks and kicks, flinging him against one of the cots bolted to the floor.

"It's OK," says Prakesh, sweat pouring down his dark skin. Neither he nor Carver have shaved, and bristly stubble covers their faces. "We just sit tight. They'll come get us."

We all stare at the door. The alarm is still blaring, and the hull of the ship is screeching now, like it's being torn in two.

"They're not coming, are they?" says Carver.

"Just hang on," says Prakesh. "Let's not—"

"They would have been here by now," says Carver, horror and anger flashing across his face. "They're not coming, man."

I close my eyes, trying not to let frustration overtake me. He's right. The Earthers – the group who took control of this ship to get back to our planet – don't trust us. Not surprising, given that I tried to destroy the ship's reactor in an attempt to prevent them from leaving.

There's no way of stopping the ship. It'll be travelling at 18,000 miles an hour, even after it's passed through the upper atmosphere and burned off the asteroid it's tethered to, acting as its

4

makeshift heat shield. Getting off the ship means being in one of the two escape pods, and it's easy to picture the chaos as the Earthers rush to get inside them. They've either forgotten us, or decided that we aren't worth saving.

I scan the walls and the ceiling, looking for an escape route that we missed the previous dozen times we tried to find one. Not that we tried that hard – after all, if we got out of the medical bay where else would we go?

Carver half swims, half crawls his way over to the door, pushing Prakesh aside and twisting the release catch up and down. When that doesn't work, he kicks at it, but only succeeds in pushing himself away.

Prakesh stares at him. "What are you doing?"

"What do you think?" Carver makes his way back to the door, kicks it a second time. It shudders but stays firmly shut.

"It's locked, Aaron."

Carver swings round, staring daggers at Prakesh. "You think I don't know that?"

"Then why are you still doing it?"

"Because it's better than doing nothing, like *some of us*!"

"I'm trying to—"

"Both of you! Shut up!" I shout. I can't afford to have them bickering now. They've been sniping at each other ever since we were locked in here – Carver has feelings for me, and he's still furious that I turned down his advances to stay with Prakesh. It's something I've tried not to think about, a problem I've pushed to the back of my mind again and again, not wanting to make a choice, not even knowing how to start.

"We kick together," I say. "All at once."

I don't have to explain. I see Carver's eyes light up. He moves next to me, bracing himself against the wall.

"Aim for just above the lock," I say, as Prakesh gets into position on my left. "Hit it on zero. Three! Two! One! *Zero!*"

The door bangs as our feet slam into the space above the handle, but remains stubbornly shut. The force pushes us backwards, nearly knocking us over. Somehow we manage to stay upright.

"Again," I say. There's a hold on the wall, and I grab onto it with an outstretched arm, bracing us.

"Three! Two! One! *Zero!*"

The door explodes outwards, the lock ripping off the wall, and we tumble into the corridor. The alarm is piercing now, ear-splitting. Carver pumps the air in triumph.

The ship jerks sideways. For a second, the wall is the floor, and everything is a nightmare jumble of limbs and noise. Prakesh falls badly, his head slamming into the metal surface with a clang that I feel in my bones. In the moment before the ship flips back, I see his face. His blank, uncomprehending eyes. A trickle of blood runs down his forehead.

2

Okwembu

The ship's movement knocks Janice Okwembu onto all fours.

She staggers to her feet, leaning against the wall, trying to control the nausea. There's a blur of movement on her right, and one of the Earthers shoves past her, pushing her out of the way.

Okwembu tries to stay calm, but she can't stop her hands from shaking. She barely makes it to the corridor hub before she stumbles again. Her green flight jacket is bulky, but she can feel the frigid floor plates through the thin fabric of her pants.

The asteroid was supposed to have held up, dissipating the massive heat and shock wave of re-entry. Every calculation they did showed that the vibrations wouldn't start until they were deep into the atmosphere. But they got it wrong – a missing variable, something they didn't take into account. The asteroid is fracturing, leaving everyone on board the ship to scramble for the escape pods.

She looks up. Mikhail Yeremin, the leader of the Earthers, is at the other end of the corridor. His greasy hair frames a face

7

locked into deep panic. In that moment, it's as if he doesn't even recognise her.

He vanishes, ducking out of sight. Okwembu curses, tries to get to her feet, but the ship lurches again. The back of her head smacks into the wall, and bright stars glimmer in her vision.

There's a hand reaching for her. It's another Earther, a young woman – one of those who went outside the ship, using plasma cutters to shape the asteroid. She's wearing a ship jumpsuit two sizes too big for her, and her eyes are bright with fear. Okwembu grabs her hand, lets the woman haul her up.

The movement of the ship stops, just for moment, then becomes more violent than ever. Okwembu goes over backwards. The Earther reaches out for her, misses, her fingers brushing the front of the fleece she wears under her jacket.

They snag on the lanyard around her neck.

It pulls tight, the cord pinching against Okwembu's spine. The hold keeps her upright – just – but it's stretched to breaking point. The woman's hand is wrapped around the green plastic data stick at the end of the lanyard, her knuckles white. Any second now, it's going to snap right off.

With an effort of will, Okwembu balances herself, planting her back foot on the floor. The pressure on her neck drops, and the woman lets go of the data stick. It bounces against Okwembu's chest.

"You OK?" the woman says, trying to hustle her along, holding her by the shoulder. She shakes loose. She's got her balance back now, and she's feeling calmer, more focused. "I'll be fine. Just go."

The woman wavers, then bolts. Okwembu's hands find the data stick, holding it tight.

For the past week, while they prepared for re-entry, all Okwembu has done is scrape data, putting every scrap of information she could onto this one little stick. None of them know what's down there, what it's really like on the planet's surface – all they have is a garbled radio message, talking about how part of the planet has somehow become habitable again. So Okwembu spent her time downloading everything off the ship's antiquated operating system – water filtration methods, studies on the best soil for growing food in, atmospheric data, reactor blueprints. Maps and charts and graphs, petabytes of information. She doesn't know if any of it will be useful, or if she'll even be able to access it on the ground, but she's not going down without it. The *Shinso Maru* is worth nothing now, but its data is a price beyond jewels.

The lights in the ceiling are flickering, and the few Earthers she does see are panicked, moving like mindless insects. Contempt boils inside her, but she tells herself to stay focused. Contempt can become anger, which can mutate into panic. She can't afford that. Especially not now.

The escape pods are a short distance away, and Okwembu moves as fast as she can.

Riley

No matter how hard I shake Prakesh, I can't make him open his eyes.

Carver crouches down, shoving his head under Prakesh's left arm, hoisting him upwards. I do the same on the other side, heart pounding in my chest. Prakesh is amazingly heavy even in low gravity, his feet dragging on the ground between us as we try to keep our balance in the shaking passage.

There are shelves along the walls, with small plastic crates strapped onto them. One of them comes loose as we walk past it, slipping out of its fabric straps, and we have to pull to the side as it bounces off the walls and floor. The ship's jagged motion turns it into a pinball.

I pull Carver's head down as it flies towards us. Not fast enough. The crate just scrapes across his forehead, and he hisses in surprise, staggering into the wall. His hiss turns into a growl as his shoulder takes the hit.

Somehow, we manage to get moving again. I'm getting better at it now, bending my legs, anticipating the ship's movements. Carver is doing it, too. The screeching of the *Shinso*'s hull has been replaced by a crunching, grinding noise, as if bits of the ship are being ripped off by the friction of re-entry. I don't even want to think how fast we're going. I don't want to think at all. If those escape pods leave without us . . .

Just keep going.

We pass a window in the corridor, looking into what appears to be a gym. The treadmills and weight machines are straining against their brackets, slowly working loose. I catch our reflection in the window. We're a mess. All of us are wearing badly fitting flight gear – grey jackets and T-shirts that are too big for us. Stray strands of hair stick to my face in greasy lines. Prakesh's face is ash-grey, blood still dripping from his head wound. Carver's arms are straining, his face contorted as we pull Prakesh along.

I tear my gaze away, focusing on the passage ahead. "How long do we have?" I ask.

"Not nearly long enough," says Carver. I flash back to when we first came aboard the *Shinso*, when he asked me to use his first name: Aaron. I still haven't been able to shake the habit of using his last name.

We reach the junction. There's a sign on the wall, grubby with age: *Mining, Astronautics, Engines.* I jab a finger at the corridor on the left. "Astronautics. Let's go."

Prakesh groans again. It's like he's trying to fight his way back. I put a hand on his chest to steady him –

– And trip.

I try to catch myself, but my legs get tangled underneath me. I go down on one knee, struggling with Prakesh, Carver grunting in surprise.

Fire rolls out from the back of my knee, travelling up my leg and down into my ankle. I wait for it to pass, gritting my teeth.

Back on the station, a psychotic doctor named Morgan Knox implanted explosive charges in the muscles behind my kneecaps, blackmailing me so I would break Janice Okwembu out of prison. I cut one of the explosives out of me when I tried to destroy the *Shinso*'s fusion reactor, tried to stop the Earthers abandoning Outer Earth. It didn't work. And after we were captured, I had to beg the Earthers to take the second explosive out of me. It took a few days, but they finally did it, numbing my leg with anaesthetic and slicing me open. I'm slowly healing, but there are bandages on the backs of my knees. Both the wounds hurt like hell.

Everything that happened on Outer Earth feels like a distant dream. We still don't know if anybody on the station survived. Even if they're did, we're much too far away for them to reach us.

I push upwards, straining against Prakesh's weight. The corridor is even narrower here, and at one point Carver and I have to turn sideways to get him through a door.

The escape pods are right ahead, three sets of airlock doors built into the corridor, with big letters stencilled on either side in black. EMERGENCY USE ONLY.

While some Earthers worked on the asteroid, others worked on the escape pods. They turned them from space-going vessels into something that might actually be able to land on Earth, creating makeshift parachutes from material found on board the *Shinso*.

The pods themselves are too small to have their own fusion reactors, so they run off conventional liquid fuel. They're housed inside specially designed airlocks. There are Earthers everywhere, helping each other inside the first pod's open door, stumbling, panicked. An orange light above each airlock door blinks on-off, on-off. The floor of the airlock is slightly lower than the floor in the corridor, and I feel my knees jarring as we step through.

Carver and I pull Prakesh into the pod. There's a cockpit at the front with rows of seats along each side. Each one is a mess of thick straps, with a neck guard protruding from the seat back. Oxygen masks hang from the ceiling, swinging wildly as the *Shinso* bucks and writhes. I badly want to see outside, but the only thing visible through the cockpit glass is the outer airlock door.

The pods can take twelve people each, plus a pilot. All but three of the chairs are full. Mikhail Yeremin is there – he's checking his straps, his long hair hanging down over his face. There's lettering above his head: ESCAPE VESSEL 1. Underneath it, in smaller black letters, is a vessel name: *Furor*.

Carver perches on the edge of an empty seat, pulling Prakesh onto the one next to him. I lean in to help, yanking the straps down and buckling them tight. Carver does the same with his own straps, snapping himself in. We made it.

I stand up, intending to take the one remaining chair in the escape pod, opposite Prakesh. Any second now, they'll shut the door and we can –

Carver's eyes go wide.

Two hands grasp my shoulders, pulling me backwards. I cry out, my feet tangling up in each other, catching the edge of the pod's entrance. I land on my coccyx, cracking it against the floor plates in the airlock.

Janice Okwembu is looking down at me.

I haven't seen her since the day we came aboard. She's a former Outer Earth council leader who went rogue, joining up with the Earthers. The expression on her face is completely blank.

"No!" Carver shouts, fighting with the straps holding him to the chair. "Leave her alone!"

I scramble to my feet, moving as fast as I can. Not fast enough.

Okwembu looks down at me, reaching over to one side of the frame for the control panel. "Goodbye, Ms Hale," she says.

And the door closes in front of me.

4

Okwembu

Aaron Carver finally gets loose.

He shoves Okwembu out of the way. She collides with one of the seats, almost falling on top of its occupant, a man with tangled black hair and an acne-speckled face. Okwembu ignores him. She lifts herself into a seat, grabbing the straps, concentrating on buckling herself in.

Carver hammers at the control pad, but the door doesn't open. Of course it doesn't. Okwembu made sure to twist the rotary to the *Eject* position. It shuts the pod down in preparation for launch, to ensure that the door has a good pressure seal. It can't be opened again. Behind it, the inner airlock doors will be closing.

She hopes that Riley Hale has the good sense to get out while she still can.

Mikhail Yeremin is staring at her, and she doesn't like the expression on his face. She turns away, ignoring him, busying herself with her straps. She's still looking down at her buckle, and so isn't prepared when Aaron Carver slams her back against the seat. His face is inches from hers.

14

"Open it up," he says. When she doesn't respond, he barks the words in her face. "Do you hear me? Open it up."

"You should sit down, Mr Carver," Okwembu says.

He rips her straps away, lifts her up, throws her out of her seat. She hits the floor, wincing in pain as her right hand takes the impact, bending at the wrist.

Carver grabs the back of her jacket, dragging her to the door. Mikhail is almost out of his seat, huge fingers fighting with the catch on his chest. The other Earthers watch without saying a word.

Okwembu attempts to spin away, trying to get her arms out of her jacket. Carver sees the move, stops her, pulling her up so her face is level with the lock. "*Open the door*," he yells, right in her ear.

When she doesn't move, he wrenches at the rotary switch alongside it, trying to get it back to *Doors Manual*. Okwembu wants to tell him not to bother. The most he'll be able to do is tear the switch itself off the control panel.

"We need to launch *now*," shouts the pilot from the front of the craft. "Everybody better strap in."

"We're not leaving," Carver says. "Not until—"

Mikhail grabs him around the shoulders, shoving him backwards into his seat. Carver tries to get back up, but Mikhail won't let him, holding him in place as he clicks the catch shut.

"You don't strap in, you die," he says.

Okwembu takes the gap. She staggers back to her seat, heart pounding, strapping herself in. She looks up to see that Carver has stopped fighting. He's gripping his straps tight, his fingers bloodless. Mikhail is making his way back to his own seat, grabbing at the straps.

"She'd better make it," Carver says, looking Okwembu right in the eyes. "Or I'm going to *end* you."

In the moment before the pilot launches the pod, she wonders about Carver. She shouldn't be surprised at his actions. He doesn't have any sort of vision or understanding of the wider consequences of what's happening here. What he has are mechanical skills, and Prakesh Kumar, sitting next to him, has agricultural ones. The moment she saw the make-up of this pod, she knew it was the one she needed to be in.

The people inside it – Carver, Kumar, the other Earthers – all have skills that can be used on the planet below. Hale doesn't. She can run, and she can fight, and as far as Okwembu is concerned neither one is particularly useful.

It's more than that, she thinks. *You wanted to do it. You wanted to put her in her place.*

Okwembu closes her eyes, and the pod explodes away from the ship.

5

Riley

I lose control.

If the pod's door wasn't made of metal, if it wasn't completely beyond human strength to do anything to it, then my fingers would be digging long channels in the surface. I kick and hit and hammer and try to wedge my fingers into the whisper-thin gap. I scream Okwembu's name, but the only thing that comes back at me are the waves of vibrations tearing through the *Shinso*.

"What are you doing?"

It comes from beyond the inner airlock door. Syria is standing there, staring at me like I've gone crazy.

He was a community leader from Outer Earth, from a place known as the Caves. He fought hard to stop the Earthers from taking the ship, but ended up here with them. Like Okwembu, I haven't seen him since the day we boarded the *Shinso*. He must have been locked up somewhere else – there's no way he would have helped Okwembu and Mikhail. He's tough and wiry, wearing a bright red flight jacket, and his dirty hair is thick with knots.

He works his way into the airlock and grabs me, then has to do it again when I tear my way out of his grip.

"Hey!" he says, grabbing my arm. "Are you crazy? There's a second pod."

"My *friends* are in there," I shout back. At that moment, the word doesn't seem adequate enough. Carver and Prakesh aren't just friends. They're everything. They're all I've got left.

Syria pulls me through the outer airlock door. It's starting to shut, the mechanisms sliding the door closed. "And we'll be right behind them," he says. "Guaranteed."

The second pod is twenty yards down the corridor. Before I can blink, Syria hustles us inside, shoving me into a seat and buckling me in. I don't have the energy left to fight back. The seat straps are tight around my chest and stomach. The shaking is getting very bad now.

"Release in ten seconds," shouts the pilot from the front of our pod.

"We have to go now!" another voice says.

"Negative. We need to give the other pod time to get clear, or we'll smash into it," the pilot says. I can't see his face, just the back of his head. A woman opposite me is muttering something that sounds like a prayer, her eyes shut tight. The name of the pod is above her on the wall: *Lyssa*.

I think back to Prakesh and Carver, tight on either side of me, our legs raised to kick down the locked door. All of us together, acting as one. I try to hold onto it, but it sends an unexpected spasm of anger through me – and this time I'm angry at myself.

I spent a week with them in that damn medical bay, a week where I could have talked to them, a week where we could have straightened out where we stood with each other. I wanted to be with Prakesh, told Carver as much, but it didn't stop the choice gnawing at me, making me wonder if I'd made the right decision. It didn't stop me thinking about how I kissed Carver while we were dealing with the last few hours of insanity on Outer Earth. I had all the time in the world to say something, and I didn't, and now I might never see them again.

And on the tail of that thought comes another. Janice Okwembu took them away from me. When I see her again, I'm going to make her pay.

I'll find you, I say, willing the thought to reach Prakesh and Carver, knowing it won't and not caring. *I don't care what happens. I'll find you.*

"Release!" says the pilot.

But there's no bang. No shuddering explosion. Nothing happens.

The pilot hammers on the control panel, each hit more and more frantic. But no matter what he does, our pod refuses to launch.

6

Prakesh

Prakesh is back in the Air Lab on Outer Earth.

He can see the ceiling lights through the canopies of the enormous oak trees towering above him. He can smell the damp scent of the algae pools, the thick musk of soil.

His parents are there, his father's arm around his mother. He can see every detail – his father's prosthetic leg, his mother's scarf, the earrings she wears. He tries to say their names, but when he moves his lips, no sound comes out. And they're not smiling – they're just looking at him, sadness lining their faces.

Then they're gone, and Riley Hale is there, standing before him. The woman he loves. He doesn't want her to speak. He knows what she's going to say.

Resin, Prakesh. The words come in her voice, even though she hasn't opened her mouth. *Resin. It came from you.*

He doesn't want it to be true. The virus that tore through Outer Earth can't have come from him. It's a dream, that's all. A bad dream. Any moment now, he's going to wake up in bed with Riley, in their hab in Chengshi.

The Air Lab is shaking. The tree branches are swinging back and forth, groaning, as if caught in a hurricane. Riley is gone.

There's a *bang*. It explodes through Prakesh's body, filling every cell, blotting out the world. His eyes snap open. For a moment, he doesn't know where he is. Then he sees Aaron Carver next to him, his eyes squeezed shut, G-forces rippling his cheeks.

Prakesh remembers everything. His gaze darts around the packed escape pod. Janice Okwembu is near the front, her eyes closed, her head tilted back. Mikhail is a few seats down from her.

They're in-flight. They have to be. That means the escape pod jettisoned from the *Shinso*. Prakesh tries to turn his head, pushing against the Gs, and gets a brief look out of the cockpit glass. It's a mess of black and red, matted with a dull grey. *Clouds*, he thinks.

The headache comes suddenly, flaring at the base of his skull. It's like a red-hot needle, jamming upwards into his brain. There's blood on his face – where did it come from? The last thing he remembers is kicking the door down, holding tight onto . . .

Riley. Where's Riley?

At that moment, the shaking stops. The escape pod stabilises, and the roaring from outside vanishes, replaced by the gentle hum of the engines. The G-forces holding Prakesh against his seat disappear, although the headache remains. An audible sigh of relief rises from the cabin and someone gives a weak cheer.

Carver still has his eyes closed, his head tilted back.

"Everybody sit tight," says the pilot. "Parachute's out."

"What's our location?" It comes from Janice Okwembu, her voice calm and controlled.

Prakesh doesn't hear the pilot's answer. "Where's Riley?" he says to Carver.

No answer. Prakesh licks his lips. "*Carver*. Why isn't Riley here?"

"Ask her," Carver says, jerking his head at Okwembu, thunder on his face.

Prakesh's eyes find hers, surprised fury igniting inside him. "What did you do?"

Okwembu doesn't hear him, or, if she does, she doesn't say anything. Prakesh twists his head, looking back at Carver

"But they got off OK, right?" he says. "They're behind us?"

Carver doesn't get a chance to respond. There's a distant boom, almost too soft to hear, like thunder from an unseen storm.

"There goes the *Shinso*," says the pilot.

7

Riley

The control panel of the *Lyssa* is a chaos of flashing lights. The pilot is panicking, shaking the stick back and forth.

This is what my father must have felt.

The thought is clear in my head. My father was on a mission to return to Earth, to establish humans on the planet again. His ship, the *Akua Maru*, suffered a catastrophic explosion during re-entry. He must have felt this, too. The same shaking. The same terror. My knuckles have gone white, my fingers gripping the seat.

"Gunther," someone shouts. "Check the couplings."

"Couplings are fine!" Gunther says over his shoulder.

"Then cycle the software. There must be—"

The bang feels like it shatters my eardrums. The G-forces rocket up, slamming me back into the seat and holding me there as the pod spins away from the main body of the *Shinso*. My eyes feel like they're going to drill out of the back of my skull.

A moment later, there's a second bang – the *Shinso* finally tearing itself apart. The sound reaches into the *Lyssa*, ripping through it, knocking us into a crazy spin. My head snaps to the side, then the other, at the mercy of the G-forces.

The other pod got off OK. I know it did. I heard it launch. I repeat the words in my mind, one after the other.

A hand grips mine. Syria. I want to look at him, but I can barely move. Everyone in the pod is screaming, held fast to their seats.

The G-force changes direction suddenly, knocking my head back the other way. I'm still squashed against the scratchy fabric of the seat, but I'm looking towards the cockpit now. I can see right out of the glass.

There are flecks of grey vapour spinning around us. The sky behind them is a dark blue, and at its bottom edge I can just see it turning to scarlet.

In a split second, the view changes. The grey vapour blocks out the sky – we must have fallen into a cloud bank. And there's burning debris, screaming past us – huge chunks of it, trailing fire. It's impossible to tell which chunks are asteroid and which were part of the *Shinso*.

There's a *thunk* as a piece hits us. I'm almost certain that the *Lyssa* is about to tear in two, but then our spin begins to slow.

"Drogue's out!" says Gunther from the cockpit. "Looking good. Everyone hold tight."

The parachute deploys. Our wild movement doesn't just slow – it comes to a sudden halt, snapping us upwards against our straps. I'm holding onto one at my shoulder, and two of my fingers get caught underneath it, burning as the fabric bites into them.

The noise vanishes, draining away. The view outside the window is swinging, left to right. It's not just sky now – there's something in the distance, a jagged shape, brown, capped with white.

24

"Gods," says Syria. It takes me a moment to see where he's looking.

Gunther's head is lolling onto his right shoulder. His eyes are dull and glassy, and I can see his right hand, drooping off the armrest of his seat. I've seen snapped necks before – it must have happened when the main parachute deployed. Maybe his straps came loose, or he hadn't secured them tight enough.

The air rushing around us is louder now. We must be getting closer to the ground. The pod gives a sickening lurch, and the side I'm on drops, sending my stomach into my throat. I'm looking up at the people strapped in opposite me, all of them tilted forwards.

The parachute. Whatever construction the Earthers cobbled together from the *Shinso*'s supplies isn't holding. It's all too easy to imagine a hole in it, the air rushing through, our drag decreasing as we plummet towards the ground, the hole getting wider with every second. And there's nothing I can do. Nothing *any* of us can do.

Through the cockpit window I see the ground. We're close enough to pick out every rock, every crack in the terrain. It's rushing towards us, way too fast.

"Everybody hang on!" Syria says. We're skimming over the ground now – it's moving too fast, the texture of the dirt blurring as I look at it. I try to picture Carver and Prakesh, holding them uppermost in my mind.

There's a grinding, wrenching crash. The pod flips over, and then everything goes away.

8

Prakesh

They should be drifting down slowly, held up by the billowing parachute. Instead, they're moving sideways, as if the wind has caught them, tossing them like a leaf.

"Too fast, too fast, too fast," Carver says, as if that alone will be enough to slow them down. He speaks more to himself than to anyone else, but Prakesh can still hear him over the rushing air. The man opposite him is praying audibly now, invoking Shiva's name, Vishnu's, Buddha's.

It occurs to him that they might not make it. It's all too easy to see the pod slamming into the Earth at hundreds of miles an hour, vaporising on impact, turning everyone inside to burning dust.

"Listen up!" It's the pilot, shouting back over his shoulder. "We're coming in over the water, and we're coming in hot. There's going to be one hell of a bang, so everybody—"

Prakesh doesn't hear the rest, because that's when he sees the water. Whatever they're above – a lake, a river, the *ocean* for all he knows – fills the cockpit window, glittering in the distantly setting sun. It's rushing past at an impossible speed.

Okwembu turns her head away, tensing in her straps. Prakesh does the same, holding on tight, thinking of Riley, picturing her in his mind, but all he can hear is Carver screaming, *"Fuuuuuuuuuuuuuu—"*

The impact lifts Prakesh out of his seat, ripping his head back. The whiplash takes him, snapping his head forward. A bright stab of pain lances through his neck.

They're airborne again, moving above the water. He can hear the rushing air above the screams from the pod's passengers. How are they still in the air? He remembers video footage he saw once, archival stuff: a stone skipping across a pond. Get the angle and the velocity right, and that stone could skip for a hundred yards.

But the pod is no stone. Prakesh has half a second to realise that they've flipped upside down, that he's hanging awkwardly in his straps, and then they hit the water again.

The impact this time sounds muted. It's a whooshing thud, vibrating up through the pod. Prakesh fights to stay conscious, to not let the pain in his neck and head overwhelm him. He opens his eyes – it feels like it takes him days, but he does it.

The pod is still moving, but much more slowly now. It comes to a rocking halt, still upside down. Prakesh can hear rushing water. He raises his eyes to where the ceiling of the pod should be, down below him, and sees why.

The water is coming in. As Prakesh watches, one of the panels shears off and a fist of water hits the man opposite him. The man chokes and splutters, his eyes wide with shock.

We have to get out of here.

The thought comes to Prakesh from a great distance. He wants to shout it to everyone, but his vocal cords have stopped working. His fingers move on their own, finding the strap release buckle on his chest.

He has the presence of mind to take a single, deep breath. Then he clicks the catch open, and drops.

9

Okwembu

The water knocks the breath from Okwembu's lungs

For one terrible moment it shuts her body down completely. She is entirely submerged, hanging upside down in her seat. Her arms and legs won't move.

The need for air overpowers everything, short-circuiting every rational part of her mind. Okwembu throws her head forward, desperate to break the surface of the water, aware that she might not be able to. Her brain sends out a desperate signal to breathe, and she opens her mouth wide.

Air. Beautiful, wonderful, air. She can't get enough of it, and she can't keep it inside her. Her lungs can't hold onto it, shocked into uselessness by the water. But she's above the surface, and awake, and *alive*. Electrical connections short out in bursts of sparks, lighting up the pod's interior.

A moment later, the water rises over her face. In a panic, Okwembu thrusts herself upwards, but she's strapped in tight and can't keep her head above the surface. The air vanishes, ripped away.

The other passengers are just like her, upside down, the

water over their chests. They're thrashing in place, fingers fumbling at the straps, desperate to get loose. Okwembu keeps her eyes open, forcing her body to cooperate. Through the dark water, she can see a huge hole in the back of the pod, edged with jagged, torn metal. *That's* her way out.

She is going to survive this. It's insanity to think otherwise. She is going to find the source of that radio transmission, make contact with whoever is sending it and continue her life. That's all that matters.

Okwembu works quickly, unstrapping herself, pushing past the panic, working the buckles on the safety straps. They come loose, but she's tangled up in them, her left arm pinned in an awkward position. She wrenches to the side, popping it free.

She doesn't know how to swim. None of them do. Nobody in this pod has ever encountered this much water in one place. She has to work it out as she goes. The water makes fine motions impossible, the cold robbing her of control. But she can still move her arms and legs, and she propels herself towards the hole. She forces her eyes to stay open, even though it feels like they're going to freeze in their sockets.

A hand claws at Okwembu. The face behind it is upside down, eyes wide with terror, like something out of a nightmare. The fingers are in her hair. For a horrifying second, she's caught, stuck fast. Then she twists away, pushing through the jagged hole.

Her next stroke gets her clear. It takes every burning atom of energy she has to keep going, but she does it, breaking the surface.

And all she can see is fire.

It takes her a confused second to work out what's happening. The surface of the water is burning, the flames licking against a darkening sky. *The fuel.* It's draining from the pod, ignited somehow, burning hard. Smoke stings her eyes. Heat bakes the water off her face, but below her neck she's almost completely numb with cold. Her clothes are heavy with water, holding her in place.

Movement, off to her right. Coughing and spluttering. A shadow, pulling itself out of the water, heaving its way up onto –

The shore. It's visible through the smoke, close enough to get to. She can make it.

Okwembu starts swimming, winding a path through the burning fuel. But her movements are slower now. Underwater she could swim, but here it's almost impossible. Every stroke feels huge, but seems as if it propels her no more than a single inch. Her vision shrinks down to a small, burning circle.

It can't end like this. She won't let it. But the circle threatens to wink out, and she tastes the water in her mouth, cold and sour.

Then she's being lifted up. Hands under her arms, pulling her bodily out the water. She slams into the ground on the shoreline, mud spattering her face, tongue touching dirt. Her limbs twitch spasmodically. She rolls over, without really meaning to. Her clothing clings to her like a second skin, and her legs are still submerged in the water.

Mikhail Yeremin stands over her, breathing hard, his shoulders trembling.

10

Riley

What happens next comes in flashes.

The seat straps are digging into my shoulders, biting down through my jacket. They're digging in because I'm tilted forwards, all the way, on the edge of my seat. My left thigh hurts, but it's a distant pain, and it doesn't seem important right now.

The bottom of the *Lyssa* is gone. The space where it should be is filled with rocks and dirt, jagged and uneven, the shadows falling in strange shapes. The rocks are speckled with ice, painted in a dozen drab shades of white and grey and brown. Here and there is a flash of colour: dark purple, like a plant clinging to the surface.

When I open my eyes again, there's movement. Hands. Feet. Someone falls, their body plummeting past me.

I don't see them hit the ground. My eyes are already closed. All I hear is the hard thud, and the piercing scream that follows it, trailing off as I sink into darkness.

I come back when something grips my shoulder. A hand. Syria's hand. His face is taut with concentration. He's hanging

31

off the side of the *Lyssa* – the pod has been torn to pieces, the metal shredded and pierced. Torn wires spit showers of sparks.

"Come on Hale," Syria says. His voice sounds like it's coming from another dimension. "You're the last one. Don't make me wait here any longer than I have to."

I close my eyes again.

Just before I go away, I feel Syria fumbling at my chest. His fingers are caught on something.

The buckle, I think. *It's connected to the straps, and the straps are—*

My eyes fly open just as Syria pops the catch.

I drop, tumbling head first out of the seat. Syria grabs me around the wrist, holding tight. I can see the muscles in his arm straining, the drops of sweat pouring off his brow. I swing in place, clutching at him with my free hand, holding on with everything I've got.

The *Lyssa* is tilted at a sharp angle. What I thought was the floor was actually the wall opposite my seat, and there's a fifteen-foot drop from where we are to the ground below. The dark purple things on the rocks are the shredded fragments of our parachute.

There's a body on the ground. A woman, writhing in agony, clutching her leg, her blue jacket spread out around her like angel's wings. She's half lying in a pool of water. It stains the rocks, creeping up their sides.

"Just drop me," I say to Syria.

"What?"

I don't wait for him to get the idea. I shake loose of his arm and drop, tucking my legs.

For an instant, I get a clear view past the edge of the *Lyssa*. More rocks, some the size of the pod itself, resting in a sea of dirt. The ground is steeply sloped. A giant gash has been ripped out of it, the *Lyssa* tearing up the hillside. We must have come in at an angle, crashing across it. I catch a glimpse of grey sky, the clouds low and dark.

I hit the ground. Hard.

My muscles aren't primed for it. It's uneven, nothing like the hard, flat surfaces on Outer Earth. I land at the edge of the pool of water, try to roll, channelling my vertical energy at an angle, twisting so the impact travels across my spine, but my feet sink into the dirt. It absorbs the energy, trapping it, and the precise roll I was planning turns into a clumsy tumble.

I somersault, landing face first, a dagger of rock jabbing into my cheek. My thigh is screaming at me, as if someone stuck a hot knife in there and is slowly twisting it back and forth.

I ignore it, forcing myself to get up, shouting for Syria before I'm on my feet. He's halfway down, clambering past the bottom edge of the *Lyssa*. The pod itself is almost torn in two, resting up against a boulder. There's a smell in the air I can't place, thick and pungent.

"Come on!" I shout at Syria. My words form puffs of white as I speak, and I suddenly realise how cold it is. The dry air scythes deep into my lungs. I'm aware of my fingers straying to my thigh, aware of them brushing something hard that sends little sparks of pain shooting through me. I look down, but my vision is blurry, unfocused. I can't see anything.

Whatever it is, it isn't slowing me down. It can wait.

The woman in the blue jacket is still on the ground. She's passed out, and two more Earthers are dragging her to safety. Their faces are smeared with dirt and blood.

I run in, intending to help, then stumble to a halt.

The ground on the side where the woman lies is churned up, with dozens of depressions formed by everybody dropping down. Depressions filled with liquid that I thought was water.

It isn't water.

It's fuel.

Highly volatile, flammable fuel. So unstable that it's not even supposed to be exposed to air.

There's a steady stream of it trickling down the large boulder. That's what the horrible smell is. And, above us, shredded wires are raining sparks.

"Get out of here!" I scream at the two Earthers dragging the unconscious woman. All I can think about are her clothes, soaked in fuel. There are two more Earthers beyond them, sprinting across the slope.

Syria is hanging, getting ready to drop. A thin stream of sparks rains down around him, and for the first time I see that he's wounded, blood running from a huge gash in his shoulder.

He lands awkwardly, stumbling. I sprint towards him, pulling him away from the crashed pod, my feet catching on the uneven ground. I can't seem to focus on any one object – the world is a mass of grey and brown, the freezing air slicing into my lungs. I almost fall, sliding down the slope a few feet, and have to use my hands to steady myself.

There's no telling how long we have, or how big the explosion is going to be. I don't even know if there'll *be* an explosion, but I've seen fuel before and I don't want to be around if it goes up.

"What about the others?" Syria shouts, looking over his shoulder.

"We don't – *watch out!*"

I grab Syria's shoulder, stopping him cold. What I thought was a pile of rocks concealed a short drop, the mucky ground sloping away at a steep angle. There are more rocks piled at the bottom of the slope, some as large as I am.

I hoist myself over, dropping down, telling myself to be careful. There's a crack behind us, a big one, like the boulder holding up the *Lyssa* is giving way.

34

Whoomp.

For a split second the world is completely silent. There's no air in my lungs – it's been sucked away, pulled towards the *Lyssa*.

There's no bang. No explosion. Just a sound that goes from a murmur to a *roar* in less than a second.

Syria screams. I'm looking up at him, and in that instant there's a halo of white fire around his body. His jacket is burning. With a kind of horrified fascination, I see his hair start to smoulder.

Then the shock wave knocks him off the ledge. He collides with me and sends both of us tumbling down the slope.

Sky and dirt whirl around me. I roll end over end, screaming, fingers scrabbling at the ground, legs kicking out as I try to stabilise myself, my thigh sending up frantic signals of pain.

The tips of the fingers on my right hand snag something – a plant, growing out between the rocks. I don't get a chance to make out the details – it snaps almost immediately, but it's enough to slow me down a fraction. I'm on my back, my legs facing downhill. I spread them wide, my heels bouncing off the uneven ground. It's crusted with ice, rock-hard, and I can't break through.

Syria is just below me, still tumbling. For an instant, I see his back, a terrifying mess of red and black. Parts of his jacket are still smoking. Before I can do anything, he smashes into the rocks below, howling in pain.

I'm coming in way too fast. I lift my legs, using every muscle I have to get them off the slope. It looks like I'm doing a complicated stretch. I slam them back down, and this time my heels catch, smashing through the crust just enough to slow my descent.

I come to a stop, bumping up against Syria. Even that light

tap is enough to jerk a horrified moan from him. He's on his back, his face twisted in agony, breathing far too hard.

The fire has turned the top of the slope into hell. I don't know how hot rocket fuel burns, but the rocks are blistered and blackened.

I get to my feet. I'm unsteady, off balance, but I pull Syria to his feet with a strength I didn't know I had. He screams again, tries to push me away, but he's too weak.

I don't know if we can outrun the fire, but we have to try.

I wrap an arm around him. As I try to get a grip under his armpit, my hand brushes his shoulder. It's baking hot, and the surface feels wrong: crumbly and soft, all at once.

No time to check. Moving as fast as I can, I pull Syria across the slope, away from the burning pod.

11

Riley

Gradually, the slope gives way to more level ground.

We're on the edge of a vast, uneven plateau. Behind us, a peak rises to the sky, its tip buried in the clouds. The air is hazy, but I can make out smaller hills around us, their surfaces barren.

I have to keep my eyes on the ground. There's plenty to trip over down there: slippery rock, patches of crusty ice, those weird scrubby plants with their brittle tendrils. Syria is almost a dead weight, barely conscious. I'm shivering – the adrenaline is draining out of my body, and it's beginning to wake up to how cold it really is out here.

Should we go after the Earthers? Try join up with any that survived the explosion? But even the thought of trying to get Syria back up that slope is too hard to take in. As it is, each step is a small miracle. I try to push myself into a rhythm, the same rhythm I used when I was a tracer: *stride, land, cushion, spring, repeat*.

"Stay with me, OK?" I say to Syria. He doesn't respond.

The fire might be burning hot, but it's not spreading. After a few minutes, it's a distant rumble, and the insane heat fades. I concentrate on putting one foot in front of the other.

We're on Earth.

The thought forms slowly. It's hard to take in. A few days ago, I was on the station, the only home I'd ever known. Every second of my life had been spent inside a metal ring, and I never once thought that I'd step outside it. It wasn't even something I took for granted. It just *was*, a fact of my existence that was never going to change.

I can't even begin to understand how this place exists. The whole planet was meant to be a poisoned, radioactive wasteland. Humans were supposed to have been wiped out. And yet we're here, out in the open. There's sky and clouds and ground and a horizon, stretching out in front of me.

Fear starts to gnaw at me. Just because we're walking around on Earth doesn't mean it isn't killing us right now. I could be breathing poisoned air, bathing in radiation, and not know until it was too late.

Of course, there's not a single thing I can do about it. If it's true, we're all dead anyway.

The light is changing. I raise my eyes skywards, and the strangest thing happens.

I see low-hanging grey clouds, growing dimmer as the sun sets beyond them. They run from one end of the horizon to the other, flat and unbroken, featureless, capping a world of distant, snowy peaks and barren rock. But everything is much too bright. I can't focus on things, and trying to do so plants the seed of a headache behind my eyes. I screw them shut, try a second time. Same result. It's like I've put on someone's glasses – someone with much worse eyesight than mine.

I decide not to look at the sky again.

We enter a shallow depression in the hill, bordered by more rocks, and that's when Syria's legs finally give out. For a moment we're locked in a crazy dance, as if he's my partner and I'm bending him over in a complicated move. But he's heavy, way too heavy, and he goes down, thumping face first into the dirt. That's when I get a really good look at his back

It's as if an amateur artist tried to mix red and black paint to create a new colour, and didn't quite manage. Most of his jacket is gone. Parts of it are fused with skin, melted onto it, along with his shirt. There's a large, undamaged section of it near his waist, flapping loose, but even that is only hanging on by a few burned threads. The skin itself is crusted black; the burned area runs all the way from his lower back up to his neck and across his shoulders. If I hadn't climbed down onto the slope first . . .

Don't think like that. You can't. Not now.

I don't know a lot about burns, but even I'm aware just how easy it is to get them infected. And we're out in the middle of nowhere, with no supplies, and the sky growing darker by the minute.

I need help. But any Earthers who were in the *Lyssa* are long gone, and Prakesh is –

Prakesh. Carver. The longing I feel for both of them at that moment is almost indescribable. I don't even know how to start looking for them – they could be on the other side of a hill, or on the other side of the world.

My thigh spasms. I bite back a scream, my fingers straying to it, finding the hard thing again. With the adrenaline draining away, I'm starting to feel more pain, and even touching my thigh sends a thin whine hissing through my teeth.

At first, I can't figure out what's wrong. I'm feeling a hard edge, but I can't see anything, just –

Then I see. There's a piece of metal embedded in my thigh. Shrapnel from the crash. Has to be. It's two inches long, almost flush with my skin, hiding under a thin slit in my pants fabric.

The wound is on the inner curve of my thigh, a few inches below my pelvis.

I can't leave it in there. If it starts festering, it might stop me walking, and if that happens I'm as good as dead. I won't be able to help myself, let alone Syria. My mind takes this thought and amplifies it. *Take it out, take it out now.*

I slip my pants down, the cold raising goose bumps on my flesh. The fragment is deep, but there's enough above my skin for me to grip onto. It doesn't look too big – I should be able to yank if out in one movement.

But isn't there an artery in the leg? Doesn't it curve around the area the shrapnel's in? I think back, trying to recall everything I know about how the human body works. *Prakesh, where are you when I need you?*

I take three quick breaths, grasping the ragged edge of the metal. I'm on the verge of stalling when my fingers act on their own, ripping out the fragment.

12

Riley

I don't hear myself scream. But I do see all the colour in the world drain away. Everything goes grey, the pain so sharp that I almost pass out.

Somehow I stay awake, looking down at the piece of metal. It's long and thin, no more than half an inch wide. It was embedded lengthwise in my thigh, the wound a shallow cut. My fingers stray to my skin – there's blood, but nothing like the amount an artery would pump out. I hang my head, sucking in deep breaths through my nose.

The wound still hurts like hell, but it's a manageable pain. I rip a length out of the bottom of my shirt, binding the wound tight. That makes everything go grey again, but only for an instant. *You can deal with this. You have to.*

That's when I hear it.

At first, I mistake it for the noise of the fire. But that faded long ago. This is different: a distant rushing sound, so quiet that I think I've imagined it at first. But then I get a fix on it.

That's water. There's water near here.

41

Syria is awake again, groaning. I crouch down, resisting the temptation to put a hand on his shoulder.

"Hey," I say. "Can you hear me?"

His voice, when it comes, sounds as blistered as the skin on his back. "Where are we?"

"I don't know. But I'm going to get you some water, OK? I think there's some of it close by."

"Hurts," he says. "Hurts bad."

"I know. Just . . . hang in there. I'll be back as fast as I can."

I walk a few steps, picking my way up the edge of the depression, and stop.

How am I going to find my way back here? It's all very well heading for the water, but I don't know how far away it is. I could get lost on the return journey – there are no landmarks here, nothing but rocks and dirt. Syria would . . .

Syria. That's it.

I turn back, kneeling next to him. Then I snag the undamaged part of his jacket, working it loose as carefully as I can. It would be better to use my own clothing, but the bright red cloth will be easier to see in the fading light – and since I used a strip of my shirt to bind my thigh wound, I might not have enough.

I'm a little worried about hurting him, but the piece comes away easily. I start tearing it into strips. They don't need to be that big, and soon I have a dozen or so in my hands.

"Just hang in there," I say again. It's all I can think of.

I climb over the top of the depression, clambering over the rocks. One of the plants is there, its branches trembling in the frigid wind. I take a strip of fabric, and tie it on. It's caught by the wind, a bright red flag, easy to pick out even in the gathering dusk.

There are other plants dotted here and there. I make my way down the slope, skidding every so often as I lose my footing on the rocks. Just when I'm about to lose sight of the first strip I take another and tie it onto a second plant.

I don't know what'll happen if I run out of strips before I reach the water.

But the sound is louder now, somewhere ahead and to the left. My legs are shaky and uneven, and I'm conscious of how hungry I am. Cold, too, with every breath showing itself in a puff of white vapour at my lips.

My dad's ship crashed in eastern Russia. I don't how close that is to where we are right now. He spent seven years trying to stay alive, desperately trying to get back to us. I had to destroy his ship to save the station, and, in the few minutes I had to talk to him, he told me about where they landed. Kamchatka, it was called. Cold, barren, hostile to life, the air a toxic soup, the environment battered by deadly dust storms. The craziness of this entire situation crowds in on me again – how am I able to walk around out here, without freezing solid or suffocating? How am I even here?

I take a deep breath, pushing back the panicky thoughts. I don't know where I am, or what I'm dealing with. I can only focus on what's in front of me.

The slope steepens slightly. I have to place my steps carefully, stopping every so often to tie a strip of fabric to a branch.

Soon I'm down to three pieces of the fabric. A few more steps. The slope is getting even steeper now. Two strips.

I stop, listening hard. I've been heading towards the water for the longest time, but now I can't place the source of the sound. It's coming from everywhere, as if the boulders themselves are picking up on it, twisting its direction.

I look back. The third-to-last strip of fabric is just visible, flickering in the dusk.

I head to my right, where I think the water is. But the sound doesn't change. If anything, it gets even harder to figure out its location.

With a shaky breath, I tie the last strip of fabric onto a plant. I can go a short distance from here, but not too far. If I get lost, I'm finished.

A few more steps. A few more. The sound is really loud now. I have to be close. But where is it?

Come on.

And then I step through a gap in two boulders, and see the stream.

It's barely worth the name. It's a trickle of water, a foot wide, narrowing to inches in places. The noise is coming from a waterfall, maybe five feet high, spattering onto the rocks from a hollow in the slope. The rocky surroundings amplified it, made the noise sound as if it was a gushing torrent.

I stare at it, feeling absurdly cheated. And yet, as I do so, the oddest thought occurs. It's still more water than I've ever seen in one place.

Thirst claws its way up my throat. I scramble across the rocks, dropping to my knees at the edge of the water, ignoring the pain in my thigh. The water is so cold it stings my lips. It isn't like the water on Outer Earth – it's sweeter, somehow. More full. I almost laugh when I realise that, for the first time, I'm drinking water without a single chemical in it.

None that you can taste, anyway.

The thought makes me lift my mouth from the water, but only for a second. I have to use the water – and not just for my thirst. I need to clean the wound in my thigh. I debate leaving it, but decide that it's more important to flush out the dirt from the wound than worry about chemicals that might not even exist.

I unbind my wound, wincing as I splash ice-cold water on it. The cut itself looks deep, despite the tiny size of the fragment that hit me. I have no idea if the water will help keep infection away, but it's all I've got.

I pat it dry and bind it up again, then sit back. Syria's still out there. I have to get this water back before it gets too dark to see.

But how? I don't have a canteen, like I would on Outer Earth. I'd give anything for my tracer pack right now, with its water compartment.

Inspiration hits. Working quickly, I strip off my jacket and the shirt beneath it. The cold is harsh enough to make me gasp. I put the jacket back on, zipping it up all the way. It's not nearly as warm as it was before, but it'll have to do.

I make my way back to one of the plants. Their leaves are small and waxy, sickly green in colour, but it looks like there are enough of them. I strip them off the bush, grazing my hands in the process. My fingers, I notice, are getting slightly numb at the tips. *Not good.*

I head back to the stream, carrying my bundle of leaves. The shirt itself is long-sleeved, made of stretchy nylon. I turn it upside down, and tie the sleeves tightly around the front below the neck, as if the shirt is wrapping its arms around itself. I stuff the inside of the shirt with the waxy leaves, pushing them down, trying to cover as much space as I can. There. A vessel, with the shirt's hem as the lip.

But will it hold water?

Only one way to find out. I crouch by the pool again, and drag the shirt through the water, open end first. A bunch of leaves float out, and when I lift the shirt up water cascades through.

I force myself to stay calm, retrieving the leaves, packing the shirt again. When I lift the container out of the pool, my hands all but frozen, there's nothing but a few steady drips leaking out of the bottom.

I breathe a shaky sigh of relief. OK. Now I just have to get it back to Syria. It's grown even darker while I've been working, and for a second I forget my rule about not looking up. The sky is turning black, with a thin band of grey on the horizon as the day fades away. Then my vision goes wonky, like it did before, and I have to look down.

It's hard to carry the water. The vessel is heavy, and I have to hold the fabric on the shirt hem tight in both hands. The fabric of my jacket is waterproof, near enough, but the shirt is still soaked through, and before long the top of my pants is dripping wet.

I can barely see the ground. The slope is steeper than I remember, and my legs are already aching. I have to concentrate hard to spot my tags. The water swings back and forth in my hands, pattering on the dirt. Apart from the slowly fading sound of the waterfall, it's the only sound.

My thoughts turn back to Prakesh, to Carver. Are they safe? Did they land close to us? I have a sudden image of them being drawn to the stream, looking for water, just like I did. I half turn, but the thought of abandoning Syria is horrifying. I stride forward again, furious with myself. I can't leave him. I won't.

That's when I realise I can't see the next tag.

I swing round, looking for the last one I passed. There. Just visible in the fading light, wrapped around one of the thin plants. *That means the next one should be visible from here.*

But it isn't.

I backtrack. Panic is sparking in my chest, tightening around my lungs, but I push it away. I look left, then right, then turn a slow circle.

Nothing. I can't see it. Did it come loose? Did the wind take it? I look downhill, but I may as well be staring into a black hole. There are nothing but shadows down there.

All I have to do is head uphill.

I keep walking, still looking for the tag, checking back over my shoulder for the previous one. And just at the point where I can't spot it any more, the slope changes. It's as if I've walked over the crest of a small hill, because the ground drops downwards again. I didn't see that on my way to the stream.

I keep going – and walk right into a wall of soil. Part of the slope is exposed, with roots poking through it, scratching my face.

"Syria!" I shout. My voice echoes into the distance.

13

Prakesh

There's a fire.

It's not big, and it won't last the night, but it's burning well enough for now. There are trees surrounding the lake; most of them are stunted and dead, their dry branches and leaves simple to collect. It was easy for Prakesh to pull in some of the burning fuel on the water's surface, lighting a dry branch while the others build a small pile behind him.

The *Furor* escape pod has long since vanished below the surface of the lake – and it *is* a lake, long and thin, stretching further than the eye can see. The forest around them is dense and dark, the wind rattling through the dry wood. The sun has slipped below the horizon, and the sky is fading to a dark blue above their heads.

The survivors huddle around the fire. Like everyone else, Prakesh is soaked to the skin, and he can't stop shivering. Every part of him, from his ears to the toes in his squelching, sodden shoes, is numb.

And yet, despite everything that's happened, he feels excitement. These trees didn't grow in a lab: they're entirely natural, sprouting from soil that might not have been touched by humans in a hundred years. He can't wait for dawn, can't wait to see what the forest actually looks like in the daylight.

Of course, that assumes they *make* it to daylight. Prakesh is painfully aware of how poor a fire is at transferring heat. They should find something to put behind them, something to reflect the warmth back. But he can barely move, doesn't even want to try it. They're lucky they've got a fire going in the first place – without it, they wouldn't last long.

"Rub your chests," says Janice Okwembu. She's kneeling close to the flames, and her eyes land on each survivor in turn. There are six of them: Prakesh, Carver, Mikhail, Okwembu, the pilot, plus the man who was sitting opposite him on the *Furor*, the one praying to every god he could think of. Prakesh struggles to remember his name. *Clay.* That was it. He's young, slightly plump, with long brown hair tied back in a ponytail. He's rubbing the chest of the sixth survivor: the pilot, one of the *Shinso*'s original crew. The man is barely conscious, a thick trail of drool snaking down his chin. *Kahlil*, Prakesh thinks. *His name's Kahlil.*

No one else in the escape pod made it to shore.

Carver gets up. He has to do it in stages, going first to both knees, then to just one, then to his feet, tottering like an infant taking his first steps. He's breathing hard – his jacket is gone, lost in the lake, and his shirt is a sodden, steaming mass.

"So now what?" he says.

Mikhail seems to be less affected by the cold than the others. He clears his throat, but Okwembu gets there first. "Well," she says. "We—"

Carver lurches forward, moving on legs that look as stiff as the dead branches on the trees. He's heading right for Okwembu, his fists balled up.

Prakesh forces himself to his feet, his own limbs aching with the effort, and gets in front of Carver. "Not a good idea," he says.

Carver bumps up against him, tries to push past, but Prakesh moves with him. Mikhail is up, too, reaching past Prakesh, his hands on Carver's chest.

"Aaron, not now," Prakesh says, somehow managing to push the words past his frozen lips. Okwembu's payback can come later. If they're going to survive this, they're going to need every pair of hands they can get.

Carver roars in anger. He tries to push past again, but Mikhail grabs his shoulders, not letting him. Okwembu watches, her face impassive.

After a moment, Carver turns to Prakesh, his face incredulous. "Are you kidding me?" he says. "After what she did to Riley? We should drown her in the fucking lake."

"That's enough," Mikhail says. He tries to make the words forceful, but they come out slurred together.

Carver sags, then points a trembling finger at Mikhail. "Your plan sucked," he says. "How many people did you lose? How many of your Earthers actually made it down? If you can call this making it." He gestures to the lake, where isolated puddles of fuel are still burning.

"They knew what their chances were," Mikhail says. "But don't you see? We *did* make it. We're back home. We can make a new life here." His tone is pleading, as if he's trying to convince himself along with them.

"We *were* home," Carver says.

"Outer Earth is gone," Okwembu says calmly. She glances at Prakesh. "Resin saw to that."

Carver stands stock still, then tries to make a rush for Okwembu again. It takes all the strength Prakesh has to stop him, but somehow he and Mikhail manage it. Carver rocks on his heels, breathing hard through his nose.

"Actually, you know what?" he says. "I'm done."

He stalks off, muttering, heading down the shore. He's shivering, clutching himself, nearly falling twice in the space of ten yards, but he keeps going.

Before Prakesh knows what's he's doing, he's following. By the time he reaches Carver, he's feeling a little better.

"Wait," he says. Carver ignores him, only stopping when Prakesh slips around him and puts both hands on his shoulders. Aaron's face is shrouded in shadow, but his shoulders are trembling, hitching up and down, vibrating under Prakesh's hands.

"Think about this for a sec," Prakesh starts, and then Carver punches him.

He's completely unprepared for it. Carver's strength has been sapped by the cold, but he still knows how to throw a punch. His fist takes Prakesh in the side of the head, and for a moment that side of his vision is gone, nothing but black. When it comes back, he's lying on the ground, and explosions are going off in his head.

Carver is yelling at him. "Where were you? She pulled Riley out of the pod, and *you were asleep*! You just passed out!"

Prakesh tries to speak, can't. It's not just that he can't find the words – it's as if the thoughts going through his head are too big to comprehend. One of his teeth is loose, jiggling in its socket.

"I'm going to find her," says Carver, staring across the lake. "You can come with me, or not. I don't care."

Prakesh knows Carver has feelings for Riley. It was hard to miss, locked in that medical bay. He wanted to bring it up, wanted to confront him, but he could never quite figure out how. Carver danced around the subject, too, radiating undirected anger. His usual upbeat, sarcastic personality had drained away. They settled for oblique remarks, snapping at each other, circling but never attacking.

And Riley's absence is like a physical pain, deep in his gut. But it's not just her. It's everyone on Outer Earth. His team in the Air Lab. His parents. And every single person who died after being infected with Resin, the virus which sprung from a genetically modified superfood that *he* created. They're all lined up behind Riley, and all of them are staring at him.

Carver might hate Okwembu and Mikhail. Prakesh does, too. But he has far more blood on his hands than they do. Not just ten more, or twenty, but hundreds and hundreds of thousands, dead because of him. He thinks back to his parents – he doesn't even know if they're alive or not, if they survived Resin. Even if they did, he knows there's a good chance that the decompression in the station dock will have wiped out everybody in Gardens. Probably everybody on the station. That thought, too, is an almost physical pain.

The tiny group clustered around the fire is all he has left. He *has* to keep them alive. It's the only way he can make it right – or start making it right. He can't do that if he's hunting for Riley.

He closes his eyes, and says, "We can't go."

"What did you say?"

Prakesh gets to his feet. He's steadier this time, despite the pounding in his head. "If we split the group up, we die."

"Yeah? Well, that's fine by me, as long as I don't have to be near *them*." Carver jerks his finger back at the fire, and the figures around it, bathed in shadows.

"OK," says Prakesh. "Go. Charge off into an environment we know nothing about, with no map and no supplies, at night, in the cold."

"I'll stick to the shore," Carver says, but he sounds resigned now. The punch drained the last of the energy he had stored up. "Riley had to have come down close to here. If we—"

"We don't know *where* she came down. We don't even know if her pod launched."

"Don't—"

"You could hunt forever, and never find her."

"So you're just giving up? Is that it?"

"I won't if you won't. But if you head off by yourself, you'll never make it."

Prakesh twists the bottom of his shirt in his hands, wringing water out of the fabric, giving him time to articulate his thoughts. "We don't know what's out there, and we don't know what the war did to the ecosystem. Most of the planet is a wasteland, and that has a knock-on effect."

"I thought this part of the planet was supposed to be OK for humans now."

"Maybe. But there could still be extreme weather patterns, localised microclimates." Carver is about to interrupt, but Prakesh talks over him. "We could be caught in a flash flood, a snowstorm. Anything. That's without talking about any wildlife we run into, or how we actually find food."

Carver frowns. "Wildlife? You actually think anything survived long enough to get here?"

"Hard to say without data. The global population of certain species might have been decimated, but it's possible that tiny clusters could survive, assuming they adapt. If they could migrate, hunt out food sources, they might be able to—"

"I get it, P-Man."

"Right. Sorry." Prakesh is secretly relieved at hearing Carver use that damn nickname. It means he's calming down, thinking more like his old self.

He gestures to the lake. "But if we stay in a group, we can cover a wider area. We can find food, shelter, fuel for a fire. We can keep each other warm. And then I promise: we'll look for Riley. We'll find her together."

Carver hugs himself, shivering. The thunderous look hasn't left his face, but he gives Prakesh a tight nod.

"All right," he says. "But if Okwembu so much as says one word to me, I'm going to do to her what I did to you." He grimaces. "Sorry about that, by the way."

Prakesh is about to answer when he hears a panicked shout from the fireside. He and Carver swing round. Okwembu and Mikhail are on all fours, leaning in close to the guttering flames. The smoke has grown thicker, swirling in huge curls around them.

"Oh shit," Prakesh says.

He starts jogging back towards the group, Carver on his heels. He's desperately hoping that he's wrong, but even before he gets halfway back, he can see that the fire – their one source of heat – is going out.

14

Anna

The noise drags Anna Beck out of her sleep.

For a moment, she can't separate reality from the nightmare. She was lost in space, drifting, alone, unable to move no matter how hard she tried. Slowly, she convinces herself that she's awake.

The hab is dark. Her father is sitting up on the other cot, blinking in confusion. Her mother is curled up tight, still deeply asleep. There's no alarm – they cut them off to save power days ago – but she can hear running feet, raised voices.

Then the voices resolve, and Anna hears the word "Fire."

She stares into the darkness. A fire isn't a reason to panic. The sector's chemical suppression system should deal with it, stop it spreading. So why are people freaking out? Why the running feet and confused shouts?

Something's wrong.

She kicks the covers off and runs, throwing open the hab door and rocketing into the corridor, sleep falling away like shed clothing. There's a man in her way – she tries to dodge past, but she's still not fully awake. It slows her reaction times:

55

she smashes into him, and she goes flying, skidding on her ass down the corridor.

"Where's the fire?" she shouts up at him.

The man is middle-aged, stubbled, naked from the waist up. He's holding a blanket around his shoulders, open at the front. Anna can see his ribs, gaunt and bony.

She scrambles to her feet. "Did you hear what I said?"

He blinks at her, and she wants to scream at him. Then he says, "Down in the gallery." He has the voice of a man who is not entirely sure that this isn't a vivid dream. He probably thinks he's going to wake up, and that Outer Earth will be good and whole again.

No point waiting to find out. She's already running, going as fast as she can.

At least it isn't far. She's in Apex sector: home to the station's main control room, the council chambers, the technicians who kept the place running. Outer Earth suffered an explosive decompression, a breach in the dock that rendered most of it uninhabitable. Everyone still alive – a thousand people or so – is crammed into this one sector, the smallest on the station. She can be at the gallery in five minutes.

Anna has no idea what she's going to do. All she knows is that she has to be there. So she runs, barrelling through the white corridors of Apex.

The last time she ran this fast was when the dock's airlock doors gave way, after the Earthers' attack. She almost didn't make it. The rush of air when the doors gave out almost took her off her feet. But she was in one of the side corridors then, a little further away from the dock. Someone – she still doesn't know who – grabbed her, pulled her along, got her across the border. It sealed shut behind her, leaving her sprawled across the floor, gasping for air.

Just before she reaches the gallery, up in the Level 3 corridor, she runs into a group of people packing the passage. Two stompers are just beyond them, pushing the crowd back. Only one of the lights in the ceiling is working properly, but underneath it Anna can see lazy wisps of smoke curling through the air. She can smell it, too, hot and sharp.

She pushes herself onto her toes, craning her neck, trying to see what's going on. She can just see into the gallery. There are no visible flames, but the catwalk is flickering with orange light. But why haven't the suppression systems kicked in? Where's the chemical foam?

A little way past the stompers holding the crowd back, a technician is down on his haunches, doing something to the wall. One of the panels has been removed, and the stomper is messing with the wiring, cursing and swearing. He grabs a hand-held plasma cutter, sparks it to life. That's when Anna realises what's happening: the suppression systems really have failed. If they can't fix them, the fire will rage out of control.

"What's happening?" she says to a man in the crowd.

"Electrical fire," he answers, not looking at her. "Circuit in the gallery floor just blew up."

And this is when Anna realises that there's nothing she can do to help.

She can run, and she can shoot. In the past few days, after Outer Earth shrank down to this single, tiny sector, she's discovered that she's good with kids, looking after several of those who found their way into Apex, who lost their moms and dads. Right now? None of those things are worth spit. What was she thinking?

At that moment, Anna feels every single one of her sixteen years. Sure, she could fight through the crowd, use her tracer training to get all the way to the front, but what good would it do? At least it looks like the stompers got everybody out – there should be nothing in the gallery but the escape pods, which won't do anyone much good anyway. No point escaping if you don't have enough fuel to de-orbit. Even if you somehow managed it, your pod would incinerate the second it hit the atmosphere.

She leans against the corridor wall, her eyes closed, fists knotted in frustration.

Two stompers, clad in black and grey, are trying to push through the crowd. They're a few feet away from Anna when she sees that one of them has a squat, orange gas canister in her hand. Supplies for the plasma cutters being used to weld the metal across the edge of the door.

But the crowd isn't parting. They aren't letting the stompers through.

Anna moves without thinking. She snatches the canister away. It's ice-cold, the pressurised gas inside filming the metal surface with condensation.

The stomper who was holding it lashes out at her in surprised fury. Anna ignores her. She takes two steps towards the opposite corridor wall, and jumps. She leads with her right foot, planting it squarely halfway up the wall, then uses it to kick her body upwards and outwards. She twists in mid-air, and now she's high enough to look over the heads of the crowd, all the way to the door.

Anna used to have a slingshot. She called it One Mile. It was nothing more than crudely welded metal with frayed rubber strips, but in her hand it became something else entirely. She could plant a shiny ball-bearing in a target from fifty yards away, knock grown men off their feet, shatter jaws and break fingers. She was that good.

One Mile is gone, lost when she and Riley and Aaron Carver were captured by the Earthers. But Anna can still shoot. She can still aim.

She throws the canister backhanded, sending it flying over

the heads of the crowd. One of the technicians is quicker on the uptake than the others: he catches it, taking it in the stomach as he wraps his hands around it. Anna has just enough time to see him turn, handing it off to someone else, and then she crashes to the ground.

The stompers pick her up, slam her against the corridor wall. She even recognises one of them: Alana Jordan, a heavy-set woman with long black hair and a sour face.

That's when she hears the *click-hiss* of the suppression chemicals. The smell of smoke vanishes, replaced by the iodine tang of the foam.

The crowd is cheering, high-fiving each other, hugging. One of the technicians – maybe even the one who caught the canister – is shouting over the noise. "We got it. It's contained."

Everyone visibly relaxes, shaking their heads and laughing, like all their problems have just been solved. Jordan lets Anna go. She dusts herself off, a small smile creeping across her face.

A man detaches himself from the crowd. He's handsome, mid-twenties, with angular cheekbones. He's dressed in the white jumpsuit of a council member, and he looks exhausted, his eyes bloodshot. Anna's smile vanishes. Dax Schmidt is the last person she wants to talk to.

"Are you out of your mind?" he shouts at her.

No, Anna thinks. *I've only got one foot out the door.* She's on the verge of spitting the comeback right in his face, but he looks as if he wants to reach over and strangle her. His anger is unbelievable, and it stops the words in her throat.

"That canister could have exploded," he says. "You could have killed a lot of people."

"Well, it *didn't*," Anna says, furious and embarrassed at the same time. People in the crowd are looking over at her, not even bothering to disguise their interest. "Besides," Anna says, pointing to Jordan. "They weren't going to get there in time."

"What? The gas? They were doing fine. They didn't need extra." Dax looks back over to the technician – they can see him clearly now that the crowd is dispersing. He's slotting the panel back on the wall, the plasma cutter by his side.

"But the stompers were—"

"I don't know how much you know about plasma cutters," Dax says. "They use them in space. They last for a really long time. You think the tech couldn't use a single canister to cut through a couple of fused power boxes?"

"But they—" Anna stops. Every word feels like it takes a year off her age. She wants to tell Dax that she's killed people. That she had a long gun, during the siege in the dock. But she can't figure out how to say it without sounding stupid.

"It's called a *back-up*, Anna. I sent word to the protection officers to bring it over in case the first one failed."

"Leave her be, Dax," says Jordan, turning away. "She's just a kid."

Dax starts to follow, then looks back over his shoulder. "You shouldn't be here. Go home."

Anna watches him leave. The exhaustion hits her like a punch to the gut, and she slides down the wall, breathing hard. She reaches up, grabs the edge of her beanie, and pulls it down over her eyes. Her blonde hair splays across her cheeks.

She would do anything to have Riley here right now. Riley, and Carver, and Kev. She has to tell herself, not for the first time, that they're gone.

It's just her.

15

Riley

I'm breathing too fast. I try to slow it down, but it doesn't help. Each breath sucks icy air into my lungs, slicing through me like a knife.

I don't bother calling Syria's name any more. I don't even know if he's able to respond. Chances are, he's probably passed out from the pain.

The wonder I felt at being on Earth has left with the daylight. The sky above me is pitch-black now. I just walk, heading uphill, trying to ignore the fact that nothing around me looks familiar. I laugh, the sound bitter against the wind – it doesn't matter. This landscape is the same for who knows how many miles in each direction. What were the Earthers thinking, coming down here?

My thoughts wander too far, and I lose control of my water container.

I'm already gripping the fabric so hard that my hands are aching and numb. I catch my right foot in a pile of rocks, or a plant root, or *something*, and the fingers on my right hand lose their grip.

There's a panicky moment where I'm scrabbling in the dark, half hoping that I can catch the edges again. Then a deluge of icy water drenches my pants. The leaf-filled shirt flops against me, dripping the last of its load onto the frozen soil.

For a long moment I just stand there, staring out into the darkness. Then I grab the shirt and ball it up, furiously scrunching the fabric. I hurl it away, and it gives a wet thud as it slaps off a nearby rock.

I howl. That's what it is: an uncontrolled, animal howl. It's a hot anger, burning bright, as if trying to force back the cold air.

And as my voice trails off, as the howl dies in my throat, there's an answering sound.

It comes from a long way away – a coughing bark, almost inaudible. I freeze, listening hard. The bark comes again. It's deeper this time, more drawn out, but then it's gone.

Seconds tick by. I let out a breath, the cloud dissipating into the night air. There's not just anger now – there's fear, too, flooding my mouth with a familiar metallic taste.

Whatever's out there isn't a picture in a tab screen or part of a story told by a teacher in some Outer Earth schoolroom. It's alive.

And it knows I'm here.

I start walking again, reducing everything to the physical motion of putting one foot in front of the other. I don't know if I'm going in the right direction, but if I don't keep moving I know that I'll just lie down and never get up again. I keep the slope ahead of me, keep climbing. *Climb high enough, and you can get all the way to the top of the mountain.*

I'm so deep in myself, so intent on movement, that I don't realise I've found Syria until I almost trip over him.

He's lying where I left him, prone in the depression. I get my footing, then drop to my knees next to him.

"Syria," I say. He doesn't respond.

My mind is already moving ahead of my words. I lost the water, but I can still hear the stream. I'll have to take him there, over my shoulders if I have to, no matter how much pain he's in.

He hasn't moved. "Syria," I say again, shaking his shoulder. The flesh beneath my fingers is a gummy crust. Even the lightest touch must cause him excruciating pain, so why isn't he—

Then I'm shaking him, trying to roll him over, screaming his name.

The screams dissolve into sobs. I sit back, shoulders shaking, breath coming in hitching gasps. It's almost completely dark now – I can't see further than a few feet in any direction.

He shouldn't have died here. He should have died on Outer Earth, in the Caves, the place he protected and watched over. He should have died years from now, surrounded by his friends. Instead, he died alone, in agony. Thousands of miles from home.

Okwembu.

Her name arrives in my mind from nowhere. It's a strange thought, as if someone else is speaking the word. I react, hammering on the ground, once, twice, a third time, tiny rocks leaving impressions in my skin. I barely notice. All I can see is her face.

She made me kill my dad, she helped destroy our home, she took my friends away from me when she shoved me out of the first escape pod. She didn't kill Syria, not directly, but she's why he's here. Without her, the Earthers' plan would never have worked. And now she's taken away the last link I had to Outer Earth.

It all comes back to her. All of it.

I've never felt such anger. The thought is so potent that, for a time, it's all I can hold in my head. When I come back, I realise I'm shivering, shaking so hard that my teeth chatter. Everything below my waist feels like it's made of ice.

I'll never find the stream again in the dark. I barely found it in the light. I decide to stay where I am – I can survive a night without water. But I *have* to get warm. The last time I was this cold was in the Core, back when Oren Darnell had Outer Earth held hostage, and that was a cold that nearly gave me hypothermia. If I don't find a way to get warm, I'm as good as dead.

I can't make a fire – or at least I have no idea how to. It's not the kind of thing they teach you on Outer Earth, where the general idea is to avoid fire of any kind. Besides, there's nothing to burn.

Inspiration strikes, and I jump up, running on the spot. But it only makes my aching muscles hurt more, and doesn't generate anywhere near the amount of heat I'd need.

I sit back down again, hard. If he was here, Prakesh would come up with a plan. And Carver . . . he'd have some gadget stashed away, a portable flamethrower or a miniature electric stove.

I close my eyes. *They're not here. You need to think.*

The Core. I was prepared for it then, dressed appropriately, with my dad's old flight jacket and several sweaters, plus thick gloves. Here, I've got nothing on but thin pants and a jacket – a single layer against the cold.

I need insulation. But how?

I could snuggle up to Syria's body – make use of his remaining heat. I could even take his clothes, or what's left of them. The thought makes me recoil. I won't do that. If there's nothing else, if I truly can't stay warm, then I'll revisit it. But there's got to be another way.

What about the leaves? asks a quiet voice in my mind.

I don't give myself time to poke holes in the idea. I scramble in the dark, using my hands to feel for the plants. I know there's one close by, and seconds later I find it, yanking it towards me. There aren't many leaves, and those that it has are crumbly and dry, falling apart in my fingers. I let it go, and keep searching.

I find another plant, then another, stripping them bare, and soon I've gathered enough to start stuffing them into my jacket. They're scratchy and uncomfortable, but I keep going, pushing them down into the jacket sleeves.

My hands are utterly numb, and the only thing I can see is my breath condensing in the freezing air. I shove more leaves into my pants, which feels even worse. Not that I have a choice in the matter – I do this, or I die.

Something moves against my skin.

I squeal, ripping my hand away. The thing comes with it – I can feel it latched onto my finger. I shake my hand furiously, and then it's gone. A bug. Had to have been. Asleep in the leaves, until I disturbed it. The idea that there might be others, crawling close to my body . . .

The cold is making it hard to think – my thoughts are coming in quick bursts, barely coherent. My stomach sends a radiating, hungry ache up through my body, and, right then, I realise just how tired I am. It's as if all the strength has run out of my legs.

I find my way back to Syria, the leaves rustling against my skin. My thigh is throbbing. I do my best to ignore it, curling into a ball, pulling my hands into my jacket sleeves and jamming them between my legs as I try to get comfortable on the hard ground. At least I'm out of the wind, hunkered down in the depression.

I hunch my shoulders, trying to get my ears into my jacket collar, but the jacket isn't big enough.

I don't know how long I sleep, but it's dark and dreamless.

I only wake up when a sound steals into my mind. The sound is a low growl, and it pulls me out of the blackness.

I open my eyes. They adjust to the darkness instantly, as if I've had them open this whole time.

The animal is right in front of me, no more than three feet away, its jaws wrapped around Syria's leg.

16

Prakesh

They can't restart the fire.

The fuel on the lake has burned away, save for a few flickers of flame in the centre that provide a little light. No matter what they do, they can't get any other wood to catch.

And the fire isn't the only thing that's gone. Kahlil is dead. He slipped away without anyone noticing, his sightless eyes staring at the sky.

Mikhail is on his hands and knees, blowing with all his might. It would look ridiculous, Prakesh thinks, if the situation wasn't so serious. He's already told Mikhail that it's not going to work – starting a fire from scratch requires fine motor skills. It requires time and energy to gather materials. The cold and damp is taking all of it away, but Mikhail won't quit. He keeps blowing, refusing to give up hope.

"Shit," Carver says, kicking a clod of dirt into the lake. The last cinder goes out with a puff, and Prakesh coughs as a loose wisp of smoke catches him in the throat.

Clay is praying loudly, invoking Buddha this time, praising his holy name. Carver rounds on him. "Will you shut up?"

Clay subsides, muttering. Carver looks at Prakesh, shivering as the wind scythes through him. "OK, P-Man. Your action. What do we do now?"

But before Prakesh can answer, Janice Okwembu speaks up. "We need to keep moving," she says, getting to her feet and dusting herself off. "Walking will keep us warm, and we can look for food."

"No." Mikhail has finally abandoned the fire and is sitting back on his heels. Prakesh doesn't like the look in his eyes, doesn't like the naked fear he sees there. "We stay here. You heard the radio message. There's *sanctuary* out there." He leans on the word, as if it'll keep the cold away. "They'll come for us. We swim out, we get more fuel. We restart the fire."

"And end up like him?" Carver jerks his head at Khalil's body. Mikhail glares at him.

"It won't work," Okwembu says, folding her arms. "If the people who broadcast that message are out there, we need to get to *them*. We can't wait for them to come to us."

Suddenly they're all talking at once. Mikhail and Carver are shouting at each other, Okwembu trying to intervene. Clay's prayers get louder.

"Enough," Prakesh says. When nobody listens, he bellows, *"Hey!"*

Everyone falls silent. Mikhail's shoulders are rising and falling with exertion. Above his beard, his eyes are gleaming with panic.

"She's half right," says Prakesh, pointing to Okwembu. "We keep moving."

Okwembu nods, but Mikhail growls in frustration. "We'll never make it."

Prakesh talks over him. "We're too exposed here. Feel that wind coming off the lake?"

The others nod. Of course they do.

"Moving will keep us warm. And we're not going far – just until we find somewhere out of the wind. Once we're there, we group together for warmth, wait until morning. It's the best chance we've got."

"We don't even know where we are," Mikhail says. Prakesh can hear the fear in his voice.

Clay stops praying, then clears his throat. "Actually, I think I do."

They all turn to stare at him, and he swallows before continuing. "I looked at some old maps on the ship's computer before we came down here," he says, pointing to the water. "I think this is Eklutna Lake. South shore."

He swallows again, knotting his hands. "We're north-east of Anchorage. It's far, but all we have to do is head that way." He points into the forest.

Prakesh doesn't wait for an answer. He walks away from the group, moving into the trees, rubbing his arms furiously. For a long moment the only sounds are his feet crunching on the frosty ground. *They're not coming*, he thinks. *They're actually going to sit there and freeze to death.*

But a moment later he hears them coming after him. He slows down, waiting for them to catch up. No one mentions Kahlil.

The ground slopes slightly, and before long Prakesh's knees are aching from the descent. His eyes have adjusted to the dark, but it's a relative term. The forest is as dark as space itself. He can just make out the stunted trees against the black sky. Once again, he feels that excitement – a feeling that refuses to go away, despite their situation.

How can there possibly still be trees down here? Why has this part of the planet survived, when everything they know about Earth says it should be a frozen, radioactive dustball? Is the planet starting to fix itself? How long has it been like this?

Surely not long – they would have seen it when they sent the Earth Return mission down, when they were scanning the planet for landing sites. That means it's only been like this for seven years, at the most. How is it even possible?

A hundred years before, the people still on Earth were using every technological trick they had to turn the tide of climate change. Cloud seeding, messing with the ionosphere, carbon capturing. None of it really worked, and then the nukes came raining down and it didn't matter any more. But here, something has changed. Something made this part of the world different.

His thoughts return to his parents, back on Outer Earth. The regret comes rushing back, rough and familiar as an old blanket.

But what is he supposed to do? How can he possibly help anybody who might be alive on Outer Earth? There's only one thing he can do now, and that's survive. If he's going to live through the night, then he's got to shut out everything else.

The wind has got worse – it's constant now, whistling through the tree branches and every gust freezes him to the bone. He keeps hoping that the slope will deviate, that there'll be a depression or gully where they can get out of the wind. But there's nothing – no matter where they go, the ground is evenly sloped.

Carver is to his right, and he can hear Mikhail behind him, swearing as he pushes through the foliage. He can't hear Clay, or Okwembu, and he doesn't want to lose them. "Everybody still here?" he calls.

"Still here," mutters Carver. The others echo him, one by one, their voices betraying their exhaustion.

Abruptly, the trees open up. They're in a small clearing, no more than fifty yards wide. There's a sliver of moonlight, peeking down through a tiny gap in the clouds – enough for Prakesh to see some strange structures ahead of them. He identifies an old wooden table, half of it rotted away. Plants have grown into it, winding tendrils through the wood. Next to it is what appears to be a large steel drum, now rusted, most of its top half gone. The bottom is still held in place by two metal brackets.

Prakesh runs his hand across the edge of the drum. It would have been installed over a hundred years ago, and probably hasn't been visited in about as long.

One thought leads to another. If humans really have survived, then they'll have managed to keep some tech going – they wouldn't have been able to broadcast a radio signal otherwise. The excitement rises again at the thought of what else might be out there.

He pulls his hand back from the drum. Wouldn't do to get an infected cut out here.

The others stumble into the clearing behind him. Mikhail collapses on the table, which groans in protest.

"Keep moving," Prakesh says.

But Mikhail is shaking his head. "No. No. This isn't right. We stay here. We can light another fire."

"Mikhail." It's Okwembu. She's shivering, too, holding herself tightly, but her voice is as calm and controlled as ever. "Get up."

If Mikhail hears her, he gives no sign. He's still shaking his head, muttering to himself.

Okwembu walks up to him, grabs him by the shoulders. "Get up," she says, and this time there's real fury in her voice. He ignores her, rocking back and forth on the rotten wood.

Carver strides off, heading for the other side of the clearing.

"Aaron!" Prakesh catches up to him just before he disappears into the trees.

The wind has got even worse, and Prakesh struggles to hear Carver's voice. "Forget that. He wants to stay where he is? Fine! Let him!"

71

"We need to stick together," Prakesh says, but he doesn't even know if Carver can hear him. He plunges into the trees, almost tripping over a rock, and has to put his hand against one of the tree trunks to stop himself from falling. The bark is damp and frigid against his skin, speckled with frost.

"Wait!" Clay screams the word, stumbling after them. Prakesh can feel a panic of his own rising, as if the presence of the others was the only thing keeping it down. He is colder than he has ever been in his life, and every breath feels like it has to physically claw its way out of his lungs. The wind has increased now, strong enough that he has to lean into it. He can hear the trees beginning to bend, the old wood creaking.

17

Riley

I stay as still as I can.

The animal lets go of Syria, its growl extending and twisting into a snarl. There's a gap in the clouds, enough to let in a little light from a hidden moon. I can't stop looking at the creature's mouth. Its teeth are a dull white, and saliva drips from its bottom lip.

A small part of my mind, walled off from the terror coursing through me, is fascinated. Outside of those in pictures, this is the first animal I've ever seen.

As my eyes adjust further, I pick out more details. Its two ears lie flat against its head, and its eyes have a lethal, primal shine. It's low to the ground, waist height, no more, with spiky, ragged hair – or is it fur?

The growl comes again, and that's when the fascinated part of me disappears. It might be the first animal I've ever seen, but it definitely isn't friendly.

Very, very slowly, I get to my feet. The beast takes a quick breath, interrupting the growl, but then it comes back at an even higher pitch. A tongue darts out from between the teeth, liquid and agile.

Terror has a way of sharpening my senses. How many times have I felt it on Outer Earth, and how many times has it made me a better tracer? It works now, because that's when I see the other two.

One of them is on the edge of the depression, almost invisible in the darkness. It's standing stock still, its head tilted to one side. The third is on my right: smaller, its fur darker than the others, opening and closing its mouth.

I raise my hands. The white vapour of my breath is coming in quick, trembling bursts. I'm speaking quietly, nonsense words, trying to keep the fear out of my voice.

I take a single step back, and that's when the first animal attacks.

It's shockingly fast. One moment it's motionless, and the next it's crossed the space between us and buried its teeth in my leg.

There's a frozen moment where I feel its teeth crushing through the leaves in my pants. Then they pierce my skin.

I lash out with my other foot. I'm already falling backwards, my arms whirling, but my shoe takes the animal in the head. It squeals – an oddly human sound – and lets go of my leg, its head twisted sideways.

Wolf.

The memory comes from nowhere. I was once ambushed by the Lieren, an Outer Earth gang intent on jacking my cargo. One of them had a tattoo on its neck. A red wolf.

I scramble to my feet. I don't know how fast a wolf can run, but right now speed is the only weapon I have. Ice crunches under my feet as I scramble into a sprint, hyperventilating, pumping my arms.

Behind me, the wolves give chase, their barks echoing across the plateau.

There might be a little moonlight, but it's like running through a black hole. Picking out details on the ground is impossible. I barely make it twenty yards before the wolves are on top of me.

And I'm not even close to fast enough. The wolves' speed is unbelievable. One of them lands on my back: a huge, hot, horrible weight knocking me to the ground. I feel its breath, burning against my skin. I twist and roll, shaking it off before it can get its teeth into me.

I spring onto my feet, legs apart, in a fighting stance. I'm surrounded – the three wolves have me in a loose circle, with a boulder at my back. The smaller wolf was the one I threw off; it's getting to its feet, its eyes never leaving mine. The bite on my leg is itching and burning. I'm trying to remember if wolves have poisonous bites, if that was something we were taught in school, but I can't marshal my thoughts.

All at once, the terror is gone. So is the hunger, and exhaustion. All of them burn away to nothingness, replaced by that seething anger.

I glance down. There's a loose rock, nudging up against my foot. I reach for it, eyes locked with the lead wolf.

It snaps at me, darting forward, but the anger strips away all hesitation. I bellow as hard as I can, swinging the rock in a massive sideways arc. The wolf drops before I smack it in the head again, twisting its shoulders as it skips backwards. Its legs are bent, quivering with energy.

Movement, on my left. This time, the rock connects, and the second wolf gives a pained howl as I smash it to the ground. My hand is buzzing from the impact, but I bring it back, driving it down into the animal's skull.

There's a *crunch*. Hot blood soaks the back of my hand, and the wolf's body jerks, its legs beating the air. It gives one final, piteous whine, then falls still.

I look up at the other two. They're backing away slowly, their teeth bared. Their growls fill the air.

I put my arms above my head, still clutching the rock, and scream at them. I don't even know what I'm doing. It's as if the anger has tapped into a part of me that I didn't know existed – something fundamental, a survival instinct buried deep in my DNA.

The wolves take off. The big one gives me a last look, and then they're gone, slipping into the darkness.

I'm still standing there, frozen to the spot, when there's a voice from behind me. "Guess you ain't such easy prey after all."

18

Okwembu

Mikhail is panicking.

He's rocking back and forth, trembling like a leaf. Okwembu stares at him. How did she ever think he would be useful?

If he wants to stay here, fine. She may not like Prakesh Kumar and Aaron Carver, but she's a lot safer with them than she is with him. But which direction did they go? They've long since vanished into the trees. Okwembu tries to remember. Her thoughts come slowly, the cold sapping her energy.

I have to get out of the wind.

She strides back to the table. "Move," she says to Mikhail. When he doesn't respond, she climbs on top of it, barking her knees against the wood, then puts a hand on his back and shoves. He falls forward, crying out in surprise, the sound whipped away by the wind.

Okwembu doesn't wait for him to get up. She clambers off the table, dropping back to the ground. She's not used to this amount of physical activity, and her arms are already aching. The wood is soft and rotten beneath her palms, but she pushes hard, using every ounce of strength she still has. If she can lift

77

the table upright, she can make a windbreak. It's far from ideal, but it's the best she can do.

The table lifts an inch, then thumps back down. Okwembu tries again, leaning into it.

No good. She's going to need Mikhail's help. But when she turns to find him, he's walking away, hugging himself, head down.

"What are you doing?" she yells after him. No reaction. She abandons the table, shielding her eyes against the biting wind.

By some miracle, she manages to get in front of him. He doesn't look at her. His eyes are fixed on a point in the distance. He keeps walking, as if determined to get as far away as possible.

"Mikhail, no," she says, putting a hand on his chest.

He shrugs her off. "We have to go back," he says.

"What?" She can barely hear him over the wind.

When he doesn't answer, she plants herself in front of him. He finally looks at her, and that's when she sees what's really happening. The panic she heard in his voice, back at the lake, has taken over completely. It's the panic of someone who finally realises that all their plans are utterly useless.

"Listen to me," she says. "We—"

Mikhail puts a hand on her neck, and shoves her to one side. She goes down hard, twisting her ankle, bruising splayed fingers on the hard dirt.

"It was a mistake," Mikhail says, raising his voice so that it cuts above the wind. Tears are streaming down his face. "All of this. We should never have come."

He starts walking again, and that's when Janice Okwembu decides she's had enough.

No matter what she tries to do, no matter how well-meaning her intentions, she is met with stupidity and cowardice. She is confronted by people who hate her, who want her dead, who would take everything she's worked for and smash it to pieces.

None of them realise how much she's sacrificed, how much she's put on the line for humanity. They're weak. All of them.

And she is tired of weakness.

She doesn't know how she finds the rock, but suddenly it's in her fingers, almost too big for her hand. She gets to one knee, then to her feet. Mikhail is almost at the trees.

Okwembu sprints after him. He doesn't look round as she approaches, and he doesn't see her raise the rock.

She swings it into the side of his head. He goes down, his legs crumpling, sprawling on his stomach in the dirt. Okwembu doesn't wait for him to roll over. She plants a knee in his back, and brings the rock down on the base of his skull. Then she does it again. And again.

Blood spatters her upper arms, dots her face. She barely feels the wind now.

After a while, Mikhail stops moving.

Okwembu takes a long look at what's left of his head. *I should feel something*, she thinks. Guilt, triumph, sorrow. He saved her life, pulled her out of the freezing lake. He should mean something to her.

But for all that she's done, for all the lengths she's had to go to ensure her survival, Okwembu has never killed anyone. Not directly. Not before now. And as she stares down at Mikhail's body, she feels nothing but quiet satisfaction.

She met weakness with strength. Cowardice with courage.

She tries to rise, but the wind is so strong now that it almost knocks her over. She saves herself by grabbing hold of a tree trunk. Her back is to the wind, and it cuts through her thin, damp clothing, turning her skin to ice. Strength and courage got her this far, but if she doesn't get shelter soon, she's not going to live long enough to reap the benefits.

She drops to her knees alongside Mikhail, wedging her hands under his torso. Gritting her teeth, she rolls him onto his side.

Then she lies prone, curling her knees to her chest, pushing herself into the gap. The thought of being this close to his body is revolting, but Okwembu finds herself regarding the feeling at a distance, like it's someone else's problem.

She's not completely out of the wind, and she's still bitterly cold, but it's a vast improvement. They're low down on the ground, and she doesn't think a falling tree or snapped branch will hit them. She can feel the last residual heat from Mikhail's body leaching into her. Nothing to do now but wait for it to stop.

Janice Okwembu closes her eyes.

She's still lying there when bright lights illuminate the clearing.

19

Prakesh

"What the hell is happening?" Carver shouts.

Prakesh can barely hear him. It's not just the roaring wind: it's the trees. The trunks are creaking, the branches grinding together. The cacophony is unbelievable. The air is a swirling maelstrom of twigs and dead leaves, scratching at his face.

Microclimates, Prakesh thinks. *Extreme weather. We should have expected this. We should have prepared for it.* He wants to shout all of this to Carver, but there's no point. They have to find shelter, and they have to find it soon.

All three of them – Prakesh, Clay and Carver – are bent over, leaning hard into the wind. Prakesh glances back at Clay. The man's eyes are screwed shut, his mouth set in a thin line, like he's trying to pretend this isn't happening. Prakesh takes a step, then another, willing his frozen muscles to work. How strong is this wind? Sixty miles an hour? Seventy?

Carver is the first to lose his footing. He skids backwards, his feet sliding along the ground as if it's turned to ice. Then he tumbles over backwards, somersaulting, face frozen in surprise. Prakesh throws himself to the ground just before

Carver smashes into him – he feels Carver's feet thump across his back, a hand scrabbling at his jacket.

He looks up to see Carver slam headlong into Clay. Somehow, Carver manages to hold on, grabbing him by the ankle. It stops him moving. He motions Clay to stay put, so they expose as little as possible to the wind. *Smart,* Prakesh thinks. If they don't freeze to death, then they might just make it through this storm. He makes himself stay down, too, tries to control his shivering.

There's a *crunch.* Prakesh raises his head a fraction, squinting against the icy rush of air.

A huge branch is tumbling towards them. It's coming end over end, ripping up the ground, and it's heading right for Carver and Clay.

They haven't seen it. They've both got their heads down. Prakesh shouts a warning, but it's lost under the wind. The branch is bouncing off the other trees, gaining momentum, smashing its way towards them.

For a second, he's amazed that they can't hear it, that they haven't noticed the presence of something that big and that destructive. Then he's moving, staying low, leading with his shoulder. A second later, he connects with Clay, his numb body barely registering the impact. Then he and Clay collide with Carver, and all three of them tangle up, a chaotic mix of limbs and dirt and wind. The crunching and cracking is deafening now.

The last thing Prakesh sees is the branch, rushing towards them. He closes his eyes, waiting for it to hit.

A bough rips across Prakesh's cheek, scratching his skin, drawing blood. Then the air rushes back into the space above them. The branch crashes further into the forest, finally wedging itself against another tree, ten feet off the ground.

The wind drops a fraction, just enough so that Prakesh can

raise his head without feeling like the muscles in his neck are going to snap.

"Come on!" he shouts. He doesn't know if the other two can hear him, and he doesn't wait to find out. The ground is still a gentle slope, and Prakesh propels himself down it, the wind at his back. It's all he can do to keep his balance. There has to be a dip in the landscape, a large rock, *anything* that will get them out of the wind. Carver and Clay have caught up, running alongside him.

Abruptly, the ground levels out. Prakesh looks around, and for a moment he doesn't understand where they are. The uneven forest terrain has given way to hard-packed ground. It's a strip, around ten feet wide, stretching away into the darkness on their left and right.

Prakesh's body is firing on all cylinders, his heart hammering in his chest. He knows the strip is man-made, but he can't seem to think beyond that. Doesn't matter. They won't find shelter, not here, not out in the open. He yells for Carver to keep going.

Lights explode out of the darkness.

Two huge yellow circles, four feet off the ground, heading right for him. It's such a strange sight, so *alien*, that all three of them freeze. It's only in the last instant that Prakesh moves. He throws himself to the side, his hands out in front of him, but he's much too late. It's going to crush them.

There's a grinding screech. The lights swing to the side, and whatever is behind them turns sideways. Prakesh sees wheels spinning, kicking up huge clouds of dust which are instantly whipped away by the wind.

The thing comes to a skidding halt, rocking gently from side to side. It's solid enough to resist the wind – Prakesh can almost see the air skating over the top of it. It's like the vehicle that Carver put together on Outer Earth, only bigger. This one has a fully enclosed body, squat and boxy, with a slightly angled back. The wheels are enormous, resting in the tracks the thing made when it skidded sideways.

One of the doors on the side of the vehicle flies open. The figure in it is silhouetted by the interior lights.

"Get in!" the figure shouts.

20

Okwembu

Okwembu doesn't have a chance to process the sudden arrival of the others. They tumble into the vehicle, sprawling across the floor in a tangle of limbs.

The man who pulled them in screams over his shoulder to the driver. "Get us out of here!"

The woman next to him slams the door shut. The driver floors it, and the vehicle bucks and writhes as it fights against the wind.

The inside of the vehicle is cramped and low, with two rows of seats facing each other. The seats are covered in torn brown fabric, worn enough that Okwembu can feel the metal frame beneath digging into her back. The others throw themselves into the seats next to hers. She can feel Carver staring at her, taking in the streaks of blood on her face.

The noise makes speaking impossible. The wind has picked up again, and it's as if what came before was only a warm-up. She can feel the constant pressure on the vehicle's right-hand side, an angry god trying to shove them off the road. Okwembu can just see through the glass at the front of the vehicle. The headlights illuminate a world of flying debris, most of it moving too fast to identify.

A rock appears in the windshield, tumbling slowly, nearly as tall as the vehicle's front end. Okwembu flinches, but the driver is already spinning the wheel. The tyres screech as they dig into the dirt.

None of them have seat belts. Aaron Carver slams into her right side, squashing her up against the side of the vehicle. For a moment, her ear is pressed against the metal, and she can hear the true ferocity of the wind. She actually *feels* the rock scrape the car.

The skid has made them tilt, lifting the wheels on the right side an inch or so off the ground. The driver spins the wheel the other way, but the wind has them in its teeth. They're slowly tilting, inch by inch.

And Okwembu sees why. The skid has shifted everyone in the vehicle to one side. If they don't shift their weight to the other in the next few seconds, they're going to roll.

Nobody else has figured it out. They're all scrambling to stay in their seats, all panicking. She has to act, and she has to act now.

She manages to get a hand between her and the wall. But she's not strong enough. She gets her foot flat against it, half twisting her ankle, gritting her teeth against the pain.

She pushes hard, shoving them off her. Carver was a tracer, wasn't he? Someone used to movement and centres of gravity? Surely he'll see what she's doing. But when she looks into his eyes, she sees only anger and confusion. He's not going to do anything. It's up to her, like it always is.

Janice Okwembu scrambles off her seat, and hurls herself to the other side of the vehicle. The tilt pauses, just for a fraction of a second, but it's enough. And it's Clay who reacts, scuttling on all fours across the vehicle, pushing his back up against the right-hand door. The woman does the same, and *finally* the others figure it out.

The vehicle slams back to the road with a bang that rattles Okwembu's skull. The driver wasn't expecting it, and for a moment it feels as if the vehicle will spin out of control.

Okwembu closes her eyes.

When she opens them again, they're back on course. She can still hear debris scraping across the vehicle's body, but they're on a steady path, the headlights slicing through the darkness ahead of them.

Trembling, she pulls herself back onto her seat. The others do the same. She glances at Carver, but he's not looking at her. He's staring at the floor, hugging himself, shivering with cold.

"Almost out of it," the man says, raising his voice above the wind. His accent is unbelievably thick, like he's chewing a mouthful of food. "Everybody just hang on."

Okwembu can feel that they're descending, winding down the slope, away from the lake. Exhaustion and adrenaline catch up with her. She bites the inside of her cheek – she has to stay awake. Her hand moves to the data stick around her neck, grasping it through her shirt.

After a while, the road straightens out. They're still deep in the forest, but now the wind is nothing more than a low murmur.

The man in front reaches over the seats, resting a hand on the driver's shoulder. "We OK there, Iluk?" he says.

Iluk nods, and the man turns back to them. He puffs out his cheeks, shaking his head.

"You're damn lucky," he says to them. He's a big man, with short black hair and a neatly trimmed goatee under a pock-marked face. "You hadn't come out onto the old forest road when you did, we'd've gone right past you, praise the Engine."

Okwembu doesn't have time to question the strange phrase. The man keeps talking. "These storms can last for days," he says, looking up at the roof as if he expects what's left of the wind to lift it right off. "We get the real big ones once or twice a year. Real big ones. Nothing like the dust storms they get further south, though. Those things last for months."

"Who are you?" Prakesh says. His voice is a croak, and he's shivering badly.

"Hell – hang on," the man says. There's a storage locker bolted to the vehicle frame above him, and he clicks it open. Okwembu can see food containers, water canteens, equipment the purpose of which she can only guess at. And blankets.

It's these that the man goes for, passing them out. Okwembu gives him a grateful smile, wrapping one around her. It's scratchy, and smells of alcohol and sweat, but it's warm. Their rescuers pass out canteens of water, and they drink deeply.

"I'm Ray," the man says. "Iluk's doing the driving, and this here is Nessa." He gestures to the woman. She has a face that looks as if it's chiselled out of stone, framed by long, dirty-blonde hair. Like Ray and Iluk, she wears camouflage-patterned overalls, open at the neck, with a thick hooded sweater below them.

One by one they introduce themselves. Ray nods to each of them in turn. "Any more of you out there?" he says.

The others look at Okwembu. She shrugs. "No. There was just the one – the man you found me with."

Carver opens his mouth to speak, but she cuts him off. "He wanted to go back to the lake, and I tried to stop him. He attacked me."

"Gods," Clay says. His face is pale, his shoulders shaking.

"You're lying," says Carver.

Okwembu shrugs. "You heard him, back at the lake. He panicked, and I had to defend myself. I didn't have a choice."

Okwembu can feel suspicion radiating off Prakesh and Carver. Before they can say anything, Ray clears his throat.

"What about the ship you came down in?" he says. "Where'd you land?"

Prakesh lifts his head. "We hit the lake. It's gone. Anyway, it was just an escape pod, not the ship itself. That burned up in the atmosphere."

"So no supplies? Any fuel, or anything?"

"Gone."

"Ah, shit." Ray shakes his head. "Prophet's not going to like that."

He glances at Nessa, and something passes between them, something that Okwembu can't quite figure out.

"Who's Prophet?" says Clay.

"We saw your ship come down," Ray says, ignoring him. "And I said to myself, Ray, the Engine has provided for us. It has sent survivors to join our cause. Prophet sent Nessa and Iluk and me up here, see if we could find where you landed."

He pauses. "Are you really from . . ." He raises his eyes, lifts his chin towards the roof.

It takes them a moment to realise what he's referring to. Prakesh speaks first. "Outer Earth?"

"I knew it!" Ray slaps his knee, a huge grin spreading across his face. His teeth have been worn down to tiny stubs.

"Outer Earth's a myth," says Nessa. But she's glancing at Ray, like she wants him to confirm it.

"Ain't no myth," Ray says, grinning. "Told you, didn't I? Where else could they have come from?"

"Why'd you leave?" Nessa says.

"Ask her," Carver says, jerking his head at Okwembu.

Okwembu's calm has returned. Carver seems to speak at a distance – he can't hurt her, not any more. She glances at him, then turns to Ray and Nessa, lifting her chin slightly as she speaks. "Outer Earth was hit by a virus," she says. "It killed almost everyone it touched. A few of us escaped."

Carver gives a bitter laugh. "She left out the part where she and her buddies blew a hole in the side of the station dock."

Stupid, she thinks, looking over at him. *Stupid and petty and small-minded. Just like Mikhail.* She exhales through her nose. "I've already explained why I—"

"You don't get to explain shit."

Ray clears his throat. "I see you folks have a lot to work out. But you're going to be fine. We're going to get you to the *Ramona*, and we're going to look after you."

Nobody speaks. The rumble of the engine is undercut by the howling wind, not as strong as it was but still forceful enough to rattle the sides of the vehicle.

Eventually, Prakesh says, "What's the *Ramona*?"

Ray smiles again. "You'll see."

21

Anna

The smell in the amphitheatre has gotten worse.

In the past, the station council used it to hold meetings, addressing the techs and functionaries that kept Apex and the wider station beyond it running. It's a huge room, two hundred feet wide, with a dozen rows of tiered seats sweeping down to a stage below.

The rows are packed with people. They lie on the floor, slouch against each other in the hard plastic seats, huddle in small groups along the walls. It's baking hot, and the thick scent of sweat hits Anna like a fist across the face.

She's still not sure why everyone congregates here. People have occupied habs and laboratories, the gallery, the mess hall. But the amphitheatre is in the centre of the sector, furthest from the borders. It's as if Outer Earth has decided to draw itself in, as if the people inside it find comfort in spending time together here.

She looks around, finally spotting her parents on the bottom row. Her mother, Gemma, is asleep, her head resting on her knees. Her father, Frank, is deep in conversation with someone, off to one side. As Anna gets close, she sees it's Achala Kumar.

Anna only really met her a few days ago, after everyone had packed into the amphitheatre. She feels the same morbid curiosity as the first time she saw her. It was her son Prakesh who created Resin.

Achala looks as if she hasn't changed her clothes in a week. The lines on her face are like deep cuts. "Don't tell me that," she's saying to Anna's father. "Don't *say* that. I deserve a place on that ship more than anyone."

"Achala." Frank Beck puts a hand on her shoulder. "Think about what you're saying. I know you want to see Prakesh again, but—"

"I have a *right*," Achala says, raising her voice. "They can't tell me I don't."

"We don't even know if he survived." He ignores the shock and anger on Achala's face. "I'm sorry, but it's the truth."

She slaps his hand away, then turns on her heel and stalks off.

Frank Beck's shoulders slump. For a moment, he looks so defeated that Anna wants to run after Achala Kumar, scream at her, tell her to leave them alone. She settles for wrapping her arms around her dad from behind, resting her head on his shoulder. She has to stand on tiptoe to do it.

He nuzzles his head against hers. "Hey you. What are you up to?"

"Just wanted to see how you were doing."

"Fine, sweetheart. Just fine."

"What was that about?" she says, pointing at the retreating Achala.

Frank sighs. "What do you think? She wants a guaranteed spot on the *Tenshi*."

"She wants to skip the lottery?"

"Mm-hmm." He perches on the edge of a plastic chair. "Can't

say I blame her. If you were down there, I'd probably be doing the same."

Anna moves in next to him. "You don't control who gets to go. Why's she bothering you?"

"That's what friends do. They listen to each other, even when one of them isn't thinking straight." He sighs, rubbing his left eye with the heel of his hand. "You'd think her husband would talk to her. He's a good man – used to work on the space construction corps, you know . . ."

Anna tunes him out. She's thinking about the lottery.

What's left of Outer Earth is dying. The fusion reactor keeps them spinning, maintaining the artificial gravity, and it keeps the water and the lights on. But its shielding is failing. No one knows when it'll go, but once it does, it's all over. Outer Earth will become a frozen tomb.

The asteroid from the *Shinso Maru* should have fixed it. It had all the tungsten they needed to shore up the reactor. But now it's gone, taken by the Earthers.

Their only hope is the one remaining asteroid catcher in existence: the *Tenshi Maru*. And it's still three months away. When it finally arrives, it's going to attempt the same re-entry manoeuvre that the *Shinso* did before it, using the asteroid it brought back. They'll ride it down, all the way through the atmosphere, taking their chances on Earth.

There are only a few spaces available on the ship. To get there, they'll need to leave via Apex's twelve escape pods – each of which can only take three people.

Everyone else gets left behind.

Even then, the trip will be crazy dangerous. The escape pods will get them most of the way to the *Tenshi*, but they can't dock with it directly – something about airlock compatibility. Every person in the pods will need to strap on a space suit, and transfer over to it.

Anna flashes back to the nightmare, when she was drifting in space, alone and terrified. Even the thought of going zero-G is enough to make a cold sweat prickle the back of her neck.

She needs to do something normal. Something beyond just worrying and surviving. She could go back to the Apex control room – it's not good for much these days, but in the first days of the crisis Anna spent a few hours there, trying to reach the *Shinso* on every wavelength she could think of. She got nothing but static.

She dismisses the idea – there's nothing for her in the control room any more. "I'm going to go find some matt-black," she says. "Finish the painting."

Frank gives her a tired smile, a final hug. Anna heads back up the stairs. Only a few lights in the ceiling are still illuminated, and she has to watch her step in the gloom. She picks up her pace as she hits the corridor, using the movement to chase the thoughts away.

The painting she's working on is in a corridor two levels above her: a mural of Outer Earth itself, hanging above the planet. Anna's never been outside, so she has to work from her imagination. She can't say why she's doing it – a few months from now, there'll be nobody alive to appreciate it.

She uses matt-black, a gluey residue left over from water processing. It's difficult to work with, but it's perfect for painting: a deep, velvety black that no other chemical mix can replicate. Anna loves it, even if it sticks her fingers together.

Her father used to work in the water-processing facilities, and she never wanted for matt-black. That's all changed. Still, she has at least one good source for it.

The hab is on the other side of the sector, on the top level. She comes to a halt outside the door, getting her breath back, resting her head against the cool metal wall. Not for the first time, she marvels at how white the corridors are here. How impossibly clean they are.

She raps on the door. There are muffled sounds from within, as if the occupant is getting out of bed. "Just a minute," he says.

"It's Anna," she says.

"Yeah, OK. Hang on."

The sounds continue. She's still standing there twenty seconds later, about to knock again, when the door clunks open.

All the doctors Anna has ever known look like they haven't slept in years. Elijah Arroway is no exception. It's impossible to picture him without the deep bags under his eyes, without the weary slump of his shoulders. Arroway was put in charge of fighting the Resin outbreak, and he still looks as if he hasn't quite recovered.

He's been handling water processing for Apex. It was what he did before he became a doctor, and they needed that more than they needed his medical training. All of which made him Anna's number one matt-black source.

He attempts a smile when he sees her, doesn't quite manage it. "Anna. Not a good time, I'm afraid."

"Oh. OK," Anna says, frowning. It's not like Arroway to be so abrupt. She shakes it off – they're all on edge. "Just came for the matt."

"The . . . right. Of course."

He turns and walks back into the hab. It's tiny, no more than a few yards across, with a single cot tucked against the wall on the left. The door to the bathroom at the back is slightly open, and Anna can smell the tang of the chemical toilet.

There's a low table in the corner. A rectangular plastic container sits on top of it, filled to the brim with the glistening black substance. Anna leans against the doorframe, and, as she does so, she notices something odd. There's a duffel bag on the unmade bed, jammed full of clothes. The bottom half of a sleeve hangs out of it, draped across the covers.

"Here," Arroway says.

Anna pulls her gaze away from the bag. She has to take the container with both hands, and the matt-black sloshes gently as she does so. She gets her forearms under it, smiling thanks.

"Moving hab?" she says, nodding at the bag.

Arroway grimaces again. "Toilet's broken. They've got a spot downstairs I can use."

"Right," she says, and then can't think of anything else to say.

"Well," Arroway says, nodding to her. He closes the door gently, clicking it shut in her face.

She stands there for a moment. Then she shakes her head, and walks back down the corridor.

The matt-black in her arms is heavier than she expected, and she has to stop to rest several times, carefully placing it next to her on the floor. The second time she stops, she idly dips the tip of her index finger in the substance, tracing a delicate curlicue on the corridor floor. She rubs that fingertip against her thumb, enjoying the slightly rubbery give of the matt-black.

She's still there twenty minutes later. Still rubbing the matt-black between her fingers.

The fire in the gallery. Arroway's bag. The lottery.

They go round and round in her mind.

She's being paranoid. She's bored, and she's scared, and she's looking for something to distract her. The things she's seen are utterly unrelated.

Anna gets to her feet, leaving the matt-black on the corridor floor. After all, it's not like anyone is going to steal it. She rubs her index finger and her thumb together once more, then jogs off down the corridor.

22

Riley

I don't know how deep the cave goes.

There's a lantern propped by the entrance, but its light only reaches a few feet in. The space I *can* see reminds me a little of the Nest, back on Outer Earth: a total mess, with blankets and tools spread out over the uneven floor. A battered metal stove is puffing away, smoke curling out of the top and collecting near the ceiling. The narrow entrance is covered by planks of rotting wood, nailed together to form a makeshift door.

The stranger is crouched by the stove. He hardly said anything on the way over, only that his name was Harlan, and that he had a place where I'd be safe. He has dark brown skin, offset by a scraggly beard. Both the beard and his hair are streaked with grey. Guessing his age is impossible – he could be forty, he could be four hundred.

He wanted to leave Syria's body behind. I wouldn't let him. He carried it on his back, bringing it into the cave. It's somewhere behind me in the darkness. I keep wanting to look, have to force myself not to.

It crossed my mind that it might not be safe, that all this

could be a trap. I found I didn't care much. There's nothing Harlan can throw at me that I haven't survived a dozen times already.

He shuts the stove door with a clank, then gets unsteadily to his feet, pulling something from a pocket in his cavernous coat.

"Eat this," he says. He has the strangest accent, mushing together certain sounds, as if he never quite learned how to form individual words. "You were damn lucky with the wolves. They got a big pack round these parts, gettin' more aggressive every year. No idea why those three were off alone, but those leaves you used must have changed your scent some. You want to be careful, though. You pick the wrong kind of leaves, you get this rash all over your body. Itch'll drive you crazy."

I stare at him, my mouth hanging open.

He grimaces. "Sorry. I ain't talked to other people in a while. Guess I ain't used to it. Here."

I reach for the food, then hesitate. Alarm bells are going off already. But my hunger wins out, and after a moment I take it. It's like a strip of tree bark, brown and hard, with a grainy surface. I have to work to tear a chunk out.

The taste nearly knocks my head off. It's salty, like the fried beetles we used to get in the market, only a thousand times more intense. My stomach growls, and I take another bite, filling my mouth with the chewy substance.

"Good, isn't it?" Harlan says, grinning. "Cure it myself."

Cure. I suddenly realise what I'm eating. "This is . . . meat?" I say, speaking around it.

Harlan has gone back to work on the stove. There are logs piled up next to it, and he's busy jamming one of them inside. Light dances on the rock walls. "Mule deer. Caught it last spring, down near Whitehorse. First I'd seen in *years*. Didn't even think they were alive any more. Can't believe I got it before the

Nomads did, I tell you that. Set a trap, over by the falls. Sucker walked right into it."

I make myself chew slowly, savouring the taste. It's not just delicious – it's incredible. For a moment I forget about where I am, forget about everything except this, the first piece of meat I've ever eaten. I tell myself to take it slowly, not wanting to upset my stomach.

"Where are we?" I say, after I finally swallow.

Harlan glances up at me. His eyes are rimmed with wrinkles, an endless field of them, reaching all the way round to his temples. "You don't know?" he says. "Seems strange, since you crashed down here. Figured you might have had *some* idea where you were going. That space station you came from – hey, is that really true, by the way? You ain't just trying to fool me? Because if you are . . ."

I shake my head. "No, it's the truth.

He gives a long, low whistle. "Boy. Is it still there? Or did they come crashing down, too? I think everyone else you came down with is dead, or they will be soon. Can't survive long in these mountains 'less you know what you're doing." He's having trouble controlling his volume – some sentences are almost shouted, while others drop to a whisper.

I focus on the first question he asked. "I got separated from the others," I say, doing my best not to think of Okwembu.

Harlan jams a piece of the meat in his mouth, swinging round and pulling a battered backpack from its spot near the wall. He rummages in it, then withdraws something long and thin. It's paper – a whole roll of it, torn at the edges but otherwise intact.

"Scooch over," Harlan says around the dried meat, and unrolls the paper across the dirty floor.

It's a map. I've seen plenty of them before, but always on tab screens, crisp and sharp. This one is faded, the tiny place-name letters all but gone. The land on the map, marked out with thick black lines, forms an uneven, top-heavy blob. At the top, near the map's edge, the land breaks up into dozens of tiny islands.

"Hold this side down," Harlan says, tapping the edge closest to me. The paper feels fibrous under my hands, almost alive, as if it too came from an animal.

"All right," says Harlan. He rests a finger on the map, where the left-hand part of the blob begins to curve and mushroom out. "This is where we are. The Yukon. Canada. Ring any bells?"

I shake my head, but he's no longer looking at me. "Not that it matters," he says. "Canada, the States, whole damn planet far as I know. Most of it's all dust now. Everything below this line is dry as anything." His finger traces a curve across the blob, east to west, a little below the place he called Yukon.

"So why is it OK where we are?"

"Can't say. A few years ago, we were living in one of the bunkers here." He taps a point about ten inches below Yukon, his finger nudging the faded word *Utah*. "Those were bad years. Ever since I was a kid. Dust storm three-quarters of the year and frozen solid for the rest of the time. Air was nasty. You couldn't stay above ground long, not that people didn't try. We didn't get a whole hell of a lot further than Red Rocks. I remember this one time, Garrison told us about this electrical spike he was reading down by . . ." He looks at me. "Doing it again. Sorry. Just, I don't know, click your tongue or something if I talk too much."

"It's OK," I say. "But . . . what about up here?"

He shrugs. "We got word that things were changing. That you could live outside. Trees, air, whole deal. Paradise, compared to where we were. You hear that kind of thing, you go for it. Beats living in a tunnel underground, believe you me."

100

Trees. I glance at the door, thinking of the barren landscape beyond. The only trees I've ever seen were the ones in the Air Lab – the big oaks. I try to picture a forest of them, stretching to the horizon. I can't even begin to imagine it.

Harlan sees where I'm looking. "They're down at the lower elevation, round Whitehorse. Not much of a forest, but it's there. Air's good, too. Go outside anywhere south of the 49th parallel, and you gotta be wearing a full-face gas mask."

"What about the wolves? How are there . . . I mean, we thought all the animals were dead."

He grunts. "Oh, they ain't dead. Not completely. Most parts, sure, you never see 'em, but animals are funny. They find ways to survive. Probably don't need no more than a handful of 'em to do it, neither. You ask me, I think they just kept moving. Couldn't go underground, like we did, so they found places they could get food. 'Course there's been a lot more in the last few years, now the air's cleared up."

"And there are more people here? In Yukon?"

"*The* Yukon. You gonna live here, you gotta get the name right."

He turns away, letting go of his side of the map. It curls over, covering my hand. I spread it out again as he jams a poker into the stove, muttering to himself.

"Why are you up here, and not in the forest?" I say, still staring at the map. "Is it because of the . . . the Nomads?"

He grunts. "Something like that."

"Who are they?"

Harlan doesn't answer, poking at the fire.

I don't bother repeating the question. It doesn't matter. What's important is getting back out there. Prakesh and Carver must have come down close by, and if Harlan knows this place as well as I think he does, then we might be able to find them. I actually smile – the thought of seeing them both again, of coming across them, seeing their faces, feels amazing. I could bring them back here.

And then you'll have to choose between them a second time, says the small voice in my mind.

I ignore it. That can come later. I try to picture the forest again, imagining running in the sunlight, in a place where there's air and water and food. Where I can see the sky.

"So, my friends were on another escape pod," I say, trying to keep the excitement out of my voice. "I need to find them."

"Yeah?" says Harlan. "Where were you folks headed?"

The name jumps up out of nowhere. "Alaska."

His brow furrows. "Alaska?" He comes back, bends over the map, so close that his nose almost touches the paper. "The border's over a hundred miles away. Well, what used to be the border. Plus, state itself goes all the way across to the Bering Sea. Nothing but ice out there."

A sick feeling starts to swell in my stomach, as if the meat is turning toxic. I didn't have time to think about the physics of our re-entry before, but I'm doing it now and it's chasing away the good feeling I had before. At the speed we were travelling, two pods launched thirty seconds apart could come down hundreds of miles from each other.

Not good. Not good at all.

Harlan clears his throat. "Where were you supposed to end up? In Alaska?"

My mind goes blank. My finger hovers above the map, as if a name will leap out at me, but all the letters run into each other. *There's got to be a way. I have to find them.*

Then I remember. "Anchorage," I say. "We were going to some settlement in Anchorage." I scan the map for it, and let out a cry when I find it, nestled into a small bay. "If they launched when they were supposed to –"

"Kid," Harlan says quietly.

"– then they would have landed nearby. And there are other people there, so—"

"*Kid.*"

I look up at Harlan, and the sick feeling in my stomach expands, spreading through my body.

"What?" I say.

"I'm sorry," he says. "Your friends are already dead."

23

Prakesh

"We're here," says Ray.

Prakesh jerks awake. He hadn't even realised he'd dropped off. His neck immediately starts complaining – the vehicle's seats weren't designed for sleeping, and he'd passed out with his head at an awkward angle. His mind feels like it's floating three feet above him.

Iluk kills the engine, then bangs the door open and slides out. For the first time Prakesh realises that they can barely see out of the windows – they're grimed over, caked with dirt. Only a thin strip at the top of each one is still clear, and Prakesh can see the early light of dawn peeking through the windows on his left.

Ray opens the door. Prakesh has to shield his eyes against the glare.

"Come out when you're ready," says Ray. He and Nessa clamber through the door, with Okwembu following them. Nessa half closes it and Prakesh can feel the chill air licking at his exposed skin.

Carver rolls his head from side to side, massaging his shoulders. He looks exhausted, like he's aged ten years in a single night. Clay, too, is slowly blinking awake.

"Glad *you* got some sleep." Carver says, as Prakesh rubs his neck.

"You didn't?" He runs his tongue along the inside of his cheeks, trying to scare up some saliva. It doesn't work.

"Five minutes, maybe. We've been driving for hours."

"Right," Prakesh says. He's trying to get his thoughts in order, but it's like tying shoelaces with thick gloves on. There's something about these people – Ray and Nessa and the silent Iluk – that he doesn't like.

Carver gestures to the door. "You getting out, P-Man? Or we just going to sit here all day?"

Prakesh pauses for a moment, then pushes open the door and steps outside.

The first thing he notices is that the ground is soft – much softer than the tough, packed dirt of the forest. The second thing is the air. It *smells* different – a mix of a thousand scents, of salt and chemicals and decay and something else, something metallic and alien.

He looks up, and his mouth falls open.

Prakesh has seen pictures of the ocean before. They always showed blue sky, sandy beaches, white-capped waves. He didn't expect oceans like that to exist on Earth any more, but this . . .

It's a black, seething mass of water, hissing at the shore like an angry monster. There are waves, but they're stubborn little things, barely managing a fringe of froth before sinking into the edge of the water.

And there's a city in the ocean.

Or at least, what used to be a city. The buildings are half submerged, poking out of the water, tall towers reaching to the sky. In the pale dawn light, Prakesh can see that most of the towers are half destroyed, their walls and floors broken away, exposing their dark interiors to the low-hanging clouds. There are dozens of them, spread out along the shore, which curves away on either side of them.

The closest tower is barely fifty feet away – Prakesh can still see the main revolving door, water lapping at its frame, the glass long gone. The interior is dark, with gaps in the far wall that let in a little daylight. Most of the upper half of the tower is gone, the steel beams exposed like old bones.

Carver lets out a low whistle from behind him.

"Something, right?" says Ray. He has the vehicle's hood open, and is rooting around inside. With a yank, he pulls an object from deep in the engine.

"Spark plug," he says, when he sees them looking. "Make sure this old girl doesn't go anywhere." He raps a headlight with one hand. Prakesh sees that they're parked a little way off a paved road, pockmarked with potholes, vegetation pushing up through the cracks.

"What happened here?" says Prakesh. Clay is climbing out of the Humvee now, and is looking around, his eyes huge. Okwembu is standing a little way off, looking out over the water, motionless. Her blanket is loose around her shoulders, the wind playing with its hem.

Ray slams the hood closed, pocketing the spark plug. "Anchorage?" he says. "Sea claimed her, just like every other city on the west coast. East, too, for all we know. Happened long before the Engine brought us here."

There's a noise from further down the beach. Iluk and Nessa appear, dragging another vehicle behind them – a boat, the same size as the first vehicle but flat-bottomed, with a bulging motor on the back.

They drop it near the edge of the water with a thud. That's when Prakesh sees that Nessa has a gun: a lethal-looking rifle with a cylindrical scope mounted on top. Its lenses pick up the thin dawn light.

Ray reaches inside the wheeled vehicle, pulling out an empty canister and an opaque, flexible tube. He flips open a small flap on the side and winds the tube down into it. He puts his mouth around the tube and sucks in his cheeks. A second later, he turns and spits a thick stream of fuel onto the dirt, then wipes his mouth. The rest of the fuel is coming up the tube, draining into the canister.

"Where'd you get this, anyway?" Carver says, gesturing to the vehicle. For the first time, there's a glimmer of excitement in his eyes.

"The Hummer?" says Ray. "Had her for years, long before we even knew about the Engine. It was Prophet's originally. While back, some other Nomads tried to jump him, but he took 'em down and took what they had. She's still in pretty good shape, right?"

"Nomads?" says Clay.

Carver ignores him. "What's it – *she* – run on?"

"Diesel," Ray says. "Gotta look after it. Not too much around these days." He looks at Prakesh. "We were kind of hoping that you'd have some with you. Some sort of fuel anyway."

Prakesh feels a tiny drumbeat of fear in his chest, fear of something he can't quite place. Once they're in the boat, out on the water, there's nowhere to run to. He can't get over the thought, and he doesn't know why it scares him so much.

Carver hasn't noticed. "I built one, you know. Well, not one as big as this, and it didn't have the roof or anything –" he points to the top of the Hummer "– but it was *fast*."

Ray smiles and reaches inside the Humvee, emerging with a rifle of his own.

"We get animals down here sometimes," Ray says, seeing that Prakesh has noted the gun. "Wolves, mainly. Nessa swears she saw a bear one time, not that I believe her. And then there are the Nomads, of course."

He gestures to the boat. Clay is already perched on the side, and Okwembu is clambering on board. "Hop in. Iluk'll push her into the water."

"Yeah, sure," Prakesh says. He turns to Carver, who is still admiring the Humvee. "Talk to you for a sec?"

Carver looks up, but before he can say anything Ray steps between them. "Something on your mind?" he says. It's Prakesh's imagination – it has to be – but his accent has grown thicker.

"Just want to talk, that's all," he says. "The second escape pod might have come down near here. We should look for that one, too." He tries to sound natural, but struggles to keep the nervousness out of his voice.

"We just saw the one," says Ray. "Besides, we should get you fed. Cleaned up. Right?"

Prakesh tries a smile, flashes Carver a meaningful glance. "Can't leave our friend out there."

Carver stares back at him, confused and wary. Ray spits. The saliva arcs through the air, burying itself in the sand, and Prakesh smells a hint of fuel in the air. The drum in his chest is beating harder now.

Ray gestures to the ocean with the rifle. "We'll talk on the way."

So much for subtlety, Prakesh thinks. "What's the *Engine*?" he says. "Who's Prophet?"

"Get in the boat."

"Where are you taking us? What's out there?"

All the good humour has left Ray's face, and what remains is hard and cold. "Food. Shelter. A society. Just like the radio message said."

"I've been thinking," Prakesh says, deciding to plunge ahead.

"That message? So you're just broadcasting your location to anyone who can listen? I don't buy it. I'm not going anywhere until you tell us—"

Ray raises his rifle, and points it at Prakesh's face. Nessa and Iluk do the same, tracking Carver and Clay. Okwembu watches, not reacting.

Ray's smile is thin and humourless. "Get in the damn boat."

24

Riley

The silence in the cave stretches on forever. The edge of the map has curled over my hand again, but I barely notice it.

Your friends are already dead.

"You don't know that," I say.

Harlan's face is grave. He doesn't say anything. And, right then, the anger comes back. How dare he? He doesn't know Prakesh. He doesn't know Carver. Wherever they are, whatever they're dealing with, they'll be OK. They have to be.

My fist is clenched, scrunching up part of the map. Slowly, I let go, pulling my hand back. Then I take a deep breath, the anger subsiding. For now.

"What's in Anchorage?" I say. The heat in the cave has built up, drying out my tongue and blocking my sinuses.

Harlan bends down to his backpack, the cave echoing with clunks and thumps as he rummages through it. He pulls out an ancient radio, one with an antenna and a big chunky knob.

There's a crank on the side, and Harlan gives it a few quick turns. A light on the radio flickers on, growing orange, and we hear the thin sound of static. Harlan mutters to himself, adjusting the knob on the front of the radio, and then there's the voice, the message, the one I heard for the first time on the bridge of the *Shinso Maru*.

This time, the message chills me to the bone.

"– can hear us, we are broadcasting from a secure location in what used to be Anchorage, Alaska. There are at least a hundred of us here, and we have managed to establish a colony. We have food, water and shelter. The climate is cold, but survivable. If you can hear us, then know that you're not the only ones—"

"They do a new one every couple of months," Harlan says, shutting the radio off. "But it's been ever since we got up here. I don't know how they get the power to do it, but it doesn't matter."

"Who's *they*?"

"We don't know." Harlan adjusts his position. "Back when I was in Whitehorse, we had a survivor come through. Russian guy. Least, I think he was Russian. Had an accent you had to really listen hard to understand. Massive beard, too, like fur on a—"

"Harlan."

"Sorry. Don't ask me how he managed to get to here from Alaska, but he did it."

I don't know where Whitehorse is, and I have only the vaguest idea of where to find Russia. "What happened to him?" I say.

"Told us he was in a big party out of Siberia," Harlan says. "Winters had got too heavy there, so they were coming east, hoping for something better. They heard the message as they were crossing through Alaska, and decided to check it out.

"They got ambushed, even before they got to the source of the signal. Guy couldn't stop shaking when he told us. Said it was like the night just folded in on 'em. Men, women, children, didn't matter. Anchorage swallowed 'em whole. He managed to get away, along with his wife. She died on the way here."

"And you believed him?"

Harlan shrugs. "Not like we were gonna go there ourselves to find out."

"There has to be an explanation," I say, staring at the map. "Maybe something else took them. Maybe the settlement was—"

"You don't get it, do you?" says Harlan. "Don't you think it's a little strange that they're just broadcasting their location?" He waves his hands in the air, waggling his fingers. "Hey! Everybody! We got food and supplies! All you can eat! Form an orderly line!"

I stare down at the map, not wanting to think about his words.

"If they were really accepting survivors," Harlan says, "then the Nomads would have cleared 'em out long ago. Them, and anybody else who feels like livin' off what other people got. You want to know what I think? I think whoever sent this message is doing the same thing. Why go out hunting for supplies when you can just have them come straight to you?"

He puts a hand on my shoulder – then jumps when I slap it away. The anger I feel is immediately replaced by embarrassment, and I turn away, hugging myself tight. This isn't his fault.

But, right now, I feel like I did when I looked up at the sky – like the world has gone fuzzy at the edges.

"You ain't gettin' to Anchorage anyhow," he says, not unkindly. "You're four hundred miles crow flight, and you won't make it even halfway before the snows set in."

I'm barely listening. I'm back on my feet, pacing, thinking hard. Four hundred miles. It's a long way, but if I leave now I can get there in a month or two. It's nowhere near fast enough, but it'll have to do.

"The person I loved was on that ship," I say, each word carried on a hot, angry breath. "I have to find him." In that moment, I don't know if I'm talking about Carver or Prakesh.

Harlan doesn't touch me again. He just steps around until he's in front of me, leaning slightly away, as if he's afraid I'm going to lunge forward and bite him.

"I don't think you understand what you're about to do. How're you planning to feed yourself? Or navigate? That's without talking about the weather."

"I can deal with the cold."

"Can you deal with a snap that drops the temperature twenty degrees in ten minutes? I've seen that stream you were at frozen solid. And we got wind storms that come out of nowhere. They'll knock you right off your feet. 'Sides, you've already met the wolves."

He stops to take a breath. When he speaks again, his voice is quieter. "What's the biggest space you ever been in?" Harlan says quietly.

"What do you mean?"

"When we were on the way over here, I caught you looking up at the sky. Like a goddamn deer in a spotlight."

"I've been outside the station before," I say, crossing my arms. "I've been *in* space."

"Right. Right. But for how long? And I'm guessing you had a space suit."

In the silence that follows, I realise that I don't have a single thing to say.

"Your mind ain't right," Harlan says, locking his eyes onto mine. "You're snapping at every little thing, and you just ain't ready for what's out there."

I look away, refusing to give up, desperately trying to think about how I could do this. *Four hundred miles.* I'll need gear, food, a map. Maybe Harlan can help me. Maybe I can—

When I look back, I see that he's staring at my thigh.

"What's that?" he says, stepping in close.

"Nothing," I say, my mind still on Anchorage. "Just a cut."

"Lemme see." He goes down on one knee, reaching in. I shy away, startled, but stop when I see the look on his face. The worry on it.

"I told you, I'm fine," I say, baring my teeth as his fingers gently explore the cut, peeling back the fabric of my pants. "It's a flesh wound. I got hit by a piece of shrapnel, but I took it out."

He stops for a moment, grabbing a nearby lantern and bringing it closer. The heat from the glass bakes onto my skin.

"Deeper'n that," he says. "And there's still some metal in there."

"What?"

"Yeah, there, and there, and . . . yeah, hi, I see you. You didn't get it all out. This from the . . ." He lowers his hand to the floor fast, making an explosion sound with his mouth when it hits, looking up at me questioningly.

I nod, furious at myself for having missed this. The smaller shards must have broken off the bigger one when it embedded itself in my flesh.

"So we take the rest out," I say. My gut churns – more pain. I tell myself I can handle it, that it'll be worth it if it gets me moving again. It can't possibly be worse than the pain I felt when I cut that bomb out of me.

But Harlan is shaking his head, sitting back on his haunches. "Can't do it," he says. "Nope. Nuh-uh. Can't. They're too deep. Do you have any idea how much it's gonna hurt when those things come out? Do you?"

"Pretty good idea," I say, getting down to his level, stretching out. In the flickering light, the wound looks even more jagged and raw. "Just bring me something I can use. Tweezers, or pliers. A knife'll probably be fine."

"You don't understand," he says, his voice shaking. "Even *if* we get them out, I don't got the medicine to stop the cut going bad."

"You must have something," I say. I can feel my nails digging into my palm.

He shrugs, helplessly. "Had. It's all gone. Tripped and fell a few months ago when I was checking traps. Got a massive gash all the way up my arm." He points to his bicep. "Used the last of it on that. Even then, I don't know if it woulda been enough to handle what you've got."

I run through the options in my head. I could clean the cut, get the slivers of metal out, but I only have to miss one for sepsis to set in. I could burn it – pour lamp oil in the cut and set it on fire – but even the thought of that makes me want to throw up. Besides, I don't even know if that would work. It might just be inviting further infection.

"Wait a second," Harlan says. He jumps up, surprisingly spry. "This is *perfect*."

I stare up at him, not entirely sure I heard him right. "I'm going to die of infection, and that's perfect?"

"No no no," he says, waving his hands. "It's just . . . listen, I think I know where we can get the stuff you need."

"OK," I say slowly, feeling a tiny spark of hope flare up in my chest.

"We go to Whitehorse," he says.

It's a name he's mentioned before. "What's Whitehorse?"

"Town about twenty-five miles south from here, give or take. Except . . . shit, I don't know, Eric was already making noises about heading for Calgary, so there's no guarantee they'd even—"

"But they'll have supplies? If they're still there?"

"*If* they're still there, yeah. Only . . ." He stops, a strange expression of longing settling on his face. In the lantern light it makes him look a hundred years old. More.

"Only . . . what?" I say.

"You gotta do something for me," he says. "If they're still down there, you gotta tell 'em I helped you. You gotta tell 'em I looked after you, all right? Made sure you were OK."

It's such a strange request that at first I don't know how to respond. "Why?" I say, after a moment.

His expression hardens. "Does it even matter? Just do that for me. I get you down the valley, you tell Eric that I did good. That's the deal."

He's going to trick you, says the voice at the back of my mind. *He can't just want something that small. He wants something else. Something he isn't telling you about.*

I'm about to listen to the voice, but then I remember something Carver told me. It happened right after we escaped from the Earthers, back on the station. He told me that I had to let other people help me – that I couldn't do everything on my own.

I could try get to Whitehorse myself, but it's all too easy to imagine getting lost out there. If that happens, I won't survive. Whatever Harlan's doing, whatever weird game he's playing, I have to go along with it. It's the only shot I have.

"All right," I say. "Sure. I'll tell them."

He smiles, showing yellowed teeth. He digs in his pack again, tossing me another stick of dried meat. "Eat up, and get some sleep," he says. "We got a long way to go tomorrow."

25

Anna

Anna has to knock several times before Achala Kumar opens the door.

She's wearing a blue sweater with a black shawl wrapped around her shoulders. The skin on her face is puffy, her eyes bloodshot. She frowns when she sees Anna. "You're Frank's daughter."

Anna nods. "Can I come in?"

Achala considers for a moment, then shrugs, holding the door open for her.

The Kumars have taken over a hab on Level 2. It's even smaller than Doctor Arroway's, and even more spartan. Cold, too – as Anna walks in, she can just see her breath curling in the air before her.

Ravi Kumar is on the small single cot, his back up against the wall. A thin blanket covers the lower half of his body. There's a depression where his left leg should be, and Anna finds it hard to look away. Right then, it strikes her just how much his son looks like him.

Ravi smiles at her, but she can see the puzzlement in his eyes.

117

Achala closes the door behind her. "I'm sorry I can't offer you anything to drink," she says. "About earlier: I shouldn't be arguing with your father. It's not his fault."

"Achala, what did you say to Frank now?" Ravi Kumar says, his voice weary.

"Don't you start with me," Achala spits back. "Our boy is *alive*, and I'm not going to sit here while—"

"I need to ask you something," Anna says, speaking over both of them. She sits down on the edge of the bed, telling herself to stop looking at the space below Ravi Kumar's left knee.

She doesn't quite manage it. Ravi reaches over, taps the blanket. "Loader claw closed over it," he says. "Crushed the shin. I was lucky it didn't puncture my suit." His eyes bore into hers. "But you didn't come here to talk about old injuries."

Anna takes a deep breath, irritated with herself. This shouldn't have been difficult. "They keep space suits in the escape pods, right?"

"Space suits?" says Achala.

Ravi nods slowly, his eyes narrowed.

"OK," Anna says. "But do they keep them anywhere else in the sector? Extra suits, or something?"

"No," Ravi says. "There's no point – there are only a few places you can do an EVA from, and there's nothing like that in Apex." He sees Anna's confusion. "EVA – Extra-Vehicular Activity. Spacewalks."

"And you were in the construction corps, right?" Anna says, more to herself than to him. "So you'd know."

"Of course," Ravi says, even more puzzled. He glances up at his wife. "Unless Achala knows something I don't."

Achala thinks hard, shakes her head. "No. There's a workshop in Tzevya where they did suit repairs, but nothing here."

She looks at Anna in horror. "But you can't be thinking of going outside?"

118

Anna thinks back to the nightmare: drifting, weightless, in a black void. She shivers, without meaning to. "Nothing like that."

"Then why the interest in space suits?" Ravi Kumar pulls himself off the bed, hands fumbling along the wall for the cane propped against it. "What's going on?"

Anna is about to tell them, then stops. She has to be sure. She has to be absolutely positive about this before she tells a soul.

"I'll tell you afterwards," she says. She sees Achala about to speak, and ploughs on. "I'm not going outside, and I'm not doing anything bad. Promise."

She smiles, turns to go.

"Anna," Achala Kumar says, and when Anna turns back she sees that Achala is crying. Her hands are knotted at her waist, fingers clenched tight. Ravi looks down, embarrassed.

"You have to help us," Achala whispers.

Anna doesn't know what to say. She doesn't know how to tell the Kumars that she has even less pull than they do. More importantly, she can't tell them that she agrees with her father – that the lottery is the only way. The Kumars aren't the only people with missing sons, daughters, husbands, wives.

"I'll try," she says. It's not a lie, not exactly, but she feels uneasy as she says it. What she has isn't even a theory. It's a hunch, a feeling, based on a collection of things that might not even be remotely related. But what if she's right? What if this all means something? What will it mean for the Kumars?

She walks out of the hab, closing the door behind her. Then she takes off down the corridor, heading for the escape pods.

119

It's mid-morning before we reach the tree line.

We see it from far up the mountain, stretching into the distance, but it's only when we're close that I get a good look at the trees. They're nothing like the ones in Outer Earth's Air Lab. Those were enormous, with canopies that blocked out the light from the ceiling lamps. But these trees are no more than twenty feet high, and they're stunted, with stubby branches and wind-bent trunks.

Even so, I make myself stop for a moment, taking it in. These trees weren't supposed to exist. They were supposed to be gone. And yet here they are, fighting to survive, pushing back against the cold.

Harlan doesn't notice I've stopped until he's a few feet into the trees. He looks over his shoulder, nodding at me to follow. He's wearing a tattered canvas pack, his rifle strapped to the side. There are no bullets in the gun – Harlan says he ran out months ago – but it's reassuring to see it there anyway.

The ground is a mess of frost and brown leaves. It's eerily silent, and it takes me a moment to work out why that bothers me. On Outer Earth, whenever we were shown videos of forests, they were always noisy – bird calls, insects, wind. Here, the only sounds are our footsteps and the laboured sound of our breathing.

I pick one of the nearby leaves from a tree, rub it between my fingers. It doesn't feel like any leaf I've touched in the Air Lab. It feels crinkly, desiccated, and before long it comes apart in my hand.

Harlan sees me looking. "Most of this was frozen over five years ago," he says. "Kind of amazing how the forest just comes back, given half a chance. Topsoil's pretty thin, but that's changing. Twenty years, this'll be green all the time."

"How do you know it'll stay this way?" I say, dipping a hand under my jacket. Harlan gave me one of his shirts to wear under it, and the material feels scratchy against my skin.

He looks helpless suddenly, as if I've brought up something he doesn't want to think about it. "No way to tell. Better hope it does, though, or we're all done."

He strides ahead, plunging deeper into the forest, his canvas pack bouncing.

I'm trying to ignore my fatigue. My eyes are gritty with it, my muscles leaden. Harlan wouldn't let us leave until dawn – he refused to travel in the dark, told me we needed sleep if we were going to hike down to Whitehorse. I didn't want to push the issue, but even curled up in one of his blankets I only managed a couple of hours of sleep.

It didn't take long for infection to start showing in my thigh. The wound felt hot, like some of the heat from Harlan's lantern had cooked into the flesh. I couldn't tell in the low light, but it looked a little red, too. Harlan bandaged my thigh, wrapping it in a wide strip of cloth, and sometime in the night it began to itch, sending up waves of discomfort. That would have been enough, but my mind was like an engine that wouldn't shut off. It kept going round and round, throwing up every uncomfortable scenario it could think of. Most of them involved Carver and Prakesh.

I think about them now, as we head into the forest, replaying my thoughts without really wanting to. My relationship with Prakesh was supposed to be simple. After everything we'd been through, it should have been enough. We had our little hab in Chengshi, and we had each other. I didn't need anything else.

But then I kissed Carver. And no matter how many times I tell myself that it was something I did in the heat of the moment, I know it isn't true. Even then, when we were trapped on the *Shinso* and I told Carver I was staying with Prakesh, I thought I was making the right choice. But it hurt him, badly, and it was only later that I realised that it hurt me, too. More than I care to admit.

What does that mean?

I know when I find them, I'll have to make that choice again. But what if the choice gets made for me? What if I get to Anchorage, somehow, and find that one is dead, and not the other? What am I going to do if they're both dead? I know I'll have to carry on, keep surviving, but it's like looking up at the sky, like trying to take in something bigger than I can imagine.

I bring myself back. The wound on my thigh isn't slowing me down – not yet, anyway – but I can't quite hold my balance on the uneven ground, and I keep having to use the trees to steady myself. Harlan slips between them, moving with an easy grace.

It's not long before I slip, my foot skidding on a patch of ice. I have to grab a branch to stop myself falling, the bark scraping my skin.

"Whoa," Harlan says, turning. He skips back up the slope, and puts his hands under my arms. "There we go," he says, pulling me upright.

"Thanks," I say. I feel strangely embarrassed, the blood rushing to my face. I want to tell him that I'm not used to the ground, that if we were on Outer Earth, with its flat metal surfaces, I'd be the fastest person he's ever met. No point. And I don't want to think about Outer Earth right now.

"Is it always this cold?" I say instead, shaking my hands. My fingers are still numb at the tips.

"Cold?" Harlan says over his shoulder. "This ain't cold. You wait until winter."

"Does it ever get warm?" I ask.

"It's not too bad in summer. We actually get a little green, if you can believe it. That's hunting season, though, so it means harder work. Hey, am I getting better at the conversation thing?"

I smile. "You're doing fine."

"Good to know, good to know. Good, good, good."

A few minutes later, we come across a pool of water, fed by a trickling stream running down from the mountain. I fill my water bottle, shivering as my hand touches the surface, then take a long drink.

"Don't fall in, whatever you do," Harlan says. "Water that cold, it'll shut your body down in minutes. Then we'll never get you to Whitehorse. The thing you did with that man's jacket was smart, by the way."

I blink at him, trying to follow the conversational path he's laid down. When I do it, I realise he's talking about how I tore Syria's jacket into strips, used it to mark my path while I tried to find water.

"Didn't work," I say. "I still got lost."

He taps his head. "Doesn't matter. You might not know how the outside works, but you think like someone who does. The tags, getting to the water, stuffing your clothes with leaves. All smart."

"It was cold."

"Exactly. And out here, cold'll kill you faster than almost anything. You gotta stay warm. Good clothing, good fire, good shelter. You remember that, and you'll be OK. Here, let me show you something."

Without waiting for me to answer, he strides off into the trees. He's heading back the way we came, but before I can tell him that he's going the wrong direction he comes out again, carrying something in his hand. It looks like a clump of hair, only it's a pale green, with much thicker strands. When he passes it to me, the underside is slightly sticky.

"Old man's beard, we call it," he says, wetting his hand in the water. "And the gunk underneath it is spruce sap. Best fire starters nature has, these two, even when they're not together. You get a spark, these'll kindle like anything."

"How do I start a fire?" I say, stuffing the sticky bundle of fibres into my jacket pocket.

But he's off again, skipping across the boulders that ring the pool. "Come on," he shouts. "Town ain't far. I know an old forest road we can use."

The road, when we get there, is wider than two of Outer Earth's corridors laid side by side. The surface is overgrown, covered in a skin of wet leaves, but it's easier going than the forest itself. The stunted trees hug the road from both sides. Here and there, some of them have fallen, their tilted trunks slick with moss. Despite their lack of a canopy, their shapes cut the sky down to a thin sliver above us, which is just as well. I still can't look at it without getting a little nauseous.

Harlan keeps stopping to point things out, and soon my pockets are full of strange plants with even stranger names: burdock, cattail, lady fern, and a tart berry Harlan calls

124

lowbush cranberry. It's bright red, and so sour that I almost spit it out.

I want to tell Harlan to hurry – I don't know how long I have left. But if I'm going to survive down here – if *we*, as in Prakesh and Carver and I, are going to survive down here – then I'll need to know about plants like this. I can't depend on Harlan forever.

"Who exactly are these people?" I ask. I'm still turning over our conversation of last night, when he asked me to tell the people in Whitehorse that he kept me safe. I still don't know what that's all about, but maybe coming at it at an angle might get me some answers.

Harlan glances at me, as if weighing up how much I need to know. Eventually, he says, "I used to be with this group. We'd try and stay one step ahead of the Nomads, but every year we lost more people to 'em. It got harder and harder to convince ourselves to keep moving."

"Why were the Nomads chasing you?"

He shrugs. "Nomads don't have anything against us, specifically. They just take down anybody who isn't them, grab as much supplies as they can, and keep moving. Lot of different tribes around here, all with the same MO. And believe me, you don't want to run into them."

He goes silent for a minute. I'm about to prompt him, but then he says, "We found this old hospital in Whitehorse. Place had been abandoned for decades, but it had a basement you could seal off. Plenty of space, and plenty of visibility around it."

"And if the Nomads came?"

"If the Nomads were in the area, we could hunker down, wait them out. They never found us. Not once." He gives me a toothy grin. "We had food, we had power, we even cooked up a water—"

I'm walking with my head down, moving carefully over a boggy patch, when I nearly bump into Harlan. He's stopped dead in the middle of the road.

"Hey—" I say, but then my voice cuts off when I see what he's looking at.

There's a wolf in front of us, mouth closed, eyes bright. Its fur is dark, matted with dirt and leaves, and its ears are pricked straight up, as if it's scanning the forest around us. My eyes go wide as I realise that it's the wolf from the night before – the first one that attacked me.

"Don't move," Harlan says.

My first instinct is to run at the wolf, scare it off. I've come too far, been through too much, to get scared away by a single animal now. In the daylight, it looks scrawny and malnourished. I can see the bones of its ribcage through its dirt-caked fur.

I step forward, a shout forming on my lips, but Harlan whacks me in the chest with his arm.

"I said don't move," he says, enunciating each word.

I'm about to tell him to let me past, but then I see the others.

They're on both sides of the road, silent among the trees. Dozens of them, low to the ground. Some are no more than pups, but others are huge adults, with ears the size of my palms. All of them are thin, hungry-looking.

The smaller wolf opens its mouth, letting its tongue roll out. Saliva drips from huge, gently curved teeth, and it gives a long, low growl.

27

Okwembu

The boat scythes across the bay, winding its way around the submerged buildings. Every time they hit a wave, or when Iluk turns the rudder a little too sharply, Okwembu feels a lurch in the pit of her stomach. The top half of her body is freezing, drenched in sea spray.

The only place to sit is on the side of the boat, on the stiff rubber pontoons. Ray and Nessa sit on one side, their feet braced against the centre stanchion. Okwembu and the rest of them sit on the other. Prakesh Kumar is staring up at the buildings, and the low clouds beyond them. Clay looks shell-shocked, his eyes flicking between their captors. His fingers grip the short lengths of rope on the side of the boat that serve as handholds, holding them tight.

Aaron Carver is different. He looks as if he wants to reach across the boat, grab Ray by the neck and launch him into the surf. He doesn't dare. Nessa still has the rifle, and she's pointing it squarely at his chest.

Nobody's said a word since they took off from the beach. But as they come around one of the buildings, Iluk eases off the throttle a little, compensating for a sudden swell, and Carver speaks.

"I don't get it," he says, talking to Ray but keeping his eyes on Nessa's rifle.

"Get what?" Ray is jovial again, like they're out for a pleasure trip.

"The whole act. Like we were safe, like you were going to welcome us into your *society*." He spits out the last word, like it has a bad taste.

"You *are* welcome," Ray says. "So long as you can earn your keep." He knots his hands between his knees, leaning back slightly as the boat crests a rolling wave. "There are only two kinds of people. Those who can serve the Engine, and those who can't. Some people find it hard to accept their place. They need a little encouragement. But it's a lot easier if they come of their own free will."

Iluk accelerates, powering over a wave. A second later the throttle drops and Ray says, "Nessa jumped the gun a little, so to speak. You know, when your friend started getting antsy?"

Prakesh raises his head, the expression on his face just as murderous as Carver's.

There's a haze over the water, soft and damp. Their visibility drops to a few yards. Iluk slows the boat, the motor puttering. The last of the buildings passes by on their right: a black shape in the fog, torn and twisted. Okwembu looks over her shoulder, taking it in. At some point in the past, moss began to grow up the walls. It's blossomed over the years, turning the first three levels a dark, almost luminescent green.

Aaron's thigh is just touching Okwembu's, and she can feel it twitching. All his energy and anger is bottled up, kept in one place by Nessa's rifle. At some point – maybe in a few moments, maybe in a few minutes – he'll make a play, go for the gun. It's inevitable. And if he doesn't, Prakesh Kumar will. Neither of them can see past the current situation, see the need to do nothing until they know what they're dealing with. If Ray and Nessa had any intelligence, they'd shoot them and be done with it.

Should she say something? Try to calm him down? No. He wouldn't listen anyway.

But Prophet might.

Society. That's the word Ray used. And judging by what she's seen so far, from the vehicles and weapons and the radio message, this isn't a disorganised group. It's what she's been looking for: a community, a collective of people away from the insanity of Outer Earth. It's this, more than anything else, that keeps Janice Okwembu calm, that keeps her compliant. For now.

She felt a spark of worry when the woman, Nessa, attacked Prakesh. When these people, whoever they are, showed their real faces. But it hardly matters. *They* hardly matter. They're foot soldiers, advance scouts. Prophet, whoever he is, is where the real power lies. What can she offer him? Everybody has something they want, and if she can understand his she can survive this.

First, she will make herself indispensable. Then, she will make herself powerful.

Clay's shocked intake of breath rips her out of her thoughts, and she looks up.

It's as if there's a hole in the fog: a huge, looming, black void. Not a building. It's something much bigger, rising a hundred feet above the water's surface, curving inwards like a giant wave.

"Holy shit," Carver says. He actually scoots back a little, bumping into Okwembu. For a second, she has the crazy idea that they've hit the horizon – that this *thing* stretches hundreds, maybe thousands of miles. She tells herself not to be so stupid.

She can see the metal surface now, see the openings in it. But this isn't a building. It's not part of Anchorage. They're out into the bay, which means –

A ship.

A distant memory jogs her. A history lesson from far in the past, their teacher talking about the war, about different armies ranged against one another. Their ancestors used these ships to transport fighter planes across oceans, between theatres of conflict. They were nuclear-powered mobile command centres, symbols of military might.

Ray is beaming. "Welcome to the USS *Ramona*," he says.

They turn, tracking alongside the aircraft carrier's hull. Awe overrides her fear. She never thought she'd see one, not in a million years. And yet, somehow, one of them is here, parked in the waters off Alaska. Okwembu sees the same moss that was on the buildings climbing up the curved metal, its tendrils burrowing into the seams between the plates. How long has this ship been here?

And right then Okwembu notices two things simultaneously.

Ray and Nessa are both looking up at the *Ramona*, their heads tilted back.

And Aaron Carver is looking at the rifle.

He moves before Okwembu can, exploding off the side of the boat. He wraps his hands around the rifle – one on the barrel, another halfway down the stock. Nessa comes alive instantly and the gun goes off.

But Carver's move knocks the barrel upwards, and the bullet passes over their heads. Clay screams, and Prakesh rockets to his feet. Only Okwembu stays seated, her heart hammering, as Carver wrestles Nessa for the gun. The boat rocks back and forth, threatening to upend them into the icy water.

Ray and Iluk react, trying to shove Carver away. But he's

ferociously strong, and in the next instant he's got the gun away from Nessa. He smashes Nessa right in the chest with the butt of the gun. She grunts, tumbles over the side, splashing into the water.

Iluk reaches for Carver, but the tracer dodges back, out of range. He's up on the front of the little boat, his foot on the edge, and he brings the gun around, seating it against his stomach.

Okwembu doesn't dare move – he'll shoot her just as easily as he'd shoot the others, without a second thought. Nessa is splashing somewhere out of sight, trying to pull her way back into the boat.

"Aaron," Prakesh says. "Just—"

"OK," says Carver, almost shouting. "I have had it up to *here* with this *bullshit*. You and you—" he swivels the gun between Ray and Iluk. "In the water. Now."

But Ray is laughing. He's sniggering to himself, shaking his head, as if Carver has played a prank on him.

"Something funny?" Carver says, stepping off the prow, lifting the gun towards Ray's face.

Ray grins. "Look up, son."

Carver gives a laugh of his own. He jerks the gun at Nessa, who has somehow managed to get both arms over the edge of the boat. "Go for a swim. Take her with you."

Okwembu looks up, and smiles.

"Aaron," says Prakesh.

"You got three seconds," Carver says.

"*Aaron.*"

Finally, Carver looks up. Okwembu gets the sense that he intends it to be a quick glance, a little upward flick of the eyes, but when he sees what's above them he can't look away.

There's an opening in the side of the ship – huge and rectangular, lit from within by a yellow glow. There are faces in the opening. A dozen of them, men and women, as ragged as Ray is. Okwembu can just make out their military camouflage. Each of them is holding a rifle, just like Nessa's, and each rifle is pointed right at the boat.

Ray sniggers as Carver lowers his gun. "That's not even the best part."

He points at the edge of the deck, far above them. There's something else there – a large metal cylinder, tilted off the end of the deck. There's a long, black tube at right angles to the cylinder – a gun barrel, Okwembu realises. It's pointing right at them.

"See, even if they missed," Ray says, pointing at the faces in the opening, "Curtis wouldn't."

"Curtis?" Prakesh Kumar's voice sounds flat and featureless.

"Took us a hell of a long time to get the Phalanx gun up and running," Ray says conversationally, folding his arms. "But Curtis kept at it. That's his baby. Hardly ever leaves. He did a test-fire the other day, and he got off a thousand rounds in one pull of the trigger. He shoots now, and you'll be in heaven before you can spit."

"So will you," Carver says. Clay is quaking behind him.

"That may be. But I doubt Curtis'd hesitate. He's always been a little bit too . . . *enthusiastic*, if you get my meaning."

It's everything Okwembu can do not to yell at Carver. She doesn't dare. One wrong move and they'll be shot to pieces.

That's when the idea comes to her. It arrives fully formed, blazing hot. Her bargaining chip. The thing she can offer Prophet. It's right there, but if Aaron Carver doesn't see reason she'll never get a chance to act on it.

Ray puts out his hand, looking Carver in the eye. "Now give me the gun."

Iluk pulls Nessa out of the surf. She collapses in the boat, the centre of a pool of icy water, staring daggers at Carver. For a moment, he does nothing. Then his shoulders slump and he hands over the rifle.

"Good boy," Ray says.

28

Riley

"Harlan?" I say, keeping my voice low.

The wolf barks – a high-pitched, almost whining sound, then gives another long snarl. I can feel my heart beating hard enough to punch through my chest wall.

Harlan ignores me. His eyes are locked on the lead wolf. Slowly, he reaches into his jacket, hunting for something, never taking his eyes away from the wolf. The others are moving now, coming in from both directions, low to the ground. They're just as thin and undernourished as the lead wolf, but their teeth are knife-point sharp.

This must be the pack Harlan mentioned. I hear his words in my head: *Getting more aggressive every year.* I flick a glance at the rifle. With no bullets, it'll be next to useless – and even if it was loaded, there's no way we shoot them all.

We have to get out of here. We have to run. I have no idea if we'll be able to outpace the wolves in a flat sprint, not if they're as fast as I remember, but we don't have a choice. There's no way we're taking out this many.

I look round. There's a gap in the closing circle of wolves, at my two o'clock. If Harlan and I run at the same time, we should be through it before they take us.

"All right," I say, my voice now barely above a whisper. "See the gap? We're going to go through it. Run as fast as—"

"Stay put," Harlan says. He's found whatever he was looking for, and is drawing it slowly out of his jacket. "Gotta face 'em head-on."

Adrenaline is starting to shoot through me, a thousand tiny blades dancing on my tongue. "Too many," I say, hissing it out the side of my mouth.

"Just *wait*," Harlan says.

The thing in Harlan's hand is a metal cylinder, bright orange, about three inches tall. There's writing on it, too scratched and faded to make out. A large black nozzle sits on the top of the can, made of dented plastic. As I watch, Harlan moves his thumb, flicking open a safety catch. The lead wolf growls.

Harlan slams his thumb down on the nozzle. A jet of fine mist shoots out of the can, dull orange in colour, curling and drifting across the ground. The moment it touches the wolves, they squeal in pain, pawing their faces, snorting, shaking their heads. I catch the scent of the spray and it makes me want to put my own arm over my face. It's like food that's been heavily spiced, then left out for days to rot.

Harlan sprays in quick bursts, targeting different groups of wolves. They all react to the spray, and one or two of them take off, hurrying back into the woods.

But not enough of them. Not nearly enough. And the spray is dissipating, vanishing in the cool air. Harlan's bursts are getting weaker – whatever propellant is in the can is being drained off with each hit.

"Come on now," says Harlan, as if pleading with the can to work. He gives it a vigorous shake. Something inside the can clacks as it swings back and forth.

"Harlan, if we don't run—"

"*Never* run," he says, as the remaining wolves circle around. "They'll chase you down like a damn dog. You can't outrun wolves."

"Yeah, but that stuff's not working."

The circle is getting tighter. A couple of the wolves are darting forwards and backwards, snapping their jaws. Everywhere I look, more of them are emerging from –

The trees.

There's a fallen one close to the side of the road, its trunk tilted at forty-five degrees. I follow the trunk – when it fell, it landed on one of the thick tree branches, which is still supporting its weight. That branch is about ten feet off the ground.

At that moment, the lead wolf attacks.

It moves with a languid grace, appallingly fast. I can see the muscles rippling under its fur, see its ears flatten against its head. But I'm moving, too, pulling Harlan with me. He's off balance, and the wolf flies past him on the left, jaws snapping at the air. It slams into the ground, spraying up clods of dirt, legs scrabbling for purchase.

I can feel the other wolves pounding the earth as we sprint towards the tree. One of them appears in front of me. Its head is turned sideways, jaws open wide. Its mouth is a gaping black hole, flecked with a stardust of saliva.

I swing my fist in an arc, smashing into the side of the wolf's head. It's like punching a wall, but it's just enough to knock the wolf away. Its jaws snap shut on open air.

I can still smell the spray from Harlan's canister. It's as if a red-hot poker is being jammed into the back of my throat. My eyes are streaming, itching like crazy. I have to fight to keep them open.

I jump, my feet landing squarely on the trunk. There's no time to look back, no time to check if Harlan's all right. I move up the trunk as fast as I can. It's too steep to rely on just my feet, so I use my hands, moving on all fours in an awkward crouch. My heart is hammering, urging me to hurry.

Harlan screams.

I look back. One of the wolves has him around the ankle, its jaw locked on his foot. It's twisting its head back and forth, as if trying to rip the leg clean off. Blood wells up around its teeth. Harlan is on his backside, pulling his way up the trunk, trying to kick at the side of the wolf's head with his other leg. The wolf barely notices his blows.

I lunge backwards, lifting my leg so it travels over Harlan's right shoulder. My foot slams squarely into the wolf's muzzle. It lets go of Harlan, yelping, and topples sideways off the trunk. Its claws scrape along the bark.

The move has left me off balance again. I manage to right myself just in time, breathing hard, focusing on the top of the trunk, which is resting cleanly on one of the thick tree branches.

I reach the top, climbing onto the branch and steadying myself against the trunk. I look down without meaning to, and it almost makes my heart stop. The ground is a snarling, biting, furious mass of teeth and fur.

"We have to keep going," Harlan says. His voice is ragged with effort.

But where? There are no other fallen trees around us, no convenient branches to clamber along. We're trapped.

Think, Riley, says the voice inside. *Find a way.*

My gaze snaps to one of the other trees. It's upright, but only just – its roots are sticking out of the soil, the trunk hanging on by threads. Its branches are thin and insubstantial, but there's a tree a short distance away that has thicker ones. I track the trees, mentally jumping from one to the other. There's no telling where this is going to take us. But it's the only choice we have.

It's an easy jump to the almost-uprooted tree – a few feet,

no more. I've jumped wider gaps on Outer Earth. But I have to shut my eyes for a second, *will* myself to do it. I turn my head sideways as I hit, just in time to avoid breaking my nose. The impact knocks the tree out of alignment, and I can feel it tilting.

I'm slipping, so I tense my legs, locking myself to the trunk. Below me, the wolves are throwing themselves into a frenzy.

With a crunching, crackling sound, the tree topples over. I hang on tight as it slams into the one alongside it, crashing down onto the branch. The impact nearly knocks me off, but I manage to hang on, my legs still wrapped around the trunk. I scramble up it, heart hammering in my ears.

It's just as well I made the jump first. There's no way Harlan would have managed it if I hadn't knocked the tree over. Even then, it takes him twenty seconds to make the jump, psyching himself up for it. He almost doesn't make the landing, but then he gathers himself, scrambling up the trunk. The wolves try to follow, hauling themselves over the destroyed roots, but there are too many of them, and they're too frenzied with hunger – every time one of them gets close, another one tries to push past. Harlan's eyes are glazed with fear, and his boot is soaked in blood – I can't smell it, but it's a sure bet the wolves can.

There's another branch above me, to my left. I swing up onto it, making room for Harlan. The wolves aren't giving up. As I look down, I see that they've made it onto the fallen trunk. One of them is a few feet up, trying to dig its claws in, but it topples backwards, landing on two of its friends.

Stopping, even for a few seconds, drives the situation home. We're moving away from the road, and we can't stay in the trees forever. But I feel elation, too. It worked. Wolves can't climb. As long as we stay up here, they can't get us. They can't—

I slip. I don't know whether it's a wet patch, or just bad balance. One second I'm crouched on top of the branch, and the next I'm falling. My fingers claw at the bark, hunting for a grip, and get nothing. The familiar, sickening feeling of gravity takes hold of me, and then I'm tumbling down towards the snapping wolves.

29

Riley

It's only at the very last second, right when my legs are about to leave the branch entirely, that I realise what I have to do.

My left leg is still in contact with the branch. I swing my right leg upwards, fighting against gravity, forcing my burning muscles to react.

My ankles slam together, locking me to the branch. I start swinging, upside down now, swinging back and forth. I look down, and a pair of jaws slams shut inches from my face. The wolf falls back to earth, vanishing in a sea of barking, growling fur.

Harlan is reaching down for me, his face contorted in pain. He grabs for my hand, misses, tries again. I'm swinging too wildly. I have to tighten my ankles on the branch, slow myself down. As I do so, I feel them slipping, inching away from each other.

I bend from the waist, my torso screaming at me. It's just enough. Harlan snags my fingers, then his other hand grabs my wrist. I can see the sweat standing out on his face.

But he's got me. He's pulling me up, around the side of the branch. Away from the pack.

He wrenches me upright, and I sit, my legs dangling on either side of the branch, breathing hard, trying not to let the panic take over. The branch itself is bending and creaking, threatening to break under our weight.

The wolves are milling around below us, growling and snapping at one another, as if arguing about what to do. I risk a look down, and several pairs of eyes meet my own, bright with hunger.

Harlan is talking, more to himself than me, his words coming fast. "That was much too close. Too close. Not like that time in Dawson when we had warning. Goddamn spray. It should have worked, it should have. Eric'd know what to do. He'd get us out of here."

My nose is running, and the stinging in my eyes has changed to a horrible, maddening itch. "We have to go," I say, forcing the words out.

Harlan is still muttering to himself. I swing round and look at him. "Hey. We can do this. All right?"

He looks up. He's trembling, although I don't know if it's exhaustion, or fear, or both, but I see him nod. Moving as slowly and as carefully as I can, I make my way across to the next branch. The wolves see the movement, snarling, grinding up against the trunk of the next tree. Some howl: a noise which feels like it's going to pierce my eardrums. They're frenzied at the thought of prey, nostrils flaring, teeth bared.

Harlan is slower than I am, but he's staying with me. We move higher into the trees, testing branches, contorting our bodies as we stretch between them. It's hard going: several of the branches are covered in slippery moss, and there are others that won't take our weight. Once or twice I place a foot on one, only to have it snap and fall, crashing down onto the pack. It feels like there are more of them, like they're calling their friends from all over to join them. There's no way to tell. Everything down there is teeth and fur and horrible, burning eyes.

Even as we make progress, I know we can't keep going like this. My arms are already burning with exhaustion, and Harlan looks like he's about to fall over.

I can see sky through the trees ahead of us, the grey clouds level with my eyeline. There must be a hill, with the forest sloping down it, away from us. We can deal with that. We just have to be careful.

Then I reach the edge of the forest, and a horrified moan escapes from my lips.

It's not a hill at all.

It's a cliff.

The trees run right up to the edge of it. I could take a few more steps out onto the branch I'm on, and have nothing below me but air. The cliff itself must be fifty feet high, formed of weather-beaten rock, grey and white. It extends a long way to our left and right, curving away from us, as if we're at the apex of an enormous circle. Here and there, plants cling to the surface, small branches thrusting outwards, like they're trying to escape.

The wolves reach the cliff. We've managed to get a little way ahead of them, and at first there are only three or four, growling, running in mad circles. But then the rest arrive, bunching up against the edge.

I don't see it happen, but, suddenly, one of the wolves is falling, legs kicking at nothing. It gives a puzzled bark, and then it smashes into a jutting part of the cliff. Its head detonates, gore exploding across the rock, and the pack's howling gets even louder.

Harlan is whimpering. "We have to go back," he says.

"What?"

"We can't go down there. We can't."

142

"We don't have a choice." I say it knowing full well that I have no idea how we're even going to get to the cliff, let alone down it.

I look at the wolves. The small one, the leader, is staring up at me. Every other wolf is in a mad rage, pacing and turning, but the leader is still. He's waiting. Calmly, patiently. He knows that sooner or later we'll need to come down.

I lean out over the edge and scan the cliff, looking for something, *anything*, that will help us.

I see it.

Then immediately wish I hadn't.

"Harlan, listen to me," I say. "We're going to have to jump."

"*What?*"

I have to force the words past my lips, because what I'm proposing is completely insane. "We grab hold of that," I say, pointing. There's a tree growing out of the cliff face, fifteen feet down, slightly to the right of us. It's got two branches, shooting out at right angles to the rock face, sprouting tufts of leaves. They're not nearly as thick as the branch we're standing on, and there's every chance that they'll snap the second we hit them. But it's our only shot.

Harlan has stopped talking. Now, he's just shaking his head rapidly, back and forth, hugging the tree even tighter.

I'm not going to convince him. I could stay up here forever, and never talk him down. I've seen panic before. If you try to take a panicked person somewhere, they won't just refuse to go – they'll fight you, desperate to stay where they are.

I have to show him.

The howls get louder, rippling up from below. I look down at the plant on the cliff. It seems impossibly far away. If I miscalculate this, if I'm off by even a foot . . .

No. Don't get scared. Stay angry. Stay focused.

I inhale once. Exhale. And jump.

30

Riley

Most times, when I'm airborne, things slow down. It's my body's own safety mechanism, the adrenaline working to make sure I survive whatever I'm trying to do.

Not this time. This time, things *speed up*.

Almost immediately, I can tell I'm moving way too fast. I've overcompensated, overshot the jump, and the only thing on the other side is open air.

The branch knocks the wind out of me. I hit it so hard that I keep moving, somersaulting over the top. I have just enough presence of mind to bring my hands down, wrap my fingers around the wood, and then everything goes upside down. I get a momentary look at Harlan, his mouth open, and then I'm hanging, swinging in the wind.

My swing goes too far, and one hand comes loose.

This time, everything *does* slow down.

One hand. Four fingers and a thumb. That's all I've got between me and a fifty-foot drop. I can feel the grip on my thumb sliding away as the swing pulls it around the branch.

But swings go both ways, and this one doesn't travel quite

144

far enough to pull me off. As I come back, I throw my free hand up, grabbing hold of the branch again. Slowly, I come to a stop. When I look up, I see a dozen animal faces staring down at me, saliva dripping from open jaws. The wolves are barking, harrying each other, not sure what to do.

"Are you OK?" Harlan is shouting, over and over again, the words blending into one another. I don't answer – not yet. Instead, I move along the branch towards the cliff. It creaks and bends, but it feels like it will hold. Twigs jab at my cheek, spiky and intrusive. Now that I'm down here, the adrenaline has started to ebb, and an awful worry has replaced it. What if the rock is smooth? What if I can't find handholds?

But the rock is cracked and fissured, and there are more shrubs dotted here and there – none with long branches, but they should be enough. I move carefully, placing my feet first, positioning them on a convex piece of rock. Then I jam my fingers into one of the fissures, bending my body so that my legs can take the weight. At the back of my mind, fear is trying to grab hold, but I won't let it. Not this time. If I can climb a surface on Outer Earth, I can climb one down here.

"Riley! Help me!"

I look up. The wolves have forgotten about me. They've turned their attention to Harlan, crowding around the tree below him. He has to jump. It's the only way.

"It's OK!" I shout. It still hurts to speak, my throat stinging from whatever Harlan sprayed at the wolves. "It'll take your weight."

"I can't do it."

He's still in a panic. Not good. If I don't get him down here soon . . .

Leave him.

The voice speaks from nowhere, and this time it's so forceful that I can't ignore it. *Leave him. You can find Whitehorse on your own. He'll only slow you down.*

I actually feel my hand start to move, as if I'm about to make my way down the cliff. I clench it deep into the fissure, horrified.

I'm not leaving him. I won't do that. He's only here because of me – he might have offered to take me to Whitehorse, but I was the one who ran for the trees, the one who led us here. More than that: he's not physically equipped for this. I'm asking him to do something that even I found nearly impossible, and I've been a tracer for years. Wherever that horrible thought came from, I can't give in to it. I have to help him.

Going first wasn't enough – I'll have to talk him through it.

"It's closer than you think," I say. "I know you can make it."

Harlan moans.

"I'm going to move further out of the way." I slide along the cliff, hunting for a hold. "We're going to go on zero."

"Can't do it. Can't."

"Yes, you can. We're going to get down there, and then we're going to go to Whitehorse. You're going get me there safe, and I'm going to tell them you were with me every step of the way."

I don't give him the chance to back out. I just start counting. "Three . . . two . . ."

Harlan jumps.

I'm looking at the branch, so I don't even see him do it. Suddenly there's this *scream*, and then a thud as he slams into the branches. He hits them exactly as I did, toppling head over heels. But he doesn't have my instincts, and he doesn't grab hold of the branch as he goes over.

I rip one hand out of the crack in the rock, lunging for him. My fingers grip the collar of his coat.

Then gravity takes over, and he nearly wrenches me off the cliff face.

He slams back into the rock, roaring with pain and fear. I grit my teeth, plant my feet, do everything I can to keep my other hand buried in the cliff. I can feel the skin tearing off my fingers.

Somehow, Harlan doesn't fall. He finds one hold, then two, then he's being supported by the cliff. My hand is clenched so tightly around his coat that it's an effort to actually let go.

"Still with me?" I say, trying to inject a little humour into my voice. I'd almost forgotten about the wolves, but they're howling and barking, furious at the loss of the kill.

Harlan grunts. It's good enough.

"I think we'll be OK," I say. "You need to go first, all right? Just take it slow. I'll be right behind you, I promise."

He stays frozen for a long moment, long enough to make me think I'm going to have to talk him into it again, but then he starts making his way down the cliff, inch by inch. I wait one breath, two, then I follow.

More than once, I get stuck, dead-ended in an area without any holds. I have to backtrack, climbing up the cliff, and somehow those are the worst parts, the times when I come closest to letting gravity take me. But soon we're thirty feet above the ground, then we're twenty. There are more shrubs now: scrubby, insubstantial things clinging to the rock. We grab them as close to the roots as we can, clenching them in our fists. At ten feet above the ground, I take my deepest breath yet, and drop.

I'm used to landing on hard surfaces, and the soft ground catches me off balance. I tuck into a roll, feeling dead leaves and frozen, clammy dirt under my hands. I come up onto my feet, gasping.

Harlan is just below where I was on the cliff. I consider

telling him to jump, but he might not know how to land properly – he could crack an ankle, or worse. I direct him, pointing out the holds, talking him down until he's a foot above the forest floor.

We're in a large clearing, on the edge of another part of the forest. Huge boulders lie scattered across the ground, as if they fell from the cliff long ago. When I look up, the wolves have gone.

"Harlan," I say. "I am so, so sorry. It was the only thing I could think of, I . . ."

Harlan is making an odd sound. He's standing, hands on hips, gazing up at the cliff edge, and he's laughing. Actually laughing.

"You like that?" he shouts. "Try to mess with old Harlan, eh? That's what you get! Hope your stomachs are rumbling good and proper, you bastards. Can't catch old Harlan, not in a million years. That cliff goes for *miles* in each direction. You'll never find us."

He collapses in howls of laughter again. I take a few deep breaths, feeling my heartbeat get slower and slower.

"What was in that thing?" I say, when Harlan subsides. My tongue is dry and heavy in my mouth, and it's hard to speak.

"What thing?"

"The spray can. The stuff you used on the wolves."

"Oh, that?" A dark look crosses Harlan's face. He digs the canister out of his jacket, staring at it like it personally betrayed him. "Bear spray," he says. "Guess it doesn't work if there's more than one wolf, right?"

"*Bear* spray?"

"Should never have traded for it in the first place," Harlan says. "Goddamn useless piece of shit. Now, if I was younger, I'd go back and find the guy who traded it to me and bust his head in two." He raises his voice again, shouting at the clifftop.

"Just like I'll do to the next mangy rat-eared *fleabag* that comes anywhere near me! You hear?"

He grins. "Come on," he says, the volume of his voice returning to normal. "Whitehorse ain't far."

He limps off, heading for the trees. I follow, the wound in my thigh throbbing like a broken tooth.

31

Okwembu

Okwembu is the last one up the ladder.

It's made of rope, frayed and salt-stained, and it's all she can do to persuade her exhausted muscles to hang on. A bitter wind slices through her clothing as she climbs.

There are plenty of faces above her when she reaches the top, but no hands help pull her over. She has to do it herself, crawling over the lip of the opening. It's only when she's on all fours, shivering, that rough hands find their way under her elbows. She is yanked upright, and the first thing she sees is a rifle barrel, pointed right into her face.

They're in a wide cavity in the side of the ship, with ridged metal walls. There are fluorescent bulbs in the low ceiling, just like Outer Earth, and only half of them appear to be working. The space goes deep into the ship – Okwembu can see passages branching off it, sealed with thick doors.

Her captors say nothing. There are around twenty of them, men and women. Most of them appear to be around her age, and they're all dressed in overalls with the same pattern of grey and blue splotches. Both their clothes and their faces speak of hard use, of long years spent fighting against the wind. Edges are frayed, knees torn, and their shoes are as mismatched as their weapons – rusted rifles that have seen endless repair jobs.

Carver, Prakesh and Clay are all being held at gunpoint, just like she is. Behind them, she can hear Ray grunting as he pulls himself over the top of the ladder.

That's when she sees the man at the back of the group.

He's around fifty, she guesses, and completely bald, his head gleaming under the lights. His right eye is gone, the lid sewn shut. The stitch job is clumsy, with dark lines criss-crossing his skin; it reminds Okwembu of a bad tattoo she once saw on Outer Earth. In this case, she's almost certain that nobody has ever told this man how ridiculous it makes him look. There's something about the way he carries himself – he's not tall, or muscular, but there's a set in his shoulders that speaks of power.

Okwembu waits until he looks at her, and smiles. "Hello, Prophet," she says.

A murmuring rumbles through the crowd at her words. She can feel Aaron Carver staring at her, his eyes drilling into the side of her head. Not that it matters – *he* no longer matters. None of them do.

Ray gets to his feet behind them. "We got 'em, Prophet. These're the only ones who survived the crash. Only ones we could find anyway. If we—"

Prophet starts laughing.

The sound is musical, the laugh genuine and throaty. It transforms his face completely, his mouth opening wide, the skin around his one good eye crinkling.

He strides towards them, still chuckling. "Welcome," he says. His voice is deep and resonant. He claps a hand on Carver's shoulder, gripping tight, then looks at each of them in turn. "You're safe now. Praise the Engine!"

He booms the last sentence to the roof, and every other fatigue-clad figure on the deck echoes him. Most of them pump their fists in the air, but Okwembu sees that a few of them look down at the floor, their words almost inaudible.

Ray clears his throat. "They came down in an escape pod. Right into Eklutna. Reckon we could go back up there, get a diver down to attach a tow rope, but—"

"Ray," Prophet says, drawing out the syllable. "We will take whatever the Engine sends us, and be grateful."

He glances at Okwembu when he says it. She stays silent, telling herself to wait.

Carver gives an exasperated sigh. "You know what?"

"Just—" says Prakesh.

"No." Carver raises his chin, looking right at Prophet. "I don't give the tiniest shit about your Engine, whatever the hell it is. Your guys brought us here *at gunpoint*, so don't give us this line about being safe."

"But you *are*." Prophet hasn't taken his hand off Carver's shoulder. "All the Engine asks is that you give of yourself before you can rise into its grace, and all of us here –" he looks around at his group "– have given everything we could."

Clay makes a break for it.

Okwembu doesn't see him do it. One moment he's being held firmly, and the next he's running, bolting towards the edge of the deck.

Prophet doesn't blink. He holds out his hand, and Nessa thrusts her rifle into it. In one fluid movement, Prophet seats it in his shoulder, aims down the scope with his good eye, and fires.

The gunshot is a thunderclap in the enclosed space. The bullet takes Clay in the middle of the back. He spins a full three-sixty, arms wheeling, then vanishes off the edge of the platform. A moment later, there's a heavy splash.

Carver goes crazy. He fights against the men holding him,

Rob Boffard

managing to get his arm around a neck. One of the others steps forward, driving a fist into Carver's stomach, dropping him to his knees.

Ray brings his rifle around, aiming right for the centre of Carver's forehead. Okwembu tells herself to stay calm.

"No no no!" Prakesh says. "We'll do it. We'll do what you want."

Okwembu glances at him, surprised that he'd submit so easily. Then again, she doubts that Prakesh would let anyone else be killed – not after he himself was responsible for so much death.

Carver subsides, staring daggers at Prophet.

Prakesh is still talking. "We can help. I can grow you food, and Aaron here can fix anything. Just *don't shoot*."

The smile is back on Prophet's face – just as radiant, just as genuine. He passes Nessa her rifle, then clasps his hands behind his back.

"A wise decision, brother," he says.

He gives no signal, no nod or raised eyebrow, but their captors move instantly. They march Prakesh and Carver away, into the ship. One of them hauls open a door further down, spinning the huge valve set into the front. Their captives are hustled inside, and the door slams behind them, almost as loud as the gunshot that killed Clay.

"And what about you?" says Prophet, his calm grey eyes finding Okwembu. "Will you serve the Engine?"

"No," she says. "I won't."

Nessa grunts in annoyance, raising her gun. A sadness comes into Prophet's eyes.

"Your Engine is broken," Okwembu says. "And I'm going to help you fix it."

153

32

Anna

Anna comes to a halt just before the gallery, jogging to a stop in the corridor. She stands for a moment, hands on her knees, shoulders rising and falling as she waits out the stitch gnawing at her side.

The gallery is a giant, cavernous, echoing space, reaching all the way up the levels, criss-crossed by catwalks. Most sectors have two or three galleries, but Apex has just the one. It's in better repair than the others – or it was, before the fire. At least the lights in the ceiling above her actually work.

She hears a voice, and looks up. Alana Jordan strides across the gallery, moving away from her. Amazingly, her stomper jumpsuit is still immaculate, stretched tight across her shoulders. Her dark hair is pulled back in a ponytail, which flicks from side to side as she walks. There's a huge, black burn on the gallery floor, several feet wide. Surrounding it are puddles of dissipating foam. The air stinks of chemicals. Anna watches as Jordan skirts them, then she looks beyond her, to the escape pods.

There are twelve of them, behind large circular doors, each

with a small window. Anna's too far away to see any details through them, but she can just make out the interior wall of the airlocks housing the pods.

Every sector has some – or had, anyway. They were next to useless. A design screw-up in the station's distant past meant that each sector didn't have even close to enough pods for the people inside it. You could get three people in them, four at a push, and they barely had enough fuel to make it out of the station's orbit. They were token, and everyone knew it.

Not that it stopped people from taking them – people who wanted out, who wouldn't listen to warnings about lack of fuel and maximum range. There are still stories about them: ghost pods, floating in the void, carrying nothing but skeletons and evil spirits. Apex is the only sector which still has all its pods. For most of the station's history, it's been guarded well enough that no one's actually managed to take them.

There are stompers around the pod doors. Of course there are. They lean against the wall, pacing the floor, looking bored and irritable. Their grey jumpsuits stand out against the gleaming white surfaces.

Anna knows why they're there – to keep people away from the pods, to deter anybody who wants to make a break for it. She counts seven of them, but it may as well be seven thousand. There have already been a few souls who have tried to get the hell out, coast away into the void. The stompers have shut them down.

She has to get a look in those pods.

Anna pulls her beanie off her head, rolling it in her hands. After the breach in the dock, the other stompers closed ranks, shutting Anna out. Alana Jordan was the worst: she'd been a stomper for her entire adult life, and didn't exactly like the idea of someone as young as Anna sticking around. Is there any way Jordan would still listen to her? But even as the thought occurs, Anna realises it's useless. The remaining stompers are a tight-knit group, determined to hold the station even if it's going down. She tries to get past them and they'll just laugh at her.

There's a burst of childish laughter. Three kids dart into view on the gallery floor, skipping around the puddles, giving the burn mark a wide berth. They can't be older than seven or eight, and it sounds like there are more of them, just out of sight.

She sees Jordan turn, hears her shout something at the kids. But it's a distracted shout, and she immediately turns back to her colleagues. One of them reaches the punchline of a joke, and the group collapses in laughter. Jordan laughs as well, but gestures at them to keep it down, casting a worried glance towards the playing children. *Must have been a nasty joke*, Anna thinks.

And then: *they don't mind the kids being there*.

Anna's eyes widen. Any adult who came near the pods would find themselves looking down a stinger barrel. But the kids aren't a threat.

There are at least ten of them, kicking a ball back and forth – a tatty thing made of rags that looks like it'll fall apart at any moment. Three of the kids are involved in another game of their own devising, one that involves a lot of running and shouting. Anna's looked after a few children before, keeping an eye on them while their parents get some sleep, but she doesn't recognise any of these kids.

And there's one standing apart from the others: a girl, younger than the rest, with dark hair that looks like it's been drawn in matt-black. She wears a faded red sweater, hanging down over her knees, and she's walking in a slow circle, lost in thought.

Anger almost overwhelms Anna. When the Earthers headed

out for the *Shinso*, these kids were some of the ones left behind. They didn't deserve that. No one did.

"Hey," Anna says, trying to keep her voice quiet. Too quiet, as it turns out: the word is lost in the shouting from the ball game. Anna tries again, and this time the girl looks up.

Anna waves her over, glancing at the stompers, who are still clustered in a loose circle around Jordan.

The girl scrunches up her face, reluctant. Anna fights back frustration – she can't go out onto the gallery floor, not unless she wants the stompers to spot her.

After what seems like an age, the girl wanders over. "I'm not supposed to talk to people I don't know," she says, folding her arms.

Anna smiles. "Then why are you talking to me? Aren't you gonna get in trouble?" She sits down on the corridor floor, crossing her legs. Now she's looking up at the girl, instead of the other way round.

"You're weird," the girl says, scrunching her face up again. It's like she's seen an adult doing the expression, and is trying to copy it.

"Maybe I am," Anna says. "But you're kind of funny-looking yourself."

She regrets the words the instant that they're out of her mouth. But the girl just giggles, her eyes bright.

"What's your name?" Anna says.

"Ivy."

Anna tries to keep her face neutral. Because, right then, she recognises Ivy. When she, Riley and Carver got taken captive by the Earthers, Riley used Ivy as a hostage so they could escape. She held a knife to the little girl's throat. Anna can only hope that Ivy doesn't remember that she was there.

"I'm Anna," she says, leaning forward and resting her elbows on her knees. "Can I tell you a secret?"

Another face-scrunch. "You don't have to treat me like a little kid, you know. I'm almost six."

Anna exhales. "Right. Sorry."

Someone from the ball game shouts Ivy's name. "I have to go," she says, turning back, about to skip away to join them.

"Wait," Anna says, a little too loudly. She drops her voice. "Can you do something for me?"

Ivy looks over her shoulder. "I'm not supposed to talk to –"

"– people you don't know. Right. But it's nothing big. You don't even have to leave the gallery."

"What do you want me to do?"

"See those doors? Over on the other wall?"

Ivy looks. "Mm-hmm."

"Do you think you can look in the windows for me? I want to know how many space suits are inside each one." She thinks back to what she knows about escape pods. "They should be strapped into lockers on the wall. Each locker has a little window in it, so you should be able to see inside them."

"Why?" Ivy says.

"Why what?"

"Why do you wanna know about the space suits?"

"I just do, OK?"

Ivy folds her arms. "If you don't tell me, I'm going to go and tell Mrs Alana that you're here, and she'll come and throw you in jail."

"All right, all right," Anna says. She gets up from her sitting position, squatting on her haunches, beckoning Ivy closer. "I think there's something bad going on."

Ivy eyes light up. "Bad?"

"Real bad. And I think the space suits have something to do with it. I can't count them, because Mrs Alana will chase me away." She looks Ivy in the eyes. "Can you do that for me?"

"No," says Ivy, shaking her head. Anna's heart sinks.

But then Ivy points to the ball game, to a particularly tall boy of about eleven or twelve, wearing a dirty blue pair of overalls. "I can't see in the windows. Marcus can."

She waves him over. Three or four children trail behind him, like a council member's entourage. Up close, Marcus is even taller than he first appeared – certainly taller than Anna, with scraggly black hair and a wide nose. The first bumps of acne are beginning to spread across his cheeks. He reminds Anna of Kev, one of Riley's tracer friends who became a stomper, too. Kev, who died when a bomb that had been planted in him –

She makes herself stop, shuts that line of thought down quick.

Anna expects him to be suspicious, but as she tells him what she wants them to do a grin spreads across his face. He starts nodding even before she's finished, rocking on the balls of his feet. His excitement is infectious, spreading to the other kids. Anna has to shush them, glancing towards the stompers at the other end of the gallery. "But you have to be careful," she says. "They can't know I'm here, or that I asked you to take a look."

"I don't like it," says one of the other boys. He has the hood of his sweatshirt up, and a froth of red hair dances under the edge of it. "We could get in trouble."

"Not if we're careful," Marcus says, echoing Anna's words.

He lifts the rag ball away from one of the other kids, tosses it back and forth in his enormous hands. Then he turns on his heel, draws back his foot and kicks the ball. It lofts across the gallery, its shadow moving along the floor, and lands squarely in the middle of the group of stompers.

Anna squashes back against the wall of the corridor as the kids barrel back into the gallery, shouting and laughing. A couple of the stompers look irritated, but the others are smiling. One of them taps the ball with his foot, sending it back towards the approaching Marcus.

In less than a minute, the kids have almost all the stompers involved in the game. Even Alana Jordan is taking part, nudging the ball with her enormous feet. Ivy takes it on the run, knocking it ahead of her, darting around another stomper as if he wasn't even there.

Anna can't help smiling. Somewhere along the way, she'd convinced herself that it wasn't going to work. That the kids would ignore her, or, worse, that they'd tell the stompers about her. But it's like Ivy said: they aren't little kids any more. Not really. They all know what's happening to Outer Earth, they're all scared, all looking for something to take their minds off the situation.

Marcus has moved away from the game. He walks casually over to the first bay door, looking over his shoulder. When he sees that the stompers are still kicking the ball around, he stands on his tiptoes and looks into the window.

Anna sinks back against the wall, looking up at the ceiling. *He's going to see three space suits in each one*, she thinks. *They're all there. You got it wrong.*

An angry shout from the gallery brings her back. She tilts her head, angling it around the corner of the passage.

What she sees nearly stops her heart.

One of the stompers has seen Marcus looking in the bay door windows. He has the kid by the front of his overalls, yelling in his face. The game stops abruptly, Ivy skidding to a halt with the ball balanced under one foot.

Anna tells herself to run. Marcus will give her up in a second, and she doesn't want to be anywhere near here when that happens. But she won't leave him. If that stomper hurts the boy, Anna tells herself, she'll tear him in half. She stays rooted to the spot, hand frozen on the wall.

The other stompers have surrounded Marcus, arms folded, all their good humour gone. Jordan is talking now, jabbing a finger in the boy's face. The stomper holding him gives him a shake. Ivy runs right at them, but the other kids hold her back, grabbing her by the hem of her enormous red sweater.

But Marcus is talking, gesturing wildly. She can't hear what he's saying, but Jordan and the stompers are listening close. The other kids are all trying to talk at once.

After a minute, the stomper lets him go.

Anna's shoulders are shaking. Before, she could hardly move, but now it takes everything she has to stay put. She wants to rush out there, drive an elbow or a knee into someone's throat, show them what happens when they threaten kids.

The game resumes – slower than before, but still enthusiastic. And Anna can't believe her eyes: Marcus is continuing to look into the bay door windows. The stomper who accosted him stays close, and he doesn't look happy at all, but he lets Marcus do his thing.

After he looks in the last one, Marcus gives the stomper a friendly wave, then returns to the game. Ivy still has the ball, kicking it up into the air now, again and again, daring someone to come and take it from her.

Ten minutes later, the game finally ends. The stompers call time – they're out of breath, standing with their hands on their knees, shoulders rising and falling. The kids take off, laughing, knocking the ball in front of them.

When Marcus and Ivy and the rest of them enter the passage, Anna is waiting, sitting against the wall. *This is it*, she thinks. If everything is still where it should be, she'll forget this insanity. She'll get her matt-black, and finish her drawing.

Marcus comes to a stop in front of her. "You OK?" Anna says. "What happened?"

He says something, but it's in a hoarse stage whisper, as if there are listening devices embedded in the walls.

"What?" Anna says, leaning in close.

"Told 'em I had a bet with a big kid," he says, grinning. "That I could touch all the pod windows without getting caught. They let me."

Anna returns the smile, more relieved than she cares to admit. "OK. What did you see?"

"There's a suit missing," Marcus says, still in that ridiculous whisper. "In one of the pods on the end. There's only two suits in the locker."

Anna sits back against the wall.

"What does it mean?" says Ivy. Her eyes are huge.

"It means," Anna says, "that we're in big trouble."

33

Prakesh

The passages are narrow – so narrow that they have to walk in single file, the struts on the walls brushing their shoulders. The stairs are the worst, steep enough almost to be ladders. The sound of their footsteps is dulled, buried by other noises.

He tries to keep track of where they're going. But exhaustion and cold prick at his mind, dulling his thoughts as they descend deeper into the ship.

He's furious at himself. He should have seen this coming. If it hadn't been for the storm and the need to get to safety, he would have. He's even more furious at the Earthers. How could they have thought things were OK down here? How could they have been so unprepared?

Without wanting to, he thinks of Outer Earth, of Riley and his parents, of his hab and his office in the Air Lab. *We should have stayed there*, he thinks. *We should have tried harder to stop the Earthers from leaving.*

Carver is still reeling from the blow to his stomach, and has to stop more than once. The second time, it's to throw up. He hunches over, hands on his knees, vomiting a thin, watery gruel.

The corridor explodes with cruel laughter. "First time anybody's ever thrown up *before* they start serving the Engine," one of the men says. He's younger than the rest, with a chin almost clear of stubble.

Another, a giant with a hooked nose, says something in a language Prakesh can't understand.

The first one laughs again. "Keep walking."

Carver puts a hand on Prakesh's shoulder, uses it to pull himself upright. He wipes his mouth, tracking thin strands of slime across his skin. It reminds Prakesh of Resin, and *that* reminds him of his part in creating it. He closes his eyes, tells himself to breathe. If they can just stay alive . . .

"Hey! I said, keep walking."

A few minutes later, the corridor opens up. The room they duck into is as big as the entrance platform, with a low ceiling that gives it an oddly squashed look. It's a mess hall – there's the kitchen off to the right, separated from the room by a large window. The sinks and countertops are rusted, pitted with disuse.

There are no tables or chairs in the main area. Just a group of people, around thirty of them, sitting cross-legged on the floor. Carver sucks in a breath behind him, and Prakesh can understand why. The men and women on the floor are skeletons, thin skin stretched over collarbones and hollow cheeks. They're all sitting in silence, spooning gruel into their mouths from battered bowls. Their overalls – rags, really – hang off their bodies in shreds of brown and black.

They aren't alone. Four people in camo, two men and two women, lean against the walls. One of them looks over at Prakesh, appraising him, and the expression on her face turns his stomach to lead. She has a rifle, as do the others, and wears a thick brown jacket over her overalls, its furry hood pulled up.

Prakesh and Carver are shoved forward, hands on their shoulders pushing them to the floor. No one looks at them. The captives just keep eating, moving like robots, spoon to mouth to bowl to mouth.

The woman smiles, icy and sharp. "New recruits," she says, sarcasm edging her voice. "Engine be praised."

She stalks off to the kitchen, returning with two battered tin bowls. Spoons stick out of them, held in place by the thick contents. She shoves the bowls into their hands. "Eat," she says. "You've got five minutes."

Prakesh wants to throw it back in her face. The meal is nothing more than disgusting slop: warm and slimy, with a thick skin on its surface. But he hasn't eaten in a day, maybe more, and his hunger overwhelms him.

He takes a mouthful and wishes he hadn't. The liquid coats his tongue, tasting and smelling of nothing at all. He chokes it down, aware that he needs to keep his strength up. Carver is doing the same next to him, breaking off occasionally to breathe in hard through his nose, trying to keep it down.

As they eat, Prakesh looks around surreptitiously at the others. None of them are speaking – they're just slurping back the soup, even tilting their bowls to catch the last drops. Heads stay down, eyes locked to the floor.

They're workers.

Whatever this ship is, whatever the Engine is, these people (*and us*, he realises with a shudder) are the ones who work to keep it going. Prophet and his followers take whatever supplies are brought in, then put their previous owners to work.

He screws up his eyes, driving the heel of a hand into his face. Then he takes a deep breath, and swallows another mouthful. What else is there to do?

The guards who brought them in have left, and the ones that remain in the room look bored, their rifles held at ease.

Prakesh is looking around, chewing as fast as he can to get the sludge down his throat, when one of the other workers catches his eye. He's young, barely out of his teens. His face is freckled, and he's just beginning to get some fuzzy stubble on his upper lip.

He holds Prakesh's eye for a second, then looks away. It's the first time any of the prisoners has even acknowledged their presence.

"All right!" the woman with the hood shouts, snapping Prakesh out his thoughts. "Chow time's over."

Prakesh and Carver don't react fast enough. The prisoners spring to their feet. As one, they march to the window leading to the kitchen and deposit their bowls on the surface. One of them stays behind, stacking the bowls, while the others line up along the wall. None of them raise their eyes from the floor.

"You!"

It comes from the guard, the one who'd joked about Carver throwing up. He's pointing a stubby finger at Carver. It's only then that Prakesh realises they're standing alone in the middle of the room, still holding their bowls. The boy with the freckles glances up at him from his place by the wall, then looks back down.

"We're going," Carver says, and starts to walk towards the kitchen.

He's stopped by a shout from the guard. "Did I say you could move?" The man's voice is contemptuous, almost teasing.

We shouldn't be here, Prakesh thinks, and at that moment real panic crashes over him. He should be with Riley right now. The thought of living here, of *dying* here, without ever knowing what happened to her, is almost too much to take.

Carver doesn't turn around, doesn't look at the guard until the man puts a hand on his shoulder. Then, in one movement, he spins around and throws the bowl into the man's face.

The slime splatters the wall, blobs of it sliding down the paint. The other guards react instantly. Prakesh is shoved out of the way and Carver is pushed to the floor, held there, a boot on the back of his head.

It's as if Prakesh is watching something unfold on a tab screen. No – it's worse. You can shut off a tab screen, put it away. This is like he's in a bad dream, hurtling along at full speed, powerless to stop it. He tries to form words, but his throat is locked up tight.

Carver disappears in a storm of bodies, roaring in pain. Some of the guards are using fists and feet, while others are swinging their rifles like clubs.

Prakesh makes himself move. He grabs the guard's shoulders, tries to pull him off, but it's like trying to shift a mountain. The guard shoves him backwards, and Prakesh crashes to the ground.

He gets one last look at Carver, curled up on the ground as kicks and punches rain down on him. *They're going to kill him*, he thinks. The thought is clear as a bell, perfectly formed.

Then someone is pulling him upright. He tries to shove them off, but it's the boy, the one with the freckles, and he holds on tight.

"D-d-don't," the boy says, so softly it's almost inaudible.

He pulls Prakesh out of the room, Carver's cries growing fainter behind him.

34

Riley

Harlan's torch barely makes a dent in the darkness. It's nothing more than a rag on a stick, soaked in oil and set alight. The chill wind threatens to snuff it out at any moment.

We've been out of the forest for an hour now, walking on what Harlan calls the Old Alaskan Highway. The surface is black and hard, unusually smooth. Some sections of it are split, plants pushing up through the cracks. It reminds me of the cliff we just climbed down.

My thigh has got worse. Not just a little worse. A lot. The pain is constant now, radiating upwards in long, sluggish waves. It's hard to pinpoint its exact location. I don't know how fast infection spreads, but the shards of metal still buried inside me are almost certainly speeding things along. My fingers keep straying to the cut. Even under a layer of bandage, touching it raises the pain another notch. The flesh is swollen, tight under the fabric of my pants, and the burning itch is almost unbearable.

And it's not just my leg. My head has started to ache, pain pulsing slowly but insistently at the base of my skull. Despite the cold, I can feel myself starting to sweat. *Fever.* Even I know it's the sign of a growing infection. If these people aren't where Harlan says they are, or if they're not willing to help . . .

Several times I catch myself breaking into a jog, and have to tell myself to drop back. I don't know the way, and Harlan won't be able to keep up with me. He's limping, his ankle swollen from the wolf bite. My own, from the night before, seems to be OK – a couple of tiny cuts, nothing more. Compared to my thigh, it's barely worth noticing.

But it does occur to me that Harlan needs to get his own wound treated. We haven't spoken much since we left the forest, and I still can't shake the guilt of having put him in danger. But he volunteered to take me, and we can't be too far now.

A building looms up out of the gloom: a squat, single-storey box, lurking on the edge of the highway.

"Edge of town," says Harlan. They're the first words he's spoken in an hour.

"How far?" I say, doing the best I can to keep the fear out of my voice.

Harlan shrugs. "Judging by the house we passed? Maybe one or two miles. Could be wrong, though – this damn fog confuses me, you know? There was this one time, I was up by the Black Rapids, tracking that deer, and got lost for—"

I interrupt him. "Tell me about these people. The ones we're going to see."

"They're just people, like me."

I take a deep breath. No point in snapping at him. "How do you know them?"

"Ran with 'em for a time. Folks tend to stick together. Gives you a better chance out here. We came up from—"

He stops.

"From?" I say

He shakes his head, a black figure cut out of the darkness

by the torchlight. "Doesn't matter. Just remember what you gotta tell 'em. Then we'll be even, you and me."

I'm about to press it, ask him why he left these people, why he wants me to tell them that he kept me safe. But then I hear the voice in my head, the one that whispered to me to leave Harlan to die. It's been silent since the wolves attacked, but now it's strident, *angry*, as if there's an actual person behind the words. *He's not telling you because he's going to hurt you. There's something he doesn't want you to know about. What is it, Riley? What's in the dark?*

"No," I say to myself, shaking my head, like I'm trying to dislodge something.

"You say something?" Harlan says.

In answer, I stride past him, moving on ahead, aware that I don't know the way but needing the movement, needing the rhythm to calm my mind. Whatever he's done, whatever his relationship is with these people, it doesn't matter. I don't have a choice. I find these people, or I die. I try to ignore my headache, which feels like it's getting worse with every step.

More buildings appear, most of them set back from the road. Like the first, they're only one storey. Some of them have dishes and antennas on their roofs. They look like alien artefacts.

At one point, we cross under a structure, built over the road's surface, fifteen feet off the ground. It's only when Harlan plays his light over it that I see it's an old sign. There are three slabs of dark green metal, each with writing on them. HAMILTON BLVD. ALASKA HWY. WHITEHORSE CITY CENTRE. There's a gap between ALASKA HWY and WHITEHORSE CITY CENTRE, like a missing tooth.

Underneath the sign, there's the oddest thing. It's a big machine of some kind, right in the middle of the road. It's only when I get closer and spot the wheels that I realise it's a vehicle.

It's like Carver's Boneshaker, only much bigger, with a

closed-in cockpit and a box-shaped back end. The metal surface is rusted, the tyres long since rotted away. Harlan pays it no attention, but as he passes its front end he runs a hand along the metal, tracing the curve, a small smile on his face. It's a strange gesture, but before I can ask him about it he's walking off into the darkness.

The road begins to slope downwards, off to the left. The buildings get bigger, with larger windows and double doors. The glass in the windows is mostly gone, smashed to pieces, and some of the buildings are in ruins – missing a wall, missing a roof, sometimes no more than a few broken pillars. There are more vehicles on the road, hulking and silent.

As we walk, I hear a very soft sound, a tiny *clunk*. Off to our right, behind one of the buildings. I stop, listening hard. The sound doesn't come again.

"Harlan," I say. "You hear that?"

"What?"

The town is completely still. I shake my head. "Nothing."

Whatever it was, we don't have time to investigate. We keep walking, heading further into town, but with each step I feel like someone is watching me. Several times I look round, thinking I'll catch a shadow moving between the buildings. But there's nothing.

I feel like it's just my imagination, but then I realise that I'm getting used to the darkness – either that or the buildings are reflecting a little light, amplifying it. I can see further down the road, and I can even make out another sign alongside it. The sign reads TWO MILE ROAD.

"Not long now," Harlan says. "Almost at the river."

A few minutes later, we hit the river itself. I'm expecting a massive body of water, but what I'm not expecting is that it's choked with objects. Barrels, pieces of wood, floating structures that looked like waterborne versions of the buildings we've

171

been passing. And there are things in the river that look a little like the vehicles on the road, only without wheels.

Boats. That's what they are. For the first time in what feels like forever, I actually smile. Back when I ran with the Devil Dancers on Outer Earth, we had one book: *Treasure Island*. We'd all read it a dozen times, burying ourselves in stories about giant ships crossing the Spanish Main, on the hunt for—

The smile drops off my face. That book is long gone. So are the Devil Dancers. There's just me, and if I don't focus, I'll be gone, too.

We cross a bridge over the river. Parts of it are gone, gaping holes in the surface, and we have to be careful as we walk around them. I manage better than Harlan, moving on the balls of my feet.

As I make my way across, I see a particularly strange boat, one I didn't notice before. It's a white, enclosed cylinder, with a cockpit up front. The cylinder is supported by two smaller ones, bobbing on the surface of the water. Along the sides of the cylinder, near the top, the metal is torn, as if something was ripped off it.

There's a light reflected in the cylinder's surface.

It's there and then it's gone – one second, no more. At first, I think it's Harlan's torch, but it was too steady, nothing like the flickering flames. What I saw is the reflection of an electric light.

Harlan saw it, too. When he turns to me, his eyes are bright. "They're still there. They didn't leave!"

I don't get a chance to answer. Harlan starts jogging, heading up the road towards the light. "Come on," he shouts over his shoulder.

The road curves sharply, and there's more forest on my right – we must be at the other edge of town. And then I see the building, bigger than any we've come across before, fat and boxy. There's a sign on the side of the road: WHITEHORSE CITY HOSPITAL.

Our path opens up onto a wider apron in front of the building, strewn with abandoned cars. My eyes have adjusted to the dark now, and I can see the double doors set into the front of the building.

Harlan slows down as we reach the doors. He's bent over, wheezing, but as I come to a stop alongside him he flashes me a huge smile.

"They're really here," he says. His accent has grown thicker, spurred on by his excitement. He pushes open the door. "We'll get inside, we'll sit down with 'em, and then they can take those things out of your leg. Then you tell 'em – tell 'em how Harlan saw you right. Tell 'em how—"

His words are cut off as a bullet blows a chunk of concrete out of the floor.

35

Okwembu

"Leave us," says Prophet.

The two guards glance at each other, then obey, quietly slipping out of the door and closing it behind them.

Okwembu doesn't know where they are in the ship. Every corridor looks the same, every stairway identical. She thinks they're somewhere high up, possibly near the deck, but there's no way to tell for sure.

The room they're in is a hab – or what passes for one here, anyway. There's a single cot, the creases in its bedding razor-sharp. A folding chair. A table, clear of everything except a battered plastic bottle of water. There are no windows, no decoration of any kind. The only light comes from a bulb in the ceiling, hidden behind a wire grill.

Prophet perches on the edge of the table, arms folded, looking at her expectantly. Okwembu says nothing. She knows that one wrong word will get her sent to wherever Prakesh Kumar and Aaron Carver have gone, so she waits for him to make the first move.

Eventually, Prophet does. "So who are you?" he says.

"My name is Janice Okwembu. I was, until quite recently, head of the council on Outer Earth."

If he's surprised, he gives no sign. "And how, exactly, did you come into the service of the Engine?"

"That's not what you're really interested in."

Okwembu looks around her. "This ship," she says, "was probably built at the same time as my station. They both run off the same type of power source: a fusion reactor, yes? Devices like that were saved for the biggest structures and military units."

She stops, raises her eyes to find Prophet's remaining one. "But yours isn't working."

Prophet smirks. "Oh?"

Okwembu starts walking, slowly making her way around the room, trailing a hand along the wall. "You're broadcasting a radio message in an attempt to gather supplies from travellers seeking sanctuary. Your colleague, Ray – one of the first things he asked about was whether any fuel had survived the crash."

"We have vehicles. Boats. The humvee. They need fuel."

Okwembu raises her finger, turning it this way and that. There's a little dust on the tip, and she rubs it away with her thumb.

"Boats can be propelled without using the motor. And your Humvee is a luxury, not a necessity. You have everything you need right here." She pauses. "Including, I assume, a steady stream of workers and supplies, thanks to that radio message."

Prophet gives a good-natured shrug. "The Engine provides for its people. We just try to save as many as we can."

"You need the fuel to run your ship. You need it to power your lights and your water purification systems. But why? After all, you have a perfectly good fusion reactor sitting right here, don't you?"

She pulls the chair out from behind the table and sits down on it, crossing her legs. Without asking for permission, she picks up the bottle of water and twists off the cap. It's tangy with purification chemicals, but it quenches her thirst.

"Your Engine is broken," she says. "Or, at least, it isn't functioning as it should do. It doesn't matter what you believe, or what you worship. Belief doesn't fix a broken machine. I think your men know that."

Prophet stiffens. Okwembu stops, wondering if she's gone too far. Belief can be a dangerous thing – people will question what's right in front of them, but swear that something invisible exists. What if she—

But then Prophet smiles. And for the first time, Okwembu sees past the mask he wears. What's underneath it is as cold as the forest wind.

"And you have a spare fusion reactor, do you?" he says. "Hidden somewhere?"

"No," Okwembu says, putting the bottle back on the table. "But I know how to fix yours."

With that, she reaches into the neck of her shirt and pulls out the data stick.

She holds it up, letting Prophet get a good look at it. Then she bends forward, removing the lanyard from around her neck, and places it on the table between them.

Prophet says nothing.

Okwembu nods to the stick. "The ship we used to enter Earth's atmosphere was an asteroid catcher. Back on Outer Earth, the asteroid would have provided us with resources, but in this case we used it as a heat shield. We spent a week in orbit, while some of the crew shaped the rock for re-entry."

Prophet picks up the data stick, resting it in his palm.

"I spent that week on that ship's bridge," Okwembu says, "downloading everything I could from the ship's computer.

176

The operating system was ancient, but I managed to get it all into a useable form."

"Data," says Prophet, not asking a question. It's as if he's trying the word out, rolling it around in his mouth. "What kind of data?"

Okwembu shrugs. "Water filtration specs, data on plant growth, maps. Things I thought might conceivably be useful on a planet we knew nothing about." She takes another sip of water. "As I said, I took as much I could. I didn't have time to sort through what I had, and since the stick had more than enough space, I decided I didn't have to. So there's information on the ship's fusion reactor. Specifications, repair protocols, parts listings, emergency procedures. This stick contains everything you need to put a broken reactor back together."

"And yet," says Prophet, deadly quiet, "you offer it in place of yourself. Like you're above serving the Engine. People have died here for much less than what you've just done."

Okwembu has gambled a good deal in these last few minutes. She hates having to do it, hates the uncertainty, but knows that it's the only choice she has. There is a society here, a stable one, with structure and order and control. There are hierarchies, chains of command. There are workers – she saw one of them, back bent, mopping the floor as they passed what looked like a mess. There is water, and there is power. Everything she needs. She could integrate herself into the *Ramona*'s society, gather allies, make it her own.

And all she needs to do that is a little time.

"You can't afford to kill me," she says.

"No?"

"No." She folds her arms. "The computers on this ship are over a century old. I'm the only person here – maybe the only person *alive* – who can get the data off that stick in a useable form. You let me stay, you let me join your . . . *faith*, I suppose

177

is the word. I download the data for you, and you get your reactor back. No more depending on fuel."

"We could torture you," he says, the grey eye never wavering.

"But you won't. You've done it before, and we both know that it never quite works. Isn't it simpler just to make the trade I'm proposing?"

She gets to her feet, steps closer to him. "You need me, Prophet. The data is there, and I'll get it for you. You just have to trust me."

He looks at her, as if sizing her up. She smiles back at him, serene. He'll do as she asks, because he's like her. He knows how to get on top, and stay there. He's created a society out of nothing – stable, controlled, self-sustaining.

There are only a few people with the will to do that. And they're very good at recognising each other.

Without another word, Prophet turns and strides to the door, flinging it open. He looks over his shoulder at her, and as she looks back into that lone grey eye, she has another unwelcome flicker of doubt.

"Come with me," Prophet says. "I want to show you something."

36

Riley

Harlan leaps backwards, yelping. His torch goes flying, extinguishing itself as it bounces across the floor.

My eyes aren't used to the darkness, and I can't see a thing. I think about running – either sprinting forwards, shoulders down, making myself harder to hit, or back through the door, putting a wall between myself and the shooter.

Before I can decide, Harlan cries out. "Wait! Don't shoot! Eric, don't shoot. It's me."

Silence.

I hear Harlan take another step forward. My eyes have adjusted now, and I can see him, a shape in the darkness. "Listen to me, there's—"

A second gunshot rings out. Harlan falls to his knees.

I'm almost certain he's been hit, the thought striking me like an iron bar. But he just lost his balance. I can hear him breathing, ragged and heavy.

There's a snap, then a hiss. A burning white light appears at the back of the room, spewing thick smoke. A flare of some kind. Tears prickle at my eyes as they adjust a second time, and I hold a hand up to my eyes. I can see people, silhouetted by the light, but it takes me a minute to see their faces.

Amira is standing in front of me.

I blink, startled, on the verge of saying her name. But it isn't Amira. It can't be. Amira's dead.

Then I get a better look at the figure. It's a man, not a woman. He's tall – six five, six six, easy. His dark hair is tied back in a ponytail, and his face could be carved from rock. It's lined and weathered, the mouth set in a thin, jagged line. He wears grey pants and a dark shirt under a knee-length coat, and he's carrying a gun – a black rifle, chunky and angular. The coat as battered as his skin; on the breast, I can just make out a logo: a bird in a golden circle, with the words ROYAL CANADIAN AIRFORCE stitched beneath it.

He has the oddest thing around his neck – a necklace, a piece of cord with something white and curved hanging off it. A tooth, as long as my little finger.

Eric doesn't move. He's looking at Harlan, and there's no mistaking the expression on his face.

"You," he says. "You'd better have a good reason for coming back here."

Harlan is smiling, getting up off the floor, glancing at me as he does so. "Oh, I do, believe me. It's good to see you again, Eric, it really is. Can we talk? I—"

"Who's she?" Eric says, jerking his head at me.

I'm about to speak, to tell them about the wound in my thigh, but Harlan cuts me off. "She's the reason I'm here. I wanted to bring her to you. She crashed outta the sky, and I looked after her. She'll tell you." He looks at me again, and it's impossible to miss the pleading note in his voice. "Go on. Tell him. Like you said you would."

Eric turns on his heel and walks away, not glancing over his shoulder. "If they aren't gone in one minute," he says to someone in the darkness, "shoot them."

I don't know if these people can help me, but I'm not letting them leave without finding out. Whatever is between Harlan and Eric, however they know each other, I have to get past it.

"Wait!" I say.

Eric keeps walking.

My mouth is dry, my head pounding, but I make myself form the words. "There's shrapnel in my leg, and I can't take it out myself."

He doesn't stop. Doesn't even register that he's heard me. I swallow, trying to keep my voice calm. "Please. You're all I've got."

Eric turns back to look at me. It's impossible to decode the expression on his face, so I don't try. I just start talking, being as clear as I can. I tell them where I come from, what's happened to me. I tell them about how I got injured, about how it's infected. And I tell them that Harlan brought me down the mountain, that he kept me safe.

I look at Eric as I say this, but his expression doesn't change. Around us, the room is silent, with nothing but the very slight shifting of bodies. Harlan, Eric and I could be the last people on the planet, locked in this circle of light.

"Why should we help you?" Eric says.

"Because I'll die if you don't."

Eric doesn't even blink. "So?"

"*So?*" Harlan's eyes are huge. "Eric, you can't do that, she's—"

"Shut up, Harlan." Eric looks at me. "You got anything to trade? Anything we can use?"

I'm ready for this. I might not have anything I can give them, but I've still got the most important thing: my skills as a tracer.

"I can run," I say. "Back on Outer Earth I was a tra . . . I

181

carried packages and messages and things. I can help. I can go wherever you need me to."

But even as I say the words, I'm aware of how pathetic they sound. I'm not even halfway through before Eric is shaking his head. "Don't need any of that," he says. "Time's up. Get out of here. And *don't* come back."

For the second time, he turns and walks away.

"Eric," says Harlan. "Eric, please."

But it's not going to work. Not this time.

So I do the only thing I can.

I've always been quick from a standing start, and I'm on top of Eric before anyone can stop me. I reach out, spinning him around. In the same movement, I grab the butt of his gun and plant the end of the barrel on my forehead.

That knocks the sour expression off his face – for a moment, real terror shoots across it.

Guns are being pointed at me from a dozen directions, warnings being shouted, but nobody really knows what to do. After all, how can you seriously threaten to shoot someone already holding a gun to her own head?

I've got Eric's weapon with both hands, one under the barrel, the other under the stock. The fever is doubling and tripling my vision, and my thigh is screaming at me.

"I don't get to walk away from this," I say through gritted teeth. "And you don't get to leave me to die slow. Harlan said you could help me, but if you can't, or won't, then do me a favour and kill me now."

Nobody moves. Behind me, Harlan moans.

Eric's finger is just outside the trigger guard. A second's worth of movement, and it's all over. No pain. No more fighting.

No Prakesh, no Carver. No Okwembu, either. Do you really want that? Do you really want to lose that chance?

Eric wrenches the gun away, so quickly that the edge of the

barrel scratches my forehead. I hear hurried footsteps behind me, Eric's group closing in, but he raises a hand, and they stop.

I keep my eyes locked on his, breathing hard. Inwardly, I can't believe I just did what I just did. It was like someone else was in control of my body.

"Let me help her, boss," says someone to my left. I can't see who it is.

Eric closes his eyes briefly. "What are you even doing up here, Finkler?"

A man steps into the light. He's Eric's polar opposite – podgy, with rolls of skin under his chin. He has bright, mischievous eyes, and his ears are enormous, sticking out from the side of his head like handles. He wears a torn T-shirt with the words *Yukon Horsepacking* across it, in big, curving letters. His arms are bare, but if the cold bothers him he gives no sign.

"If she's still walking," he says, "then we've still got time. Couple of minutes with the old tweezers, some antibiotics, and she'll be good to go."

"Not going to happen," Eric says, but he sounds less sure now.

Finkler looks at me, tilting his head. "Where'd you get hit?" he says.

I don't want to take my pants off in front of everyone, so instead I point, my finger brushing my inner thigh. I have to make a real effort not to scream – not just at the pain, but at how hot and puffy the flesh feels, even under my pants.

"I took the main piece out," I say, my mouth dry. "But there's still a few shards in there."

"I can handle that." Finkler turns to Eric. "Come on, boss. I need the practice anyway."

For a very long minute, nobody moves. Everybody is looking at Eric. I don't dare speak, don't dare make a single move. I definitely don't try to think about the word *practice*.

183

"You got spine, I'll give you that," Eric says to me. He looks back at Finkler. "Do it. And stay up top – I don't want her going anywhere she's not supposed to."

"No problem," says Finkler. "I've still got a few supplies up here anyway."

I don't get a chance to thank Eric. He raises a finger, pointing it at me. "But once he's done, you're gone. Both of you."

Without another word, he turns, marching off into the darkness. Harlan tries to follow, but is brought up short behind me, two of Eric's people stepping in to block his path. They're muttering to each other, as if they aren't quite sure what just happened.

"OK then," Finkler says. His voice is high and musical, elated, like Eric just gave him a new toy. "Come with me, and we'll fix you right up."

He ducks through another set of thick double doors. I follow, too stunned to speak.

The interior of the hospital is a wreck. I can see the sky through the lobby ceiling. The corridors leading off it are dark, but Finkler seems to know where he's going. He moves surprisingly fast for a big man, his feet nimble as he skips around a pile of rubble.

I'm still trying to process the last few minutes, and it takes me some time to find my voice. "Thank you," I say.

"Don't sweat it," Finkler says. He smiles at me, his teeth picking up the light from outside. His voice is slightly nasal, like he's speaking through a pinched nose.

"I'm Riley."

"And I," he says, turning mid-stride and pulling off a weird bow, "am Finkler. Pleased to meet you."

He bashes through a set of double doors, sending them swinging wildly. "This way," he says over his shoulder.

I trail behind him. The corridor is almost pitch-black, but it

184

doesn't stop Finkler. He's looking left and right, hunting for something.

"In here," Finkler says, waving me over. He ducks into a room off the corridor, and when I follow him he's lighting an oil lamp, adjusting the light level using the wheel on the side.

The room we're in is so similar to Morgan Knox's surgery that it shakes me a little. It has the same kind of bed, the same wheeled machines and sets of drawers lining the walls, the same instruments laid out on metal trays. But there's a mattress on the bed, ancient and stained, and Finkler is bustling around collecting bottles and meds, lighting more oil lamps. He's whistling to himself – notes that almost form a tune but not quite.

The horror I felt before drips through me like poison. This is going to happen. He's going to cut into me. Right here, right now.

Finkler sees me standing in the doorway. "Come on," he says, patting the bed.

The mattress is scratchy and wet under my hands. I shuck my shoes, and slide my pants down my legs. The air is cold, goose-bumping my skin – I'm self-conscious in my underwear, but Finkler barely notices. He's pulling on rubber gloves that look like they've been used to clean out a septic tank. I lie on my back, head towards the door.

I feel Finkler unwrapping the bandages, and raise my head just in time to see him grimace at the wound. "Yeesh," he says. "Good thing you got here when you did. You say this happened yesterday?"

I nod.

"Hmm. Infection's taken faster than it should have done. Must be the metal in the leg. Nothing some meds won't cure, but it's good you got here when you did. Few more hours, that'd be that."

I decide not to look. I rest my head back down on the mattress, telling myself to breathe.

"I'm going to give you some local anaesthetic, 'kay?" Finkler says. "Some of the fragments look to be buried pretty deep, so I need to cut around them a little. Sorry I can't knock you out or anything. Don't really know how."

"But you *are* a doctor, right?" I say, trying not to let my nerves show in my voice. "You've done this before?"

Finkler smiles, not in the least bit concerned. "Yeah, totally. Air goes in and out, blood goes round and round. Long as that's happening, you got nothing to worry about."

I stare at him.

He sees the expression on my face. "Stop being such a nervous nellie," he says, slipping a syringe into the top of bottle and drawing the plunger back. "Honey, I learned medicine by doing medicine. Fixing broken legs, digging bullets out of people."

He resumes his whistling, bending over me, and running a hand down my right leg.

"This'll sting a little," he says, then laughs. "I've always wanted to say that. Usually the people I operate on are unconscious, or passed out from blood loss. It'll be nice to have someone to talk to."

The needle goes in. I hiss, without really meaning to. Finkler scoffs. "You big baby," he says.

The needle comes out, and numbness creeps up and down my leg, radiating outwards from my thigh. Finkler is pottering around, lining up instruments – tweezers, a pair of forceps, a scalpel. A memory blindsides me – Morgan Knox's surgery again, waking up after he put the explosives inside me. I shiver, shutting my eyes tight.

"Alrighty," says Finkler. "Here we go."

I feel pain when he cuts, but it's a distant sting, nothing

more. I can get through this – it's far from the worst insult my body's suffered. Sweat stings my eyes, and the fever is making it hard to form thoughts. But I'm already thinking ahead, to what'll happen when Finkler is done. Somehow, I need to work out how to get to Anchorage. Maybe I can persuade Harlan to come with me . . .

That's when I hear voices from the corridor. Raised ones, shouting commands back and forth.

"Finkler?" I say, not opening my eyes.

"Yeah?"

"Everything OK out there?"

"What? Oh yeah, yeah, fine, they're probably just—"

The door behind me bangs open. The volume of the voices increases, and I look up to see Eric leaning over me. His face is upside down, but there's no mistaking the fury on it.

"You led them right to us," he says. A fleck of saliva hits me on the cheek, and I have to resist the urge to brush it off.

"Led who?" I say. I twist my shoulders around without thinking, looking back at the door – Finkler has to put a hand on my leg to stop me. I can feel pressure in the wound – he's still got an instrument in it, nestled inside.

There's the sound of running feet in the corridor, and I see Harlan in the doorway, his face pale with fear. "You and him," Eric says, jabbing a finger at Harlan. "Nomads."

"How many?" Finkler says. He doesn't move his hand from the wound.

"Lots." He looks back at me. "They must have been tracking you, and now you *brought 'em right here*."

I don't know what to say to that, but I'm saved when Finkler speaks up. "Scouts said they'd left the area," he says. It's impossible to miss the worry in his voice.

"Guess they got it wrong. And now it's coming down on top of us."

He doesn't wait for me to respond. "Finkler," he says. "Get below. Right now."

"You got it," Finkler says, and I feel him slowly withdrawing the scalpel. "Sorry about this, but we're gonna have to postpone—"

He stops speaking, and that's when I notice a different sensation in my leg. Not pain, exactly – it's more a feeling of tension, like how my muscles feel after a long run.

"Oh, fuck," says Finkler quietly.

I lift my head. He's got the scalpel in the wound – I can just see his fingers wrapped around the handle – and there's a *lot* of blood. It's spattering his gloves, dotting the skin on his forearms. Eric is staring at him, his eyes wide.

"It's OK," Finkler says. "I just . . . I think I might have nicked your femoral artery."

"What?" Harlan and I say at the same time.

"Leave it," says Eric, striding over to Finkler, trying to pull him away.

He shakes Eric off. "No way," he says. "Gotta fix this."

"Finkler."

"If I don't, she'll bleed out."

"Not our problem. I can lose her, but I can't lose you. Get below, right now."

I thump my head back down on the mattress. This is not happening. *This is not happening.*

"I'm not leaving her," Finkler says. There's a note of steel in his voice, one I haven't heard before now. "She stays, I stay."

"No."

"You can't just leave me here," I say, horrified. I'm feeling strangely lightheaded now, and I recognise the sensation – this isn't the first time I've lost blood.

Eric ignores me, speaking to Finkler. "Don't be stupid. You're putting everyone in danger."

188

"What's the matter, boss?" he replies. "Can't handle a few Nomads?"

He sees Eric about to explode, and speaks quickly. "She's my patient. I screwed up, and I have to handle this. Boss, I *have* to. I've got clamps and sutures – it won't take me long."

There are a few seconds when I think Eric is going to win. He's going to drag Finkler away, and leave me to die. But then something passes between them, a look I can't even begin to decode. Eric swears loudly, turning and running for the door. I see him grab Harlan, pushing him out into the corridor. "We'll hold them off as long as we can," he shouts back at us. "Just hurry."

"You'll be OK," Harlan says. "He knows what he's doing."

Finkler starts whistling again, and I hear the first gunshot echoing down the corridor.

37

Riley

I lay my head back, trying to remember to breathe. I tell myself that there's nothing I can do, that I have to let Finkler work.

"Goddamn it," he says, talking more to himself than to me. "Stupid thing. Keeps slipping."

More gunshots ring out, closer this time, like they're coming from *inside* the hospital. "Please hurry," I say, clenching my teeth so hard that my jaw twinges. It helps keep the lightness in my head at bay.

"Sorry. Never done this before. Artery, I mean."

I hear running footsteps, and tilt my head back to see people sprinting past the door, yelling at each other. A face appears in the doorway. Eric. His eyes are dancing, alive with the heat of battle.

"How're we doing?" Finkler says, without looking up.

In response, Eric swings away from the door, letting off a round of shots at someone we can't see.

A moment later, he strides into the room, then reaches around behind his back and pulls out a handgun.

I'm so wired that, for a moment, I'm convinced he's going

to shoot me. But he just holds it out to Finkler, who gestures at him to put it on the table.

"They're coming in from all sides," Eric says. "We have to split our defences. You see anybody come in that's not us, shoot them."

"Got it."

"There are too many of them. They must have been lying low, camped somewhere we couldn't see."

"Got it."

"We're going to hold this corridor, but they're coming in from everywhere, and we don't have nearly enough people. If we—"

"I said I got it, Eric! I'm working here!" Finkler waves him away. Eric vanishes, exploding out of the door, loosing off another volley of shots.

Finkler keeps operating. He's working with stitches now – I can feel the thread jerking through my artery. I try not to imagine what it looks like. The anaesthetic is still there, but the pain is winning, hot and sharp, shooting up from the wound.

It isn't enough to hold off the fogginess in my mind.

There's a shout from the doorway. My eyes fly open to see Finkler grabbing the gun, loosing off two quick shots. The bangs are enormous, and the shots ricochet off the corridor wall. I have just enough time to see a shadow there before it vanishes, ducking out of sight.

"Yeah!" Finkler shouts. I look over to him, in time to see a fresh spurt of blood jet up from the wound.

He sees it, too, and his brow furrows. "Here," he says, holding the gun out to me.

I take it in one shaking hand. It's heavier than the stingers we had on Outer Earth, the surface slimy with oil.

"You've got to be kidding me," I say.

"It's easy," he says, raising a scalpel. "You point it at someone and pull the trigger. Bang."

"I know how a *damn gun works*!" I say, shouting the last three words as the anaesthetic gives way, a shrieking pain blasting up from my thigh.

"Sorry," Finkler mutters. He doesn't stop, using his teeth to hold the end of the thread. His arms are soaked in my blood. I don't know how much I've lost already, and I *really* don't want to think about it.

I keep my eyes on the door. I have to tilt my head back to look at it, so it's upside down. "How will I know who to shoot?" I say, tasting sweat.

"What?" Finkler is barely listening.

"What if I shoot one of your guys?"

A second later, a Nomad comes through the door, and I realise that that's not a mistake I'm going to make.

The man is tall, with pale skin and lank dreadlocks. He wears a sleeveless T-shirt and torn pants. At first, I think his face is scarred, but then I see that it's paint: long slashes of it, red and grey, curving around his nose and mouth.

He has a gun, long-barrelled, battle-scarred, around his neck on a sling. He leads with it, kicking open the door and flying into the operating theatre. For a second, he's brought up short, not expecting to find an operation in progress.

One second is all I need.

I raise the gun and fire, not thinking, not *wanting* to think. I pull the trigger again and again. The kick from the weapon nearly takes my head off. My view is upside down, and my wooziness makes it tough to aim: two bullets go wide, but the third finds its mark, tearing away half of the man's neck. He goes down, full ragdoll, spinning as he hits the floor.

"Jesus!"

Finkler ducked when I fired, pulling the scalpel out of the

192

wound. The pain rockets through me, delayed by my adrenaline but finally shooting home, and I let loose an animal cry. The air is thick with the smell of gunpowder.

Finkler gets back up, wiping his forehead, staring down at the wound. "Shit. I think I sliced a muscle."

"*What?*" The word is almost a shriek.

"No, hang on. It's fine. I just have to be careful." I feel Finkler's fingers in the wound, opening it further. "Hang on . . . got it. There. Artery's patched up. No harm done. We're fine."

He's barely finished speaking when another Nomad bursts into the room. This one is even more terrifying – his head is shaven, and the paint goes right over the top of his skull, as if his head is some kind of ancient totem. He's bare-chested, and he's already raising his gun.

I raise mine faster. I fire once. Twice. Both bullets go wide. I pull the trigger again, and the gun clicks empty.

The Nomad grins, takes a step forward. His eyes move from me to Finkler. He lets his gun drop, and takes a wicked-looking knife out of his belt. Its blade is long, slightly curved, the edge notched and gouged. *Smart*, I think, not wanting to but doing it anyway. *He doesn't want to waste ammo.*

I hurl the gun at the Nomad. It's a last-ditch move, awkward from my position, and it doesn't even come close to hitting him. Finkler cries out – a high, warbling yell. But he doesn't move away from the table. Instead, he moves around it, trying to shield me.

The Nomad smiles, sauntering towards us, taking his time.

The room swims in front of me. I blink, and there's something around the man's neck. It's a rifle, and behind it is Harlan, yanking it backwards, pulling tight.

The Nomad grunts, tries to fight him off. He's strong, and when he wrenches his body to the side, Harlan is lifted clean off his feet. He screams, but refuses to let go, pulling the top of the rifle into the man's throat.

I will myself to move, but it's as if my mind is no longer attached to my body. I don't know if it's the fever or the blood loss. I can't do anything but watch.

The Nomad reaches behind him, slamming his fist into the side of Harlan's head, who lets go, tumbling away. But the Nomad is focused on Harlan, and he doesn't see Finkler lunge forward, doesn't even realise he's there until the scalpel is buried in the side of his neck.

His knife clatters to the floor. It's the last thing I hear before I sink into oblivion.

38

Prakesh

Everything hurts.

The ache in Prakesh's legs radiates upwards through his spine. His arms are in agony. It's his shoulders that hurt the most – every time he takes a step, the enormous bag of soil presses down on them.

He concentrates on putting one foot in front of the other, blinking away the sweat dripping into his eyes. Then he's at the mustering point, the other bags of soil appearing in his field of view. With a groan, he rolls the bag he's carrying off his shoulders. It thumps on top of the rest, starts to slide back. For a horrible moment, Prakesh thinks it's going to slide right off – he'll have to pick it up, and that means crouching down, which he's not sure he can do at that moment.

The bag comes to a quivering halt. Prakesh straightens up, tries to ignore the pain in his upper body. He places his hands at the small of his back, rolls his neck.

"Move it," the guard says.

He's sitting on a nearby crate, elbows on his knees, and his voice has a high-pitched, needling quality to it that Prakesh has already learned to hate. The guard has told him to *move it* every time Prakesh has brought another bag of soil, and he doesn't vary his tone no matter how quickly Prakesh heads back to the other side of the hangar.

Out of the corner of his eye, Prakesh sees another prisoner stumbling towards him, almost collapsing under the weight of the bag of soil. Prakesh sidesteps smartly, but something under his shoe causes him to slide, a slick of oil, maybe, and he over-balances. His windmilling left hand brushes the bag on the worker's shoulders, and he has to stop himself from grabbing hold. He finds his balance, exhaling hard. The worker glances at him as he offloads the bag. He looks brittle, like his bones are made of thin glass. Every prisoner is like that, moving as if each step will make their shins crumble.

"Move it."

Prakesh walks back across the hangar, past the line of trudging workers, back towards the dwindling pile of soil bags. He's counted twenty-eight prisoners here besides him, plus six guards spaced around the hangar. He wonders how many people are actually on this ship, the ratio of prisoners to guards, but then realises he's too tired to care. The gruel they ate a couple of hours ago barely registered inside his body, and his throat is screaming for water.

The hangar is in the centre of the ship, and it's enormous – not as big as the Air Lab, but still a couple of hundred feet from end to end. It's baking hot, shimmering with a wet, sticky heat. There are stacks of crates everywhere, rusted together, their tops and sides ripped off in places. A disused forklift is parked near the wall, missing two of its wheels. There's even a plane in a corner of the hangar, hulking and silent, covered with frayed netting like a captured animal.

Most of the floor space is given over to huge troughs, filled with soil, running wall to wall. The troughs are badly made, little more than sheet metal clumsily welded together. The soil is poor quality. The few living plants that Prakesh can see are wilted, feeble things: tomatoes and beans and cabbage and squash.

The irony is, there are a dozen ways he could improve the yield: space the plants properly, introduce interplanting, create better fertiliser. He tries to think about the procedures, hoping to distract himself, but he's just too damn tired.

Prakesh reaches the first pile of soil sacks. He focuses on the one he has to pick up – the pile is low to the ground now, and the sack is at knee level. Like the others, it's made of thin brown fabric, harsh on the hands, with grains of dirt leaking out between the fibres. He's going to have to crouch after all.

Move it, Prakesh thinks, and bends to pick up the sack.

There's movement in front of him, flickering at the edge of his vision. He looks up to see one of the prisoners fall – a woman so thin that her collarbone appears to be holding up her body like scaffolding.

The woman hits the ground with a staggered thump, her arms splayed out on either side of her. She gives a thin, rattling breath, then falls still.

Prakesh tries to cry out, but his throat won't cooperate. He takes a step towards the woman, reaches out to her—

A hand lands on his chest, pushes him back. One of the guards, her face utterly bored. She has long hair running down her back, deep red in colour.

"Back to work," she says.

Prakesh stares at her. "She—"

"I *said*, back to work."

And Prakesh knows that the woman is dead. Knows it down to his bones. Is he really the only one who sees this? He looks over his shoulder – the other prisoners are looking at him, glancing up as they trudge, but nobody is coming to help. Not a single person.

The scene swims in front of him, and a burst of nausea propels itself up from his stomach. He reels in place, bent double, aware that he has to throw up and not sure how to stop himself.

The guard doesn't tell him again. She doesn't wait for a response. Prakesh senses that she's raised her rifle, that she's turning it in her hands. Any moment now, the butt is going to crash into him, and that'll be that. If she hits him, he's not getting up. Not that he can do anything about it.

At least I'll see Mom and Dad, he thinks. *Maybe Riley, too.* He's aware that he's trembling, but he doesn't know how to stop.

"No!" It's a different voice, high and reedy. The speaker steps between Prakesh and the guard. "He's n- he's n-"

Whoever it is gulps, two quick sounds, then says. "He's n-n-new. He d-d-doesn't kn-kn-know how it w-works, that's all."

There's a pause. The guard's rifle doesn't crash into him.

A canteen appears, raised by a thin, grimy arm. Somehow, Prakesh gets hold of it, and manages to drink. It's a few seconds before his throat responds, and then it's almost too much, like he's trying to drink the ocean.

Somehow, he manages to keep it down. When he lowers the empty canteen, he sees the kid with the freckles staring back at him. He's just as emaciated as the others, but his eyes are alive. The guard, the one with the tattered boots, is standing off to one side, looking sour. The woman's body is still there. Two of the guards are bending down for it. (*Her*, Prakesh thinks. *Not it.*) The man holding the wrists says something Prakesh can't hear, and his partner actually laughs.

The kid with the stutter bends down, and with a grunt, hoists a sack of soil. Prakesh does the same, trying hard not to look at the body, trying not to think about what he just saw.

The thoughts come anyway. *How long before you end up like that? How long before they work you to death? A month? A week?*

He and the kid trudge back to the empty troughs in silence. It's only when they're halfway there, when no guards are nearby, that that kid speaks.

"J-J-J-" he says, scrunching up his face, trying to get the word out without raising his voice. "Jojo. My n-n-n-name's J-J-Jojo."

"Prakesh."

They reach the second pile of soil bags, and heave their loads onto it. A puff of dirt shoots up from the pile, the motes floating in the air in front of them. As Prakesh looks up, he sees that the two nearby guards are turned away, muttering to each other.

Prakesh speaks as quietly as possible, keeping his head down, aware of the guards. The water is having an effect, and his head is starting to clear. "How many guards?"

"Wh-what?"

Prakesh gestures to the nearest one, then raises a questioning eyebrow.

Jojo bows his head, hunches his shoulders. He starts walking a little faster, and Prakesh has to up his pace to stay level. Jojo shakes his head – a quick, almost imperceptible movement – then his mouth forms a single word.

Later.

39

Okwembu

Prophet leads Okwembu down through the vessel, through endless corridors and T-junctions, walking for so long that she's given up trying to keep track.

They're below the waterline now. They must be close to the outer hull – she can hear the ocean lapping at the walls, the echoing sound of the metal creaking in the cold water. Okwembu's clothes are still damp, and she shivers as they walk, rubbing her arms. Prophet hasn't said a word since they left his quarters, hasn't even looked at her.

Eventually, they come to what looks like a dead end in the corridor. No – not a dead end. The lights in the ceiling have burned out, and as they get closer Okwembu can see a massive set of double doors. A track runs down the centre of the corridor, with a single wide rail set into it. Chunks of the rail have rusted away – when this ship was still in service it must have been used to transport heavy equipment.

There are three guards outside the door. Two leaning against it, and one sitting up against the corridor wall, spooning food into his mouth from a can. All three are heavily built, camouflage tight across their shoulders, and all three carry rifles. The two standing men stiffen as Prophet and Okwembu approach, fingers just touching their trigger guards.

The man on the floor stops eating, his spoon halfway to his mouth, eyes tracking between them. He gets to his feet, dusting himself off.

"Brothers," Prophet says, spreading his arms wide. He sees where the men are looking. "She is under my purview, for now." He gestures to the door. "Open her up."

The other men keep looking at Okwembu, not moving. She meets their eyes, her face expressionless.

"I said, open it." Prophet's voice has become very soft.

The two guards by the door look at each other. The one on the left nods almost imperceptibly, and his partner fishes a key out of his uniform. The key isn't like anything Okwembu has seen before: it's long and flat, the metal scored with a line of precise circles.

There's a slot in the left door, at ground level, and the guard has to crouch down to insert the key. He grunts as he turns it, and within the door a locking mechanism clicks back.

Prophet watches, his arms folded, as the two men haul the doors apart. Metal screeches on metal, and a shiver of rust falls from the top of the doors, flakes drifting to the ground. Okwembu peers into the space beyond, but there's nothing but darkness. What little light there is from the corridor reveals a grated metal surface.

"Thank you, brothers," says Prophet, walking past them. As he does so, one of the men mutters to himself.

Prophet whirls, getting in the man's face. "You say something?"

Okwembu expects the man to quail, to protest. He doesn't. Above his trim black beard, his eyes are cold.

After a moment, he shakes his head. "No, Prophet."

"You got anything to say to me, you can say it to my face. Or I'll see you taken to the stern, Engine's my witness."

The man breaks his gaze, looking away. "Nothing, Prophet."

She expects Prophet to persist, but he just turns and strides past the doors. "Kyle. Vladimir," he says over his shoulder. "Lock it behind us."

"Yes, Prophet."

"Yes, sir."

Curious, Okwembu thinks, as she falls in behind him. Perhaps Prophet's control isn't as iron-clad as she thought. That's good. It could make things easier.

Prophet turns the lights on. Okwembu's mouth falls open.

They're standing on a platform above a hangar, as wide as one of the galleries on Outer Earth. Banks of high-power lights are clicking on in the ceiling, one after the other. On the floor of the hangar are several massive containers – Okwembu counts twelve, stretching to the back wall. They remind her of the vats in the Recycler Plants on Outer Earth, the ones that treated human waste. It's as if an entire plant's worth of vats have been laid on their side, placed end to end.

She leans on the platform's railing, looking closely at the nearest container. It's been made in the past few years – there's very little rust. The seals have been badly done, as if each one was put together from spare parts. There's a hole cut in the top of each container, as wide as three men. Okwembu glances up: there are half a dozen thick pipes hanging down from the roof, their ribbed surfaces crinkling as they gently sway in place. The pipes disappear into the mess of girders in the ceiling.

And there's the smell of fuel. It fills the air, thick and oily.

"Why are you showing me this?" she says.

"We came to this ship ten years ago," Prophet says, and there's something in his voice that wasn't there before. The bright tone he had while taking about the Engine has disappeared. There's a set of metal stairs leading to the floor, and he marches down them, his hands clasped behind his back. "We were tired. Tired of living underground. The elders told us that the whole world was dust, but we decided to see for ourselves."

They reach the floor, and Prophet idly trails a hand along the vertical pleats of a giant container. "We thought if we went east, the land would be different. So we got as many air filters and supplies as we could, and made the crossing. The journey was . . . well. We were tested."

He pauses, as if gathering himself. "We were hugging the coast, and found this ship out in the bay. There'd been some sort of battle. We don't know who they were or what they were fighting over, but none of them survived. There *was* a fusion reactor, broken, beyond our capability to repair. And they had this fuel stored down here. Enough to last us a while."

He taps a container, and a boom echoes off the walls. It's the sound of an empty vessel.

Okwembu waits for the echoes to vanish. "But not long enough," she says.

"We could always use more fuel, hence the radio message," says Prophet. "Survivors provide that, and more. They provide their hands, their labour. This is a big ship, and we can only do so much."

He smiles. "Do you have faith, Janice Okwembu?"

She knows enough to stay silent, letting him fill in the gap. He obliges. "We all do. Even in the worst of the Alaskan winter, where the wind would take your mind if you let it, we had faith. Even when we had to burrow down into the dirt, wait out the dust storms, we had faith. We would be provided for. And we were."

He raises his hands to the ceiling. "Not just with the *Ramona*. Not just with the fuel. But with the *Engine*."

He shakes his head. "It took us a little while to get it working. We had to figure out how to run it on the fuel we had. But once it did, it smiled down on us. It changed the air, allowed us to go outside without masks. It raised the temperature, brought the trees back. It gave us the land, and we used it. No more hiding under the dirt, scared of the world above."

"Wait," Okwembu says, shaking her head. "I don't understand. The Engine . . . you're using gasoline to run a fusion reactor? That isn't possible."

Prophet ignores her. "We are running low on fuel, Janice Okwembu. I am a man of faith, but even I know that miracles are most often based in reality. There are fewer and fewer survivors coming in, and when they do, they bring less and less fuel. We have barely enough to last one more winter. If we run out of fuel, this ship will die. And the Engine will die with it."

He raises his eyes to the ceiling. "Some of my men think we should let it. That we should stop feeding the Engine with fuel, and let the land starve. The climate here is so fragile – even a year without the Engine's influence would destroy it."

Abruptly, Prophet turns and stalks away, striding down a line of containers bigger than he is. Okwembu follows, her mind reeling. "Prophet, wait," she says.

"You asked why I'm showing you this. It's to illustrate the consequences of lying to me." He doesn't turn to look at her, but Okwembu can hear the razor edge in his voice. "We need that reactor. We need it to keep the Engine alive, and to free us from our dependence on this."

He taps the container again. There's a thin line of fuel running down from one of the containers, dripping out of a microfracture in the metal. Prophet runs his finger along it, the liquid coating his skin.

"You're right," he says. "I'm not going to torture you into retrieving that data. I'm going to torture you if you *can't* retrieve it. And once it starts, there'll be nothing you can do to make it stop."

Okwembu makes herself speak. "Prophet, I don't understand this at all. *What is the Engine?* If it's not the fusion reactor . . ."

Prophet's smile grows wider.

And he tells Janice Okwembu what the Engine really is.

40

Riley

When I awake, I'm still lying face up on the bed, and my thigh is bandaged tight. Finkler is in a chair, leaning against the wall, fast sleep. His mouth is open, with a thin slick of drool on his chin, and he's snoring gently, snuffling through his nose. His arms hang by his side, and I see that he still has his gloves on.

I try to sit up, but something pulls at my right arm. A drip, the needle buried in the vein. The fluid bag is suspended on a slightly rusty pole, and it's almost empty, with only a half-inch of yellow liquid remaining. Wincing, I slowly pull the drip out. There's a tiny spurt of blood, but that's all.

The events of the night before come back to me. When I look around the room, I see an enormous patch of blood on the floor, parts of it still liquid. I'm still a little fuzzy, and it takes me a minute to remember what happened. The Nomad bursting through the door, Harlan fighting him off, Finkler stabbing him through the neck.

I give my leg an experimental flex. It hurts like hell, but it's not as bad as I thought it would be. I swing my legs off the bed, take a deep breath, and stand up, moving even more slowly than when I pulled the needle out. My thigh groans, but it can handle the weight. I take one step, and then another. The floor is freezing cold, but I don't mind. I can walk.

I think about waking Finkler to ask him if he has some painkillers, but I don't. He saved my life. He even treated the wolf bite on my leg – it's bandaged, too, with yellow disinfectant leaking through. The least I can do is let him sleep.

I pull my pants back on, slipping them over cold skin, taking it very gently. There's a bottle of water balanced on top of one of the shelves, almost full. I drain half the bottle before I realise that it might not have been for me, and I put it back, feeling a little guilty.

The water wakes my stomach up. There are still some plants in the pocket of my jacket, and I chew on one as I walk down the hospital corridor. It's cattail, I think – Harlan showed which parts I could eat, the white centres at the base of the leaves. The taste is fresh and sharp. I follow it up with the last of the meat strips, savouring them.

The hospital looks different in the daylight. There's no telling what time it is, but the parts of sky I can see through the shattered ceiling make me think that it's early morning; the clouds are lightening, their dark grey fading away. I make it to the entrance, seeing things I didn't see the night before. Plants have grown across the floor, as well as the desk at the back of the room. The old signs are still up on the wall, still legible after all this time: OBSTETRICS, GYNAECOLOGY, OUT-PATIENTS.

And there are bodies, stacked in the corner.

They're all Nomads, from what I can tell. Maybe six of them. A mess of limbs and ugly paint. I don't see any of Eric's people, but that doesn't mean they weren't hurt, or that they don't keep the bodies somewhere else. For a horrible moment, I could swear that I see Syria among them, but it's just my mind playing tricks.

The bodies are being tended by a man and a woman, who

are dragging another one across. Neither of them glance at me as I walk past them. I think about talking to them, saying something, but realise I don't want to. Not now.

Every atom in me wants to go, to head right out of the front door, keep going, and not stop until I get to Anchorage. But it's not hard to picture Carver, picture him shaking his head, telling me that I need a plan first.

He's right.

There are stairs on the other side of the entrance hall. I climb them slowly, knowing that my leg can take the pressure but not wanting to push it too hard just yet. The pain has settled down to a low throb. I'll have to wait until Finkler is awake to know if there's any lasting damage, but from the feel of things, I should be OK.

I don't really know where I'm going. Right now, just moving is enough.

The stairs take a ninety-degree turn to the left, leading out onto a corridor on the second floor. It's a mess. There are a couple of upturned stretchers, and the floor is covered in dead leaves and plant roots. The only light comes from an open door a little way down. As I get closer, I hear voices.

It's Harlan. ". . . suffered enough", he's saying. "I'm out there, by myself, with nobody to help me. I survived for over a year in those mountains."

"Oh, don't make out like you're some kind of hero." Eric's voice is sharp and hard. "After what you did? You think you have any right to come back here?"

"Eric—"

"And bringing *her* . . . what, did you think we'd just open our arms? It's a cheap trick, Harlan. You know it, I know it."

"I saved her. I did. You can't take that away from me. She told you herself. That has to mean something, whatever you say about it."

208

"Fuck you, Harlan. You need to leave. Not tomorrow. Not later today. Now."

The space outside the doorway is a balcony – a wide rooftop space, empty except for a single plastic chair by the waist-high railing. Puddles of foul water dot the gravelly surface. I can see out across the river, across the low buildings of Whitehorse to the mountains beyond. There's a gap in the clouds, just a tiny one, and the rising sun has turned it to a gorgeous, burning orange slash. It reflects off the surface of the river. The space before the bridge is clogged with debris, but the water runs clear downstream of it, the river growing larger as it filters into a lake.

For the first time, I find I can look at the sky without my vision going weird. Maybe Harlan was right – up until yesterday, the largest space I'd been in was outside the station, and that was only for a few minutes. My body's slowly adjusting to having a horizon, getting used to not being enclosed in a tiny metal ring.

Harlan and Eric haven't noticed me. They're standing over by the balcony, facing each other, close enough to touch. They're wearing the same clothes they were the night before. Eric's airforce jacket is dark in places, crusted with dried blood, and Harlan's ankle is wrapped in a bulky bandage.

"You think I'm kidding?" Eric says, jabbing a finger in Harlan's chest. "You play games with me on this, and I'll shoot you myself."

"You'd like that, wouldn't you? Then you wouldn't have to think about me."

I shouldn't be here. I'm intruding on something very private. I try to remember why I came up here in the first place, and find that I can't. I turn to go, automatically shifting onto the balls of my feet, and that's when Harlan says, "Oh, hey – you're up."

I close my eyes briefly, then turn. They're both looking at

me, silhouetted slightly by the burning sky. Harlan is smiling, relieved, but the look on Eric's face is thunderous.

May as well make the most of it. I look up at Eric. "I wanted to say thank you," I say, stumbling over the words a little. "I don't know how I can pay you back, but . . ."

Eric crosses the space between us in three long strides, and slaps me across the face.

It's a backhand hit, not as hard as a punch but still strong. I raise my hand to block it, but I'm not fast enough. It takes me across the mouth, and my teeth cut into my top lip. I taste blood, harsh and salty.

"Eric!" Harlan says.

My first instinct is to hit back, to take a swing at him, but I don't. I just stand there, watching his shoulders heaving.

"I don't know what happened to you," Eric says, "and I don't care. I want you gone."

The slap has brought the anger back, instantly, like it was waiting to happen. And that awful voice again, bitter and strident: *You hit me again, I'll break your arm.*

With an effort of will, I bring myself under control. Eric must see something on my face, because he takes a step back.

"I'm sorry," I say, picking my words carefully. "I didn't have a choice. There was no one else who could help me."

Eric stalks away before I'm finished, coming to a stop by the railing, leaning on it like he's admiring the sunrise. My cheek is throbbing, and I can taste blood in my mouth.

Harlan shuffles over. "You OK?"

"Fine," I say.

"Don't mind Eric. He'll come round. Nomad attack wasn't too bad – couple of his folks got hurt, but nothing serious."

I look down at my feet, then back up, into his eyes. Before he can do anything, I pull him into a hug. He's taller than me, and I have to stand on tiptoe to put my head next to his.

"Then thank *you*," I say. "For everything."

"It's OK," he says, laughing a little, patting my back, as if he's not quite sure how to take this. I pull away, and he nods, two quick dips of the head.

"I'm going to head out," I say. "The sooner I get moving, the better."

A dark expression crosses Harlan's face. "Come on now. You aren't still talking about—"

"They're out there," I say, thinking of Prakesh, and Carver. *And Okwembu.* "I have to find them."

"You got nothing between those ears of yours?" he says, tapping his forehead. "You. Won't. Make. It. Nobody would. Even the Nomads don't go that far west."

He pats the air, like he's trying to calm the situation. "Listen. Listen, now. Why don't you just come with me? You can make a life out here for yourself. Plenty of people have. There aren't a lot of us, but we do all right. It's better than dying out *there*, when you don't even know if your friends are alive or—"

"Stop," I say.

Harlan doesn't. "It's suicide," he says, angry now. "It's insanity. You almost got dead from that infection, and now you want to walk to *Anchorage*?"

"Anchorage?" Eric is still angry – I can see it in the way his mouth is set – but he's confused, too. "What the hell is she going to Anchorage for? Doesn't she know what happens out there?"

"I *told* her!" Harlan's eyebrows skyrocket. "She won't listen."

"I'll be fine," I say, but neither of them is paying attention to me now.

"We can't let her go, Eric. She'll die out there."

"That's on her," Eric says. "And you, since apparently you didn't do a good enough job of telling her how bad an idea it is."

"But she'll—"

I stick two fingers in my mouth, and whistle. The piercing sound explodes across the rooftop before drifting off into the cold morning air. It brings both of them up short.

"I'm going, OK?" I say. I turn to Eric. "You won't see me again, I promise. Just let me say goodbye to Finkler, and I'll be on my way."

Eric nods. "Good. Listen to Harlan, though. You're insane, thinking you'll make it to Anchorage."

I've managed to contain my anger so far, holding it back with an effort of will, but Eric's words almost make that will fail completely. I want to grab him, shout at him, *make* him understand.

In my last months on Outer Earth, I was scared. All the time. Scared of people who want to hurt me, scared of losing the people I love, scared of getting someone killed. I thought I could do it – I thought I could live with it. But it didn't matter. I ended up losing them anyway. And in the process, everything I know was ripped away.

So I'm done being scared. I'm sick of it. Eric thinks I'm insane? No. It would be insane to not go, to *not* try and get my friends back. If I don't, I'll spend the rest of my life wondering if they're still out there. I'll spend the rest of my life knowing that I had a chance to track down Okwembu, and didn't.

I don't say any of this. Somehow, I get that anger back under control. Because Eric doesn't deserve it – not after I put him and his people in danger. Not after they helped me.

"OK, Eric, listen," Harlan says. "If she's gonna be hard-headed about it, then at least help her out with some supplies. A better coat or something. I saw your people wearing some pretty heavy gear, and I know Marla's still got a full storage locker, saw it when I was down there."

Eric says nothing. When Harlan speaks again, he sounds like he's panicking. "What about the seaplane?" he says, pointing. "That one, in the river? I know it's rusted all to shit, but we could fix it up!"

"Good luck with that. Believe me, we tried. Thing's shot to shit. You'd be better off asking the Nomads for theirs." He turns, looking Harlan dead in the eyes. "You want the one out front? You're welcome to it. Just get the hell out."

He turns and stalks past me, almost shoving me out of the way. I jump back just in time.

"Wait a second," Harlan says, jogging after him. "The Nomads have a seaplane? Since when did that happen?"

Seaplane . . .

As Harlan and Eric vanish down the passage, I jog over to the railings, doing it without thinking, pleased to feel my leg take the speed. From up here, I can see across to the river, clogged with trash and debris. The dilapidated boats bob in the current. I notice the one that caught my eye the night before – the enormous white cylinder, supported by two pontoons, bobbing on the water's surface.

I know what a plane does, although I haven't needed to think about it until this moment. It's not exactly the kind of thing worth teaching people who live on a space station. That thing must be able to fly – or did, a very long time ago. Right now, I'm amazed it's even able to float.

And the Nomads have one. One that sounds like it's still working.

I don't give myself a chance to consider the flaws in the idea. I push off the railing, and start jogging after Eric and Harlan.

41

Prakesh

They sleep ten to a room, curled up on the floor. There used to be bunk beds on the walls – Prakesh saw the places where cots were bolted on – but they're long gone. There's no light in the ceiling, and when the door behind them is banged shut the room is in total darkness. The bodies inside it quickly raise the temperature, and the smell of sweat mixes with the coppery tang of dried urine.

At least the room is large enough for all the workers. They huddle in small groups, sitting against the wall or trying to stretch out on the hard floor. Prakesh tries to find a spot, tripping over outstretched feet more than once.

He's too tired to sleep, and too wired to do anything but sit and stare into the darkness. The last few hours passed in an exhausted blur: more soil bags, another dose of slop in that mess hall, some water, a chance to use the bathroom. Then this . . . *hole*. He saw Jojo come in with them, caught a glimpse of his face before the door was shut, but he doesn't know if he should call out for him.

He keeps seeing Carver, vanishing under a hail of feet and

fists. Keeps seeing the look on his face. Prakesh curls his hand into a fist of his own.

Jojo's voice comes out of the darkness, so close that Prakesh nearly jumps. "Hey. Y-y-you . . . uh, awake?"

The kid is right next to him, his mouth by his ear, but Prakesh can't see a thing. "Yeah," he says, keeping his voice low.

Jojo's stutter seems to be less prominent, as if the fact that it's too dark to see him means he finds it easier to speak. "W-we can talk now, if y-y-you want. W-what's it like?"

His question catches Prakesh off guard. "What do you mean?"

"Outside the sh-ship."

Prakesh tries to marshal his thoughts. It's hard to even know where to start. "We weren't out there long," he says. "We got picked up by Ray and Nessa."

"I hate them. R-R-Ray 'ssssssspecially. So w-where are you from? I'm f-f-from Denali, up north, or I w-was before my p-p-p-" He stops, and makes two of those gulping sounds again. "Parents brought me here. Th-th-they n-named me J-Joseph, but th-they always called m-m-me Jojo. Everyone d-d-does."

"Where are your parents now?"

"D-d-dead." He says it without regret, like it's a simple fact, and that alone is enough to make Prakesh's stomach clench. It's enough to remind him of his own parents, on Outer Earth. Thinking about them is like walking on the edge of a gaping hole. He knows he'll never see them again, but even trying to comprehend that fact is like leaning out over the hole, daring gravity to take him.

"B-b-but I'm g-gonna get back there," Jojo says. "My uncle st-stayed b-b-behind. He's w-waiting fffff-for me. I know he is."

Prakesh nods, knowing Jojo can't see him, but not sure what else to say.

Jojo saves him the trouble. "So w-where *are* you from?"

Prakesh takes a breath. "Outer Earth."

"Like the ssss-space station?" Jojo says. It's impossible to miss the excitement in his voice.

"That's right."

"But that's a m-m-million m-miles away! W-why did you come down here?"

Because I unleashed a virus that destroyed the station. Because we couldn't stop people from leaving. Because no matter how hard I tried, I couldn't do the right thing.

"Doesn't matter," Prakesh says. "We're here now, and that's all there is."

Jojo pauses, as if turning this over in his mind. Prakesh takes the moment. "Jojo," he says, leaning in closer. "How many people on this ship? How many prisoners?"

Jojo shrugs – Prakesh can feel it, feel JoJo's shoulders brushing his. "Th-thirty of us in the farm. M-m-m-maybe another thirty somewhere else?"

"What about the guards?"

"Twenty-f-f-five, I think? B-but they got all the guns and they never let us near them and th-th-they—" He stops, and takes a couple of hitching breaths.

"How long have you been here?" Prakesh says.

Another shrug. "A c-c-couple years. I d-d-don't r-really know. L-lost time. But P-P-Prophet says we have to w-work for the—"

He stops, coughing, like he hasn't talked this much in years, and isn't used to it. "Engine," he says eventually, without a single hitch in the word. "The Engine."

"And what *is* the Engine?" Prakesh says.

"W-we don't know. It's b-b-below decks, and they d-d-don't l-let us go there."

"You've never been?"

Jojo makes a negative sound. "Th-they keep their f-f-f-f-f-*fuel* down there, right at the bottom of the sh-sh-ship. Th-th-they won't l-let anyone near it." A note of excitement creeps into his voice. "One day w-w-we're gonna burn this place down. All of it. G-go off and f-f-f-find a suh-spot of our own."

Prakesh hears movement – someone scrabbling across the floor in front of them. He feels hot breath on his face. "You two shut up. Shut up right now."

"We were just—" Prakesh says.

The man cuts him off. "I don't give a shit. I don't want our rations taken away because you felt like a conversation."

"Hey *f-f-f-f-f-*" Jojo says in a harsh whisper, not quite managing to get the curse out. He swallows loudly. "I'll talk if I w-want. Just 'cos you got n-n-nothin' good to say . . ."

He trails off. For a moment, Prakesh wonders if the other man is going to retaliate, but then the hot breath on his face vanishes and he hears the man withdrawing to the other wall.

Jojo shifts his body a little. "F-f-fraid he's right. We shouldn't r-r-really be talking. I'll s-s-s-s-s-see you tomorrow."

He turns away. Someone snores loudly, groaning in their sleep.

Prakesh sits in the darkness, thinking hard. And the more he thinks the angrier he gets.

He's been on the edge of a long drop before, only that time it was for real. After Riley brought him the news about Resin, that it was his genetic experiments that caused it, Prakesh almost took his own life. The grief and despair was almost too much to take. He stood on the roof of the Air Lab control room, seconds away from stepping off. It was only a last-second thought that stopped him.

He was going to save as many people as possible. It didn't matter where they ended up, whether they stayed on the station or came to the planet below: he was going to dedicate the rest of his life to that goal. It was the only way to atone for what he'd done.

It's what he thought he was doing, when he helped stop Riley from destroying the *Shinso Maru*'s fusion reactor. *Saving lives.*

But it didn't work. Everybody he tried to help is either dead, or trapped here. His colleagues, his friends, his parents – another clench of his stomach muscles, an involuntary reaction. And Riley – gods, even the thought of what happened to Riley is enough to make him want to pound the walls, scream and roar until they come in and knock his head right off his shoulders.

What would Riley do? If she were here right now?

That's when Prakesh has a thought that is as clear and sharp as the one he had on the control room roof. *She'd fight. She'd do whatever it took to get to safety. She'd never give up, never, no matter how bad things got.*

As sleep finally takes him, Prakesh has time to think one last thing. He's going to escape. No, not just escape. He's going to do what he promised himself, and get the rest of these people off this ship.

218

42

Riley

I put on an extra burst of speed, coming alongside Harlan as
he reaches the stairs. My legs grumble, but I ignore them.

Harlan is still shouting at Eric. "There's a working seaplane
out there, E? And you haven't gone to check it out? Are you
crazy? That's what you've always wanted!"

We've reached the lobby. Eric ignores us, striding right past
the desk at the back, not looking at the pile of bodies stacked
in the far corner. He glances up at the mezzanine, where a
guard is staring into the distance, half hidden behind a pillar,
his rifle held at ease on his shoulder.

"Eric, wait up a second," I say, aware of his short temper
but not caring.

"Jesus," Eric mutters, not breaking stride. "Finkler!" he
shouts, bellowing down the passage where Finkler has his
surgery. When there's no response, he starts striding towards
it, only to be brought up short when the guard on the mezzanine speaks.

"He ain't there," the guard says. "Went below."

Eric's face twists in irritation. He turns on his heel, heading

219

deeper into the hospital. "Come," he says to me. "I'll let Finkler look you over once more, and then you get the hell out."

I lag behind him and Harlan, my mind moving at light speed. I don't have the faintest idea how I'm going to get to the seaplane, but I am damn well going to try.

We head deeper into the hospital. It's not until we've actually gone down the second flight of stairs that I realise we're underground. It's quiet down here, and warmer. What was it that Eric told Finkler, before the Nomads arrived? *Stay up top*.

The corridor we're in is dark, but there's a dim glow coming from round a corner. As we turn it, I see a small door set into a dead end, with a glimmering fluorescent light above it. There are two guards outside, both wearing thick, bulky black jackets. They spring to attention when they see Eric, dropping their rifles.

Eric nods to them, and pushes open the door.

It's the sound I notice first. It's like the noise of a gallery on Outer Earth – the hum of people, the almost subsonic rumble of machines, the clanking of old metal. In the galleries, the lights were set far above the floor – here, they're just above our heads, intensely bright. I have to squint to see.

We've come out onto a small metal platform in the top corner of a huge open space. After the closed-in passages, the size of it is startling. The floor below us has been cordoned off into discrete sections: a vegetable garden here, a common area there, an enormous section with cots and mattresses scattered around it. Wood panels separate each section. A group of children sit cross-legged on the floor in one corner, with two adults showing them something on a board that's been stuck to the wall. It's as if the entirety of Outer Earth has been condensed down into a space around half the size of the station dock.

There's a narrow metal stairway leading down from our platform. Eric descends, not bothering to check if we're following.

As we get closer to the ground, I see that the space isn't as regular as I first thought. Jagged sections of concrete jut out of the wall, flat on top, with bent metal bars poking out of the sides like stray hairs on skin. Previous floors, perhaps, long since fallen away, opening the space up. And there's an even stranger structure diagonally across from us: a curving ramp, also made of concrete, with a high lip around its outer edge. It rises from the floor, bending back on itself. It must have been used for vehicles, like the ones Harlan and I saw on the road.

It stops before it reaches its highest point, ending in an explosion of metal rods. There's a depression in the wall beyond it, what looks like an exit to the outside world, now completely bricked up.

The moment Eric hits the floor, he's besieged on all sides, asked a thousand questions, his input begged for, his attention needed. The people – *his* people – are all thin, all dressed in threadbare clothing. Plenty of them are missing hands, or arms, or legs. He has a few seconds for each one, never lingering, giving clipped, direct answers to every question thrown at him.

Some of the people glance at me, with a few of the glances lingering longer than I'd like. I feel my face going red, a hot flush creeping under the skin. When I brought the Nomads to their door last night, I didn't know I was risking . . . *this*.

"They used to put cars here."

Harlan is standing next to me, gazing around the space with pride. "Not that there's been a car down here for a thousand years. There used to be whole floors of 'em, just lined up next to each other. That'd be quite something, wouldn't it?"

I nod, more stunned than I'd like to admit. "How do the Nomads not know about this place?" I say.

"Eric's smart. It's why I married him. He—"

"Wait, you and Eric were married?"

"Sure. Twenty years and counting."

He flashes me a smile. I decide not to mention the fact that Eric apparently doesn't want him around any more.

"Anyway," he says. "Eric keeps scouts in the field. They get food, supplies, report back whenever Nomads move through the area. They get close, Eric locks the hospital down. Haven't been discovered yet."

He sees my expression of disbelief. "Oh, they've been in the building plenty of times, but they never managed to get into the basement."

I shudder. I had to get the wound in my thigh cleaned, didn't have a choice, but I'm appalled at the destruction I nearly brought down on Eric and his people. No wonder he wants me out of here.

Eric leads us to the far end. There's a tiny space, in the shadow of the giant concrete ramp, separated from the rest of the floor by scarred metal plates that look as if they were cut from something much larger, then propped up so they form a vertical barrier. There's a gap in the plates, guarded by another man with another gun. He starts when he sees us, but Eric waves us through and he relaxes.

I take in the space. A bent and twisted table, its surface empty, balanced on wobbly legs. Two straight-backed metal chairs. A duffel bag squats under the table, clothes spilling out of a half-open zip. There's a cot in the corner, a faded mattress on top of it. No blanket or pillow. The only decoration is on one of the walls: a map, like Harlan's, but in even worse condition. It doesn't show as much land mass, just what looks like the surrounding area. Printed on the map, running in large, spaced-out letters, are the words: THE YUKON.

"Stay here," Eric says. "Both of you. I'll get Finkler."

He steps out through the gap between the plates, and I see the guard slide into place, blocking off the exit.

"Harlan," I say. "Where would this seaplane be? The working one?"

"Goddamn fool," Harlan says, staring at the door. "Always was stubborn. That's what I liked about him. Even back when—"

"*Harlan.*"

"Kind of hard to say." He saunters up to the map, running his finger along it. After a moment, he taps a segment on it where the brown land gives way to a splodge of blue. "My guess is Fish Lake."

I blink. It takes me a second to dredge up the meaning of the word *lake*. The idea of a body of water that size is almost impossible to imagine.

"I was on the north shore few months ago, spotted smoke," he says. "Got a look through my binocs – seemed like they set up a camp of some kind." He shrugs. "Weren't no seaplane there, though. Not then, anyway."

"I thought you said the Nomads moved around?" I say.

"They do. Camp might've been temporary. But if I was a Nomad with a seaplane around these parts, Fish Lake'd be the place I'd land it."

"OK," I say, studying the map. I spot Whitehorse, and nearly scream with joy – it's close to the lake, no more than a few miles on the map. I could get there soon. I could get there *today*.

"And they can get to Anchorage?" I say, trying to stay calm, tracing across the map with my finger. The paper feels slightly damp under my fingertip. "They can fly that far?"

"Range-wise? Sure. Assuming they've got enough fuel. And assuming they're even there in the first place. Nomads aren't exactly predictable."

My finger touches the edge of the map, right on the border with Alaska – and that's when my heart sinks.

I need someone to fly the plane. It's all too easy to picture it coming down on the water – if the angle's off, even a little bit, it would flip right over the second it touched the surface.

"The Nomads'll have a pilot, right?" I say, more to myself than to anyone else. Of course they'll have one – they couldn't fly the plane otherwise. I'll have to get hold of that pilot, convince them to get me airborne. I don't have the first clue how I'm going to do that, but it's a start.

Eric returns, entering the room without looking at us. "Where's Finkler?" I say.

"He'll be here in a minute," Eric says, crossing around the other side of the table, dropping heavily onto one of the chairs. The metal frame protests, scraping across the concrete floor.

Harlan shakes his head, incredulous. "You know, I can't believe you, E," says Harlan. "You've been wanting to get in the air your whole life, and you just leave a damn seaplane *sitting there*?"

"What?" I say, turning away from the map. Surely I didn't hear that right. "You can fly a plane?"

Harlan and Eric glance at each other, for just a split second, and something passes between them. I don't even think they know they've done it.

"I can't fly a plane," Eric says.

"Sure you can," says Harlan. He turns to me. "We grew up in the same bunker together. I always remember he had this book – about how planes work? Engine diagrams, things like that. He read it a thousand times, always talking about how he was gonna learn to fly one day."

"Harlan, if you say one more word—"

"Well, sorry, E, but it's kind of obvious now, isn't it?" Harlan says, annoyed. My eyes drift to the logo on Eric's jacket. ROYAL CANADIAN AIRFORCE.

Eric sees me looking. "You want to know why I haven't gone up there?" he says. "Because I'd just get myself and my people killed. We're doing just fine here, and we *don't* need to risk everything we've built for a goddamn seaplane."

I turn back to the map, studying it, buying myself some time to think.

Assuming the plane is still there, then somehow convincing a Nomad pilot to help me without getting captured or killed – when I don't know the terrain and all I have is Harlan's rifle and no bullets – is going to be next to impossible. There's an easier way, and he's sitting right in front of me, still arguing with Harlan.

Except it isn't easier. Because even if Eric has enough knowledge to fly a plane, I don't have the faintest idea how I'm going to convince him to help me. I don't have a single thing to offer him. Asking for more, after what happened last night? I might as well demand that Harlan pull a teleportation device out of his back pocket.

And that's when the anger comes back. I know what I'm asking is too much, but it doesn't stop me from wanting to scream at Eric, to grab him and *make* him take me to the plane. The existence of the seaplane ignited a bright, burning hope inside me, but now that hope is fading, and the anger is in its place, dark and hot. With it comes the voice inside me, speaking quietly, insistently, telling me what I have to do.

There's only one way I'm going to convince Eric to help me. And I don't like it one bit.

I close my eyes. Then I turn back to Eric, folding my arms. "I'm going to Fish Lake. I'm taking that seaplane. If you're too scared to come with me, that's fine."

Eric is shrugging off his coat, pulling on a tattered sweater. I catch a knowing smile just before he pulls it over his head. "Nice try," he says, when he re-emerges.

I take a step closer. "Because you *are* scared, aren't you?

That's why you're in here, right? That's why you hide every time the Nomads come by. You don't want to fight them."

"Careful," Eric says. But he doesn't look at me when he says it, and I hear the voice again: *keep pushing*.

"Must be nice," I say, and the spite in my voice shocks me. "Hiding out here while the rest of the world goes to shit."

"Come on, that is not—" Harlan says.

I cut him off. "This is a sweet hole in the ground," I say, spreading my arms wide. "But it's still just a hole. At least the Nomads have the guts to survive on the outside."

Eric's eyes flash with anger. "I'm here to keep my people alive. This little hole in the ground kept *you* alive, last night. Or did you forget that?"

That almost derails me. I don't have any right to say these things. Not even a little bit. But I can't let that stop me.

I cup my hands to my mouth. "Can anyone else here fly a plane?" I shout, and that's when Eric grabs me. He wraps his hands around the lapels of my jacket and pulls me close, looking right into my eyes.

He speaks very softly. "Get. Out."

I smile. Because I *wanted* that anger, that naked, white-hot fury.

"I would have hidden too," I say. "I would have kept my people around me, and kept it just us."

I can't help but think of the Devil Dancers, of the Nest. Of Amira.

"But here's the thing, Eric," I say. "The world doesn't care. It will take your friends from you no matter what you do. Now you can get angry at me –" I drop my voice a little "– or you can get angry at the nomads. You can take the fight to them. Take the seaplane for yourselves."

Harlan is staring at me, confusion on his face. I don't recognise the words coming out of my mouth. Whoever owns the voice at the back of my mind is speaking for me. It's like I'm jamming a blade into a tiny crack, twisting, finding the place where I can lever it open.

I reach up, and slowly pull Eric's hands from my jacket, clasping them firmly.

"You know I'm right," I say, whispering now.

And then a voice, from over by the entrance. "She kind of is, you know."

Finkler. He looks as if he hasn't slept: his hair is a mess, his skin sallow, and there are giant sweat stains under his armpits. He walks over to me, and without waiting for an invitation tries to pull my pants down.

"Hey!" I say, letting go of Eric, twisting away.

"Come on," says Finkler. "Either you can pull them down, or I can, but I gotta see."

He waves at Harlan and Eric. "You two turn around. Give the lady some privacy."

Eric stares at me for a long moment, then turns to face the wall, along with Harlan. Blushing slightly, I work my pants down until the waistband is just above my knees.

Finkler runs his finger along the stitched-up cut. "Good, good, good. Okey-dokey. Any pain? I'm guessing you're walking OK?"

"Yeah. Thanks to you."

"Excellent," he says, motioning at me to pull up my pants. His belly is peeking out below the hem of his T-shirt, and I see the fat wobbling slightly. "Keep it clean, drink lots of water. You'll be fine. We caught it in time. I'd tell you to rest, but I'm pretty sure you'd just ignore me." He shouts over his shoulder. "OK, now we can talk about going to get this seaplane."

"Finkler . . ." Eric says. He sounds more tired than angry now.

"No, listen," he says. "I'll admit, last night was a bit of a clusterfuck, but it doesn't stop her being right. We've known about that plane for months, and we haven't done a damn thing about it. Now I know you're in charge, man, but you know how everyone feels about this."

"You're serious," says Eric. "You actually want us to go out there? Risk everything we've built?"

Finkler snorts. "I think it's a terrible idea. But the Nomads know we're here now. Even if we move the bodies somewhere, they'll figure it out. If we strike back, let 'em know we won't just lie down—"

"That's—"

"*Plus*, maybe we get a seaplane out of it. Maybe we get whatever's *in* the seaplane. Our medical supplies could use a restock, for one thing." He glances at me, then back at Eric. "So is it *really* that terrible? There's plenty of water to land it on. We can figure out how to disable it, too, if any Nomads do come looking. Just take a few crucial pieces out the engine."

He doesn't give them a chance to answer. "I'm going with her. If nothing else, it'll be a fun day trip."

"*You* could die," Eric says. "You ever think about that, Finkler?"

He pauses a second before answering. "Yup. And you wouldn't want to send your only real medic out there with nothing but *her* for protection now, would you?" He jerks a finger at me.

I could hug Finkler. Instead, I flash him a warm smile, then look back at Eric, raising my chin slightly.

I desperately want to take back everything I just said. I hate having to do this, hate having to manipulate people to get what I want. That's what Amira would have done, or Okwembu. It's not me, and it never has been. I tell myself that I only did it because Eric left me no choice, but no matter how hard I try, I can't convince myself.

I try to ignore my thumping heart. Eric could still say no. He could still send us away. I don't know if I'd blame him.

"Hell," Harlan says. "If you're really doing this, then I'm in. I'm no coward."

He's looking at me when he says it, but there's no mistaking who he's directing it at. Slowly, Eric raises his eyes.

"OK," he says. "We'll go."

Before I can speak, he raises a finger. "It's a scouting mission *only*. The four of us, and that's it. I'm not risking anybody else on this."

I take a deep, shaky breath. "That's all I ask."

Eric calls Harlan and Finkler over. I turn back to the map, my eyes on Fish Lake.

The voice inside me is silent, the anger turned down low. But I can feel it, just below the surface. It was so easy to tap into, like a vein of energy I'd always had inside me but never knew about. I tell myself that I won't let it happen again, that I won't let that be who I am. But the quiet voice inside me knows better. If it helps get me to Anchorage, then I'll use it.

No matter what.

43

Anna

Anna finds Dax Schmidt on the stairwell that leads to the main Apex control room. He's with Doctor Arroway, their heads close together, conferring in low voices.

She moves in quietly, on the balls of her feet, and neither of them realise she's there until she puts a hand on Arroway's shoulder, spins him around and slams him against the wall.

Arroway shouts in protest, shoving her away. He's stronger than she is, but he isn't ready for what Anna does next, which is to grab his hand and twist. Hard.

He grunts, the force bringing him to his knees, his arm twisted up at an awkward angle. Anna's used the move a few times before, usually on whoever tried to jack her cargo. She knows how painful this little hold is – and from here, a further twist coupled with a strike to the elbow will snap Arroway's arm. She doesn't do that. She needs him talking, not screaming.

"You're going to tell me what's going on," she says. "And you're going to tell me right now."

Arroway looks at Dax, as if pleading for help. Anna adds a

little more torque to the twist, making sure Dax sees it, making sure he knows not to come any closer. "He can't help you. Start talking."

Fury crosses Dax's face. "Let him go."

Anna actually smiles. "There's an astronaut outside the station – I don't know how they got out there, but they did. And *you*." She spits the word at Arroway. "You're packing your bags, like you've won the lottery already. What do you know that we don't?"

Neither of them respond. Arroway is still squirming a little, but the stairway is silent, save for the hum of the station.

"Anna," Dax says again. "Let the doctor go, and I'll tell you."

Anna hadn't realised she was breathing so hard. She makes a conscious effort to slow down, but doesn't let go of Arroway's wrist.

"Please," Dax says.

After a moment, Anna lets the doctor go. He staggers to his feet, trembling. Anna looks at Dax, folding her arms and raising her eyebrows questioningly. He looks over one shoulder, as if to check that they really are alone.

"You're right, OK?" he says, leaning in and lowering his voice. "We sent one of our men outside."

"Dax," Arroway says, hissing the word.

"Shut up, Elijah." Dax holds Anna's gaze. "He took one of the escape pods. Once he was outside the station, he put on one of the pod's space suits, then he did an EVA."

Anna frowns, not understanding. Why launch yourself in a pod if you were just going to climb out of it?

Dax sees her confusion. "We had him use the thrusters on his suit to manoeuvre the pod back inside its launch bay. Nobody would know it had ever been launched, and we'd have a man outside the station."

"What about the fire? Was that part of it?"

"We had to get people out of the gallery area."

Anna stares at him in disbelief, as much for his candour as anything else. "You could have got everybody killed."

"Well, we didn't. We were always going to put the fire out. That wasn't the issue."

"What did you do? Turn off the suppression systems or something?"

"Just for long enough to get our man where he needed to be."

Anna closes her eyes, remembering the tech on the night of the fire. No wonder he was cursing. He must have been wondering why chemicals weren't spraying out, when the system was perfectly configured. That must have been why he tried to get into the power boxes, thinking the fault was inside.

"OK," she says. "Where is he now? Your astronaut?"

Dax takes a shaky breath. "We sent him to the dock. Or what's left of it. His mission was to secure one of the tug ships. Each one has plenty of emergency rations, plus a water reclaimer, so he can live out there for quite a while if he needs to."

"A tug?" Anna says, frowning. That doesn't make any sense.

"We think—" Dax says. "I mean, my advisers tell me that there's a way to construct a rudimentary heat shield on one of the tugs. Something that would ablate the heat of re-entry."

Arroway groans. Anna just keeps staring at Dax. This wasn't the confession she was expecting – although, in hindsight, she's not sure *what* she was expecting.

"But this is good," she says, after a moment. "If we can put heat shields on the tugs, then more people can escape. Right?"

"There's only enough heat-shield material for one tug," Dax says. "We made it out of epoxy and a type of copper alloy. We still had some in one of the labs."

"Then just hold the lottery now," Anna says, hating the

pleading sound in her voice, hating how young it makes her feel. "If there's a way to escape, we should take it before the reactor . . ."

She trails off, her eyes wide. How could she have missed it? Why didn't she see it before?

She shut her eyes, screwing them tightly together. "There isn't going to be a lottery, is there?"

Dax's voice is quiet, gentle. "What would you do if you were in my position?"

Anna opens her mouth to speak, but no words come out.

"We've picked engineers, Air Lab techs, doctors." He glances at Arroway. "The best and the brightest. We're giving ourselves the best possible chance of surviving once we reach the ground. Something like this . . ."

He pauses, tries again. "It's too important to be left to a selection of random people. We're talking about the survival of our species."

Anna raises her eyes to meet his. "And council members?"

"What?"

"You're going, too. Aren't you?"

He shrugs. "Someone has to lead. We're going to need structure and order down there."

For a long moment none of them moves. Anna wishes she wasn't seeing things so clearly, wishes she wasn't filling in the gaps. They'll take the escape pods – all of them. Jordan is probably in on it – probably the one who started the fire. Dax and his friends will need the suits, after all, to transfer to the modified tug. Everybody else will be left behind. Even if they're still alive by the time the *Tenshi* gets there, they won't have any way to make it on board.

Eventually, Dax says, "We can try and get you a space on the tug, if that's what you want."

It's his solicitousness, his reasonable tone, that finally kicks

Anna back into action. She almost snarls, backing away from them. "I'm going to tell everyone," she says. "They're all going to hear what you're doing."

She regrets the words the instant they are out of her mouth. She's still alone with the two of them. What if Dax has a gun? What if he tries to stop her?

"If you put a hand on me, I'll break every bone in your body," she says.

"Gods, Anna. No," Dax says, horrified. "Who do you think I am? Oren Darnell? Nobody's going to touch you."

"Doesn't mean I'm going to keep this a secret." Anna is already thinking ahead. She's still going to run, as fast as she can, right to the main amphitheatre. Her dad. She needs to find her dad. He'll know what to do.

"You're free to tell whoever you want," Dax says. "But understand this. If you let everyone know that we've got the means to escape now, there'll be anarchy. Complete breakdown. People will die."

"Yeah. Like you."

"Yes," Dax says simply. "But then what happens? You think things will go back to normal? You think this will be resolved *peacefully*?"

It's impossible for Anna not to think of Achala Kumar. Of her desperation to reach her son.

Dax smiles sadly. He walks past her, gesturing for Arroway to follow him. The doctor looks back at her, fear crossing his face.

"Think about it," Dax says. "It's up to you. But you'd better be sure you're making the right decision."

He and Arroway walk away, leaving Anna alone in the silence of the stairwell.

44

Riley

The howl stops us in our tracks.

For a moment, nobody moves. Harlan raises his face to the sky, head tilted very slightly.

The sound fades, and he visibly relaxes. "That's miles away. My guess is they don't know we're here."

He gives me a toothy smile. I try to smile back, don't quite manage it.

Eric seats his gun more comfortably in his arms. Harlan sees, shakes his head. "Doubt we'll need it. They might be aggressive, but there's easier prey than four folks with guns."

"Depends how hungry they are," says Eric, more to himself than to us. Without another word, he starts walking again.

My dark green jacket feels tight across my shoulders, padded out by the extra layers that Finkler insisted I wear. The grimy backpack on my shoulders keeps catching on branches. It's heavy with supplies: food, water, blankets, flares. *What I wouldn't give for my old tracer pack*, I think.

It's hard going. The ground is flat, but it's boggy and uneven, with plenty of frozen puddles ready to catch an ankle. There are trees, but they're spaced widely apart. Above our heads, the sky is low and grey, and there's no sound but the crunch–snap of our footsteps.

I've had some more time to think about what I baited Eric into, and it's not looking any better. It's all very well heading for a seaplane with someone who might be able to fly it, but that doesn't mean we're going to be able to walk in and take it. Harlan and Eric have a couple of those ancient rifles, now with some ammunition, but it's hard to imagine using them to take out a group of Nomads.

"Hey."

I hadn't noticed Finkler falling into step beside me. He hops over a patch of boggy ground, its surface speckled with ice, and lands with both feet. Despite his size, he seems to be doing better than all of us, even though he's wearing a bulky grey coat that makes him look even larger than he is. The ground has started to slope upwards, and there are more trees now, their bare branches reaching to the sky.

"How's the leg holding up?" he says. "Not that I'm worried or anything."

I smile, then look away into the distance. "Hurts a little, but I can handle it."

"I'm sure you can."

There are two fallen trees blocking our path, their branches standing straight up, their trunks caked with brittle moss. Finkler helps me over them, or tries to, holding out a hand to me even as he's struggling to keep his own balance. I wave him off, clambering over the trunks and hopping down on the other side. When I look up, I see that Harlan and Eric have reached the top of the slope, silhouetted against the sky.

"So what's the deal with them?" I say.

Finkler hits the ground behind me with a thud. He nearly topples over, and I have to steady him, holding his shoulder as he finds his feet.

"Who?" he says, dusting himself off. "Harlan and Eric?"

"I get that they used to be together, but why doesn't Harlan live with the rest of you?"

Finkler doesn't answer for a minute. As we trudge in silence up the hill, I start thinking that I've gone too far, but then he says, "They had a kid, you know."

"Had?" I raise my eyes to the figure of Harlan, gazing about him at the top of the ridge. Eric is swigging from a bottle of water, shivering slightly in the cold.

"She'd be about your age now," Finkler says. "Name of Samantha. Nomads killed her parents down in Utah on a raid when she was a baby. Eric saved her life, and he and Harlan took her in."

"What happened to her?" My throat is dry, and it's not because I'm thirsty. I dig in my pocket, hardly aware I'm doing it, and stick a cattail leaf into my mouth, chewing hard. My legs are burning from the climb, my upper back aching from the weight of the pack.

"They loved that kid. We all did. She had this smile like . . . Anyway, she was out hunting with Harlan one day, and they startled a bear."

"Gods," I say, more to myself than to him. I can fill in the blanks myself. I've never seen a bear, but I've seen pictures of one. Fur and teeth and muscle and claws.

"Eric had told Harlan not to take her, but that wasn't going to happen. Harlan doted on Samantha. He wanted to show her everything."

Finkler speaks in a matter-of-fact tone, which makes his words so much worse.

"The bear went for Samantha first. Harlan couldn't stop it. He tried to fight it off, but if he hadn't run when he did, he'd be dead too."

Ahead of me, Harlan laughs at something Eric said. Apparently it wasn't meant to be funny, because Eric meets it with a scowl.

"After Harlan came back," Finkler says, "Eric went out by himself."

The tooth. On the string around Eric's neck.

"Eric told him to get the hell out," Finkler says, and gives a bitter laugh. "Last night's the first time I've seen him in three years."

Harlan's face comes back to me, that night in the cave. It feels like decades ago. I remember the expression on his face – the sheer desperation. *You gotta tell 'em I helped you. You gotta tell 'em I looked after you, all right? Made sure you were OK.*

We crest the ridge. There's a flat part, an open plateau with tufts of grass sticking up through the mud. The forest sweeps away below us, and we begin picking our way down the slope. It's hard going; the ground is still slippery, and the rocks embedded in the slope aren't tight enough to hold onto. Harlan and Eric have already reached the bottom.

"Tell me something," Finkler says. "What happened to you up there?"

"What do you mean?"

He jabs a finger at the sky. "You tumble into my operating room, claiming that you crash-landed after escaping from a space station. That must be quite a story."

I open my mouth to tell him – but how do I even start? Janice Okwembu, Amira, my father, Morgan Knox, Resin, the mad escape from the dock, all of it. It's like a hunk of metal, with layers and layers of rust, the oxidation building on itself until you can't see the original shape underneath, the whole thing ugly and misshapen, with sharp edges that you have to be careful around.

"It's OK," Finkler says. He has a weird, crooked smile on his face. "I don't mean to pry."

"No, it's just—"

"But listen. You need to deal with that anger, and you need to deal with it soon."

His words stun me, although I'm careful not to show it. I shrug, but it's an unnatural motion, as if I have to instruct each individual muscle to move. "I just want to find my friends."

We've reached a steep part of the slope, and he has to watch his footing as he climbs down it. "Post." He takes a step. "Traumatic." Another, pausing to catch his balance. "Stress. Disorder."

He stops and looks at me, his eyes narrowed, breathing hard. "You think I haven't seen this a dozen times before? I've dug enough bullets out of people, done plenty of amputations. Even read a couple of books. I'm no psychologist, but I'm not stupid. How are the hallucinations?"

"What you talking about?"

"Please. I mean, don't get me wrong, I've had plenty of hallucinations myself, but they're usually self-induced? If you get my meaning? I'm not sure I want the ones you're having."

"I'm *not* hallucinating." But I can't help thinking of how I thought Eric was Amira. Such a small thing, so small I'd almost forgotten about it. And the voice inside me. Quiet, calm, insistent. Like part of my mind has decided to take over.

He goes on as if I hadn't spoken. "OK. You're not hallucinating. There's no anger in you. No aggression. You don't feel guilty that your friends might be dead, and you're a completely well-adjusted person with absolutely no fixation on a completely impossible task."

He purses his lips. "What do you want, Riley?"

"What do you mean?"

"When this is all over. After you and your buddies are back together. What are you going to do?"

I stare at him. Because, right then, I realise I don't know. So far, all I've thought about is getting to Alaska. Finding Carver and Prakesh, confronting Okwembu. I haven't even considered what'll happen after that.

I have a better idea of what I *don't* want. I don't want to be scared. I don't want to be cold, or hungry, and I don't want to keep fighting people who want to hurt me.

I don't want to be alone. And at this moment I don't know whether I want Prakesh or Carver to be with me. As long as someone is.

My thoughts are interrupted as Eric's voice reaches us. *"Finkler."*

He and Harlan have stopped dead, crouching down on top of a huge spear rock jutting out of the hill. Without looking back, he motions for us to get down. I drop to a crouch, then all fours, letting my pack slip off my shoulders. Moving as quickly as I can, I scoot across the ground until I'm level with Harlan. There's an icy wind slicing through the trees, cutting through my jacket like it isn't there.

What I see takes my breath away.

We're perhaps a hundred feet up on the hillside, with Fish Lake stretching below us. It's more water than I've ever seen in one place, more water than I could ever imagine. It goes on forever, miles long. Under the low-hanging clouds, the water is the colour of burnished metal. The surface isn't still: I can see the water forming into waves with white caps, battering against the shore. The waves look tiny, as if I could rub them out with a finger.

The forest goes right up to the shore on all sides, the trees hanging down, reaching for the water. I can see right into the distance, right to the icy mountains with their peaks shrouded in the clouds.

Finkler is cursing and grumbling behind me as he tries to come up on our viewpoint. Harlan beckons me over, and points to a spot on the shore below.

Not just one seaplane, but two. Parked nose to tail, bobbing up and down as the waves hit them. Unlike the one in Whitehorse, these have wings, each one holding a single engine and a spiky propeller. They're just offshore, next to a simple floating platform, cobbled together from barrels and misshapen wooden planks. There's a figure standing on the platform, hefting a tank. I can't make out the details, but it looks as if he's fuelling the plane, pouring liquid into the engine.

Harlan points again, and I see the tents, their grey fabric surfaces just visible through the trees. I can see the glint and glimmer of a fire, and there's a wisp of smoke snaking through the branches.

Eric has a pair of binoculars out, gunmetal grey, the lenses chipped. He's scanning the shoreline.

"How many?" says Harlan.

"Can't say," Eric says.

Eric crawls backwards off the rock, then slips into the trees. After a confused moment, the rest of us follow.

Once we're back in cover, we stand up. My legs are freezing, my toes almost completely numb. "OK," I say, thinking hard, reaching for my abandoned pack. "If we can—"

"No."

Eric isn't even looking at me. He's shouldering his own pack, making as if to leave.

Worry fills me, like an expanding bubble, pushing up through my body. "We can take them," I say, trying to keep the desperation out of my voice. "We just need a plan."

"We don't know how many there are down there," Eric says. "But two seaplanes? That means way too many Nomads."

"OK," I say again. "We wait until it's dark. They can't shoot what they can't see, right? And we can get closer, get numbers. Maybe even sneak past, take a plane."

"You don't know much, do you?" Eric says, scorn dripping from his voice. "You know how much noise a plane makes when you turn it on?"

Finkler brightens. "What about starting a fire? We could burn them out." He grins. "That'd be a lot of fun, actually."

Harlan looks around him. "Wood's too wet. No way we'd get it big enough. Even if we did, how are you planning on controlling it?"

Finkler's shoulders sag. I close my eyes, almost groaning in frustration. *There's got to be a way.* What if we could push a plane out into the lake? Start it away from the shore? No – the Nomads still have guns, and they'd still be able to shoot at the plane. We'd be a static target.

"So we come back with more people," I say. I'm grasping at ideas now, desperately trying to find *something* that will work. "We go back to Whitehorse and—"

"Wrong." Eric's voice has hardened again. "I can't ask my men to risk their lives because *you* want a seaplane. We're done."

He turns to go. Harlan and Finkler are getting ready, too, putting on their packs in silence. In the silence, another wolf howl drifts across the forest. It sounds as if it's a little closer.

"Harlan," I say.

"He's right," Harlan says. He won't meet my eyes. "I'm sorry, but we have to—"

"Tell me again," I say. "About the wolves. About how they track their prey." I keep my voice quiet and even. A tiny spark of an idea is flickering in my mind.

Harlan's brow furrows in confusion. "Well, it's like I said, they've been getting more aggressive every year. Chances are they still got a little bit of our scent, but we'll be back in Whitehorse long before they . . ."

He stops when he sees the expression on my face. I'm barely listening. The spark has ignited a fire, and the idea itself is flaring brightly. Finkler looks back and forth between us, puzzled.

"No," Harlan says, his eyes wide. "Oh no. No. That's *suicide*."

He's right. It doesn't stop a smile from spreading across my face.

45

Riley

I concentrate on my breathing.

I don't know how long I've been out here. I gave up keeping track hours ago. The night is bitterly cold, and there's nothing for me to do but try and keep my attention on the forest around me, watching for movement in the trees. My eyes are adjusted to the darkness now, and I can make out white vapour, curling in front of me with every breath.

I'm a hundred yards or so up the slope from the Nomads' camp. I can see the glimmer of their fire through the trees. I picked this spot carefully: there's a slight depression in the slope, shielded from the wind, and there's a relatively straight path through the trees to the camp. I scouted it out as the last of the daylight faded. I also made sure to test my leg, doing a couple of sprints in a clearing a short distance away. It hurts, and the cold makes the pain worse, but running won't be a problem.

Harlan begged me not to do this. So did Finkler. Even Eric was surprised that I was considering it – he told me it was the craziest thing he'd ever heard. He's probably right, but I think that's also why he and Finkler haven't left yet. The risk is all on me. If I mess this up, I die. Eric and the others can walk away, slipping back through the forest. If I don't, then Eric gets his seaplane – and this particular group of Nomads won't bother him and his people any more.

I told them to get as close to the camp as they could, and be ready to go. All they could do was insist I wear extra clothing: a thicker jacket, a scarf, a thin beanie. It helps, but only a little. I have my hands jammed deep in the pockets of the jacket, and every so often I windmill my arms to keep my body temperature up.

Around me, the forest is silent.

I breathe in, closing my eyes. I feel exhausted, but my mind is working in overdrive.

I've had time to think about what I said to Eric, how I convinced him to come out here. On one hand, it's hard to forgive myself for it – what I said was horrible. But at the same time I can't help thinking that it's the only choice I had. That's what I keep coming back to. The anger I feel – that hot, burning rage – is what's keeping me alive down here. In the end, getting to Prakesh and Carver is going to be about how hard I fight. I don't have to give in to the anger, but I can use it as a fuel, powering me all the way to Anchorage.

But the problem with those thoughts is that suddenly the voice is there, whispering in my ear. *It's not Prakesh and Carver. It's Okwembu. You want to find her. You want to make her pay.*

And that's the problem. I can tell myself I don't have to let the anger control me, but what's going to happen when I find Okwembu? When I'm face to face with her?

I exhale, and open my eyes. The moon has come out, spreading its light through a tiny gap in the clouds.

The wolf is right in front of me.

It's the leader, the small one. Its head is tilted slightly to one side, studying me, as if asking why I would be stupid enough to be alone in a forest at night.

I meet its bright eyes, just for a second. Looking into them drives a spike of terror into my chest. I look away, and that's when I see the rest of them, moving silently between the trees. Giant tongues pass across gleaming teeth. Clawed feet paw at the ground. There are too many of them to count.

"Thought you'd never get here," I say. It comes out as a harsh whisper.

Harlan was right. The wolves might be aggressive, but they're still animals. They'll go for the easy prey: a single target over a big group. They must have smelled us from miles away, tracked us here, urged on by their rumbling stomachs.

This is going to be the most dangerous thing I've ever done. Worse than running the Core on Outer Earth, worse than defending the dock. Because there is zero room for error. One mistake, no matter how small, and they'll have me.

But there's no going back. Not now.

My hands grip the flare in my jacket pocket. Slowly, oh so slowly, I pull it out.

It's a thin tube, ten inches long, the writing on it long since worn away. Eric gave me two of them. I considered using one in each hand, but I wouldn't be able to light them quickly enough.

It's only when the flare is fully out of my pocket that the wolf in front of me growls. The sound is so low it's almost subsonic. It opens its mouth, long tongue dropping from its lips.

How long before they attack? I don't even know if it'll come from the lead wolf. It could come from behind me, or from either side. I can hear them, padding through the trees.

In one movement, I reach up, grip the tab on the bottom of the flare, and pull. The tab comes out, jerking away from the body.

Nothing happens.

The wolf cocks its head to the other side. I try to keep breathing, thinking ahead, getting ready to drop the flare I'm holding and go for the second one.

With a gushing hiss, the first flare ignites. There's a white-hot flash at the end of the tube, and thick orange smoke begins pouring out. The smoke is lit from within by a cone of fire and sparks, and it turns the forest into a scene from hell.

The wolves go crazy. They bark and snap, clawing at the dirt, darting back and forth. Only the leader doesn't move. But I see his ears flatten against his head, see the orange light reflected in his eyes.

I take one last breath, sucking in the scent of the burning flare.

And then I run.

I explode outwards, my arms pumping, running at full speed towards the lead wolf. It jumps back, scared of the fire, just like I thought it would be. It's fast, but it doesn't get back far enough, not willing to give up that easily. With a yell, I swing the flare upwards, slashing it across the wolf's face. It yelps in pain, twisting away from me.

Behind me, the pack gives chase.

I'm reacting to things before I even register that they're in front, leaping over rocks, ducking under incoming branches. The wolves are on me in seconds, coming in from both sides so fast that I nearly lose my footing out of pure terror. The speed of the creatures is appalling. They're not just coming from the sides now – they're sprinting ahead of me, turning back, legs scrabbling in the dirt as they try to change momentum for an attack.

I keep going, swinging the flare behind me. The burning tip smacks into soft fur, and there's an agonised howl.

You can't outrun wolves. Harlan was right about that, too.

247

But they've never hunted prey armed with a flame burning at 750°C. Over a longer sprint, they'd take me – Harlan said that the flame only lasts for about fifteen seconds. But fifteen seconds is all I need.

There's a steep drop in the slope ahead, a few feet, no more. I see the drop less than two seconds before I hit it, but I react instantly, slashing the flare across my left side to clear some space. Then I jump.

In the sputtering light from the flare, all I can see are teeth and eyes. Jumping doesn't make me move any faster, but being in the air means I'm out of the way of the wolves – the longer I can stay airborne, the better.

I bend my knees, ready to take the landing, to roll if I have to. It's not enough. I hit the ground badly, and my ankle twists.

The movement sends a shocking, agonising bolt of pain up through my leg. A single word blares in my mind, endlessly, like a siren: *No, no, no, no.*

A set of jaws snaps shut around my arm.

I react on instinct, jamming the flare right into the wolf's face. It lets go with a yelp, and I'm up on my feet before I can think about it. Another wolf snaps at my leg, but I'm too far away, and its jaws close on nothing but air. My ankle is screaming at me. The terror blocks out everything, even sound: all I can hear is a thin ringing in my ears.

I look up, and there's a Nomad ten feet away.

He's young – my age maybe, no more. He hasn't raised his gun, which is held slack across his chest. He's staring at me, at the wolves, completely confused.

I have half a second to pick out the details: the dried scraps of face paint, the torn jacket hanging on his slender frame. Then I'm sprinting past him, and he's raising his gun, yelling at me to stop. But he's much too late, and the wolves take him, knocking him to the ground. His gun goes off, but I can't tell if it found its mark. I don't dare stop. Not for a second.

I get flashes of activity as I run through the camp. Bodies springing out of tents, shouting in confusion. An oil lamp knocked over, spreading fire across the ground. The wolves are darting back and forth, snarling, growling, unsure of what to do with such a large group of humans but driven on by hunger.

It's what I was counting on. The only way through the camp, the only way to get past the men with guns, is to make the biggest, most insane entrance possible.

Two wolves have attacked a Nomad. I see him, blood spurting from his neck as he tries to push them away. On my left, a rifle is going off, the shooter repeatedly pulling the trigger. One wolf, more determined and focused than the rest, darts ahead of me, trying to cut me off. The flare is spent, and I hurl it at the wolf. It buys me just enough time to get ahead of it.

And I can see the seaplanes. They're floating a few feet off the shore, just beyond the makeshift wooden platform. Their white surfaces glimmer in the light of the spreading fire. The door on the leftmost plane is open, exposing the dark interior.

There's a Nomad in front of them, a scrawny stick of a man. He's got his gun up, tracking me as I run towards him. I spring forward as he fires, tucking into a roll, my knees scraping across the platform as the bullet splits the air above me.

Then I'm up, leading with my shoulder, charging full speed into the man's stomach.

He topples backwards with a surprised *ooof*, the gun whirling away, bouncing off the side of the seaplane. I feel his hands on my jacket, hunting for a hold. Then we're tumbling into the seaplane, my body on top of his, my legs hanging out the side.

I don't wait for him to get his breath back. I twist around

and punch him, fist connecting with his jaw. He grunts, trying to buck me off.

I push myself upwards, and that's when the lead wolf lands on top of me.

46

Riley

It's jumped the gap, launching itself right into the plane, the back of its body hanging out of the door. Its mouth is drawn back in an enormous snarl.

I jerk away, and a second later its jaws snap shut right where my head was. I'm still on top of the Nomad, my knee in his throat. The wolf lunges again, biting, snarling, moving in a fury. I try to get my feet underneath it, try to tuck them to my chest so I can kick it off, but I can't get enough space.

The wolf rears back, its front legs straight, its head silhouetted against the light from the camp. Its eyes are alive with the hunt, its mouth open, flecks of saliva flying as it bares jagged teeth. It's smart, backing off a little, giving it a bit more space to jump. This time, its teeth are going into my throat.

I don't see Harlan coming. All I see are his hands, wrapped around the wolf's midsection. With a terrified roar, he hurls the wriggling wolf right into the lake.

This wasn't the plan. They were supposed to come when the platform was clear. I thought that the Nomads would occupy the pack, letting us steal away in the plane as the camp dissolved in chaos. I didn't count on one of the wolves following me. Not that I have time to complain – Harlan saved my life. Eric and Finkler are pounding up the shore behind him, leaping onto the platform.

I don't have time to be relieved to see them. Harlan shoves me back into the plane, scrambling in after me, and then Eric and Finkler are there and my hands are shaking and I can barely breathe.

They grab the Nomad I punched, taking him by the arms. My punch was hard enough to break his jaw, which is already beginning to swell. I'm dimly aware of my hand aching, of a feeling of wetness as blood runs down from my knuckles.

The Nomad groans as they pull him up. "Can you fly this thing?" Eric shouts at him. The fire on the shore makes the sweat on his face glisten. When the Nomad doesn't answer, Eric sticks a rifle barrel in his face, jamming it against the man's undamaged cheek. "*Can you?*"

The Nomad nods, his eyes squeezed shut. Without another word, Eric pulls him towards the cockpit.

The interior of the plane is cramped, with a bare metal floor and straps hanging from the walls. Finkler is up against the wall next to me, hyperventilating. The camp is a nightmare. Dark shapes fly across the ground, flames lick at the sky. Screams and gunfire echo across the lake.

"The plane! They've got the plane!"

The shout comes from the shore, where two Nomads are running towards us. Their bodies are dark shapes against the flames.

Harlan swings the rifle around, and fires. His first shot goes wide, and he rips the bolt back, chambering another round. This one takes a Nomad in the shoulder, sending him spinning off the wooden platform and into the water. Harlan fumbles with the gun, his fingers slipping on the bolt, and then the second Nomad reaches the plane.

He's big, with square shoulders and jagged red paint above an unkempt beard. He doesn't have a gun, but he plants his hands on either side of the door, and starts to haul himself in. Harlan swings the gun around, but the Nomad just grabs the barrel.

I lash out, hammering my elbow into him. He's not expecting an attack from the side, and it knocks him off balance just enough for his one hand to slip off the doorframe. He tries to stay on, so I grab hold of his fingers, ripping them away. He goes down, falling out of sight.

The engines start, the propellers on either side of us whirling to life. The noise is so loud that I have to clap my hands over my ears. It's like being inside the belly of a roaring monster. I can see into the cockpit, up at the front. The Nomad's hands are moving like lightning, flicking switches and pulling levers. Eric is seated on the right, head low, gun trained on the pilot.

The plane starts to move, juddering beneath us. I can just see the shore slipping sideways through one of the windows.

We're moving way too slowly. Another burst of gunfire rakes the side of the plane. Finkler grabs me and pulls me down, just in time, almost slamming my head into the bare metal.

The plane lifts, just for a second, then hammers back down onto the water. This time I do knock my head on the floor and stars explode across my vision. Finkler's hand finds mine, squeezing tight.

We lift upwards for a second time. And stay there.

My stomach is rolling, not used to the sensation of take-off. Finkler's face is split in a massive grin. He pumps the air, cheering, then grabs my shoulders and pulls my face close to his. I can see his lips moving, see him shouting something, but I can barely hear the words over the noise of the engines and the rushing air from the open door. Harlan is there, too, down on one knee, breathing hard.

I sit back against the wall, feeling the vibrations travel through me. We have a seaplane. *And we're flying.*

The relief is exquisite, so powerful that I have to close my eyes for a second, fight the tears back. We did it. I can get to Anchorage.

The feeling lasts all of three seconds. Another window shatters, the bullet burying itself in the far wall.

The second seaplane comes into view, flying alongside us.

47

Riley

For a long, frozen second, it looks like their plane is going to crash right into ours.

I can just see it through the broken window. It's coming in off our left wing, rising up from below. I can't see into the cockpit, but the door in the side of the plane is open, and one of the Nomads is leaning out. He has a rifle, and he's trying to get a bead on us again, trying to steady his shot against the buffeting air.

He fires. The bullet goes wide, and the plane drops out of sight.

"It's OK," Harlan shouts, his mouth next to my ear. "First shot was lucky. Son of a bitch'll never—"

The second seaplane collides with us.

The bang feels like the world tearing apart. My stomach plummets as our plane lists to the left, tilting sideways. It's all I can do to keep my balance. With a roar, the second plane appears on the right, its wingtip only just missing ours.

Whoever is flying that plane is insane. He'll take both of us out at once. A hit in the right place will damage an engine, shear off a wing.

The other plane drifts away, as if it's taking a run-up. Then it banks towards us, filling the windows.

There's an angry shout from our cockpit. Eric is leaning across, hands wrapped around the control yoke, pushing the Nomad pilot aside. We tilt again, the nose dropping, and the incoming plane roars above us.

The Nomad in the cockpit grabs Eric's head by a fistful of hair, smashing him into the yoke. Eric is in an exposed position, bent over, and he can't reach around to stop the attack.

I launch myself up the body of the plane. Finkler is just behind me, almost rolling across the wall. I can't do anything about the attacking plane, but I can do something about the Nomad in the cockpit.

I reach through the gap between the two front seats, and wrap my arm around the man's throat.

He tries to fight me, tries to push me off. But I brace my knees against the back of the seat, and pull. He can't stop himself being hauled upwards, even as his fingernails rake across my cheek.

I twist my body sideways, dragging the man through the gap between the seats and into the body of the plane. I can just see the other seaplane through the cockpit glass – it's coming up from below us, trying to find an angle. Eric is trying to haul himself into the pilot's seat, trying to grab the yoke.

The attention slip costs me. The Nomad lands a blow on my eye socket, setting off a burst of stars in my vision. He's wriggling out of my grip, his chin pushing against my arm.

Finkler and Harlan are grabbing his arms and legs, trying to hold him down. But we're all awkwardly balanced, the confined interior of the plane not letting us move around. The Nomad takes the advantage. With a sudden burst of strength, he rips out of my grip, his body swinging sideways. He nearly falls out of the open door, but manages to grab on, his fingers snagging the edge.

His eyes meet mine, and I can see him getting ready to move, getting ready to throw himself back inside. The second seaplane is in view, moving in from behind us, coming in fast, a white ghost against the dark sky.

I don't think. I just move. My foot slams into the Nomad's chest. He swings sideways, his fingers ripped from the edge of the door, just like the one who tried to climb in off the platform. Except this time there's nothing to break his fall.

The shock and anger on his face are unbelievable. Then he's falling, tumbling out. Slamming into the other plane.

Its wing takes him at his waist. For an instant, he just hangs there, stuck fast by the rushing air. Then he slips sideways, his upper body dropping right onto the whirling propeller.

There's a grinding bang. The propeller knocks the Nomad sideways, his body spinning out of view. The engine starts to tear itself apart. Grey smoke billows out of it as the housing comes apart in shreds, the propeller curved inward now, starting to tear up the wing itself.

The plane tilts, as if the mangled engine is pulling it to the ground. Then it's gone.

For a moment, I'm perfectly balanced in the plane's unstable interior, hands just touching the wall. I'm reliving the Nomad's expression again – that horrified shock as he realised he was falling. That was me. I did that.

I don't feel anything. Not a thing. And for the first time, that doesn't bother me.

"Eric!" Harlan shouts.

The sound drags me out of my thoughts. I turn to see Harlan leaning into the space at the back of the cockpit. Just past him, I can see Eric in the pilot's seat, hands on the controls. He's gripping them so hard that his skin has turned white.

He's never flown a plane before – never even been inside one, for all I know. He might have the knowledge, gleaned from books, but that's all he's got. And now he's at the controls, a thousand feet up. The plane starts to tilt, its nose pointing towards the ground.

I stagger up towards the cockpit, squeezing through the opening and slipping into the seat on Eric's right. It used to be fabric and foam padding, but it's been worn down to a bare skeleton, and the struts jam into my back. There's a second stick in front of me, moving in tandem with Eric's. I can just make out the dark shapes of mountains through the smeared cockpit glass.

The plane levels out a little. We're still descending, but more slowly now. Eric is staring straight ahead, mouth open. Sweat drips from his chin, landing on his vice-grip hands.

I say his name, but it gets lost in the roar of the engines. When I reach out to grab him, I find that he's trembling, his shoulder vibrating under my hand.

Finkler shoves his way through the opening, hunting for something. He reaches up behind me and jams something over my head. A pair of headphones, huge and bulbous, catching my hair and trapping it against my scalp. I adjust them, pulling the microphone stalk down as Finkler puts another pair on Eric's head.

The sound of the engine is muffled now. I feel on the stalk for the transmit switch, clicking it into place. A thin crackle of static emerges over the engine.

"Eric," I say. I have to repeat his name before he looks at me, and, when he does, there's naked terror in his eyes. This isn't the commander I saw back at the hospital. This is someone who is coming face to face with his worst fear.

I see his lips moving, but I can't hear him. I point to the stalk, and after some fumbling his voice comes across the channel: "– do it. Can't do it."

"Yes, you can," I say.

He shakes his head, letting go of the control yoke and gripping the mic stalk with both hands. The plane dips even further, sliding me forward in my seat. I grab my own control yoke, moving more on instinct than anything else, pulling it backwards. We start rising, but I've pushed it too far, overcorrecting the movement. The yoke feels heavy in my hands, the plane both sluggish and impossibly sensitive.

"Eric, listen to me," I say. "I can't do this by myself. I don't know how."

"You think I do?"

"You've read the books. You know how this thing works. Eric, *please.*"

"No." He's shaking his head. "We need to go back to Whitehorse. We'll find someone else."

It would be so easy to get angry, to scream at him. It's not just that I could – I *want* to. But getting angry isn't going to work – not this time. I don't have the first clue what I'm doing. Eric needs to figure out how to fly this thing, and soon, or we're going to crash. I have to help him understand that he can do it.

A memory tugs at me. Carver, back on the station. We'd been captured by Mikhail's Earthers, and to escape I'd taken a little girl hostage. Ivy, her name was. I held her round the throat, used her to buy us some time. Carver gave me hell for it, told me that I was trying to handle everything myself, acting before my friends could help me.

I reach out, grabbing his hands, pulling them gently off the stalk. Then I place them on the control yoke, holding them tight, before returning my hands to my own controls.

My eyes meet his. "We're going to do it together," I say. "We'll pull it up. All right?"

The terrified expression hasn't left his face. But after a long moment, he nods.

Impact

"Here we go," I say. Together, we pull back on our control yokes.

The plane levels out, and then slowly begins to climb.

260

48

Anna

Anna Beck leans over the control panel, her mouth inches from the mic set into the edge of the touchscreen.

She opens her mouth to speak, then stops.

It takes her several attempts to form the words. "*Shinso Maru*, please respond. This is Outer Earth. Do you copy?"

Nothing. Just static, ebbing and flowing.

"*Shinso Maru*, can you hear me?"

Her voice breaks on the last word, and she sits back, head bowed. This isn't the first time she's been in the Apex control room, and it's not the first time she's tried to find a sign that the asteroid catcher survived. Why should now be any different? She's not going to hear from the *Shinso*. She's not going to hear from anyone. Earth is silent – the last time any signal was picked up was decades ago. One by one, they all winked out.

Anna Beck doesn't cry. She hasn't shed a single tear, and she's not going to now.

The Apex control room is a long and narrow space, with banks of screens bordering a thin strip of metal flooring. Most of the screens are dead. The few chairs that remain are battered and worn. Anna is sitting in one of them, elbows on her knees, staring at nothing.

Nobody comes here any more, mostly because there's no point – most of the technicians who used the systems are dead, and what's left is running on automatic, humming away while they wait for the reactor to die. The control room is the one place that Anna can virtually guarantee that she'll be alone. She's afraid that if she runs into anyone she won't be able to keep Dax's plan to herself. And she can't tell anyone about it. Not yet.

Because it might be the wrong choice.

Anna laughs. There's no humour in the sound. She's thinking about the people she killed during the siege in the dock, when she squatted behind a barricade with her long gun and fired again and again and again. She's thought about them a lot in the past few days. Why shouldn't she? Nobody should have to take a life, let alone five or six of them, one after the other.

And yet, it doesn't bother her. Not as much as it should have. The choice to do it was cut and dried. Those people – the Earthers – were coming to hurt her and her friends. They wanted out, and they didn't care what was in their path. She did the right thing – no, she did the *only* thing.

This isn't so simple.

Objectively, Dax is right. That's the worst part. It *does* make sense to send the people who give them the best chance of survival. That doesn't stop it from being completely insane, a plan that takes the chance of life away from almost everyone on the station, without their consent.

Anna could let it happen. She could let them die, and give humanity the best possible chance. Or she could tell everyone, and accept that in the chaos that comes afterwards – and Anna knows it'll be chaos, knows it in her bones – there might still be deaths.

Every time she thinks she's made her decision, every time she starts to rise from her chair, she falters. This isn't just a group of people in a thought experiment. This is her parents. Achala and Ravi Kumar. Marcus, and Ivy, and the rest of the kids. These are people she knows.

Which ones will die, and which ones will live?

Without really realising she's doing it, Anna leans forward, idly trailing her hand along the onscreen frequency band. "This is Outer Earth," she whispers, not expecting an answer but not sure what else to do. "I need help. Please. If anyone can hear me, this is station control for Outer Earth. Please respond."

49

Riley

Finkler's voice comes through the channel. "Can you hear us up there?"

I twist round, looking through the gap in the seats. As I do so, I get a better look at the plane's interior. It's old – ancient, actually. The walls are caked with rust, and the floor is a mess of struts and hinges, the seats they once held long since removed. There are a few battered plastic crates scattered across the floor of the plane, and, at the back, there's a loose mesh netting hanging from floor to ceiling, with more crates stacked tightly behind it. Finkler and Harlan have found headphones of their own, pulled down from brackets mounted on the wall

Eric is staring straight ahead. "Yeah, I hear you," he says, barely moving his lips. He seems . . . not calm, exactly, but a little more focused. We're not going to crash, at least not right away.

"How much fuel do we have?" I say.

His eyes don't leave the windshield. "We're lucky. They'd filled her up. Probably getting ready to head out in the morning." He glances at me, and his face hardens. "Before you say anything: yes, I'll take you to Anchorage."

I don't know *what* to say. Despite everything that's happened, he's still got every right to turn this plane around and return to Whitehorse. He'd be putting his people's needs above mine, and I wouldn't be able to fault him for it.

He sees my confusion. "That plan of yours was the stupidest, most insane thing I've ever heard. It should have got you killed, and you know it. But you went out there anyway. That counts for something, at least to me."

There's a long pause.

"Thank you." It's all I can think to say.

"But let's get it straight," he says, and I can hear the strength coming back into his voice. "We're not sticking around. Once we get you there, you're on your own. I'm taking this thing back home. That's assuming I don't mess up the landing and kill us all."

"Fair enough."

There's a square screen to his left, full of strange shapes, and he taps it with a fingernail. "The plane's got some working nav software on it. We'll head for . . ." He checks the screen. "Cook Inlet. It's just up past Anchorage. If we get down safe, we can get you onto the shoreline. We should have enough fuel to make it back OK."

I sink back against the seat. The plane is rocking gently from side to side, steadily climbing, and Finkler and Harlan are talking in excited bursts as they dig through the containers at the back of the plane.

Eric looks around for a long minute, hunting across the control panel. "Hit that button there," he says, pointing to a spot on my side, where there's a bank of toggle switches. I reach over and grab the one I think he's pointing to, on the far left.

"No, that's the—" Eric says, and then I flip the switch and our headphones explode with noise.

My eardrums feel like they're tearing in two, like every frequency in the spectrum is trying to jam itself inside my head. I grab my headphones, trying to rip them off, but one of them is caught on my ear. Eric launches across the space between us, scrambling for the switch.

At the last second, just before he turns the switch off and kills the radio, I hear something.

Something that shouldn't be there.

"Jesus," Eric says, shaking his head as he sits back in his seat. He yanks the control stick downwards, jerking the plane back up. "That was the radio. The one I was *pointing to* is the autopilot switch, so if you could—"

"Turn it back on," I say.

"What?"

"Turn it back on. Right now." I don't wait for him to do it. I reach forward, and flip the switch. Eric stares at me, wincing at the noise. Then he grabs a dial just under the bank of switches, and twists it all the way to the left.

The sound is still a jumble of noise, but it's softer now, almost inaudible. Eric is staring at me like I've gone mad.

Slowly, very slowly, I turn the volume up. A little at time. My eyes are closed, as if it'll help me find the signal in the noise.

Nothing.

I must have imagined it. My shoulders sag. For a second there, I thought –

The voice comes across the transmission, almost buried by the noise, split in two by the static: "– anyone hear me?"

Eric is staring at me, confused. "So some kid's got hold of a transmitter. So what?"

"We have to respond," I say, my voice curiously breathless. I'm hunting the panel for a transmit button, but I can hardly make sense of the labels: DOPPLR and TFREQ, RFREQ and OFFSET.

"Finkler!" Eric shouts, not bothering to use his headset. I hear clunking footfalls, and then Finkler's flushed face pokes into the space between Eric and me.

"Mind giving us a little warning before you mess with the radio?" he shouts.

I grab his shoulder, jamming my headphones back on. "I have to transmit," I say. "Outside the plane."

"Hey, whoa," Finkler says, his face serious. "I mean, I don't know if—"

"*Please.*"

"Do it," Eric says.

Finkler shakes his head, his eyes wide, but leans forward until he's on all fours, half in and half out of the cockpit. He toggles some switches and adjusts some knobs, his tongue sticking a little out of his mouth.

"Hurry," I say.

The voice comes again, and my heart almost explodes out of my chest. The sound is fainter this time: "– Control on Outer Earth transmitting. If there's – out there—"

"My God," Eric says, staring at the radio.

Finkler twists a knob, and reaches over to flick a second switch, his arm nearly colliding with my face. Then he leans back, and touches a button on the centre console.

The static vanishes.

For a second, I think we've lost her, but then Finkler gestures at me to speak.

"Anna?" I say. "This is Riley. Come back."

Finkler releases the button. The static returns. There are more artefacts in the noise now, strange blips and clicks, as if my words have disturbed a strange god, slowly coming to life.

Then, almost inaudible, I hear Anna Beck's stunned voice. "Riley?"

Finkler and Eric are staring at me in shock. Harlan has arrived, too, his face visible above Finkler's back.

"I can hear you!" I say.

Anna's reply is fractured "– shit, you're alive! How – others, are you –"

"Anna, what about everybody up there? Is Outer Earth OK?"

"– dying. The reactor's cut out, and –"

"Anna, say again?"

"– send a ship back to Earth, but we don't know—"

"It has to be passing right overhead," says Finkler, as Anna's voice cracks apart in the static. "That's the only way this is happening." He grabs my shoulder. "You've probably got about fifteen seconds, maybe less."

Hearing Anna's voice, knowing she's alive, after the breach in the dock, is almost too much to take. I hit the button again. "Anna, listen to me carefully. If you can make it back to Earth, aim for a place called Whitehorse, in the Yukon. We'll be waiting for you." I don't know what Eric might say about that, and right then I couldn't care less.

Her voice is even fainter now. "– ley, I copy, we'll come – you. As soon as I—"

And then she's gone. There's nothing but static

"You have to tune it," I say, pointing to the radio. "Get her back."

"She's out of range," says Finkler, giving a helpless shrug.

"There's gotta be something we can do."

He reaches forward and adjusts the dial marked DOPPLR. The squelches and clicks mutate, lengthening and twisting into new sounds. He grunts in frustration, turning his attention to TFREQ, then RFREQ. After a long moment, he drops his hand.

"Nada," he says. "Doppler offset didn't catch her. She's out of range."

He looks genuinely distraught, like he's let someone die. I reach up and put a hand on his, squeezing tight.

"Were we just talking to someone in space?" Harlan says.

"Who was she?" Eric says. "And did you just seriously invite *more people* to live with us in Whitehorse?"

I don't have a chance to answer. At that moment, another voice cuts across the static.

"– broadcasting from a secure location in what used to be Anchorage, Alaska. There are at least a hundred of us here, and we have managed to establish a colony. We have food, water and shelter. The—"

I flick the radio off.

50

Anna

Riley is alive.

The implications cascade through Anna's mind as she sprints across the sector. The *Shinso Maru* made it down. The plan to use the asteroid as a heat shield actually worked. And what was that Riley said? *We'll be waiting for you.*

She barrels around a corner in the corridor, slamming into the wall but pushing off it, sprinting even faster. She doesn't have to make the choice any more. If there are people down there already, then Dax's decision – to take only *the best and the brightest* – doesn't have to be made. She doesn't have to play his game.

Riley made it. Maybe Aaron Carver, too, and Prakesh. She has to tell her dad. She has to tell the Kumars. Hell, she has to tell everyone. She runs faster, pumping her arms, and this time she opens her mouth and let loose an ear-splitting whoop of joy. It occurs to her that she could have used the station comms, which are operated from the control room. Then again, she thinks, that would deny her the opportunity of seeing the look on Dax's face.

She doesn't slow down as she approaches the amphitheatre.

The door is open, slid away into the wall, and she can hear the crowd as she gets close. She can hear –

Angry shouts.

She hesitates, and that hesitation nearly kills her. She's going too fast, and the pause shifts her centre of gravity slightly, tilting her forward. Her feet try to compensate, stutter-stepping, and then she slams into the edge of the door. It takes her in the shoulder, and a starburst of pain explodes on her collarbone.

She comes to a halt, leaning against it, and finally sees inside the amphitheatre.

Everyone is on their feet, screaming at each other, giant knots of people hurling accusations. Her father is standing on one of the chairs at the front, his hands around his mouth, yelling at everybody to stay calm. An empty food container flies through the air, bouncing down the centre steps.

There's a woman coming out of the amphitheatre, a grim look on her face. Anna pushes past the pain, and grabs her. "What's going on?" she says.

"You haven't heard?"

Anna manages to controls herself. "Tell me."

The woman shakes her head. "The escape pods launched," she says, speaking as if she can't believe the words herself.

Anna stares at her, eyes wide. "How many?"

The woman doesn't answer. She shakes Anna off, then jogs away down the corridor.

Dax.

He wasn't giving her a choice. He was just buying himself time, taking her out of the equation so she wouldn't warn anyone before he could make his escape. How could she have been so stupid?

Anna's shoulder is on fire. She ignores it. She takes one last look at her dad, down in the amphitheatre.

Then she turns, and runs.

51

Riley

"We're getting close," Eric says.

His words jerk me awake. Until that moment, I hadn't even been aware that I was sleeping, but the vibration of the plane and the whirr of the engines made me drift off. My back is kinked from the hard chair, and, despite the meat strips I ate a couple of hours ago, my stomach feels hollow and tight.

I raise myself up a little, looking out of the cockpit glass. I can't see a damn thing. Dawn is starting to glimmer behind us, but I can still barely tell the difference between the ground and the sky. It's hard to believe that Eric knows where he's going.

"Shouldn't we be seeing lights?" I say.

"We don't know what we should be seeing," says Eric. He sounds more subdued than before, a note of worry creeping into his voice. Not surprising – soon he'll have to land the plane, one way or another.

"Don't you worry about Eric," says Harlan, his voice coming crystal-clear over the headset. "He'll fly us right. Hey, Riley – come back here for a second, would you?"

I stretch briefly, kneeling on the seat. Then I clamber out

into the main body of the plane, leaving my headset behind. Eric is making a gentle right turn, and it nearly throws me off balance, but I manage to keep one hand on the side.

Harlan and Finkler have turned the place inside out. Boxes lie everywhere, their contents upended and scattered across the metal floor: scrap metal, spare parts, tools, pieces of foam rubber, articles of clothing so threadbare that it's a wonder they don't fall apart when I look at them. Finkler is on all fours, picking through a pile of seemingly identical screws. Bandages and bottles are stacked on his right. A single dim bulb, set into the ceiling, is the only light.

Harlan waves me over. He passes me an extra set of headphones, the cable running into a box bolted to the roof.

"Here," he says, bending down, once I've got them in place. There's a backpack by his feet, covered in lurid red and green stripes, the fabric torn in places. By the way he grunts as he lifts it up, it's clear that the pack is heavy.

"Food, some extra clothing, odds and ends that you might need," he says. "There's a gun in there, too, although we can't find any ammo. Still, might come in handy. Oh, and here."

He passes me a piece of clothing – his coat. When he sees my expression, he shrugs. "It's thick, you know? Thicker'n the one you got on, anyway. You'll need to keep warm."

I tell him thanks, pulling off my coat and exchanging it for Harlan's. He's right. It's scratchy and uncomfortable, but it's also warm. The fabric smells of smoke. The pockets are stuffed full – I decide not to pull everything out now, where it could roll around the plane. I'll check on it later.

"I still think we should give her those socks," says Finkler, from his position on the floor.

Harlan rolls his eyes. "They're more hole than sock."

"I'm just saying."

"She'd be better off wrapping her feet in marsh grass."

273

"Fine. Then I'll keep them. I like socks."

I try to smile at Finkler's words, and don't quite manage it. The thought of going out there by myself, of leaving them, is almost too much to take.

I crouch down to Finkler's level, putting an arm around his shoulders. He stops picking through his pile of screws, letting his hand rest on the cold metal floor. "Just get back to Whitehorse safe."

I reach over and grip Harlan's shoulder. "You too, all right? You'd better be around when I get back."

He nods, not looking at me. "The terrain down there isn't going to be what you've seen before," he says. "Alaska's a bad place."

"Bad? Like how?"

"It's tougher for things to grow. The land isn't *honest*. It plays tricks on your feet. It's all bog and swamp, especially this close to the shore. You watch yourself."

"Thought you'd never been to Anchorage."

"I ain't. But I've been a little ways west. I've seen how it gets."

Eric's voice comes over the headphones, crisp and cold. "We're coming up on Fire Island, which means Anchorage is north of us. I'll go a little way past it, down the inlet. I don't want to put this bird down in Anchorage, not when I don't know what's out there."

"Fire Island?" I say.

Harlan points to the window, and I bend down to look through it. There's more light in the sky now, enough for me to see the vast ocean stretching away from us, a thousand times bigger than Fish Lake. I try to take it all in, but the sheer size of it makes me blink with astonishment.

At the very bottom of the view, peeking over the edge of the window, is a black strip of land. Water pushes in on it from all sides. We're coming in low over the ocean, and I can just make out scrubby plants on the shoreline. Water laps against the rocks.

Almost there.

Finkler stands up, resting one hand on the wall for balance. He puts his head close to mine, gazing at the view out of the window, and whistles softly. "You keep that incision clean, you hear me?" he says after a moment. "Don't wreck my beautiful stitches."

"Wouldn't dream of it."

"Good. Because if I find out you picked up *another* infection, I'm never going to let you forget it."

And that's when the sky explodes.

It's like we've flown into a meteor shower. The plane shudders as objects pelt it from all sides, too many to count. And the noise. All at once, I'm back on the *Shinso* as it plunged down through the atmosphere, tearing itself apart.

Eric banks the plane sharply, shouting over the headset. Harlan is thrown to the floor, and Finkler and I nearly land on top of him. At the last second, I manage to grab one of the headphone brackets on the wall, and stop myself falling. But the plane rocks from side to side, shaking to pieces as the storm gets more intense. My fingers slip loose, and my knee slams into Harlan's shoulder. Finkler is on his feet, whirling his arms, desperately trying to keep his balance.

A window detonates, glass raining inwards. Something is burning, and I smell the sharp stench of fuel, shooting upwards into the cabin from an unseen puncture. It's like we've flown into some insane weather pattern, a localised storm that—

Gunfire. It's gunfire. We're being shot at, by what feels like a million stingers going off at once.

We lurch to the side, tilting almost ninety degrees. Finkler slams into me, knocking me off Harlan. I feel his arm wrapping around me, like he's drawing me into a protective embrace.

We're heading right for a closed door in the side of the plane. The thoughts come in split-second bursts: *It slides open sideways, it'll hold us, it has to.*

Finkler takes the full force of the impact. I feel the bang, and it's so powerful that it rips the door off the wall.

I don't know if the metal is too old or the rails it's on are too fragile, but one second we're in the body of the plane and the next there's nothing but open sky above us. My headphones are yanked right off my head.

The tracer part of me kicks into overdrive, adrenaline and instinct overwhelming everything. I see the plane's pontoon and grab it in the same instant, wrapping my forearm around it. With my other arm, I reach for Finkler, already bracing to take the weight.

I get one last look at him, at the raw shock on his face. Then my hand closes on empty air and Finkler is gone.

Bullets are whizzing by me like angry insects, and the roaring chatter of the gun is everywhere, coming in quick bursts now, like whoever is firing is trying to save ammo. The plane took fewer hits than I thought, but it's still holed in a dozen places, gushing black smoke.

Harlan is above me, spreadeagled in the doorway, trying to get a better grip. He sees me, shouts my name, but then Eric swings the plane back the other way.

For a moment, I'm weightless, the motion of the plane cancelling gravity out. I can see the ocean below me. The white caps on the waves look as if they're frozen solid. We're seventy feet up, maybe more.

Harlan reaches out from the doorway, desperately trying to find my hand.

Another bullet hits us. I feel the plane tilt, and my arm rips free from the pontoon.

52

Riley

I thought I knew real panic. Not even close. As I plummet towards the water, the panic that surges through me is knifepoint sharp.

I'm face up, windmilling my arms. Harlan is still leaning out of the plane, still reaching for me, as if his arm is going to extend and catch me. Then I'm falling, and I find that my mind is capable of only one thought, repeating over and over, Harlan's voice in my head. *Water that cold, it'll shut your body down in thirty seconds.*

I have to stabilise myself, brace for landing, do *something*. But my tracer instinct, so strong a few moments before, has vanished.

When I hit the water, it's with a thud so loud that it feels like it cracks my skull open.

It's as if someone has flicked the switch, turning out all the light in the world. I try to breath, and suck in a mouthful of seawater. It's foul, as cold as space itself, but forcing it back out is almost impossible. Somewhere, very distant, the muscles in my back are screaming at me. My lungs are on fire. I'm panicking, thrashing in place. I don't even know which direction to swim in.

Light. A tiny glimmer, no more. It takes me a good three seconds to get my muscles to push me in the right direction. My chest has turned into a supernova, and with every foot I swim, my vision gets smaller, shrinking down to a tiny circle.

My sight is almost gone when I break the surface.

I breathe too soon, before I'm fully out. I suck in a mouthful of water, coughing and spluttering. My eyes open so wide that it feels like they're going to tear right off my face.

The water is so cold that it's as if it's burning me, scourging my skin. It's slate-grey, spattered with white foam, hissing like an angry monster. There's a black shape rising out of it, an uneven jumble of contours.

Fire Island. I have to get there, and I have to get there *now*.

It takes every ounce of effort I have to keep my body above the icy water, but I manage it, kicking hard to stay afloat. More than once, the panic grips me, like a tentacle threatening to pull me under. I have to fight it off, willing myself to keep kicking, using my hands and forearms to push through the water.

I'm not going to last much longer. The muscles in my back are dull and useless, and the cold is shutting my body down, robbing me of energy. A chemical reaction in my cells. Prakesh would know . . .

The thought of him makes me force my exhausted arms to keep going. Prakesh is just over the horizon, and Carver, and Okwembu, and I did *not* come all this way just to drown here.

Kick, stroke, breathe. Kick, stroke, breathe.

Soon, the only sensation I can feel are my trembling lips. I can hear the teeth behind them chattering, my tongue a dead slab of flesh in my mouth.

And then something changes. I try to make a stroke, and my hand bounces back at me.

I keep going. My forearms slam into dirt, and I'm raised up on my knees. I start crawling, and when I fall, face crunching into the dirt, I pull myself along with my hands.

I don't know how long it is before I stop moving. But I can feel another sensation now: grains of sand, rubbing against my lips.

I'm out of the water. I'm on land. Wonderful, amazing, solid land.

I blink. Or I try to, anyway. The second I close my eyes, I discover that I don't want to open them again. They feel like they're welded shut, and what's behind them is too sweet to turn away from.

Don't.

It's the voice – the one at the back of my mind, the angry one, except this time it's not angry. It's distraught, crazy with fear, pleading with me. *You have to get up.*

It's like waking from a deep sleep, where you've stayed in one position all night and your arm or leg has gone dead. I have to focus on my fingers, slowly clenching them into a fist, then pull backwards until I'm resting on the forearm.

I raise my head. A muscle in my shoulder twinges, sending a sharp, shooting pain down my back. I push a clenched, angry noise through gritted teeth and open my eyes.

Black sand gives way to jagged rocks, sloping steeply away from me. I can see plants pushing up between the rocks, but they're withered and stunted, barely alive. There are a few trees further inland, their branches bare. The sky beyond them is ash-grey, and the only sound is the pounding of the ocean, the steady swish of water around my ankles.

My clothes are soaked. Streams of water fall off me, soaking into the sand. The wind has picked up, and it's like a blast from an open freezer, chilling me to the bone.

I look at the rocks again. There's something there, something splayed across them.

Finkler's neck is broken, his arms twisted at unnatural angles. The shocked expression is still on his face.

53

Okwembu

Okwembu's eyes fly open. She sits bolt upright, so quickly that she nearly hits her head on the underside of the bunk above her.

She listens hard. There: distant, humming bursts of gunfire. The Phalanx gun.

Okwembu kicks the thin blanket off her legs and slides off the bed. She's been given her own room, a tiny space on one of the upper levels of the ship, with low ceilings and a bunk bed bolted to the wall. She has to hammer on the door three times before the guard outside unlocks it. Okwembu ducks under his arm and strides down the corridor, only stopping when he grabs her above the elbow.

"What do you think you're doing?" the guard says. He's in his thirties, with blond hair and an angular, almost blocky face. His voice is alert, but Okwembu can see the fog of sleep in his eyes.

She shrugs him off. "I'm going up to the bridge," she says.

"Get back inside, right now."

Okwembu has a sudden, surprising urge to reach out and

wrap her hands around his throat, to squeeze until that bright voice is extinguished. She shakes it off. "I'm going up to the bridge," she says again, her voice cold. "Touch me, and you'll have to answer to Prophet."

Another burst of muted gunfire rumbles down through the ship. The guard must see something in her eyes, because he stays rooted to the spot. She starts walking again, not looking back. He follows, but at a discreet distance, and after a few steps she forgets that he's even there.

The bridge is at the top of a central tower on the deck of the ship. Okwembu pushes herself up the last flight of stairs, ignoring her protesting legs, and pushes open the door.

The space reminds her of the main control room on Outer Earth. It's longer, and wider, but it has the same banks of screens and uncomfortable wheeled chairs, the same sickly fluorescent lighting. There are three large tables in the centre of the room, spread with yellowing maps and charts. Floor-to-ceiling windows line the wall to her right, looking out across the deck of the ship to the ocean beyond. Through the glass she can see the first faint glimmerings of dawn.

The bridge is packed with people, most of them still blurry with sleep. She picks out the alert ones instantly. They're the ones holding rifles, the ones who were on nightshift, or whatever these people call it. She can feel their eyes on her, hear their whispered, angry mutterings. Ray and Iluk are there, hunched over one of the tables. Ray's eyebrows almost touch his hairline when he sees her.

She spots Prophet immediately, standing before one of the windows. He's holding something up to his face, using both hands – some kind of binoculars, black and bulky. It's still dark outside, so Okwembu supposes they must have some kind of night vision.

She strides around the bank of screens, ignoring the suspicious stares. "What's going on?" she says, when she's standing next to Prophet.

He glances at her, irritation slipping on and off his face in a microsecond. "You should be sleeping."

"Just tell me."

He doesn't speak. She's about to ask again when he says, "An aircraft came in over the water. Our gunner caught it."

"Aircraft?" Okwembu squints, looking out over the water.

"Seaplane. Haven't seen one of them in years. Could be Nomads."

"Did you shoot them down?"

"Not sure. Definitely hit 'em, though, Engine be praised."

The words are taken up by the others on the bridge, rippling out from Prophet. Just as before, Okwembu can't help but notice a few people who conspicuously fail to praise the Engine.

She turns back to the window. "Who were they? Do you know?"

"Prophet." The voice comes from one of his men, standing off to their right. He has an identical pair of binoculars, and he's leaning forward, resting them on the window glass. "Got something."

"Where?" Prophet raises his own lenses again.

"Over by the island."

The murmuring on the bridge drops even lower. Prophet scans the horizon, tracking right to left.

He shakes his head, lowering the binoculars. "I don't see anything."

"Could have sworn," the other man says. "Right around the rocks on the western point."

"Nothing could have survived a fall from that plane," Prophet says, more to himself than to anyone else. "Not even if they hit the water."

He falls silent, still holding the binoculars at chest level, staring out across the water.

Janice Okwembu has always trusted her instincts. Sometimes, she thinks that they are all that has kept her alive. They've led her here, up to the bridge, and now she understands why. Despite the belief in the Engine, despite the military uniforms and the rudimentary chain of command, Prophet and his followers aren't good at reacting to the unknown. They're fine as long as new workers keep coming in, as long as there's a constant stream of supplies. She's an anomaly: a potential worker who somehow managed to avoid her fate, to position herself next the ship's leader. That seaplane is an anomaly, too. It's upset the balance, disrupted the status quo.

Which gives her the perfect opportunity.

"You need to send some men out there," she says, careful to address herself to Prophet – she's not at the stage of giving orders. *Not yet.*

Prophet looks at her, his eyes wide. "You forget your place."

She pushes on. "You need to be sure. If there's someone on that island, they might be able to tell you about where the plane came from."

"She calling the shots now, Prophet?" says someone from behind her. Prophet's eyes are dark, but Okwembu holds his gaze. *Strength over weakness.*

After a moment, he turns away. "The Engine has brought her to us for a reason. We'll take her advice, for now. Ray: take Iluk and get out there. Bring Koji with you – if there's any debris, I want him to take a look at it first."

Okwembu turns back to the window, looking back out into the darkness.

54

Riley

Crying or screaming isn't enough. I want to turn and go back into the ocean, stop swimming, let myself sink into the blackness.

He saved my life. He helped get me to the Nomads' camp. He got me all the way here, and now he's dead. Just like Amira, and my father, and Syria, and everyone else. I can't save any of them.

My legs stop supporting me. I drop to my knees, bent over, digging furrows in the dirt with numb fingers. The tears finally come.

Maybe I shouldn't try to find Prakesh and Carver. They're not safe around me. Maybe I should just . . . vanish.

Listen, says the voice inside me.

And I do. I listen as it tells me what I need to do next. Because, right then, I realise that it's something that will never let me down. It'll help me, and it'll keep me alive. As long as I trust it. As long as I pay attention to it.

What was it Finkler said? Post-traumatic stress disorder. The result of bottling everything up, pretending that these horrible things never happened. Not any more. I'm not going to bottle this up. Finkler isn't going to have died for nothing. I'm not going to die. I'm going to find Prakesh and Carver, I'm going to take out Okwembu, and I'm going to make sure that this *never* happens again.

Somehow, I manage to get to my feet. I stumble over to the rocks, retching and coughing. When I'm a few feet away, my legs give out again. I go to one knee in the sand, breathing hard. I make myself get up, make myself pull Finkler's body off the rocks. It takes almost all the strength I have to do it, and when I feel that there's still body heat under the clothing, it nearly stops me in my tracks.

I pull Finkler's clothes off him, working his pants down around his ankles, rolling him over to get to his jacket sleeves. What I'm doing is awful, like spitting in his face, but I do it anyway, because I don't have a choice. I need dry clothes.

I strip naked, right there on the beach. The tips of my fingers have gone blue, and it takes everything I have just to stay upright. The enormous grey coat, and the shirt and sweater underneath it, almost swallow me whole. The pants balloon around my waist. My skin is still wet, and the remaining water makes the clothes a little damp, but I barely notice.

His boots are far too big. My feet slide around in them, threatening to slip out at any moment. In the end, I have to wear my own shoes. They're soaked, and the water bites through the dry socks instantly, but it's better than nothing.

I stand up, shivering in the wind, clutching my arms around me with my hands jammed in my armpits. I'm still far too cold, my thoughts coming in sluggish waves.

Harlan and Eric.

My eyes go wide. How could I not have thought about them? It was as if what happened to Finkler took up all the space in my mind. I scan the sky, hunting for the plane, listening hard for the noise of the engine. Several times I think I spot it, a black dot against the clouds, but then I blink and it's gone. *They're* gone.

I try to tell myself that they stayed in the air, try to make myself believe that they're OK. But how can they be, after that barrage? I squeeze my eyes shut, fighting off the despair.

There's nothing you can do for them, the voice says. *You need fire.*

That's what Harlan said, too. Clothes, shelter, fire. Whatever happened to him, he'd want me to keep going.

Finding shelter here isn't an option – it's rocks and sand and scrub as far as the eye can see. Fire it is. But how? Harlan never showed me how to make it. Back on Outer Earth, we'd use fuel oil, drenching rags with it and igniting it all with a lighter . . .

I jog over to the discarded jacket. It feels frozen solid when I pick it up, but I manage to keep hold of it, turning it the right way up and digging in the pockets. I feel something, pull it out. It's the bear spray, the one Harlan gave me. I growl in frustration, stuffing the spray into the pocket of Finkler's jacket, then keep digging. There are a couple of meat strips, a spare scarf, also soaked through, and a folded-up map. I shake it out, but it's too wet to even think about using as kindling.

There's something else in the pockets, something round and solid. A flare. Harlan was the one who gave me two of them to use on the wolves – he must have kept one for himself.

It's soaked, what's left of the label peeling off. Shivering hard, I clamber up the rocks towards the trees. I'm finding it more difficult to flex my fingers, and it's tough to get a good grip on the rocks, but somehow I manage it. I don't dare strike the flare until I have something to light it with. I try not to think about what will happen to me if this doesn't work.

The trees are spaced widely apart, pushing their way out of

the uneven ground. They're tilted at odd angles, as if they've been frozen in the act of trying to escape. It takes me a few minutes to find some old man's beard. I let out a harsh, ragged cry of joy when I find some, and one of my fingernails breaks as I scrape it off the bark. It's a tiny amount, no larger than my palm, but it will have to do.

Harlan didn't explain how to keep a fire going after you start one, but that's not hard to work out. I dump the flare and the old man's beard in a clearing, and start collecting twigs. The ground is frosty beneath my shoes, and my feet have gone completely numb, but I keep going.

It seems like hours before I have enough. I crouch in the clearing, back aching, and squash the old man's beard into an uneven lump. I reach out for the flare, but it's not there any more. My fingers scramble at the ground in horror. Have I lost it? Did I take it with me? The cold is making it hard to focus. My mind keeps drifting, and it's hard to pull it back.

Then I spot the flare, a little way behind me, and grab it as if it's a lifeline. With shaking fingers, I turn it upright, and pull the tab. If it doesn't work . . .

It hisses like an angry animal, burning bright. It happens so quickly that it burns my eyes. I snap them shut, feeling the heat bake onto my hand, then jam the flare onto the old man's beard.

Nothing. There's smoke, lots of it, and some pieces of moss start to catch, but it's not working. The moss is too damp, too—

Flames. Shooting upwards. With a cry of triumph, I jam the flare deeper into the moss, and start piling sticks on the fire.

The smoke is unbelievable now, acrid and hot. The flames start to lick upwards as I add more twigs, little by little, and it's not long before the fire is a foot high. I get as close as I can to it, hugging my knees, letting the heat bake onto my face. The wind has grown worse, but I just manage to shield the fire from it with my body, kicking off my wet shoes and propping them as close to the heat as I dare.

I don't know how long I'm out for, but when I wake up the fire has burned down to cinders, and it's daylight – or what passes for it, under the grey clouds. Slowly, I pull my shoes on. They're still damp, but much less than before. The wind has died down, and I'm not quite as cold.

The faces of Harlan and Finkler and Eric swim to the surface of my mind. I push them away. I can't mourn for them now, not if I want to make it through this.

I try to picture Fire Island as I saw it from the air. It didn't look too big – I can probably make it to the far shore in a few minutes. I stand up on shaking legs, and start walking.

The pain in my back has settled into two burning rods at my shoulder blades, but I make good time, pushing through the scrub and stumbling onto the rocky beach. The ocean in front of me is enormous. It's become choppier, the waves slamming onto the sand. I can just make out the land on the horizon, a dark line above the water, reflecting the grey sky.

There's something else there, too. A black shape, separate from the line of the land. I squint, putting a hand up to my eyes, but I can't figure out what it is. It's too far away.

My shoulders sag. It doesn't matter what it is. I have to get across this expanse of water, and I don't have the first clue how to do it. If Carver were here, he'd—

Voices.

I stop, listening hard, then hear them again, coming from further down the beach. I react fast, hurling myself to the ground. Sand scratches against my palms as I crawl behind a nearby rock. I put my back against it, trying to ignore the pain in my shoulders.

The voices are coming closer. I can't make out the words yet, but I can hear that the speakers are male. Their footsteps crunch on the sand.

". . . the whole damn island," I hear one of them say. His voice is gruff.

Another one speaks. He's using a language I've never heard before, all elongated vowels.

"There's nothing here," says a third. "We would've found them by now."

"In the water, you think?"

"Then what about the dead guy? What happened to his clothes? Unless you're telling me they stripped him, *then* threw him out of the plane."

Finkler. They know about him, which means they know I'm here. Any second now, they're going to come round the side of the rock. I have no weapons, and I can't even imagine fighting three people in this cold. I close my eyes, trying to stay as still as possible.

"You're sure you saw—"

"*Yes*, Koji, I'm damn sure. Two of 'em, clear through the binocs."

There's a pause. The footsteps stop.

"Let's get back to the boat," the first one says.

When the reply comes, it's in an angry burst of that strange language.

"Tell you what, Iluk. *You* can stay here and double-check. Me, I'm going back to my booze and my bed. Only thing the *Ramona*'s good for any more."

I lick my lips. These people, whoever they are, have a way off this rock. I can't let that slip away.

But the second the thought occurs, so does every problem with it. I can't fight them – not in my current state, with no weapons.

I could follow them, track them across the island. I've done it before, on Outer Earth, when I followed a psychotic killer named Arthur Gray onto the monorail tracks. But this isn't Outer Earth – here, the ground is uneven, littered with rocks and branches, and staying silent will be difficult. I could try and get ahead of them, make it to the boat before they do, but I don't even know where it is.

There's another way, the voice says.

I stand up, turning to face the men, my legs burning as I push up off the sound. Then I cup my hands to my mouth and yell, "Hey!"

55

Prakesh

This time, Prakesh pays more attention.

He hardly got any sleep, but even a little is better than nothing. He's more alert now, looking for anything that he can use.

They're back in the farm, carrying the last of the soil sacks to their new position. Some of the workers have already begun filling the troughs, and the hangar is alive with the thumping, scratchy sound of dirt on metal. As Prakesh drops a sack on the pile, he takes a closer look at the guards.

It isn't hard to see how they've kept control. The workers might outnumber them three to one, but they've got all the guns. And they're smart about their positioning, too, spacing themselves out around the edges of the room, always keeping the workers in view. It would be easy to see a coordinated attack coming – and even if it succeeded there's no telling how many workers would die in the attempt.

Prakesh looks back at the troughs. They stretch all the way from the middle of the hangar to the far wall. Each one is waist-height, around forty feet long. *Easy enough for a man to hide behind.* If he could slip out of view, he could find a way out. And once he's out into the ship . . .

But there's no way he'll be able to get to a hiding place before being cut down. It would take an extraordinary amount of luck. For a moment, he entertains the idea that the guards have set movement patterns, but then discards it. They aren't robots.

Frustrated, he starts walking back the other way, his shoulders groaning under the heavy sack. Jojo passes him on the right, not looking at him. He hasn't said a word to Prakesh since the night before, as if the act of talking as much as he did has exhausted him. Prakesh can't help thinking of their conversation – how Jojo shut down the man who tried to stop them talking. He may have a stutter, may not even be out of his teens yet, but the other workers respect him.

The sack slips a little, sliding down Prakesh's shoulder onto his upper arm. He stops, shifting it back, and that's when the idea comes.

It's not just what Riley would do in this situation. It's what Aaron Carver would do, too. Carver, whose first response to any situation was to use a gadget or a tool, to use something he'd made. Carver, who was (*is*, he tells himself) always looking for new equipment.

Carver wouldn't just rely on what was here. Carver would be looking to see what he could do with it.

Prakesh stands there for a moment too long, and one of the guards shouts at him to get moving. He bobs his head in apology, hefting the sack as he starts walking.

He can't take out the guards individually. None of them can. But what if he could take them all out in one go?

They move to the troughs, all of them unloading the soil now, dumping it in and mixing it with fertiliser. The stuff comes in foul-smelling buckets, the white granules gritty and slightly slimy. There's insecticide, too: yellowish dust that Prakesh recognises as sulphur. He spotted it earlier, off to one side in a pair of grimy containers. It stains his hands and prickles the inside of his nose. You're supposed to handle this stuff with gloves – it can irritate the skin, causing blisters if you use a lot of it.

Jojo is next to him, head bent, patting the soil down. Prakesh doesn't look at him. Keeping his voice low, he says, "Jojo."

No response.

"Jojo," he hisses, a little louder. Out of the corner of his eye, he sees Jojo's hand flick the air twice. *No. Not now.*

"Then don't talk, just listen," Prakesh says.

It doesn't take him long to explain his plan. Jojo does nothing, doesn't even register that he's heard, but Prakesh isn't worried. *He wants this more than you do*, he thinks, pushing a handful of fertiliser under the soil.

When Prakesh is finished, Jojo doesn't respond for a long minute. Then his right hand forms a quick thumbs up.

It takes a long time for Jojo to tell the rest of the workers the plan. He has to be careful, changing places only when the guards' attention wanders, conferring with them in an almost inaudible voice. Eventually, he makes his way back to Prakesh, and flashes another thumbs up, more emphatic this time.

Prakesh lifts his hands out of the soil. He can feel the other workers watching him. There's a guard close by, a stick-thin woman with a shorn head, and Prakesh slowly starts to walk towards her.

The guard sees him coming before he gets within twenty feet. Her rifle goes up instantly, finger in the trigger guard. "Stop right there."

Prakesh can feel the other rifles on him, like needles sticking into his back. For a moment, it's as if all activity on the floor has stopped. He can't hear anything but the roaring of blood in his ears.

"Back in the line," the guard says, jerking her rifle. "We'll take a break in an hour. You can piss then."

"I don't need a piss. I need to ask you something."

"I said, *back in the line*."

Prakesh looks over his shoulder, gestures to the troughs. "I can make your fertiliser better."

The guard's eyes narrow. "What?"

"Fertiliser. I used to be a plant technician, a biologist—"

He feels the bullet before he hears the gunshot. It *spangs* off the floor a few feet away, the gunshot echoing around the hangar. Prakesh jumps, and the workers hit the deck, throwing themselves to the floor.

"Move away!" shouts a voice. One of the other guards. "If she doesn't shoot you, I will."

Prakesh puts his hands above his head. He speaks as loudly and clearly as he can. "I can make it so everything grows faster. OK? Faster and stronger. I can make you a new batch of fertiliser. We can grow new plants – tomatoes, fruit, whatever you want. I just need a few things to do it."

Silence. The guard still has her gun on him. He tenses, sure that at any second a bullet is going to slam right through him.

But he guessed right. A grow-op like this won't give them a lot of variety in their diet. He's offering them some new tastes, and he can see them looking at each other, thinking it over.

One of the guard's colleagues wanders over, and they have a whispered conversation. Prakesh watches, not wanting to move, not wanting to give the others any reason to shoot.

Eventually, the first guard looks over at him. "I'll pass it up the chain," she says. "Keep working."

56

Riley

The three men stand frozen, staring at me like I'm a ghost.

One of them is young, still in his twenties, with a round face and tiny bud of a mouth. The man on his left is enormous, a neat goatee covering his chin, the skin above it lined and scarred. The one on the right has a hooked nose and prominent chin that look like they've been carved from stone. Somehow, I know he's Iluk – he looks like his name sounds. The one with the round face must be Koji.

All three are wearing thick jackets, and all three have rifles. I have just enough time to take this in, and then I'm face down in the dirt, my arms twisted behind me. The ice-cold tip of a gun barrel is shoved into the back of my neck, and I can feel grains of sand digging into my cheek.

All three men are shouting – two in English, and one in that strange language. The man with the rifle shouts at the others to shut up, digging it harder into the back of my neck.

I have to tell myself to breathe. This is the only way. If I want to get off this island, I have to go with them. I don't know what happens after that, but I'll figure it out. Somehow.

"You alone out here?" the man says. When I don't answer immediately, he shoves the back of my head. I feel sand in my mouth, rough against my tongue. "Answer me."

"I'm alone," I say, the words muffled.

"You sure you're telling the truth there, girl?" I feel the gun barrel shift, as if the man holding it is getting a better grip on the trigger. "Because if you're not . . ."

I raise my head, just enough to get my mouth out of the sand. "I'm the only survivor."

"Now I know you're lying. There were more people in that plane of yours. It was still flying, even after Curtis shot 'em full of holes."

The pressure comes off my back, and the man flips me over. I try to get an elbow underneath me, but then the gun is in my face. It's hard to look anywhere but the huge black barrel in front of me.

"Where'd you come from?"

There's no point lying to him. Unless they've got planes of their own, they're not getting to Eric's people. "Whitehorse," I say.

He laughs. "That so? Long way to come. You want to tell me why you're all the way out here?"

To find my friends. To kill someone.

While I'm trying to think of something to say, he lifts his foot and slams it down on my stomach.

I curl into a ball. I don't have a choice. The pain is hot and feverish, radiating up from my abdomen in long waves. I feel Ray digging through my pockets, pulling out the contents, grunting as he stuffs them into his jacket.

"Jesus, Ray!" says Koji. Iluk spits a sentence I can't understand – I don't know if he's angry with Ray, or goading him on.

"You want to come back with us?" Ray's mouth is inches from my ear. "Fine. But you're going to wish you'd stayed here."

57

Riley

My hands are bound behind me, held in place by rusty metal cuffs. The edges are worn and jagged, and I have to keep my hands as still as I can to avoid cutting the skin. The floor of the boat is hard plastic, cold and wet under my cheek.

It goes against everything I am to lie still. I want to take these people down, one by one, take that rifle away and shove it in their faces, listen to them beg. But the voice tells me to be calm, and I'm learning to listen to it.

Ray sees me looking up at him, and shakes his head. "The second you come off that floor, I'll put a bullet in your kneecap."

The sides of the boat are large tubes made of grainy rubber, tapering to a point at the front. A wave slaps the side, its tip launching over the tube, spraying me in the face. There's a motor at the back of the boat, which Iluk controls using a long handle.

We crest another wave, and the engine coughs and splutters, threatening to give out. Iluk says something back in that strange language, irritated. Ray stands up, moving to help him. "Watch her," he says, jamming the rifle into Koji's hands.

I clear my throat, looking up at Koji. He seems calmer than Ray, less likely to lash out. "Where are we going?" I say.

No response.

"Am I the only new person?" I say. "Or are there others like me?"

Koji looks down, then back up at me. For the second time, I see something in his eyes, something I can't quite read.

The engine starts up again. Ray straightens, satisfied, then glares at me. "You speak when spoken to, you hear?"

I fall silent, desperate to know more, but aware of how fragile my position is. Underneath me, my bound hands are in agony.

And then all at once, there's something above us. Sliding into view, impossibly huge. It's like a mountain decided to shoot up from underwater. I squint up at it, trying to work out what it is.

This was what I saw from the island – that strange shape against the skyline. It's man-made, built from giant metal plates, leaning over us at a sharp angle. The plates are discoloured for a few feet above the water, painted with green fungus and brown rust. Over our heads, I see the letters A-11 marked on the metal. Each letter is white, outlined in thick grey paint, and each one has to be four times the size of a man.

There's a wide rectangular gap in the plates, twenty feet above the waterline. Faces peer down from it. Iluk cuts the motor, and one of them shouts, the words lost in the rush of the ocean. Ray cups his hand to his mouth and yells back. "Nah, just the one. Throw us the ladder."

The face vanishes. A second later, a rope ladder unfurls, clanking against the hull and splashing into the water. Koji reaches out for it, pulling it towards us, while Ray secures the boat. There's an upright piece of metal that's been welded to the hull, sticking out from it, and Ray ties the boat to it with a thick, wet length of rope.

Iluk's face appears above me, upside down. He grabs me by the shoulders and hauls me to my feet. The rocking motion of the boat nearly topples me over, and he has to grab me by the scruff of my jacket, only just stopping me from falling in.

"How's she gonna climb?" says Koji.

"What?" says Ray.

"Her hands are tied."

Ray makes an annoyed sound, then grabs hold of me, spinning me around. The cuffs snap off my wrists, and I resist the urge to cry out as the blood rushes back, pins and needles digging deep into my hands.

He brings me back the other way, pulling my hands together and cuffing them in front. This time, the cuffs aren't quite as tight.

"Climb," he says, jerking his thumb upwards.

It takes one or two tries to grab the swaying ladder. The sides are rope, but the rungs are made of rough wood, and splinters bite into my palms as I move. The cuffs make the climb even more awkward. Halfway up, I glance back over my shoulder. Fire Island is there, and the impossibly empty sea beyond it. I look for the seaplane, but it's nowhere to be found.

"Keep moving," Ray says from below me.

As I reach the top of the ladder, strong hands pull me over the edge. I roll onto the deck, my heart pumping. The people standing above me are all variations of Ray, with beards and grimy skin and dark, angry eyes.

I look past them, to the space we're in. It's huge – big enough to park two seaplanes across, wingtip to wingtip. The walls are made of ribbed metal, with curved struts every couple of feet. Oversized fluorescent lights criss-cross the ceiling.

"This is all you came back with?" one of the men says, prodding my shoulder with the tip of his boot. "Doesn't look like much."

"We'll let Prophet decide that," Ray says. Now that he's in here, his voice is quieter, as if shouting won't be tolerated. He and Koji lift me to my feet, and the crowd parts in front of us.

I'm hustled through a door into a narrow corridor – so narrow that we have to walk single file: Iluk and Ray in front, Koji behind. The corridor has heavy, ribbed walls, like the entranceway. The lights are sparse, one every twenty feet or so, each one covered by a wire cage. There are enormous pipes running along the ceiling, cocooned in thick, silver insulation.

There's no chance of escape here, nowhere to go, no door that isn't sealed tight. Frustration starts to build – Carver and Prakesh are somewhere on this ship, they have to be, but I can't see any way I can escape.

And there's something behind the frustration. It takes me a moment to pinpoint it. A weird sense of déjà vu, like I should recognise my surroundings. Like I've been here before.

I close my eyes, irritated with myself. My mind's playing tricks on me, just like it did when I looked at the sky for the first time. I breathe deep, letting the frustration fade, letting it be replaced with anger. I have to trust that anger – it's kept me alive so far, and it's going to keep me alive now.

The passage opens up a little. There's a stairway leading up to the next level: impossibly steep, with steps even narrower than the corridor. Ray and Iluk are already climbing it, and Koji gives me a push from behind, his hand on the small of my back.

Another door, with a valve handle. When Iluk cranks it back, bright daylight shoots into the corridor. I try to raise a hand to my eyes, forgetting for a moment that I'm cuffed. Ray reaches for me, pulling me through the door.

We're outside, on a long balcony bordered by waist-high railings. Below us is the deck of the ship: a massive space, bigger than any gallery on Outer Earth. Its surface is covered with strange markings, yellow chevrons, white stripes, warnings in huge lettering.

There are a dozen planes, lined up in rows along the deck. They aren't like the seaplane: they're sleek, predatory, with needle-like noses and enormous tail fins. But as I look closer, I see that their surfaces are caked in rust. The surface of their wheels has rotted away, and several of them list to one side.

We move along the balcony. My shoulder blades are hurting a little less now, and it's getting easier to move. I keep sneaking glances at the deck. There are things I missed the first time round, like the metal plates angled at forty-five degrees to the deck. There's a strange structure on the edge, too: a massive cylinder, capped by a dome.

Ray sees me looking, claps a hand on my shoulder. For a moment, he sounds almost jovial. "That's the Phalanx gun. Still got plenty of ammo left. But you and your friends in the plane figured that out already, right?"

As I watch, the gun gives out a metallic whirring noise, turning a few degrees to the right. Its barrel comes into view, sticking out at right angles to the cylinder.

A moment later, we duck through a door, coming out into another narrow stairway. There's more light here, and it's a little quieter than down below.

Another set of stairs. Then another. And then Ray is cranking open a door, much larger than the others, and he and Iluk pull me through.

We're in a control room of some kind, not much larger than the one in Apex on Outer Earth. The layout is immediately familiar: banks of screens, chaotic groups of chairs, low lighting. There are large windows overlooking the deck, and I can see the fog just starting to lift.

The room is packed with people. Some of them are gathered around screens, while others are off to one side, talking in small groups. Several of them have rifles, slung across their chests or hanging down their backs. I feel their eyes on me, sizing me up, taking in my mismatched clothing and bound hands.

My gaze falls on a table in the middle of the room. There's a map spread across it, like the one Harlan showed me, only much larger. Alaska, the Yukon, other areas I can't name.

Ray reaches into his jacket, pulling out the items he took from me: the scarf, the bear spray, the meat strips. He lines them up on the table in front of him, then clears his throat. "Prophet."

One of the men clustered around the table raises his head to look at us. He wears a stiff, brown jacket over a dark shirt, and one of his eyes is gone, sewn closed with ugly, amateurish stitches.

And sitting behind him, bent over a computer screen: Janice Okwembu.

58

Okwembu

Before Okwembu can do anything, Hale somehow gets away from the men holding her.

One moment she's being held by her arms, the next she's twisted free. Her hands are still cuffed in front of her, but it's as if she barely notices. She's at the table in two strides, launching herself across it. Her left foot lands squarely on the map, planting itself on the border between Alaska and Canada, crumpling the paper, and then she's diving for Okwembu.

Prophet's forearm takes Hale on the collarbone. Okwembu has just enough time to step to the side before Hale crashes across the floor.

Everyone on the bridge is on their feet, racking the bolts on their rifles. Ray plants a foot on Hale's stomach, forcing her to stay down.

Okwembu finds her eyes, holds them. She may not know how Hale managed to get here, to escape the *Shinso* and make it all the way to Alaska, but it doesn't matter. Her shock is starting to give way to anger, to pure righteous fury. She holds her ground, breathing hard, keeping her expression neutral.

Hale is a mess. Her clothing is ragged, mismatched, soaked from sea spray. She has a cut on her cheek, and dark rivulets of blood have dried on her face. She's struggling, spitting mad, her eyes never leaving Okwembu's. "You," she says. "You. You. Y—"

Ray hits her, driving a foot into her stomach, and her body shakes from the impact. Okwembu's hand strays to the data stick, still hanging round her neck. She was about to take it off when Hale attacked her. If it had been damaged . . .

Prophet looks at Ray. He's deeply rattled, his lip shaking with fury. "What in the name of the Engine did you bring her up here for?"

"She's from the plane," Ray says, giving Hale a shake. "Her friend didn't make it."

Prophet walks over, lifting Hale's chin.

"Now why would the Engine send you?" he says. His expression hardens. "Let's start with the aircraft. Where did you take off from?"

Hale tries to get loose again, wrenching her shoulders back and forth. She doesn't succeed, and this time Ray hits her across the face, his fist landing with a sound like a gun firing. Hale falls limp, blood dripping from her mouth, pattering softly on the floor.

Prophet leans in close to her. "I'll ask again," he say. "Where did the plane come from?"

Hale says nothing, flexing her jaw left and right, eyes squeezed shut. When she speaks, it's to Okwembu, not Prophet. "Where are they?" she says. The aggression in her voice is like an open wound. She's speaking around the blood, and more of it drips between her lips, coating her teeth "Prakesh. Carver. Are they here?"

"Now you listen," Prophet says, grabbing Hale's chin and

turning her head towards him. "That plane. Are there others like it? How many people were with you?"

Hale stares at him, like he's speaking another language. After a long moment, she swallows hard, then says, "Out of Whitehorse. Just the one plane."

"Good. How many of you were there?"

". . . Four."

"And why did you—"

Hale cuts him off, speaking to him but looking directly at Okwembu. "I hope you realise who you've got on your ship. Whatever she's told you, it's a lie. That's what she does. She lies. You let me walk out of here with her, and—"

Iluk grabs Hale's hair and yanks her head back. She barks a cry of fury, and he spits something at her in Inuktuk.

Okwembu can feel Prophet looking at her, his eyes searching. She ignores him, looking right back at Hale. *Get control of the situation.*

"She's the one who isn't being honest," she says. "I know her from Outer Earth. She's responsible for the virus that nearly wiped us out."

Hale tries to speak. It earns her another punch, snapping her head sideways and sending dots of blood onto one of the screens.

"Then why did she attack you?" Prophet says.

Okwembu shrugs. "She disagreed with some of the decisions I made."

Silence. Okwembu keeps her eyes on Prophet. She suppresses the urge to elaborate, letting the seconds tick by.

"Should I take her downstairs, Prophet?" Ray says. "We lost another one yesterday. They could probably use the extra hands."

Prophet shakes his head, looking Hale up and down. "She's

violent, this one. Something tells me she won't be so comfortable serving the Engine."

He turns away. "Take her to the stern."

59

Anna

By the time Anna reaches the gallery, her shock has turned into a righteous, roaring fury. Every stride she takes feels like it drives an electric bolt of anger through her body.

She skids to a halt on the Level 1 catwalk above the gallery floor. There's a muted alarm blaring somewhere, along with the recorded voice advising evacuation. The escape pod bay doors are still closed, with nothing but darkness through their viewports.

For a moment, Anna is confused. Where were the stompers? Why didn't they stop Dax and his group from . . .

That's when she sees them. Two bodies, clad in grey stomper jumpsuits, sprawled face down on the floor. It's impossible to miss the blood pooling under them.

Another electric bolt shoots up through her, and she pounds her fist on the railing in frustration. Jordan. That must have been her price. Places in the escape pods for her and her buddies. Did the two dead stompers refuse? Did they try to stop them?

A strange sound pulls her out of her thoughts. It takes a

second to place it: someone is crying. No – not just someone. A child.

Anna launches herself over the catwalk railing, turning one-eighty degrees in mid-air, using a hand on the railing as a fulcrum. She comes down with her toes in between the railings and her heels hanging out over the edge. She relaxes into the landing, then pushes herself off the catwalk.

It's not far down – ten feet, maybe, no more. She lands with a thud, not bothering to roll, staggering a little on impact. The crying is coming from her left, and she turns her head, hunting for the source.

Ivy.

She must've been here when it all went down. She's huddled by the wall, sitting with her back against it, her hands wrapped around her knees. Anna sprints to her, pulling the trembling girl into an embrace.

"It's all right," Anna says. She says it again, then a third time, as if she needs to convince herself.

There's nothing she can do. She should take Ivy back, find somebody to look after her. She gets to her feet, cradling the girl. Ivy is still crying, but the sobs are silent now, and she snuggles into Anna's shoulder.

That's when Anna notices the last airlock.

The viewpoints in almost all the airlocks are dark, but the last one is different. There's the faintest glimmer inside it, so faint that at first Anna is sure she's imagined it.

She crosses the floor, avoiding the two dead stompers. As she reaches the bay door, she sees that the viewport is just out of her reach. But she didn't imagine the light – it's a little clearer now, like the glow cast from a tab screen.

Her heart beating faster, she drops to one knee, whispering in Ivy's ear. "I have to put you down, OK? Just for a second."

Ivy doesn't move. Slowly, Anna disengages the girl's hands

from around her neck, and places her gently on the floor, making sure she's not looking at the stompers. Then she gets on tiptoe, straining to get as high as she can, and looks into the viewport.

The escape pod is still there.

Anna doesn't know why they didn't take it. Maybe someone got cold feet. Maybe they left so quickly that there wasn't time to inform everybody. It doesn't matter. Not now.

She crouches down, putting her hand on Ivy's cheek, feeling still-warm tears as her fingers touch the skin. The girl's face is deathly pale.

"Ivy? Honey?" she says. "I want you to do something for me."

Ivy starts to answer, glancing at the stompers.

"No," Anna says. "Don't look at them. They can't hurt you. I promise. Now, what I want you to do is run. Fast as you can, far as you can, until you find a grown-up. Can you do that for me?"

Ivy stares at her. Anna is about to repeat herself when the girl nods. Her enormous brown eyes prickle with fresh tears.

"Good," Anna says, forcing a smile onto her face. She hugs Ivy one more time. "Go. Now."

Ivy skims across the floor, her oversized red sweater trailing out behind her. She only looks back once. Anna stays put, anticipating the look, and even manages a wave. Then Ivy is into the corridor, and out of sight.

Anna turns back to the pod. Her fingers brush the release catch next to the door. "Oh, this is a very bad idea," she mutters to herself.

She clambers into the airlock, pulling open the door of the escape pod inside it. The pod itself is tiny. There are three soft-backed seats arranged in a triangular formation at the front. A transparent locker on one side holds three space suits. Anna can't see a thing through the cockpit viewport, which stretches around the seats. The only light comes from the controls themselves, from the multiple touchscreens on the U-shaped line of controls around the front seat.

I shouldn't be doing this, Anna thinks. But then she's clambering over the seats, dropping into the foremost one, fumbling with the safety belt. There are straps, clicking into place at her sternum. Three touchscreens in front of her, black and silent. There's a single joystick beneath them, with two thick plastic buttons – one on the top, one on the front.

She doesn't know that much about Outer Earth's escape pods. She remembers being told once that they're relatively simple to operate – they have to be, given the situations they might be used in. But how do you turn them on? How do you launch them?

Breathing fast, she gives the nearest touchscreen an experimental tap. Somewhere behind her, she hears an engine kick into action, rumbling through the little craft. The airlock around the pod comes to life. A rotating light near the ceiling comes on, and the door to the station seals shut behind her with a grinding noise.

A dozen readouts appear on the screens: fuel capacity, estimated range, attitude, thruster locations. Anna stares at them, horrified. A half-second later the displays dim, and a message appears on the centre display. LAUNCH?

Anna raises a finger. Stops.

She is out of her depth. The fear is setting in now, crawling out of her nightmares and tearing its way into the real world. *You're going to die out there*, she thinks, and it's almost enough to send her flying out of the chair, back into the station, back to her parents. *There has to be someone else who can do this.*

And then, before she can stop herself, her finger touches the screen.

60

Prakesh

It takes a while for the guard to return. She strides over to Prakesh, rifle swinging. "Higher-ups say to do it. Get going."

He doesn't waste time getting to work, already aware of what he needs. The ammonium sulfate is easy. Prakesh can get that from the slippery white fertiliser pellets. Same with the sulphur – that's the yellow insecticide. They give him a plastic cup to use as a scoop, but some still gets on his hands, prickling at his skin.

The calcium hydroxide is the tricky part. He needs calcium oxide first, and the usual source of that would be a stick of chalk. The guard assigned to watch him just stares blankly when Prakesh asks for some.

He tries to keep the frustration off his face. "What about shells?"

"Shells?" the guard says slowly. He's not much older than Prakesh, with dark brown skin and a shaggy mess of black hair, but he holds his rifle like it's an extension of his arm. Like it would be the work of a single thought to bring it up and pull the trigger.

"Yeah, like—" Prakesh can feel the word, dancing on the tip of his tongue. *What the hell are those things called?* The name snaps to the front of his mind. "Barnacles. They'd be stuck to the ship? Right at the waterline. I just need two or three."

He takes a step forward, moving without thinking, and is brought up short by a rifle barrel in his face.

"You don't move," says the guard. "I'll get them."

Slowly, he lowers the rifle, then calls one of the others over to spot for him. He stalks off, his boots tapping on the metal floor of the farm.

They've got Prakesh in one corner of the hangar, set up with a couple of old tables. There's a portable gas ring, purloined from the mess hall. Fresh water sloshes in a big metal drum. They've even managed to find him some tongs, their metal surface blackened with age.

It's not even close to perfect. The chemistry he's about to perform is unbelievably inefficient, the kind of procedure that would make his old Air Lab colleagues burst out laughing. But it's all Prakesh has.

He waits, hands on the table, head bent. Jojo and the others are still at the troughs, working on the soil. Every few minutes, a guard will pull some of them away, letting them take a piss break.

Please let this work.

The guard returns with a handful of barnacles: lumpy, misshapen things with jagged white shells. He dumps them onto the table. "Ruined my knife getting these off," he says, tapping a chipped blade hanging from his belt.

"Sorry," Prakesh mutters, gathering the shells.

He gets both hands under one of the metal drums, lifts it up, then smashes it down on the shells. They're hard, weather-worn, and it takes a few hits before they begin to crack.

The gas burner is tricky to get going – Prakesh can't stop

his hands from shaking, and he keeps fumbling the butane lighter. Eventually, he does it, and a scorching blue flame rises up from the plate.

Prakesh holds the smashed shells over the flames until they smoulder and crumble, kicking off a thin white smoke. He catches the fragments in one of the plastic beakers. He can feel the heat singeing the skin on his fingers, and bites his lip, pushing through it. Soon, the beaker is full of clumpy, off-white powder. Calcium oxide, or something close to it.

He dumps it in the water-filled drum, using the tongs to stir it. There. Calcium hydroxide.

The guard leans in. "So how does it work?"

"Huh?"

"This chemistry shit." He gestures at the drum.

"Oh," says Prakesh. "Well . . . calcium hydroxide from the shells will react with the existing fertiliser, and it should make it more potent, so . . ."

"Right." The guard's actually interested, his gun lowered, tilting his head to one side as he regards the drum. "My mom showed me this stuff in a book once. Didn't really know how it all worked but I always wanted to try it."

The drum goes on top of the burner. Prakesh has to get the guard to help, which he does willingly, handing his rifle off to one of the others. Even then, they nearly send the entire mess flying when the guard's fingers slip. Prakesh pulls it back at the last moment, exhaling a shaky breath.

"There," says the guard, dusting off his hands. "What's next?"

Prakesh's mind goes blank for a moment, surprised at having such an eager lab assistant. "Uh . . . the sulphur. Right over there."

"Yeah, you got it."

The guard brings it over. Working quickly, Prakesh dumps several scoops of the sulphur into the pot, then stirs it all together. The ammonium sulfate fertiliser goes in last, followed by a thick sheet of scrap metal as a makeshift lid.

"So shouldn't there be some sort of, what's it called, reaction now?" the guard says.

Prakesh shrugs, trying to ignore how much his shoulders hurt. "It'll take a little time, but sure."

"Nice," says the guard, hands on his hips. "Guess you'd better get back to work." He sounds genuinely apologetic.

Prakesh walks with his head down, sliding in next to Jojo. The kid says nothing, doesn't even look at him.

Prakesh digs his hands into the soil, and tries not to look at the metal drum.

They carry me off the bridge. I try and stop them, kicking and thrashing, screaming at them to let me go. It doesn't do any good. My hands are still cuffed, and while Ray holds my upper body, Iluk wraps his huge arms around my legs, pinning them together. My eyes keep being drawn back to Okwembu, like light getting sucked into a black hole.

Iluk lets go when we reach the bottom of the stairs. Ray lifts me up, spins me around and slams me back against the wall. I bang my head, sending flickering sparks across the edge of my vision. My face is numb, and the ache in my stomach is rolling up through my body.

"You got a choice," Ray says. "You can go to the stern as you are, or you can go there with broken arms. Your call."

I stop struggling. There's got to be a way out of this, there must be, but I won't be able to act on it if I'm crippled. After a few moments, I raise my chin then give Ray a tight nod.

"All right then," he says.

Ray drags me down the corridors, Iluk and Koji following behind us, down more flights of stairs, until eventually we reach another rectangular opening in the side of the ship. I can see white clouds through it, hanging low over the gently whispering ocean. Unlike the way we came in, there's no one else here. The space is completely empty.

Ray and Iluk drop me on the metal floor, right on the edge. There's nothing between me and the world outside.

"Maybe we shouldn't do this," Koji says.

"One more word, Koji," Ray says. "Just one."

I look back, and see that Ray has a new gun.

I don't know where he got it from. It's a rifle, the wooden stock polished to a high sheen. He's loading it carefully, almost tenderly. Iluk stands with his arms folded. Koji is cowering behind him, as if he's being forced to watch.

Ray sees me looking. "Sorry. Prophet says you're gone, you're gone." He racks the bolt. "You can die on your feet, or on your knees. I don't much care which."

I barely register his words. There's a taste of copper in my mouth, the metallic tang of fear. My hands are shaking. The whole way down here, I was looking for anything I could use, and got nothing. Even if I somehow managed to escape, I'd still be stuck on the ship, trapped in the narrow corridors. And in the next few seconds Ray is going to put a bullet through me.

But the anger I feel is stronger than the fear. Even after everything I've been through, there's one thing that will never change. I'm a tracer – no, more than that, I'm a *Devil Dancer*, and I've come too far and fought too hard to let it end here.

Slowly, I get to one knee. Ray glances down at the gun again, and that's when I act.

I launch myself forwards, head down, leading with my shoulder. Ray sees me coming, raises the gun, but I'm moving way too fast for him. My shoulder bends his body in two, the air leaving him in an explosive rush.

Iluk is there, his hands on me, trying to push me to the floor. He's strong, much stronger than I am, and if I let him get ahold of me I'll be a static target for Ray to aim at. So I throw my head back, and feel bone shatter as it crunches against Iluk's nose.

Ray jerks the gun around, snapping the side of the barrel against my cheek. It's a glancing blow, but it's enough to knock me off balance, sending me to my knees. I twist to one side, and the gun goes off, right by my head – I feel the kick power through me, the bang slamming my ears shut.

Ray's hand goes to the bolt again, starts to pull it back. That makes him vulnerable. I use the tiny window of time it gives me, and throw myself towards him.

My hands are still cuffed in front of me. I lift them high, then bring them down on the other side of Ray's head. It looks like I'm embracing him. I rock backwards, the handcuffs digging into the back of his neck, pulling with every ounce of strength I have.

He grunts, trying to plant his feet. For a horrifying instant he feels too heavy, and I don't know if I'll be able to throw him off balance. But I'm faster than he is, and his centre of gravity is way too high. As I roll backwards, he comes with me, his weight pressing down.

His hands pull at my jacket, but I've got momentum on my side. I keep the roll going, using my thighs and abdominal muscles to transfer the energy to him. He somersaults, landing flat on his back. I look back, the world upside down suddenly, and I can see that his feet are hanging over the edge.

I roll over, pushing myself upwards with my bound hands. Koji is backing away, terrified, and Iluk is lying face down on the floor. There's a pool of blood spreading out from around his head. One of his hands is tucked under his neck, as if trying to seal the bullet wound.

Ray is up on one knee. Somehow, he's still holding the gun. He pulls the trigger, but there's no bullet in the chamber – he never got a chance to pull the bolt back before I threw him over.

Tough luck, Ray.

He curses, hands flying to the bolt. I sprint towards him, and drive my fist into his temple.

I can almost see the pressure waves moving through his flesh. He doesn't fall, but his head snaps to the side, and I feel a burst of bitter pleasure as I regain my balance. My hearing is coming back, and Ray's moan of pain is crystal-clear.

I snatch the gun away, gripping it by the top of the barrel. Then I lean back, and kick Ray in the chest.

The move disrupts my own centre of gravity, and I fall flat on my ass. It doesn't matter. Ray is in mid-air, his eyes wide with terror. A half-second later he's gone.

No time. There's still one more.

I can feel the prolonged effects of adrenaline starting to take hold, making my hands shake and my vision blur. I rock forward, launching my body upright. I'm holding the gun wrong, my hands around the barrel – and it's a big gun, heavy, my wrists already aching from keeping it up. It's useless in this position, unless I want to use it as a club. If Koji's got a weapon of his own, that decision might cost me.

There's only one thing I can do. I launch myself into a sprint, heading for one side of the opening, the gun held out in front of me. I feel the shock wave as the stock slams into the wall, but I'm ready for it, letting my hands travel down the body, twisting sideways to let the barrel slide past me. It works. My fingers find the bolt, and I have just enough grip to swing the gun, letting the stock seat itself in my stomach.

I'm already thinking ahead – I have to draw the bolt back, chamber a round, reseat my hands so I can pull the trigger, draw a bead on Koji, and fire. It's going to have to be perfect. One mistake, and he'll do to me what I did to Ray.

My hands turn sideways, catching the bolt, snapping it backwards. I feel a round enter the chamber, and I'm already hunting for the trigger guard when Koji yells out, "Wait! Don't shoot!"

I look up. He's standing a few feet away, his hands up, terror on his face. "Don't shoot," he says again.

My finger finds the trigger. My skin is soaked with sweat, and a drop falls into my eye, blurring my vision, stinging with salt. *Aim. Aim now, while he's standing still.*

"I knew John Hale," he says. "Your father. I knew him."

62

Prakesh

The liquid in the drum is bubbling, the metal lid clanking up and down. The sound scratches at Prakesh's eardrums.

It's taking too long. He should be smelling something by now. They all should. But there's just the loamy, thick fug of the soil, accentuated by the tang of the fertiliser.

Prakesh tells himself not to look, but does anyway. The guard is hovering near the drum, watching the reaction.

Prakesh looks back down. *It didn't work. They're going to figure it out. It's over.*

At that moment, he hears the guard shouting at him.

The guard doesn't know his name. He's just shouting, "Chemistry guy!" Prakesh looks up, feeling all the blood drain from his face.

"Is it meant to smell that bad?" the guard shouts.

Slowly, Prakesh walks over. Every step feels awkward, every motion forced.

The guard watches him approach. He bangs the drum with the butt of his rifle, and it wobbles slightly on its perch. "Starting to stink. Worse than before. Is that supposed to happen?"

And that's when Prakesh smells it. The makeshift lid has kept most of it inside, but some has escaped, and it scours the inside of his nostrils.

"Let me see," he says, stepping behind the table. His heart is pounding.

"I gotta say, though," says the guard, "this is by far the most interesting shift I've had in a long time." He claps Prakesh on the back. "Can't wait to eat those first tomatoes. I had one once, when I was a kid."

Prakesh forces a smile, bending over the barrel, trying to hold his breath.

"So?" says the guard. He looks more eager than ever, almost excited, like a child getting a toy. Prakesh actually feels a little bad for what he's about to do.

"It's ready," he says.

Then he puts a hand on the side of the drum and shoves it off the table.

The barrel crashes to the floor, spilling its contents everywhere: pale green slurry, with slimy lumps floating in it. A second later, the full force of the smell hits Prakesh.

It's as if boiling acid has been forced into his lungs. He bends double, trying to raise a hand to his nose, not quite getting there before his stomach reacts. He vomits, the liquid forcing its way out of his lungs, spraying across the floor.

The guard is vomiting, too. He was right next to the barrel, and got a full dose of the fumes.

Sulphur, ammonium sulfate, calcium hydroxide. Water. Heat.

Clunky, but effective.

Prakesh has enough presence of mind to pull himself behind a nearby crate. He gets there half a second before the shooting starts. Bullets explode off the metal floor around him. One hits the gas canister, which flies off across the floor, whirling like a child's toy.

The smell is spreading. The hangar is big, but the stench is powerful enough to penetrate every corner of it. Prakesh can hear the other guards coughing, hear them starting to heave. That sets him off again. He retches, spilling more slime onto the floor by his head. The smell is so strong that he feels like it's a living creature clamped onto his face, forcing itself down his throat.

There's nothing more he can do. He curls into a ball, his hands over his mouth and nose, and waits for it to be over.

It takes him a few moments to realise that the shooting has stopped. His ears are ringing, but the hangar is silent. No – not silent. He can hear voices now, muffled, shouting orders to one another. And soft thuds, like boots being driven into flesh.

He gets to his knees, dry-heaving. The smell has ebbed, just a little, but it's still enough to set off a coughing fit. When he looks up, wiping gunk from his lips, Jojo is standing over him, holding the bottom of his shirt to his face. The shirt is wet, soaked with urine, blocking out the smell. Prakesh sees that every other worker did the same thing, clamping wet fabric over their noses and mouths. It gave them just enough time to take down the incapacitated guards.

And all of them are dead. Prakesh can see that. Or, if they're not dead, they will be soon. His eyes fall on the one who helped him. The man's eyes are staring at nothing, blood leaking out of a massive head wound. Prakesh feels an odd sense of loss, a feeling he doesn't quite understand.

"Nnnn-" Jojo gulps twice, the wet fabric across his mouth muffling the sound. He helps Prakesh to his feet. "Not bad."

Prakesh finds it hard to keep his balance, especially when the other workers start slapping him on the back and pulling him into massive bear hugs. Someone passes him a soaked strip of cloth – it's revolting, having to hold it up to his mouth, but it's a million times better than the smell.

For a long moment, nobody moves. The workers are looking around them, unsure, cradling the guns.

Jojo breaks the silence. "S-s-see that?" he says, pointing upwards. Prakesh follows his finger, landing on a clunky security camera bolted onto the wall. "W-we gotta mmmm-move f-fast."

Prakesh groans, irritated that he didn't see it before. Their revolt will be noticed – assuming the camera works, there'll be reinforcements arriving at any moment.

"Y-you two – generator room," Jojo says, pointing at the other workers. His words are muffled by the fabric. "Heard the g-g-guards t-talking about it earlier. It w-w-won't be too heavily g-g-guarded. D-D-Devi, t-take a few p-p-people w-with you and g-go and secure the b-b-b-boats."

The workers split off from the group, charging away across the hangar.

"What's in the generator room?" Prakesh says.

"Th-th-th-the other workers. W-w-we're n-n-not gonna l-leave them here."

Prakesh's head snaps up. *Other workers. Carver.* If he's still alive, that's where he'd be. But the moment the thought occurs, so does the memory of those fists and feet raining down on him. Prakesh desperately wants to believe he's still alive, but he knows the odds aren't good.

"What about the rest of us?" says a man behind Prakesh. "I say we take the bridge."

"We'll never get near it," someone else says. "Not unless our man's got another batch of those chemicals somewhere."

"N-n-no," says Jojo. "We c-c-c-c-can't go to the b-b-bridge. It's t-t-too heavily guarded."

"So then what do we do?" It comes from an older woman. She's holding one of the rifles like a newborn baby.

Jojo gulps twice. "W-we blow it up."

There's a stunned silence. "What, the bridge? Or the ship?" says the woman.

"The shhhhh-ship. We hit the f-f-f-fuel hangar, lllll-light it up. T-torch the p-p-place."

"Jojo, that's crazy," the woman says.

Jojo talks over her. "We g-g-get in, t-take some f-f-fuel for ourselves, then burn the r-r-rest."

Prakesh finally finds his voice. "What about the other workers? The ones you just sent off? Shouldn't we warn them?"

"They know how to get to the b-boats," Jojo says, barely glancing at him, excitement chasing away most of his stammer. "W-w-we won't leave without 'em. D-don't w-worry."

"What do we do about weapons?" Prakesh says.

But Jojo and the rest of the workers are already heading for the hangar doors. A couple of them loose shots into the ceiling, ignoring Jojo's stuttered shouts to save ammo. Prakesh has no choice but to follow them.

63

There's no way Koji just said what I think he said. I keep the gun pointed at him. The only sound is my breathing, harsh and hot.

"I knew your father," he says. "I was with John Hale on the *Akua Maru*. I—"

"*Shut up.*"

I get to my feet slowly, keeping a very, very tight grip on the gun.

"Look," Koji says, spreading his hands slowly. "My name is Koji Yamamoto. I was born on Outer Earth, in Tzevya. I was a junior officer on John Hale's crew. We crash-landed in eastern Russia eight years ago."

This isn't possible. The *Akua Maru* was thought destroyed, lost forever. It wasn't. My father was still on Earth, and with Janice Okwembu's help, he managed to repair the ship, intending to use it to destroy a station he thought had abandoned him. We thought the rest of the ship's crew were dead.

"You're lying," I say. But is he? How could he know any of this? How else would he know the names *John Hale* and

Akua Maru? Could Okwembu have told him? But why would she?

"How do you know who I am?" I say.

Koji lowers his eyes. "You look just like him."

I lift the gun a little higher, and he starts speaking more quickly. "I knew he had a daughter, but I never thought . . . you have his eyes. You *are* his daughter, right? Riley?"

"The *Akua* landed in eastern Russia," I say. "That's a long, long way from here."

He nods. "Kamchatka. Some of us survived the crash. We decided to head east, see if we could find anything. We crossed the Bering Strait, ended up here."

"Why tell me this now? Why not say anything before?"

A pained expression crosses his face. "I was scared. All right? They would have killed me if I tried to help you." He points to Iluk's body.

"So you wait until I'm the one with the gun," I say. "Convenient."

"I'm telling the truth, I swear." He's trembling now, overcome with emotion. "I don't know what happened to your father – he wanted to stay with the ship, but if you—"

"Shut up," I say for the second time. I have to calm my racing mind. I have to think.

Right now, it doesn't matter who Koji is, or where he came from. What matters is that he might be the only person here who could help me. There's no chance of taking Okwembu down yet – not with one gun, not when she's on the ship's bridge. But she's not the only reason I'm here.

"Uncuff me," I say.

He gives a helpless shrug. "Ray had the key. I'm sorry."

I bite back the frustration. Nothing I can do – I'll just have to live with it. "I'm looking for two people," I say. "Their names are Aaron Carver and Prakesh Kumar." I have to assume that they're alive – I almost physically recoil from the alternative.

Koji shakes his head, and I feel my stomach drop a couple of inches. "We've had some new people," he says. "I don't know their names."

"Tell me about these arrivals. What happens to them?"

"They get put to work. All across the ship."

"Where?"

Sweat is trickling down his face. "All over. Depends on what needs doing. But the closest is probably the generator room. We've been having some power problems, so—"

"Take me there," I say. "Right now."

I make him go first, keeping my gun up, ignoring the burn in my cuffed hands. We're almost at the corridor entrance when he says, "Wait. You need to give me the gun."

"Are you serious?"

"You don't understand," he says, licking his lips. "What do you think is going to happen if someone sees you marching *me* at gunpoint?"

"They'll do nothing. Because if they do, I'll shoot you." The words sound hollow, even to me.

"You think they care?" Koji shakes his head. "If we're going to find your friends, then you're going to have to trust me."

"Why should I?" I say.

"Because—" He stops, looks away. "Because I owe your father. I owe him everything."

I don't move.

"Please," he says.

My finger tightens on the trigger.

Then slowly, very slowly, I pass him the gun. I'm already visualising the angles, anticipating what he'll do. The moment he brings the gun around, I can swing my hands into the side of the barrel, knock it away, then shoulder-charge him, which should—

But he holds the gun as if it's an unexploded bomb, keeping it pointed at the floor. He tries a smile, but it's gone before it can fully form.

We resume our walk down the corridor. Every so often, Koji will tell me to turn left or right, directing me deeper into the ship. He's visibly trembling, trying to look everywhere at once. It's hard to imagine someone like him surviving in this place.

"How did you end up here, anyway?" I say.

"Me and two of the crew – Dominguez and Rogers," Koji says. "We left the crash site. Rogers, she . . . she didn't make it."

He goes silent for a moment. Then he says, "There was this radio message. Talking about food and shelter."

"I've heard it."

"It was a lie. Obviously. I got put to work like everyone else."

"But you're not a worker any more."

"No. I figured out what the Engine—"

At that moment, a shape blocks out the light from the passage above us. Koji swears quietly, not looking up. I keep my gaze on the corridor ahead.

Footsteps descend the stairs behind us. "Hey," a voice calls out.

Neither of us responds – I'm waiting for Koji to say something, but he stays silent.

"Hey," says the voice again, louder this time, and now it's accompanied by heavy footsteps, clumping down the corridor behind us.

Koji looks round. "Just bringing her to the work detail at the generators," he says, nodding at me.

I keep my eyes on the floor. The man is wearing thick work

boots, much too big for him, as if he took them from somebody else.

"Where's Ray?" says the man, his voice gruff.

Koji shrugs. "Probably with Iluk somewhere."

"Go find them. Something's happened in the farm, we need every available . . ."

He trails off. I flick my eyes upwards, and that's when I recognise him. Sandy hair, red face. He was on the bridge when I was brought in, and I can see recognition sparking to life in his eyes, see the yell forming on his lips.

64

Prakesh

The cleaner air outside the hangar is like a splash of cold water. Prakesh takes a huge breath, letting the strip of urine-soaked cloth fall to the floor.

The workers push through a door ahead of him, exploding out of the corridor into a larger space. It's an old weapons bay – there are empty racks everywhere, running floor to ceiling, some of them still carrying ancient ordnance, their labels cracked and faded. Computers line the wall, the screens black and dead.

By the time Prakesh gets there, the gunfire has started.

There are at least two guards, firing from behind one of the racks. Prakesh hits the ground, going down hard. He has no weapon, nothing to protect him. All he can do is stay down. The gunshots are deafening.

One of the workers takes a bullet, his arm almost torn from his shoulder. He collapses onto the floor, twitching, and Prakesh sees that it's the man who wanted to take the bridge. He pushes himself away, rolling across the floor.

The shooting stops. There's a split second where Prakesh thinks they've lost, that one of the guards is about to come round the corner and put a bullet through him. But then he hears Jojo's voice. "L-l-let's go!"

The rest of the workers roar in agreement, and he feels feet pounding on the metal surface. He tries to get up, but as he does so his hand slips in the blood pooled on the floor, and he crashes back down, knocking his chin on the metal plating.

Jojo pulls him up. He's surprisingly strong. He and Prakesh stumble to the exit, and that's when one of the racks gives way.

Its supports are riddled with bullet holes. It gives off a metallic screech as it comes down, collapsing in on itself, kicking up clouds of dust as it goes, spewing its cargo across the floor. Prakesh pulls Jojo back just in time.

The sounds of the crash die away, replaced by Prakesh's ragged breathing. Their way to the passage beyond is blocked. A woman, the one who told Jojo that it was crazy to hit the fuel hangar, is staring at them through a gap in the debris, her eyes wide. Her lank hair hangs down her forehead in streaks of wet grey.

Prakesh moves to climb the wreckage, but Jojo grabs his shoulder. "There's an-n-n-nother way r-round," he says

He doesn't give him a chance to respond – just plunges back the way they came, ducking into the passage. Prakesh takes one last look at the woman, and then follows.

Prakesh struggles to keep up with Jojo. He moves at a brisk pace, the rifle swinging back and forth. There's an alarm blaring somewhere, distant but urgent, and he swears he can hear more gunfire, as if the ship has finally woken up to the threat inside it. At each junction and stairway, Jojo pauses for a split second before picking a path and heading down it. Within minutes, Prakesh is lost – he knows they're heading deeper into the ship, but he has no clue where they are.

Eventually, he catches up to Jojo at the top of a set of narrow stairs, where he pauses a little longer than normal. "Hang on a second," he says, gasping out the words.

"Gotta k-k-keep g-going," Jojo says, starting down the stairs.

A few minutes later, they reach a T-junction in the corridor, marked by a rotating yellow light that casts strange shadows across the walls. Jojo stops, peering around the side of the junction, as if he senses something up ahead.

Prakesh stumbles to a halt, hands on his knees, blood pounding in his ears.

"Jojo," he says.

"J-j-just g-gimme me a s-s-second." He starts down the passage, then abruptly turns, heading back in the other direction.

Prakesh raises his head, and Jojo glances back at him. "I haven't b-b-been d-down here b-before. B-b-but I th-think this is—"

"Wait," says Prakesh. "How do we get out after we torch the fuel?"

"I t-t-told you. W-we g-get to the b-b-boats."

"What if there aren't enough? What if we get ambushed again?"

"W-w-won't happen." Jojo's eyes are alive. "I b-b-been planning th-this for a l-long t-time. I'm g-gonna g-g-g-get out, and th-then I'm g-g-going back to D – to D—" His voice cuts off, and he swallows hard: ". . . Denali. Up n-n-n-north."

"We can't—"

"*No.*" Jojo's tone of voice is almost pleading, as if he's trying to make Prakesh understand. "I have to g-g-get out. M-m-my uncle c-c-can't s-s-survive if I'm n-n-not there. He's g-g-g-got a b-b-bad leg. I g-g-gotta find him."

Prakesh puts a hand on the wall, breathing hard, forcing oxygen into his lungs. *This is all happening too fast*, he thinks. He assumed Jojo had a coherent plan, latched onto it, desperate to get out of this place. It's a mistake that might get him killed. There'll be no ordered exit, no regimented attack on their captors. Jojo doesn't even know where he's going. The whole thing has already gone to shit, and there'll be more deaths by the time it's done. He can't let that happen. He won't.

Jojo tilts his head. "Th-that was p-p-pretty clever b-b-back there," he says, glancing down at the rifle. "W-w-w-with the sssss-st-st-stinker."

"Thanks." Prakesh doesn't know what else to say.

Jojo grins, hefting the rifle and stepping into the corridor. "OK. I th-think I know w-where we are. Let's—"

The bullet takes him in the side of the neck.

65

Riley

I'm on the guard in two steps, aiming a knee right for his groin. He sees it coming, manages to half turn, but he's not even close to fast enough. My knee crunches into him, and he doubles over, wheezing. I shove him sideways, and his head bangs off the corridor floor.

"Shit," Koji says, his voice curiously breathy.

"No choice," I say as I get to my feet. I'm amazed that I can speak, even more amazed that he hears me over the blood pounding in my ears. But if he'd used the gun, it would have brought others running.

"No, I mean, shit!" Koji is pointing down the corridor. I look up – and that's when the bullet buries itself in the wall next to me.

There are two more guards by the stairway. One of them is already turning, using the rail to swing himself around, shouting for help. The second is raising his gun again, taking careful aim.

I don't turn to see where the bullet ended up. I run with my head and shoulders tucked in, zigzagging in the narrow corridor,

336

presenting as small a target as possible. I can hear Koji behind me, hear his panicked breathing and stumbling footsteps. Another gunshot: this time, the bullet ripples the air above my head.

"Go right! Go right!" Koji shouts. Another corridor branches off the one we're in, and I have to dig into the turn hard to stop myself from crashing into the wall. I scrape my shoulder along it, barely feeling it through the thick coat.

We crash down another steep stairway, tumbling into the corridor beyond. "Where's the generator room?" I shout.

"Just ahead," Koji says. He can barely get the words out.

Another left. Another right. The pumping noise is louder now, coming from all directions. But then another sound eclipses it. Gunfire. And it's coming from in *front* of us, from further down the corridor.

"There," Koji says. The corridor ahead of us opens up into a larger space, terminating in a vertical drop of a few feet. The floor is slightly curved where it meets the wall, the metal racks of equipment stretching beyond my field of view. I can smell engine oil, and, over it, the sharp stench of gunpowder.

There are two guards hugging the door on either side, their backs to us. One of them is blind-firing into the room, but the other – a man with powerful upper arms and thick dreadlocks hanging down his back – is picking his targets, aiming carefully. He squeezes off a shot, and there's a howl of pain from inside the room.

These guards aren't shooting at us. They don't even know we're here. What is this?

I don't waste time trying to find out. If that's the generator room, then it means the guards are firing on the workers. I don't know why, or why it's happening now, but something tells me I've got a much better chance with the people in that room than I have on my own.

The two guards haven't seen us yet. I go faster, sprinting

right for the entrance, pumping my arms from side to side, head down, eyes up, muscles on fire.

Dreadlocks whips his head round, finally noticing us. There's no time for finesse here. I stutter-step, closing the distance, and launch myself towards him.

The first thought is to lead with my elbow, or my knee. But I launched a little too late, with no time in the air to line up the strike. The man's head collides with my torso, the impact spasming through me, and then he and I are tangled up in a confusing embrace, everything spinning, my leg knocking into the door, smacking my head on the ground, trying to tuck into a roll, not quite doing it. I come to a stop, skidding on my back in icy water

The floor is under an inch of it, foaming with muck, and it immediately soaks through my clothes. The air above me is full of gunfire and angry shouts and screams of pain. I try to get up, propping myself on one elbow, then have to throw myself down again as a gun goes off. In the dim light, the other people in the room are nothing but silhouettes.

The gunfire has stopped, and now people are shouting, talking over each other. I can't see Koji at all. What I can see is the other guard, the one who was blind-firing. He's slumped over the edge of the door, blood trickling into the water.

"Get the door! Shut it!"

"Can we lock it from the inside?"

"Anybody hurt?"

"They'll be more coming. Hurry."

We're in a chamber with rusted walls, bare bulbs hanging from the ceiling. Generators squat on low tables, looking like alien artefacts, all black piping and tarnished silver blocks. Tools are half-submerged in the water, spinning in place: wrenches, screwdrivers, welding goggles, something that looks like a primitive plasma cutter.

I look from face to face: men and women, less than a dozen, all dirty, all thin. Workers – have to be. I don't see Carver, or Prakesh. I spot Koji – he's managed to get inside, but whoever these people are, they've identified him as a guard. They've got him pinned to a wall, an elbow at his throat.

"No no no!" I shout, forcing myself to my feet. I can't have them shoot Koji. I still need him. "He's here to help."

The workers look between me and Koji, suspicious, not sure how to proceed. I open my mouth to speak, and then feel a hand on my shoulder.

I'm still too wired from the run, and I spin round, my body moving before I can stop it, bringing my arms up, ready to fight.

Aaron Carver puts his hands on top of mine, and slowly pushes them down. There's the strangest expression on his face – like he's expecting me to vanish, like I'm a dream that he's about to wake up from. His face is mottled with bruises, his lip split. A dried crust of blood marks his forehead like warpaint.

He reaches out, his fingertips brushing my face.

He's going to say something smart, like he always does. He's going to make a crack about always having to save my ass, or about me making an entrance. He's going to—

Then he pulls me towards him, wrapping his arms around me.

And just for a second, I'm safe.

66

Okwembu

Prophet is hunched over a bank of screens, staring down at the scenes unfolding on them. His eyes flick back and forth, terror on his face. Gunshots flare on the screens, washing out the cameras.

Riley Hale is there. Okwembu saw her moving through the corridors, saw her take out one of the guards. *She's still alive.*

She looks around the bridge. It's packed with people, all of them watching Prophet, all of them waiting for an order. On one of the screens, something explodes, sending another flare of white light across Prophet's pale skin. His lips are moving, but no words come out.

"Sir?" says one of the men, standing by the map table. He's older than Prophet, more grizzled, but it's impossible not to see the fear in his eyes.

Okwembu looks at him, then back at Prophet. He doesn't react to the question, his eyes locked on the screen.

"Prophet?" the man says, more urgently this time.

Okwembu doesn't hesitate. Prophet's thin veneer of control

is cracking open, and she's not going to let the opportunity pass.

"You, you and you," she says, pointing. "Lead your men down there and provide support. Get word to the gunner: if anybody tries to get off this ship, blow them out of the water. It'll stop anyone else from trying to leave."

She ignores the surprise on their faces. "You three," she says, turning to face the others. "When they're gone, you lock this bridge down."

The man by the map table sneers, disgust winning out over fear. "I don't take orders from *you*."

For the first time since she killed Mikhail, Okwembu loses it. "*I don't care who you take orders from.* If you don't stop this right now, you lose control of the ship."

She jabs a finger at Prophet, who hasn't reacted to the outburst. "It's exactly what he'd order you to do if he was thinking straight. Now get moving."

A dart of worry shoots through her, but she ignores it. She's lived through revolutions before – usually, all it takes is a few deaths, and then the instigators stop fighting. They should be able to keep the majority of the *Ramona*'s workforce.

A ripple of emotion travels around the room, borne on glances and nods. The ones at the back move first, hefting their guns, then jogging for the doors.

"One thing," Okwembu says, talking over the rising tide of voices. "The woman who Ray and Iluk brought in earlier. If you find her, I want her alive. Bring her to me."

Prophet is finally looking at her, but she ignores him. She drops her head and closes her eyes, just for a moment.

Okwembu is tired. Tired of trying to keep people safe. She's sick of it. She has tried, over and over, but no matter what she does, it never works. She has suffered, been imprisoned, nearly tortured. Whenever she has found supporters, they've been snatched away. And now, just as she finally finds a place she can keep safe, a place of order which she can control, Riley Hale comes along.

A woman she respected. A woman she had high hopes for. A woman who hates her, and wants to destroy everything she would build.

On some level, Okwembu understands Riley's hate. She knows she deserves it, after what happened to the *Akua Maru*. But Hale is about to destroy the one thing she has left, and Okwembu will not stand for it. Not this time.

She is going to kill Hale herself.

67

Anna

All Anna Beck can see is stars.

There was no sound when the pod ejected. No roar of rocket engines. The airlock is designed to open completely in a fraction of a second, letting the vacuum shoot the pod away from the station. Anna's heart has climbed up her throat and into her mouth – she's struggling to breathe, as if she can't push the air around its mass. The G-forces have welded her to the chair.

The touchscreen displays are alight, each one incomprehensible, as if the craft is daring her to take control. The pod is spinning, the stars give way to Outer Earth's massive hull, moving from the top of the viewport to the bottom, vanishing before she can pick out any details. Three seconds later, it appears again, and Anna is sure she's going to smash into it.

The feeling passes. Her hand is still locked tight around the joystick, and she makes herself push the top button. An engine bursts into life behind her, rumbling up into her spine. The pod tilts on its axis, the stars yawing to the right. A million tiny pinpricks, more than she could ever have imagined. The sun flashes into view, filling the cockpit with an awful glare.

Anna pulls the stick towards her – gently, almost tentatively. A different sensation this time, as boosters on the side of the pod fire. Dimly, Anna realises that she's weightless. There's a ripple of nausea in her stomach, and her sinuses feel strange, like they're slowly filling with mucous.

With a tiny rasp of fabric, her beanie comes loose from her head. It was dislodged by the launch, and now gravity floats it above her eyeline, mocking her. She grabs it, pulling it back on.

"Fuck," Anna says, the sound more of a breath than a word, horrifyingly loud in the silence.

Slowly, carefully, she stops the pod from moving. Outer Earth is no longer appearing in the cockpit viewport, and she has no idea where she is in space, but the stars have stopped moving. That's good enough for now.

Tiny movements are best. Little flicks on the stick, no more. The two buttons control her thrust – the top one sends her forward, and the one on the front of the stick causes a burst of white smoke to shoot from a nozzle on the front of the craft, out of sight below the cockpit.

Outer Earth comes back into view. She nearly loses it, brings it back, and holds it.

For a few seconds she can't tear her eyes away. Outer Earth is a monolith: a scarred, grey, ancient relic, hanging in the black void. The sun is behind the escape pod, and its light picks out the station perfectly.

The dock is easy to spot. It's as if a giant monster locked its jaws around the station, and tore away a huge chunk. The wound is marked by a haze of debris, glittering in the vacuum.

Anna doesn't know exactly where the tug will be – Dax didn't tell her – but the dock's her best bet. Pushing back the fear, she thumbs the thruster. The pod responds, and Outer Earth begins to get larger. It's hard to control – the station keeps sliding away, only for Anna to overcorrect and send it veering in the other direction. How much fuel does she have? She doesn't dare look down at the gauges to find out – if she does that, she feels like she'll never be able to look away. The thought of being lost out here, trapped in the void forever, is enough to send her heart back into her mouth.

The hull looms in front of her, and she brings the pod around so that the nose is pointing towards the dock. It's a little further along the station's curve, but she can see the debris. Slowly, ever so slowly, she heads towards it, keeping a close eye on the nearby hull.

The debris takes shape. A crate here, a destroyed tug there. Half of the dock's smashed airlock door. The mag rails that pulled the tugs inside the station are twisted and torn, spinning gently, as if they weighed no more than a human hair.

There's an urgent beep, and one of the displays flashing a warning. PROXIMITY ALERT.

The hull. It's too close, swallowing the right half of the viewport. She jerks the stick, and the pod drifts to the left, silencing the alarm.

There. She sees the other pods, just inside the destroyed dock. They're widely spaced, rotating on their individual axes. Their doors are open – Anna can see inside one of them, right out of the viewport on the other side. Dax and the others have got their space suits on. They'll be transferring to the tug, clambering aboard, getting ready to depart.

Anna thinks hard, picturing the dock as she remembers it. A huge hangar, packed with tugs and equipment. If she can manoeuvre her pod inside, if she can spot Dax's tug, she can ram it. If it's damaged, they won't be able to use it, which means their only option will be to return to Outer Earth.

Except . . . *shit*. She's not wearing a space suit. She didn't even think to put one on yet. An awful image comes to her mind: the escape pod hitting the tug, cracking down the middle. She's heard stories about what happens to a body in space – everybody on the station has.

There's no time. She's coming up on the debris. Anna pulls the stick, trying to steer her way through. Something scratches across the roof of the pod, and she yelps in fear.

She can see the tug. It's hanging right in the middle of the dock, facing outwards. It dwarfs her escape pod: a bulbous, misshapen thing, with a prominent nose and small fins on the sides. There's something on its underside, just out of view, something gold-coloured and thin. The heat shield.

Anna steers herself between two escape pods. *Almost there*, she thinks. Maybe she can come to a stop, let herself drift while she straps into a suit.

For a second time, the proximity alarm explodes to life. Anna's head snaps to the side, expecting to see the wall of the dock creeping up on her. But there's nothing – she's through the pods, past the debris, so what—

She has half a second to register the man in the space suit, half a second to see the horrified expression on his face. Then he slams into the viewport with a bang that shakes the tiny escape pod.

68

Riley

I don't try to process what I'm feeling: the relief, and joy, and fear, all tangled up in a big knot. I just let Carver hold me.

It's a full minute before he lets me go. By then, the fabric of his overalls is wet from my tears, and my face is red and puffy.

He cracks a smile. One of his teeth is gone. "Nice of you to join us," he says.

I smile back, wiping away more tears. "Not like I had anything better to do."

There's splashing ahead of us, and we turn to see a worker lifting one of the guards' rifles from the water. He's painfully thin, with lank hair and a gaunt, scarred face, but his hands are sure as he checks the gun. Another worker is at the door, a woman with a closely shorn head and a nasty scar across the back of her neck. "Does anyone know how to lock this?" she shouts over her shoulder.

"Riley, I don't . . ." Carver stops, shaking his head. "How are you even here?"

I open my mouth to tell him, but then I realise that explaining everything that happened to me would take longer than we have. Instead, it's Prakesh who jumps to the front of my mind. I look around again, certain that I'll see him among the other workers, but he isn't there.

"I'll tell you later," I say. "Promise."

"Seriously, what—"

"Right now, we need to get Prakesh, and then we're going to find Okwembu. Where is he? Was he with you?"

"I can't lock this," the woman by the door shouts. A couple of workers respond, wading over to help out.

Carver looks at me. "We got separated. I sort of maybe mouthed off to the guards."

He sees my expression. "Yeah, I know. Not smart. Ended up getting the shit beaten out of me. Bastards still put me to work, though – yesterday we were cleaning out the guards' quarters, and today it was here." He gestures around the dank space. "Water was leaking in and fried some of their generators. They put us to work repairing them."

I point at the worker with the rifle. "But if you were working, then what happened with—"

"Beats me. One minute we were fixing holes in the hull, then the next a bunch of other workers burst in here and start shooting. Took the guards by surprise."

He pauses, looking over at the man checking the rifle. "At least, I think they're workers. We haven't really had a chance to get to know each other."

"We're workers, all right," the man says. He finally decides the rifle isn't worth using – water-damaged, probably, and throws it aside, disgusted. "We were in the farm. The new guy did something – had us all soak our shirts in piss, then knocked out the guards with . . . hell, I don't know *what* it was. Some kind of chemical stuff. Never seen anything like it."

Carver raises an eyebrow. "Oh yeah. That makes total sense. Thanks."

Chemicals. Prakesh.

Before I can say anything else, there's a panicked yell from behind us. We turn to see one of the workers standing over Koji, a hand wrapped in his jacket at the scruff of his neck. He has a gun in one hand, one that doesn't look like it hit the water.

I get between them. "Don't even think about it," I say. Koji is on his knees, shaking in fear.

The man stares at me. "He's one of *them*."

"I *told* you. He can help us."

"Who are you?" the man says, glancing at my cuffs. "What are you even doing here?"

Carver steps between us. "Back up, Adam," he says.

The man – Adam – spits, his saliva plopping into the water. He jerks his head at Koji. "These people don't deserve to live."

"This one does," I say.

Adam holds my gaze a moment longer, then turns away, disgusted.

"What's his deal?" says Carver, nodding to Koji.

"Long story," I say. "But I need him."

"Come on," says the gaunt worker from behind Adam. "Jojo said to get to the boats."

"The hell is Jojo?" Carver says.

"Forget the boats," Adam says. He points to the body of one of the guards, face down in the water. "We leave without taking care of the rest of 'em, they'll come after us. Hunt us down."

"You're gonna get yourself killed, man," says Carver. "You and everyone else."

"He's right," Koji says, and everybody turns to look at him. "Believe me, you aren't getting to the bridge. It's too heavily guarded."

Adam tries to speak, but the gaunt worker talks over him. "Then we get as many weapons as we can," he says. He looks

349

over his shoulder, raising his voice. "Find 'em, bring 'em here. I'll check 'em for any water damage."

As the workers start to move, Carver looks down at my hands, frowning as he takes in the cuffs.

"Hang on," he says, casting about him. He spots what he's looking for, and holds up the old-fashioned cutter. It's acetylene, not plasma, and he aims it at the metal join between the two cuffs. I wince as the torch singes my skin. But within a second my hands spring apart. I badly want to get the actual cuffs off my wrists, but a cutting torch isn't the way to do it.

The voice inside me speaks, reminding me that Prakesh isn't the only reason I'm here. "Carver, was Okwembu with you? What happened to her?"

"Gods know," he says, running his fingers along the cuff on my right wrist. "Lost her when they took me and Prakesh." He sees me about to protest, and talks over me. "I know you probably want to throw her off the side of the ship right now, but it's too dangerous. Let's just get out of here."

"Hold on," says the woman by the door. "There's—"

She doesn't get a chance to finish. The door flies open, smashed from the other side, knocking her and the others aside.

Gunfire deafens me. Adam flies backwards, his arms stretched over his head, like he's calling out for his own personal god. I feel blood speckle my face, and then his body slaps the surface of the water.

A split second later, something else comes through the door – a small cylinder, squat and black. I get a momentary glimpse of it before it vanishes under the surface, bumping up against Adam's body.

Koji moves faster than I would have thought he could, grabbing me and Carver, pulling us down. "Flash-bang!" he shouts.

Everything goes white.

69

Prakesh

Prakesh squeezes himself against the wall. He can't take his eyes off Jojo's body, sprawled across the floor in the corridor junction. Half of the boy's neck is torn away.

"Got him!" someone shouts, speaking over the noise of the fading gunshot. The voice is shockingly close.

"See any others?" says another voice.

Prakesh starts to edge away from the T-junction, moving as quickly and quietly as he can. He glances to his right – there's a turn ten feet behind him in the corridor, with a corner he can slip around.

Bam.

Another gunshot. Prakesh snaps his head around, half convinced that he's hit. But whoever shot Jojo is blind-firing, the barrel of the rifle pointed around the corner. Another shot comes, the report deafening in the cramped space.

It feels like all the blood in Prakesh's body is rushing to his head. But he keeps moving, sliding along the wall. The turn is three feet away. Two.

Prakesh slips around the corner. At the very last second, he sees movement out of the corner of his eye. A head, poking round the edge of the junction.

They've seen me. There's no way they didn't.

Jojo's blood is still speckled across his face, slowly going tacky. It loosens the muscles in his legs, and he has to work very hard to stay upright, pushing himself against the wall. He realises he didn't know how old Jojo was, if he had a last name, anything about him except for the fact that he came from somewhere called Denali and he wanted to get off this ship more than anything else in the world.

He pauses, his knees bent, trying very hard not to breathe.

The voice comes again. "Nobody here. Guess he was the only one."

"I don't buy it, man. Why come down here by yourself?"

"Doesn't matter now." There's a muffled thump, and it takes Prakesh a second to realise that it's the sound of a boot colliding with Jojo's body. He has to fight down a wave of nausea. Could he keep moving? Slip away silently? He tells himself to move, but he's frozen to the spot.

Another pause. Then the sound of metal scraping on metal – Jojo's gun, being lifted off the floor. The sound is followed by footsteps, trailing off into nothingness.

Prakesh counts to ten. Then twenty. Silently mouthing the words, telling himself to move. It's only when he gets to thirty that his legs kick into gear.

He peeks around the corner.

Deserted.

In ten steps, he's crossed to the T-junction. He pauses, holding his breath. There's more distant gunfire, quick bursts of it, but the area around him is silent.

He glances down at Jojo's body, immediately looks away. There's nothing he can do. He can't even take the body with him – not if he wants to get out of here alive. And he has to make it out, otherwise Jojo died for nothing.

He should try and find the fuel hangar. Link up with the others. He keeps walking, listening hard for any footsteps coming his way, keenly aware that he doesn't have anything to defend himself with.

The corridor opens up into a wider hub area, with various passages leading off from it. There's a sign bolted to the wall, but the letters are rusted over, faded with age. Prakesh can just make out the words AIRCRAFT ELEVATORS, but the rest of the sign is illegible.

The boats must be on a lower level, surely, so all he has to do is—

What is that?

There's a subsonic hum, almost inaudible. He has to focus to hear it, and focus even harder to work out where it's coming from. It's emanating from his left, down a corridor that's even narrower than the others.

Prakesh hasn't been on the *Ramona* long, but he's become familiar with the sounds of the ship, the rumbles and clanks and bangs that echo through its rusted body. This is different. This is something he hasn't heard before.

Jojo told him the Engine was below decks. He said they didn't let the workers get close to it. His curiosity overwhelms him, and before he can stop himself, he's walking down the corridor, treading as quietly as he can.

A light flickers in the ceiling as Prakesh makes his way down it, the buzzing and clicking accenting the machine hum. He's holding his breath, and has to force himself to exhale. There aren't any more guards that he can see, but he still proceeds carefully.

The passage turns right, then left, and then Prakesh is in a high-ceilinged, brightly lit storeroom. The walls are lined with racks, just like the one that nearly took him and Jojo out. The shelves are brimming with equipment, a hodgepodge of frayed wires and oversized batteries and rusted cutting torches, nestled up against machinery whose use Prakesh can only guess at.

He focuses. There's a set of double doors in front of him, shut tight, with two folding chairs off to one side. The two who killed Jojo must have been guarding it. For a few moments, Prakesh wonders why they abandoned their post. They must have decided to join the fighting on the upper levels.

The doors are twice his size, as if heavy equipment needs to be moved in and out. A metal plaque is bolted to the door, faded words picked out on it in black lettering. *HAARP MOBILE UNIT 2769X-B8 AUTHORIZED ACCESS ONLY.*

Prakesh takes in the letters. The split in the doors bisects the B in *MOBILE*, and the first C in *ACCESS*.

HAARP.

He knows what that is. He's sure of it. But it's like something glimpsed out of the corner of an eye, vanishing the moment you turn to look at it.

Prakesh knows he has to get to the boats, knows that it won't be long before the other workers escape. But it's as if his feet have stopped listening to his mind. He looks around, then walks towards the door. There's a chunky keypad on the wall by the door, but as he gets closer he sees that it's dead, its digital display blank. And the doors aren't sealed completely. There's the tiniest gap.

The hum rumbles in Prakesh's stomach.

He puts his fingers in the gap, braces his arms, and pulls.

The doors resist for a moment, then give way, moving so fast that they almost knock Prakesh off balance. The hum is even more powerful now. He steadies himself, then raises his head and looks inside.

Nothing but darkness. Prakesh is on a metal grate, and he can feel empty space below him. He moves along it, hands touching the wall. A line of switches slides under his fingers, plasticky to the touch. Taking a deep breath, he flicks them up.

Banks of lights begin to click on, one after the other. Huge spotlights in the ceiling spring to life, making Prakesh blink, chasing away the shadows.

He's standing above another hangar – this one slightly smaller than the others. Most of the space is taken up by four enormous cubes, at least fifty feet on all sides, their surfaces dull grey metal. There's a thin passage below him, running between the cubes. The floor is covered with thickly insulated cables, tangled up in each other, running up the walls of the cubes and into them via giant connectors. Some of the cables go higher, vanishing into the ceiling. Prakesh's nostrils haven't recovered from the chemicals he cooked up, but he can still pick out the sharp stench of ozone.

He puts a hand on the railing, trying to work out what he's seeing. Again the word tugs at his mind. *HAARP.*

There's a ladder hanging off the end of the platform he's standing on. He swings himself onto it, climbing down, wincing as the noise of his feet on the rungs echoes across the hangar. He's more careful as he hops off onto the grated floor and walks between two of the cubes.

He keeps walking, running his hand along the side of the cube. It vibrates ever so slightly under his fingers. The hum is loud now, so loud that Prakesh wonders why the whole room isn't shaking. There must be some kind of inertial dampening, shock mounts built into the floor and ceiling . . .

He looks up as he comes round the corner of the cube. There's a rectangular, rusted metal plaque, mounted on the side of the next cube along. Prakesh moves closer, reaching out to touch it. At the top of plaque is a triangle with an exclamation point inside it, its bright yellow turned ochre with age. There's a litany of warnings underneath it – Prakesh's mouth moves as he scrolls down it. "Unauthorised personnel . . . risk of electric shock . . . safety equipment . . ."

He reaches the bottom. There's a set of barcodes, slightly raised off the metal surface. Underneath them are the words *Mobile High-frequency Active Auroral Research Program – Installation 2769X-B8.*

HAARP.

Prakesh's heart starts beating faster. This is the Engine, he's sure of it, but why can't he remember what it does? He knows he's heard the word HAARP before, somewhere on Outer Earth – a lesson in a schoolroom, a snatched conversation somewhere, an archived article on a tab screen.

He starts walking faster down the passage. At the very end, near the wall, is a screen built into the side of the cube on his right. It's dusty, and as Prakesh wipes it off, it springs to life, flickering under his fingers.

The screen is old. Prakesh can see plenty of dead pixels, and there's a crack that extends almost all the way across it. But he can still read the information displayed. He flicks across it with his finger, scrolling faster and faster. It's data – complex scientific data. An analysis of radio frequencies, breaking them down by different values.

He moves further along. The second screen doesn't work – the touch function has degraded, and it's glitched out. But the third, which he finds at the back of the room, shows something different. It's displaying complicated electrical diagrams, each one showing the flow of current.

Prakesh taps one, and a new window appears, displaying a separate graph. The lettering at the top of the window reads, *Fluxgate Magnetometer Data File Reviewer.*

He frowns. A fluxgate magnetometer measures the Earth's magnetic field. But why would—

The puzzle pieces slot into place, and Prakesh's eyes go wide.

HAARP. It's weather control. A way of altering the make-up of the ionosphere to control climate.

Before the war, Earth's governments tried to get various HAARP projects off the ground, but they didn't manage to do it before the missiles fell. Except this HAARP unit is here. And it's working. Prakesh puts his hand flat on the side of the cube, feeling the vibration travel up his arm.

This is why the area has become habitable. Why humans have been able to establish themselves here. This is the sacred Engine, the life-giver, the reason Prophet and his followers have thrived. Prakesh can't believe something like this still exists, can't believe that Prophet worked out how to get it running. It's *beyond* belief.

And the workers are going to burn the fuel supplies. They're going to sink the ship. And when they do, whatever this HAARP unit is doing to the climate will stop. It'll be lost at the bottom of the ocean. This part of the planet will go back to the way it was before: a frozen wasteland. It'll never recover.

Prakesh turns, and runs.

I close my eyes a split second too late.

The flash jabs hot needles into my retinas. The bang finishes the job, slamming my ears closed, filling them with an awful, high-pitched whine. A spray of water splashes across my face.

It feels like a whole minute before I can open my eyes. When I do, the generator room is exploding around me. I see a worker go down, his head snapping backwards as he takes a bullet. A guard is out of ammo, using his gun like a club, swinging it back and forth as two workers dodge out of range. A generator tips over, sparks flying as it lands on top of a prone guard, pushing her under the surface of the water.

Carver helps me, pulling me to my feet. Somehow, he's got hold of one of the rifles, and is trying to load it, yanking at the bolt. The mechanism is jammed, stuck halfway. He gives up, swinging it at an approaching guard. The butt takes the man in the face, and he spits a thick gout of blood as he topples sideways, crashing against the wall.

The impact from the hit travels up Carver's arm, knocking the rifle out of his hands and into the water. I don't wait for him to retrieve it. I just grab him and go, heading for the corridor. He pulls me back at the last second, just as another volley of bullets explodes past the door.

"We'll never make it!" he screams. I can barely hear him. Koji appears behind him, hyperventilating, hardly able to stand upright.

He's right. That corridor is a death trap – a couple of guards hanging back will be able to cut down anyone coming out of here. I cast around for something to use, and that's when I see the man Carver took down. More importantly, I see what's on his belt.

A squat cylinder, just like the one that came through the door. What did Koji call it? *Flash-bang.*

I sprint over to him, skidding onto my knees in the water, grabbing the cylinder. It crosses my mind that the water might have damaged it, but there's no time to check. We lose nothing by trying.

"Koji!" I shout. I can't tell how loud my own voice is. It hums in my ears, sounding as if it's coming through thick padding. He looks over to me, and I toss him the grenade.

He catches it with two hands, almost fumbling it, but then he reaches up and pulls a pin out of the cylinder. He spins around, hurling it underhand into the corridor.

The bang is just as loud, but this time we're prepared for it, hands over our ears, our eyes closed. And a second after it goes off, Carver and I rocket out of the door.

For a moment, it's almost like we're tracers again, running through Outer Earth. I can feel him behind me, hear his feet pounding the metal, like we're sprinting through a sector with me on point. The corridor is filled with thick smoke, stinking of gunpowder. A guard appears in front of me, on his feet but unsteady. I barely pause as I knock him aside, elbowing him in the ribcage.

"This way!"

It's Koji, pointing at a turn-off from the corridor. Somehow, he's managed to stay with us. I'm closest, and I skid to a halt alongside it, quickly peeking my head round. Deserted.

The surviving workers clamber out of the generator room, coughing and blinking. We can't leave them here – not after everything they've been through. I motion them to follow us, and they accept the order without comment. Two of them, I see, have managed to retrieve rifles. I almost ask them to test-fire the guns, check if they work, but decide not to. Last thing we need is someone getting hit with a ricochet in the tight corridors.

We keep moving. There's no telling how far this little worker rebellion has spread – not without a way to communicate with Prakesh's group. An alarm is blaring somewhere, harsh and guttural, but there's no more gunfire. I make Koji take the lead – the bowels of the ship are impossible to figure out, every corridor identical, with the same ribbed walls and recessed doors.

I'd give anything to have Harlan and Eric here. The seaplane could give us a way out. But thinking about them hurts too much, and I make myself stop. Even if they're alive, they have no way of knowing what's happening on the ship.

Ahead of us, the corridor opens up into a mezzanine level, with railings on the left. I can see a set of stairs leading down from the railings a few feet into the room, but it's only when we sprint through the entrance that we see what's in there.

It's some kind of storage hangar. Planes – the same as the ones on the ship's deck – are parked wingtip to wingtip, with their noses angled diagonally towards us. Close-up, they're enormous, at least fifty feet long, with cockpits like huge eyes. Puddles of old oil and grimy tyre tracks dot the floor beneath them. Huge rolling pallets rest up against the plane wheels.

There's an enormous roller door on the far wall of the hangar; it's hard to imagine these planes flying in here, so there must be an elevator platform beyond it, something to get them to the deck. The railing on my left has a thick coating of dust on it, and the whole place looks like it hasn't been touched in years.

"Over there," says Koji, pointing. I can make out the opposite end of the hangar, six planes away. It's identical to ours, with its own mezzanine.

"That get us to the boats?" says one of the workers. It's the woman who was trying to lock the door – somehow, she survived the assault. Even scored herself a rifle.

"Quickest way," Koji says, resting his hand on the railing. "Once we get there, we need to—"

The bullet ricochets off the railing next to his hand, burying itself in the wall. Another goes wide, pinging off the wall below us. The workers scatter. The woman with the rifle tries to fire back, then hurls it away when nothing happens.

I can see figures running across the floor, using the planes as cover. There's nowhere for us to hide – not up here, exposed, with nothing but railings between us and guards. Carver and I share a split-second glance, then in one movement, he and I hurdle the railing, bringing our legs up to our chests. We land on the closest wing with an enormous bang, hitting it so hard that the plane rocks in place, tilting on its three wheels.

They want to use the planes as cover? Then so will we.

The jump to the wing wasn't high enough to need a roll. I take a second to catch my balance, centring myself on the metal surface. Then I take off, sprinting up the plane's body. There was no time to explain what we were doing to Koji and the other workers. I look back over my shoulder, and, as I do so,

I hear the voice in my mind again, speaking the same words it did when Harlan and I were hanging off that cliff near Whitehorse. *Leave them. They'll just slow you down.*

But Koji has already jumped, crashing onto the wing, sending shock waves through the metal. Two of the others follow. I keep moving, pushing into a full sprint, leaping over the plane's body. The gap between the first and the second plane is no more than five feet, and I land easily, momentum carrying me forward. I see a guard, his face hidden by the body of his rifle, and only just leap across to the third plane when he fires.

The bullet passes above me, but I can't stop myself ducking. The movement pushes me off balance, and it happens right when I hurdle the plane's body. I land awkwardly, try to correct it, nearly manage, and then my feet tangle and I crash onto my side onto the third plane's wing.

At the last second, I turn my body so I'm sliding feet first. It's just enough. I tuck my body as I come off the wing, rolling, smacking my shoulder on the floor. But the momentum's on my side now, and I use it, angling my body forward as I come up to my feet, going from a roll to a sprint in half a second. Somewhere, deep inside me, my heart is pounding hard enough to shatter my ribcage.

Another gunshot. No telling where the round went, or where any of the others are. I start zigzagging – it slows me down, but that's better than a bullet in the back. There aren't any guards on the floor in front of me, and I don't dare risk looking over my shoulder.

I spread the zigzag, sprinting between cover on the floor, using the tool pallets and wheel struts as cover. I'm at the fifth plane when one of the guards, smarter than the others or maybe just more controlled, gets a real bead on me.

He must have been tracking my movements, looking for where I'm going to be instead of where I am. I dive, skidding on my stomach across the floor into cover, just as the space above me fills itself with gunfire.

"Riley!"

Carver has made it to the other end of the hangar. He's got hold of one of the wheeled pallets, and is pushing it towards me, using it as mobile cover. I flatten myself to the floor, crawling towards him. We meet at the edge of the fifth plane, and I squirm into position behind the box. There's no telling where Koji is – he could be on the planes, or he could be bleeding out somewhere.

"I'll go left, you go right," I say to Carver. "Now!"

Open floor. Gunfire. Shouts. Stairs. Railings. Mezzanines. Stumbling. Almost falling. Running. Koji has made it – he's standing in the door, waving us in. I get there half a second before Carver, skidding into the passage, and then Koji slams the door shut. He and Carver spin the valve, locking it tight.

The noise from the plane hangar vanishes, replaced by the thrumming sound of the ship. Carver leans against the wall, breathing hard. Koji looks like he's about to throw up – his face is ash-grey.

"What about the others?" Carver asks.

He shakes his head, and Carver kicks the corridor wall in a fury.

The corridor we're in is wider than the others. It's a hub, with several other passages branching off from it. The choking smell of gunpowder has made it out here, and I can see dust motes caught in the light from the bulbs in the ceiling.

"We need to keep moving," I say, turning to go. "We don't know if they can open the door from the other—"

The guard is fifteen feet away, calm and ready, squinting down the barrel of a rifle. It's pointing right at me, and I can see him starting to squeeze the trigger.

I can't close the distance between us. Not fifteen feet, not before he squeezes the trigger. I don't have a single thing I could use as a weapon.

Then I see Prakesh, sprinting out of one of the side passages.

He's wearing a ragged pair of overalls, identical to Carver's, and there's blood streaming down his face from a cut below his eye. He looks exhausted and terrified but in that instant I don't care because *he's alive*.

I see him look towards me, see the disbelief on his face, see his mouth start to form words.

I see the guard's surprise, see him swing his gun around, hunting for the movement.

I don't see him pull the trigger. But I hear the shot. And I see Prakesh stumble, his hands reaching out towards me. Then he's on the ground and I can see blood and all I can do is scream.

71

Riley

Carver crosses the fifteen feet in an instant, driving a fist into the guard's face.

The man crumples, his legs collapsing under him, his gun clattering to the floor. I barely notice. I'm already past Carver, skidding to my knees next to Prakesh.

I can't see the bullet hole. There's too much blood. Prakesh looks at me – there's a momentary flare of recognition, and then his eyes close, and they don't open again.

I fumble for his hand, gripping it hard, *willing* him to squeeze back. Nothing. I can hear footsteps around me, more than just Carver and Koji, and the corridor is suddenly filled with voices. But I can't look up. Carver has his hands on Prakesh's chest, hunting for the wound, trying to put pressure on it.

And that's when the voice inside me speaks.

I don't want to listen. But the voice is everywhere now, filling me with white-hot light, the anger burning away everything else.

This isn't just about the man who shot him, it says. *It isn't about the people on this ship. It's about the chain of events that led you here, to this exact spot. There's someone at the start of that chain of events. She's responsible – for everything. And it's time for her to pay. Not tomorrow. Not later on. Now.*

Slowly, I get to my feet.

"Riley, what are you doing?" Carver says. I glance down at him. His arms are red from fingertips to elbows, pushing down on Prakesh's chest. I should help him. Prakesh is dying in front of me, and I'm standing here, just looking at him.

You can't save him. Just like you couldn't save Amira, or your father, or Royo or Kev or Yao. You can't save anyone. The only thing you can do is avenge them.

The corridor is packed with people. Three of them are locked in an argument with Koji. The others are in a loose circle around us – other workers, wearing the same threadbare overalls. I recognise some of them as the ones who followed us from the generator room, but there are others I haven't seen before. The new arrivals have guns, rifles that they must have taken from the guards. And they've got supplies: containers of fuel, food, water canteens, as if they grabbed whatever they could on their way here.

I look past them, and that's when I find the source of the strange feeling: the déjà vu I had when I first arrived on the ship.

I know these corridors. I've spent my entire life moving through ones just like them, using their walls and ceilings and angles and obstacles to craft the fastest, most efficient routes. That's what I do. I'm a tracer – nothing more, nothing less.

I don't know why I didn't see it before. The guards might run this place, they might have weapons and they might have numbers. But in this environment? In this warren of corridors and right angles and hard surfaces? I'm in control. I am the single most dangerous person on this ship.

"Ry, you have to help me," Carver says.

Rob Boffard

"Get him out of here," I say. My voice is as calm as still water. "Get to the boats, get off the ship. Keep him safe."

And before anyone can say anything, I start running.

72

Prakesh

Everything comes in flashes.

Prakesh is awake, being dragged down one of the *Ramona*'s corridors. Something is wrong with his chest. It's like his ribs is made of hot coals. Every time he tries to breathe, they flare up, searing him with impossible pain. He can hear someone screaming. By the time he realises it's him, he's falling back into darkness.

Another flash. He's outside, looking at the sky. No: not quite outside. The hull of the *Ramona* curves above him, a black mass blotting out the clouds. He's in one of the ovular entrances in the ship's side, lying on his back.

"How many boats down there?" It's Carver's voice. *He's alive.*

"Three. Should be enough for us and the supplies both," says someone else.

He saw Riley. He's sure of it. Where is she? Is she here? He tries to speak, but he can't get enough air into his lungs. He was shot. Why was he shot? He was on his way to find the other workers, to stop them from . . .

He doesn't know. He almost has it, but holding onto the memory is almost impossible.

Carver appears, leaning into view above Prakesh, arguing with one of the workers. His arms are soaked in blood, streaked up to the elbows. Dimly, Prakesh realises that it's his blood.

"You did *what*?" Carver is staring at the man, his eyes wide.

"There's enough time," the worker says. Sweat is pouring down his face, and a cut on his cheek spills blood down his jawline. "We put down a long trail of fuel. It'll take a while to really catch."

"No way," Carver says, jabbing a finger at the ceiling. "Riley's still up there. I'm not leaving without her."

"Fine," the man says. "Then stay. But we can't come back for you."

Carver turns away, on the verge of leaving. Prakesh struggles to speak, desperate to remember. But it's too much effort, and he feels his eyes starting to close again.

HAARP.

Prakesh's eyes fly open. He has to find a way to tell them. If they let that fuel catch, the detonation will sink the ship. There's got to be a way to stop it.

His throat is dry as old bone. He tries again, and this time sound escapes. It's a moan, low and weak, but it's enough. Carver looks down at him, just for a second.

Please, Prakesh thinks. And somehow, he finds the strength to form words.

"HAARP," he says. It's a rough bark, barely a word.

"You're going to be OK," Carver says, squeezing his shoulder. He's getting ready to leave.

"HAARP," Prakesh says again.

This time, his voice is stronger. Carver glances at him again, and there must be something on Prakesh's face, because he drops to one knee next to him, concern on his face. "What's that?"

"There's a HAARP," Prakesh says. He tries to keep going, but his voice gives out, and he coughs. Pain envelopes him, and he blinks away hot tears.

"A *what*?"

Prakesh doesn't have much left. He can already feel himself slipping back into unconsciousness. He gives it one last try. "There's a HAARP unit," he says. "On this ship. Climate control. Weather. You can't let it burn."

It'll have to be enough. There's nothing left.

"What the hell is—" Carver says, and stops. His eyes go huge.

It was all Prakesh could do to provide the information he did, but he can see that Carver has put it all together. He understands. They're both scientists. He grows things, and Carver builds things, but they still come from the same place.

The worker appears in Prakesh's field of vision. "What's he saying?"

"You stupid, *stupid* son of a bitch." Carver rockets to his feet, so suddenly that the man has to jump back. "This ship – it's got bulkhead doors, right? Where's the closest door to the fuel stash?"

"Door 6 on C deck, I think, but—"

"How do I close them? *Tell me*."

Good, Prakesh thinks. *That's good.*

And he sinks into oblivion.

73

Riley

The fastest a human being can run is twenty-six miles an hour. Thirty-eight feet per second.

Back on Outer Earth, the other Devil Dancers and I used to argue about whether anybody would ever break that record. I was sure someone would do it someday, even hoped I might do it myself. Yao and Carver insisted that it was impossible.

I don't know how fast I'm going. But right now, it feels like I've taken that record and doubled it. *Tripled* it. My legs are a blur. White-hot fury is exploding through me, acting like rocket fuel, propelling me through the corridors.

I have never moved this fast, or this cleanly. There's a T-junction ahead of me, and I barely slow down, leaping towards the wall, hardly aware of my own movements. I use my left foot to cushion the impact, then push myself to the side, zero momentum lost, the air roaring in my ears, my heart thundering in my chest.

It doesn't matter that I don't know the way. I just have to keep moving upwards, to the bridge. Okwembu will still be there. I'm sure of it. It's the safest place on the ship. It'll be heavily guarded, but I can figure that out when I get there. Right now, I feel like I could blow past them before they even raise their weapons.

I fly up a stairway, my feet hammering on the steps, four at a time. The anger inside me, the sheer *rage*, is like a miniature fusion reactor all on its own. An endless source of energy.

Two guards appear in the corridor, running towards me, guns up. One fires just as I jump, and the bullet scorches the air on my right as I jump towards the wall. I use the tic-tac to push myself higher, scalp scraping the ceiling, foot landing on the opposite wall, then pushing off again and driving my knee into the first one's face. I roll over him, taking out the second guard at the knees, and all the while the voice inside me is screaming. *Faster. Go faster.*

My lungs are burning, but I take that burn and use it, pushing myself harder. At one point, the access to the level above me is gone, the stairs ripped out. I don't even slow down. I angle my run and tic-tac off the wall again, grabbing the ledge, ignoring the jagged metal biting into my skin. The momentum I have swings my body, and I pull it back, using it to launch myself upwards. I get an elbow on the ledge, then two, and then I'm up and running.

There's an entrance ahead of me, like the one leading into the generator room. The room beyond it is flooded with natural light – there's an opening in the wall on my right, another rectangular entrance port. The hangar itself is empty, an open space big enough to hold another six planes. I lean into the run, pushing myself harder. Okwembu can't be far, two more levels, then—

The door at the far end starts to slide open. It's big and heavy, moving on screeching metal rollers. There are shapes behind it in the darkness. Guards.

There's half a second when I think about running towards

them. But even at the speed I'm moving, I won't reach it before the guards burst through. They can blanket the hangar with gunfire. I can't dodge bullets, no matter how fast I'm going.

I skid to a halt, back-pedalling, then lunge for the only cover I can see: the rectangular opening. I stop myself just in time, my foot skidding over the edge. There's nothing below me but cold sea. I can see Fire Island in the distance, dark and brooding under the cloudy sky.

The frame of the door is two feet wide – just enough to hide my body. I'm cursing the loss of momentum, but the anger is quickly replaced by fear. There's nowhere else to go. I can hear them, moving across the hangar, and I can tell by their voices that it's a big group of them. And then I realise – they're not sweeping through the hangar. They're heading towards the opening. I sneak a look, just peeking my head around the side of the frame. They're coming right towards me, guns low.

I thought I could get past them, wait until they'd cleared out, then keep moving. But it doesn't matter how much adrenaline I have, or how confident I am – they're going to find me. They'll be on me in seconds.

I look out at Fire Island, and realise that I know where I am. I can place myself on the ship. And at the same time, Koji's words come back to me. *We'd need a lot more guns to even think about getting to the bridge.*

Maybe we don't need a lot more guns.

Maybe we just need one.

74

Riley

I lean out over the edge, and crane my neck upwards. The frame of the opening extends a foot or so beyond the wall, and the deck is thirty feet above my head. At first, I see nothing but smooth metal, and fear rises up inside me, a black spot in the angry, white heat. But then I see the rivets, each the size of my closed fist. There are small openings in the hull, too – miniature ovals, with ancient, rotted cables hanging out of them like tongues.

You can do this.

The voices of the guards are getting closer. I take two quick breaths, then make my move.

I don't have time to be scared. I don't have time for anything. I reach for the nearest cable, fingers snagging, jerking it sideways. Then I swing myself off the edge.

I slide down the cable, burning the skin on my hands. My foot catches something, a rivet, and it brings me to a jerking halt, with one leg cocked at an awkward angle. The air is cold on my face, the wind wicking sweat from my forehead.

I start climbing, moving as fast as I can. My muscles scream as I haul myself up the cable, lunging for the ovular opening. I get a hand in it, then thrust upwards, hunting for a second one. My body moves faster than my mind, and I jam myself against the other side of the frame, out of sight. I nearly fall, my foot slipping on the surface. I have to be still. For five seconds, I don't dare move.

I can hear the guards in the doorway. If one of them looks around the frame, they'll have a clear shot. The only thing protecting me is the illogical nature of what I just did. Nobody in their right mind would try to climb up the side of the ship.

"Did she jump?"

"I don't see her."

"Forget it. If she's in the water, she's dead anyway. Let's go."

The voices fade. I wait five seconds, then five more. It lets the guards get out of earshot, but it gives me a chance to consider where I am. I make the mistake of looking down and out, and the sea feels like it's rushing towards me, as if I'm already falling. The clouds reflect off the surface, the glare bright enough to make me squint.

Grunting, I turn myself until I'm face up against the wall, and start climbing again. One hand at a time, focusing on planting my feet. The rivets are evenly spaced – I use them to hold my feet up while I hunt for handholds. I can feel the wall starting to curve, tilting me outwards, but I just push my torso into it, refusing to let it defeat me. The sound of gunfire inside the ship reaches me, elongated and warped.

Then, suddenly, there are no more handholds. The section of hull above me is completely smooth. Worse than that: the curve is more prominent, jutting out above me as the deck extends over the water. I keep my breathing deep and even, cheek flat against the surface. The metal is freezing cold, damp with condensation and sea spray, speckled with gritty rust. I have to find a way. I can't stay here, and the thought of climbing back down is enough to make my stomach lurch.

I look to my right. There's platform bolted onto the edge of the deck – a metal grate, five feet wide and ten long. It has a pair of antennae hanging vertically off the bottom, spaced maybe four feet apart. Each of the thin metal tubes has a fist-sized bubble at the end, and they're swaying in the breeze, the metal creaking gently. They must be radio antennae – maybe they're even the ones that broadcast the message.

Suddenly, I'm back in the Yukon, trapped on that clifftop by the wolves, preparing to jump to the branch jutting out of the rock. That was nothing compared to what I'm about to do. Here, I have to jump sideways, with no gravity to help me on distance.

My foot slips off one of the rivets. I cry out, my fingers aching as my foot flails at the air. Somehow, I manage to get it back on, manage to get myself flat against the wall again. Wind whips at my clothes. I can't stay up here. I either jump now, or I fall.

I lean to my left, as far as I can go. Then, in one movement, I throw myself the other way, towards the closest antenna.

My world shrinks down to my forearms, my hands, the tips of my fingers. I touch metal, my fingers wrapping around the cylinder, and then my hands slam into the top of the bubble. I can feel the antenna straining, reaching its limit. If I swing too far, it'll snap right off.

I lift my legs up, gritting my teeth, controlling my swing. I come to a stop, hanging with my arms extended, my numb fingers wrapped around the antenna. Instantly, I realise my mistake. I should have used my swing, channelling the momentum into an upwards lunge. Nothing for it: I'm going to have to do this ugly.

I can't pull my entire body up the antenna. My arms won't

take it. I need something to take the weight, and that means I need to get my ankles wrapped around the second antenna.

I throw my legs up, trying to snag it. My first attempt is a failure, and I feel my fingers slip a little. The pain in my arms is getting worse. My muscles are taut cables, stretched almost to breaking point.

I try again. This time, I make it. I'm face up, my hands wrapped around the first antenna, my ankles gripping the second. It'll take some weight off, give me some leverage. I close my eyes, ask my arms to do this one last thing for me, and start pulling myself up the first antenna. I tense the muscles in my legs and my core, teasing out every bit of leverage I can.

More than once, I slip, sliding down the pole, the metal biting into my hands where they got scorched on the cable. I tighten the muscles in my legs, gasping as I keep pulling myself up.

It feels like it takes hours. Eventually, I'm standing upright, my feet perched on the bubble at the bottom of the second antenna, my fingers gripping the edge of the platform. I take a breath, then climb onto it, forcing my body upwards, letting my arms take the weight.

I roll onto my back, my tortured fingers clenching, my lungs and arms on fire. I'm on dangerous ground: rage might keep me going, but my body can only take so much of this.

I let myself lie there for a full thirty seconds. There's plenty of noise – the howling of the wind, the creaking of the hull, the smack of waves against metal, far below me.

And bursts of gunfire from the Phalanx gun.

It's targeting the boats, firing out into the ocean. Whoever is operating it doesn't know I'm here yet. I roll onto my stomach, then prop myself up on my elbows and look around the deck. There's no one around. The old, silent fighter jets are lined up in front of me. The bridge itself is on my right, a tower at the edge of the deck. Its windows reflect the white clouds.

Get up, Riley.

I clamber to my feet and start moving, going from a walk to a jog to a sprint, staying as low as I can.

75

Prakesh

The voice comes from a long way away. "Hang in there."

It takes Prakesh a full minute to work out what's happening. He's lying in one of the boats, propped up against the prow. The boat is full of people and equipment, and Prakesh can see that they're speeding across the water. He can hear the roar of the boat's engine, feel it buck as it climbs the waves. There are three other boats, moving alongside, all of them packed with workers.

Another sound explodes across the water – a guttural roar, ripping through the frigid air. One of the boats tears in two, its surface shredding before Prakesh's eyes. Its crew spill into the water, the surface churning with froth and blood.

Prakesh's boat reacts instantly, veering to one side. Someone collapses on top of him, and that's when the pain in his chest *really* wakes up. He tries to scream, but can't get enough air into his lungs. There is something very, very wrong down there.

The boat changes direction again, digging into the water. The roar is coming in bursts now, seconds apart.

"Hold on!"

"Goddamn Phalanx gun—"

"It's gonna cut us apart."

"Turn. *Turn!*"

Prakesh hears the motor throttle up another octave, its pilot pushing it to the limit. But it's not going to be enough. They won't be able to outrun bullets.

He opens his eyes, and sees one of the other boats running straight towards them. Its pilot is panicking, turning the boat hard, desperately trying to get away from the hailstorm of bullets. Pain explodes through Prakesh as the boat collides with theirs. He feels the floor tilt underneath him, then it slams back down onto the water.

The bullets are sending up spikes of white froth, getting closer by the second. Prakesh can't look away.

76

Okwembu

The *Ramona* has been torn apart from the inside out.

The screens on the bridge are still displaying camera views, and each one shows nothing but fire and smoke and spitting sparks. The bridge itself is locked down tight – its doors barred, the men and women inside all armed with rifles. But that doesn't stop worry from churning at Okwembu's gut. It's all slipping away from her, all of it.

The people on the *Ramona* should have planned for this. Their setup – spacing their people, never letting the workers get hold of weapons – was clever. But they didn't think it through. They didn't think about what would happen if things went wrong. They were stupid. Sloppy. She won't let that happen again.

Prophet is still standing over the control panel, still in a mute trance. Okwembu looks across the screens, hunting for something she can use. She can't even tell if there are any workers left on board, and there's no way to see if the Phalanx gun is hitting its targets. She's already thinking ahead – should they give chase? Round up any stragglers?

"How many boats do we have left?" she says, not looking away from the screens.

She hears the guards shifting behind her, and lowers her voice to a growl. "How many?"

"One or two," says a voice. "There should still be some left on the C deck ramp."

"Go and secure them."

There's no movement behind her, and she doesn't have to turn around to picture the guards – to picture the lazy, slow expressions on their faces. She closes her eyes for a moment, then turns to Prophet. If she can just get him to—

But as she does so, she gets a look out of the window.

There's a figure on the deck, sprinting across it, running between the line of disused planes. It's heading right for the Phalanx gun. Okwembu stops, her eyes narrowing. In an instant, the figure is gone, covered by the wing of a plane. But Okwembu saw the dark hair, recognised the body shape.

"Hale," she whispers.

And then raw terror floods through her.

She doesn't waste another second. She walks over to Prophet, grabbing him by both shoulders and turning him towards her. "You have to talk to the gun operator."

He stares at her as if he doesn't know who she is. "Curtis?" he says, after a long moment.

Okwembu has to work very hard to keep her voice level. She desperately wants Hale alive, but she doesn't have a choice now. "Yes. Curtis. We need to talk to him."

Moving slowly, way too slowly, Prophet bends over a bank of screens. There's a radio, attached to the edge of one of the screens on a coiled cable, and he unhooks it and pulls it towards him.

"Curtis, are you there?" he says.

Okwembu snatches it away from him, hammering the transmit button. "You've got a runner heading towards you on the deck. Take her out. *Take her out now.*"

77

Riley

I can feel my body starting to rebel. The muscles in my shoulders and upper back are roaring in pain, and my arms hurt from my climb up the side of the ship. But I have to keep going. I *have* to get to that gun.

Somewhere in the back of my mind, I realise that it's stopped firing. Has it run out of ammo? Are Prakesh and Carver out of range? I sneak a glance to my left, off the edge of the deck, but I can't see any boats from where I am.

I keep running. The body of the planes are too low for me to move between the wheel struts, but there's just enough room for me under the wings. I'll need to stay in cover – I'll be too exposed out on the open deck.

Ahead of me, one of the planes is tilted sideways. One of its wheel struts is missing, and the tip of its wing scrapes the surface of the deck. I tilt my body, leaning into the turn, already plotting my angle of attack.

There's a roar of gunfire, and the plane in front of me rips apart.

Great gouges appear in the body. The cockpit glass shatters, raining down on me, and one of the wings almost shears off. If I hadn't started to turn, if I wasn't in the process of running around it, I would have gone right into the bullets.

I switch direction, adjusting my angle, sprinting away from the planes – onto the open deck.

There's no choice. Behind me, the line of planes is being ripped apart. The noise is unbelievable. Something explodes – a missile, a fuel tank, no way to tell. I keep my head down, my feet hammering the deck.

The gun stops firing, just for a second. Under the ringing in my ears, there's a thin mechanical whine. The barrel is tracking me, turning in my direction, trying to aim ahead of me.

I can't outrun bullets. But I can outrun that barrel.

The gun starts firing again. Bullets dig divots out of the deck behind me, so close that metal shrapnel bites through the leg of my pants. The fragments are tiny, nothing like the one that buried itself in my leg when we crashed the escape pod, so I ignore them. Acrid smoke stings my throat, but I ignore that, too. I couldn't stop, even if I wanted to.

The bridge tower is on my right. For an instant, the bullets stop coming, the person inside the gun not wanting to shoot the tower itself. I seize the advantage, pushing myself harder, hurdling a chevron-striped ramp. But the gun is still tracking me, and, a moment later, whoever is inside hits the trigger. Bullets split the air behind me. Gods, how many does he *have*?

I'm ahead of the barrel's targeting line – no more than a few feet, but it's enough. I'm getting closer, leaning into the turn, coming up on the gun. A cry bursts out of me as I sprint the final few feet, and then I'm out of the line of fire, under the barrel itself. The bullets stop coming, the barrel shuttling left and right, hunting for a target.

The gun looks even more menacing up close. It's foundation is a metal box with rivets on it as big as the ones on the side of the ship. There's a mess of machinery above the box: a rotating platform, with two wings bracketing a curving chain of bullets, each one the size of my ring finger. The gun barrel itself is like something out of hell, blacker than space itself, longer than I am tall.

I move to the seaward side of the gun. At first, I think I've made a mistake – that the gun is controlled from the bridge. But then I see the door, set into the side of the platform, its surface caked with rust. There's lettering across the door, in stencilled capital letters: PHALANX CLOSE-IN WEAPONS SYSTEM AUTHORISED PERSONNEL ONLY.

There's no valve lock – just a simple handle. The door is slightly open, and as I move towards it I see movement. Someone behind the door, trying to close it, lock me out.

Not today.

I sprint to the door, dropping my shoulder, driving hard. It slams backwards – whoever is behind it shouts in surprise, almost knocked off balance. They recover quickly, try to close it again, but they're not fast enough. My follow-up kick almost knocks the door off its hinges.

A man lunges at me. He's pale from lack of sunlight, his lank hair hanging down his face in thick, gungy strands. He throws a clumsy punch, aiming for my face. It's the work of half a second to grab his arm, turn the strike against him. I shove him backwards, then come in after him.

I see screens leaking green light into the gun's interior. There's the most awful smell – stale sweat and rotting food, mixed into a horrible miasma. I try to ignore it, dodging another of the man's punches. He's off balance, and I take the gap, grabbing the back of his head and smashing it into the wall.

He mewls in pain, but his hand keeps moving. I look to the side, and see a rifle on a nearby chair – one he's hunting for, feeling his way towards it. I stop him, gripping his arm, turning him around in one move and twisting it behind his back. The mewling noise becomes a yell, deafening in the tiny space. I make a fist with my other hand, then slam it into the pressure point on the back of his neck.

I give him a shove. His body sprawls across the floor, his head thumping off it. He's twitching slightly, his eyes rolled back in his head, but I barely notice. All my attention switches to the screens.

Some of them are radar displays, others internal readings from the gun. One of them shows the deck, where the gun is currently pointing, and there's a complicated target reticle overlaid on top.

I slide into the chair. The seat underneath me is still warm. My hands slide over the control panel, stopping when I find a small joystick with a prominent button on it. I give it an experimental push. The body of the gun vibrates around me as the motor kicks in, and the view on the screen changes, moving to the left. Slowly, the bridge slides into view.

"OK," I say to myself. "Here we go."

78

Okwembu

Okwembu can't see Hale any more. The tracer vanished when her path took her along the wall of the bridge tower. It doesn't help that the deck is shrouded in drifting smoke, obscuring the Phalanx gun. Half of the planes are on fire, their fuselages hanging in shreds.

The bridge behind her is silent. No one speaks. They're all staring out of the windows, their faces illuminated by flickering screens.

Okwembu tries to control her breathing. *There's no way Hale survived that. Nobody could. Not even a tracer would be able to outrun—*

The gun starts to move again.

The barrel raises itself in short jerks, as if the operator isn't quite sure of the equipment, still trying to get the hang of it. Prophet is muttering under his breath. "Engine's gonna save us," he says, more to himself than to anyone else. "The Engine will keep us safe."

Okwembu reaches out, gripping his arm. "You have to shut the gun down. Right now."

He stares at her blankly, as if he doesn't know who she is.

"The Phalanx gun," she says. *"How do we shut it off?"*

He shakes his head. "It's manual control," he says. "Only Curtis can do that."

Okwembu looks back out of the window. The Phalanx gun is turning in a slow circle, the barrel moving upwards.

Aiming for the bridge.

"Get out!" Okwembu shouts. She throws Prophet to the side, launching herself towards the doors. "We have to get out now!"

And Riley Hale opens up.

79

Riley

The bridge *implodes*.

That's the only word for it. The structure folds inwards, its struts bending and snapping under the barrage. Part of the roof caves in. In seconds, the entire bridge is wreathed in smoke, glitchy and pixelated on my screen. It's like the bullets brought a black hole to the bridge.

The whole gun shakes around me, the vibrations travelling up through my chair. I laugh, and my laughter vanishes under the roar of the gunfire.

I keep my finger on the trigger until the ammo counter on the screen blinks a big fat zero.

The only sound is my breathing, close in the cramped space. There's a water canteen off to one side, balanced on the control panel. It's half full. I drain most of it in one go, then tip the rest over my head, soaking my hair and neck. I take one last look at the smoking, sputtering wreck of the bridge, then step over the unconscious gunner and push my way out of the door.

The harsh daylight makes me blink, the smoke worming its way into my lungs. My body chooses that moment to really wake up, my muscles burning, protesting against everything I put them through. A sudden wave of nausea rolls through me, and I drop to one knee on the deck, retching.

My shoulder blades are twisted rods of red-hot steel, and there's something wrong with the muscles on my right side. Every movement sends a sharp arc of pain up into my armpit. It's like a stitch that's got out of control, taking on a life of its own. I'm pushing my body to a level it hasn't gone to before, and if I'm not careful I won't going to make it out the other side.

You're not done yet, says the voice.

I look over my shoulder at the bridge. It's a smoking ruin. There's no way anybody survived that. But I can't walk away, not until I see Janice Okwembu's body, not until I know she's paid for everything she's done.

It's hard to get moving again, but I do it. Each step hurts, and I have to grit my teeth to keep going, gripping my right side as if I can massage the pain away. I hear a bang, and look up. Something on the bridge has exploded, gushing even more fire and smoke.

There's a buzzing sound, growing by the second, and a shape explodes out of the smoke. No – not out of it. *Above it*. It takes me a moment to realise what I'm seeing.

The seaplane.

I stare at it, open-mouthed, as it soars above me. I can just see Harlan through the blown-off door, hanging on for dear life. The plane's body is damaged in a hundred places, bullet holes standing out like acne scars. It banks, descending towards the sea, vanishing past the edge of the deck.

How did they survive? Did they land somewhere? No way to tell – and they don't dare land on the deck, not without wheels. It doesn't matter. They're alive. *They made it.*

The knowledge makes me want to punch the air and throw up, all at once. I hadn't realised how much it was weighing on me. Ever since I saw Finkler, lying broken on the rocks of Fire Island, I thought they were gone. I told myself that I didn't know for sure, but I never really believed it.

If I can get to them afterwards, we can get back to Whitehorse. Carver and Prakesh and I can . . .

Prakesh. My good feeling vanishes. My stomach gives another sickening lurch, and I squeeze my eyes shut. When I open them again, the buzz of the seaplane has faded, and I'm looking back up at the bridge.

Later. That can all come later. You've got a job to do first.

It takes me a few minutes to find an entrance. I have to go nearly all the way round the bridge structure, to the far side of the ship. I hesitate for a moment, not wanting to enter the pitch darkness of the interior again.

But there's no choice. Not this time. I take a deep breath of cold ocean air, then step inside.

80

Anna

Anna can't get control of the escape pod.

She's wrestling with the stick, willing it to do what she wants, but every time she tries to correct her course she overcompensates, sending the pod into a flat spin. The destroyed dock revolves around her, tugs and debris orbiting like miniature planets.

With an enormous bang, Anna's pod collides with the wall of the dock.

It hits rear-first. Anna lurches forward in her seat, and that's when she sees the crack.

It's spreading slowly across the cockpit viewport, moving in tiny jerks, growing larger and larger. She can't take her eyes off it, can't focus on anything else.

She doesn't know whether the crack came from the impact on the wall or when she collided with the astronaut. Doesn't matter. Her fingers scrabble at her seat belt, digging into the catch. It snaps back, and she floats upwards, feeling a fresh wave of nausea roll through her. The crack is bigger now, almost to the other edge of the viewport.

Space suit. I have to get to a space suit.

She pulls herself to the back of the craft, hammering on the suit locker's release button. She has no idea of the right way to put on one of these suits, and there's no time to find out.

An alarm starts beeping on the escape pod's console. It's not like the proximity alarm – this is the harsh cry of a machine that knows it's dying. Anna ignores it, pulling the suit out of the locker. It's made of tough, rubber-like material, with the seam running down the torso. She forces it open, then tries to spin her body so she can jam a leg inside it. She misses the first time, her foot grazing the outside of the suit. She's breathing too hard, using up too much oxygen, unable to think of anything but zero gravity, of being lost in space, floating forever.

One leg. Then the other. Then the arms. It's like being entombed. The material holds her body fast, and she has to make an effort even to move her fingers inside the gloves. Anna knows enough about these suits to be aware that the helmet is integrated – all she has to do is activate it.

There's a control panel on her wrist. Slowly, she moves her other hand around, pushing at the large buttons. A second later, there's a hiss, and the faceplate slides up and over her head, using the rigid arches on the suit's shoulders to guide itself, locking into place with a heavy click. The heads-up display winks to life in front of her. Oxygen, power levels, a thousand other things she can only guess at.

She doesn't hear the cockpit viewport give way. The first she knows about it, she's tumbling out the front of the escape pod, sucked out by the pressure loss, rolling end over end. The fear is potent now, like a toxic gas that she's sucking deep into her lungs with every breath.

A piece of debris heaves into view, a piece of a mechanical arm, and Anna smashes into it before she can stop herself. It knocks her sideways. Fingers fumble at her wrist controls, fat and useless.

With a thud that jars her body inside the suit, Anna comes to a stop. It takes a confused few seconds to understand what happened. She's ended up in one of the top corners of the dock – somehow, she's wedged in it, as if the oxygen pack on the back of her suit is being held by the walls as they join up.

She can see the tug. The heat shield is hanging off the bottom of the vessel. It's a thin sheet, dull gold in colour, wrinkled and malformed. It's been joined to the main body by a series of ugly-looking welds.

The rear ramp of the tug is open, surrounded by space-suited figures. A few of them are looking in her direction, although they're too far away for her to see their faces. She has to get to them. She has to *stop* them.

But how? What exactly is she supposed to do? Drag each one of them out of the tug? It's absurd.

What if she could talk to them? Persuade them not to do it? It's a million-to-one shot, but it's the only one she has. She prods at the wrist control. Seconds tick by before she works out which one turns on the radio – she hesitates half a dozen times, unsure about what each button does.

Static swells in her helmet, and then voices penetrate, coming over the suit radio.

"– anybody see that?" It's Arroway, sounding more panicky than ever.

"Jordan's gone."

"We've got someone else in a suit out here. Who is that?"

And then Dax: "Identify yourself."

Anna can't help it. She screams Dax's name, the sound reverberating inside her helmet. It's only when he doesn't respond, when the chatter continues, that she realises she doesn't have her transmit button activated. It takes her another few seconds to find it.

"Dax," she says, quieter now, but still determined. "Don't do this."

"*Anna?*" he says. "What are you doing out here?"

"I can't let you leave." Her voice is husky, her throat tight with anger.

"I don't—"

The words cut off. She has a horrible moment where she thinks her suit radio has died on her, but then the static returns, fizzing in her ear.

"Say again?" she says.

"I don't see how you're going to stop us."

Arroway cuts in "Dax, maybe we should—"

"No, Anna. You come with us. You've earned that much."

What would Riley do?

Easy. She'd find something. She'd *make* it work.

Anna makes herself stay calm. She lowers her breathing, pushes back against the fear, and starts looking around the dock.

"Anna," Dax says. "Come with us or stay, but we're gone in three minutes."

She sees nothing but debris. Torn metal, bullet casings, strands of broken mag rail. The mechanical arm she smashed into. Bodies, too: frozen, twisted, curled in on themselves. *Keep looking. There's got to be something.*

Anna's eyes track along the far wall of the dock, and come to a sudden halt.

There's no way. It's not possible.

But it is. It's right there, caught on a ceiling support.

The long gun.

Her rifle. The one she used during the siege of the dock. She thought it was lost. She thought she'd never see it again. But there it is. Anna doesn't know if guns work in space, if the gunpowder will even ignite, but she has to try.

Slowly, she brings her wrist control to her face. The moment she pushes the THRUST button, her suit springs to life. She feels pressure in her shoulder blades and at the base of the spine, like she's being punched from multiple angles, and the suit launches forward. The heads-up display changes, displaying a diagram of the suit with six thruster points highlighted. She senses mechanical movement at her stomach, and when she brings her right hand there, she finds a joystick has popped out from the suit's midsection.

"Anna, be reasonable," says Dax. "We're offering you a way out. It's more than anyone else on this station will get."

It takes more than a few false starts to get the hang of it. Anna goes into a spin more than once, aware that she's attracting more attention from the tug, aware that a couple of the suited figures are moving towards her. But she's too far ahead of them, and within a minute she's at the gun. She can pick out the details: the thin black barrel, the fake-wood-grain stock. The scope, perched on top. It's wedged into the wall, at the bottom of the triangle formed by the roof support. She reaches out for it, fingers questing.

Too fast. You're coming in too fast—

Anna slams into the wall, so hard that her head bounces off the back of the helmet. The gun is knocked away, spinning out into the void.

Anna grips the joystick at her stomach, propels herself off the wall. She's running out of time. The rest of Dax's group have given up on her – they're heading back to the tug. If she can't grab that rifle soon, it's over.

She boosts herself towards it. Three yards. Two.

"I'm sorry, Anna." Dax sounds almost regretful.

Her hand touches the barrel. She clenches her fingers, gritting her teeth as her skin scrapes against the inside of the suit glove. But she's got hold of the rifle.

She's still moving, heading towards the gaping mouth of the dock. No time. She turns the rifle round, welding the stock to her shoulder and using her right hand to steady the barrel. She jams the finger of her left hand in the trigger guard. It is a tight fit, almost too tight, and her stomach lurches again when she realises that she didn't even think about that. If she hadn't been able to pull the trigger . . .

The rifle is bolt-action, but the bolt itself is gone, sheared off. She won't be able to load another round.

Sighting down the barrel is impossible. She can't move her head. She's going to have to do this on instinct, trusting her arm to find the aim.

She finds the tug, then the heat shield, glimmering in the light from the sun. Slowly, she brings the gun towards it.

81

Okwembu

Janice Okwembu picks herself up off the floor of the bridge.

As the bullets tore through the walls, she threw herself behind the thick map table, skidding across the floor. There was nothing she could do but put her hands over her ears, and wait for it to be over.

Slowly, she gets to her feet. She's unsteady, her ears ringing. She isn't injured – the table was thick enough and low enough to protect her – but her face and the backs of her hands are scratched and bloody.

The interior of the bridge is a sparking, smoking mess, as if what they saw on the cameras earlier has come through the screens, exploding into life around them. The windows are gone, smashed apart. Part of the roof has collapsed, opening the bridge up to the sky. The banks of screens have disappeared. There's thick, white smoke everywhere, and the wall behind Okwembu is completely shredded.

But not as shredded as the bodies.

Mercifully, most of the men and women on the bridge are dead. But there are still a few moaning in pain, pulling themselves across the floor, their camouflage fatigues stained black with blood. Okwembu sees Prophet, lying face down. His left arm is almost gone, ripped off at the shoulder. As Okwembu watches, his body twitches slightly.

She tells herself to help him. But there's no point – he's dead, whatever she does. Instead, she finds herself stumbling over to the space where the windows used to be, pushing her way past the destroyed screens. A part of her knows she should stay behind cover. Hale might have more bullets, might be waiting for her to show herself.

She ignores the impulse, reaching the gap, looking out across the deck. The Phalanx gun is still shrouded with thick smoke, and several small fires have started among the ruins of the planes.

There's a flash of movement. Okwembu looks down, just in time to see Riley Hale sprinting towards the base of the bridge tower. In an instant, she's gone.

Anger, hot and bright, fills every space in Okwemb's body.

She turns, and almost immediately sees what she's looking for. There's a narrow metal support, up against the wall. It's been blown in half: a four-foot segment has come loose, attached to the bottom part of the support by a tiny shred of metal. It reminds her of Prophet's arm, but she doesn't dwell on the thought.

With a strength she didn't know she had, Okwembu grabs the displaced segment, trying to wrench it loose. But she can't get it free from the strand connecting it to the main body. She casts around, finds another chunk of metal, something hot and misshapen, and hammers it against the support. It snaps free, the metal giving a tortured shriek.

Okwembu discards the debris, then hefts the support, testing its weight. She strides over to the door, positioning herself along the wall to its left, and waits for Riley Hale to walk through.

82

Anna

The long gun's recoil knocks Anna sideways.

There's no sound, but she feels the kick, feels the butt slamming its way past her right side. It sends her spinning again. She fumbles with the joystick, tries to right herself, but every move makes the spin worse.

The wall of the dock rushes towards her. She hits it faceplate first, the heads-up display shuddering and fracturing as the transparent material takes the impact. The material holds, and Anna finds herself moving away from the wall, still turning in that sickening spin. Somehow, she brings herself to a halt. Her fingers are trembling inside the gloves, holding the stick tight, but she's not spinning any more.

Slowly, Anna raises her head and looks for the tug. She doesn't want to know. If she missed, then she won't be able to stop them from leaving.

The tug's heat shield is torn in two.

It may be strong enough to withstand the intense, even heat of re-entry, but the direct, shearing impact of the bullet sliced right through it. The two halves are still rigid, but there's a gaping hole in the crinkly golden material, the edges bending slightly in the vacuum. It's beyond repair – even if they managed to patch the two sides back together, the heat of re-entry would worm its way through.

The tug itself is spinning slightly from the impact, and as the gold heat shield angles towards her, as it picks up the light from the sun, Anna can't help smiling. *Guess guns do work in space, after all.*

The suit's radio is going insane: a dozen confused voices, all clamouring for attention. Dax cuts through them. "What's happening?" he shouts. "We—"

The radio cuts off again, stays silent for a few seconds, then roars back.

"Some sort of impact. I can't see it."

"Hey, Dax," Anna says, keying the transmit button. "How's that heat shield looking?"

She doesn't wait for him to respond. Moving as carefully as she can, she turns herself until she's facing the mouth of the dock, then uses the thrusters to steer herself out. She keeps each burst short, aware that her supplies are limited. Still, it should be enough to get her back to the pod bay.

Dax is swearing at her over the suit radio. She turns it off, almost absentmindedly.

She feels drained. But it's a good feeling. She survived. It didn't matter how young she was – she made the right call. She saved the station, just like Riley did. That's enough.

Anna doesn't know if the people in Dax's group will be able to make it back inside, but there's nothing she can do about that. They don't have a choice – if they don't make it back, they'll die.

She's outside the dock now, moving along the curve of the station. She's gone past most of the debris, gently spinning, letting herself drift. She sees the others start to make their way out of the dock, moving in short bursts, close to the station's hull.

She's drifting too far away. As she activates the thrusters to correct her course, Anna sees the curve of the Earth below her.

She stares for a moment, mesmerised. The planet is brightly lit, the clouds swirling, scraps of brown land only just visible. It looks alien, forbidding. And yet, somehow, it's the most beautiful thing she's ever seen.

Riley is down there. Waiting for her.

Anna makes herself focus. She can see the pod bays now, just dimpling the hull at the point where it starts curving away from her. She angles herself towards it – she's really got the hang of this now. The nausea is still there, but she feels it at a remove, as if it belongs to someone else. There's a readout on her display – a vertical bar, decreasing every time she hits the thrusters. She's still got a third of her fuel left: more than enough to take her right into the pod bay. *Almost home.*

Something smashes into her from behind.

In the half-second available to her, Anna thinks it must be a piece of debris – something she missed. But whatever it is is *holding* her, pulling her tight to itself. She's spinning out of control, the station whirling away from her.

Dax's face slides into view, inches from her own. Behind the transparent helmet, his face is contorted with hate.

83

Riley

The smoke sears the back of my throat, scratching my eyes. It gets thicker the higher I climb, and I have to pull the top of my shirt over my mouth and nose. It's damp and sticky with sweat and dirt, but it's better than nothing.

Most of the lights are dead. There's an alarm blaring, and I can smell fire. A sprinkler springs to life above me, soaking me with a short spray of cold water before sputtering out.

As I get closer to the bridge, I see that part of the stairway has collapsed. There's a gaping hole in the wall, the metal shredded and torn. The Phalanx gun's barrage ripped the stairs away. I allow myself a small smile. *Should have aimed a little more carefully.*

I climb up, hauling myself onto the remaining steps. This time, getting up is harder, the muscles in my right side clenching in pain.

I've come up onto the bridge level in the same corridor that Ray and Iluk used to bring me in. The door to the bridge is firmly shut, although the wall to its right is pocked with bullet holes. I grip the valve lock hard, and wrench it down, pushing the door inwards.

I can barely see a thing. The smoke is a solid white wall, pushing me back. I hold my shirt fabric tight around my mouth, and step inside. The windows of the bridge have been blown away, and daylight is leaking in from the massive holes. Sparks from destroyed electronics shower the floor.

There are bodies everywhere.

They lie sprawled across the floor, collapsed across chairs. Some of them still have their rifles, their fingers locked around the triggers. The floor is a sticky mess of blood and bone fragments. Prophet is there, too. One of the bullets caught him in the shoulder, almost tearing his arm off.

All dead. Because of me.

I should feel something. Remorse, guilt, anything. But I'm done with that. I've felt all of those things before, and they didn't help. They didn't bring the dead back to life. All I've got is an emptiness, like I've given out all the emotion I have, and there's nothing left inside. I just want to do what I came to do, and get out of here.

Movement. Behind me. Janice Okwembu. She has a metal pole, and before I can react, she smashes it into my side.

84

Okwembu

Riley Hale goes down in silence.

Okwembu can see her screaming, howling in pain as she clutches her side. But she can't hear a thing. Even the ringing in her ears has disappeared.

It's the strangest sensation, like she's standing outside herself, watching her body lift the metal support over her head.

In that instant, she doesn't even feel anger. She feels nothing but a quiet satisfaction.

And yet Hale is still alive. She rolls away across the floor, and for an instant Janice Okwembu loses her in the billowing smoke. But only for an instant – Hale is injured, struggling to get to her feet, and in two steps Okwembu is on her. She brings the support down. It's more a diagonal hit than a vertical one, the weight robbing it of momentum. But it still hurts, crushing into the small of Hale's back.

This time, Okwembu does hear her scream.

The girl is writhing on the ground, her legs kicking. She throws an arm out, tries to catch Okwembu in the ankle, misses. Okwembu didn't hit her nearly as hard as she should have –

she was hoping for a crushed vertebra, at the very least. It's a cold, clean, satisfying thought.

Why is she bothering with trying to maim Hale? Why is she waiting? She should have aimed for Hale's head, or better yet, retrieved a rifle from one of Prophet's men. She's not in her right mind, not thinking straight. It's the same mistake Amira Al-Hassan made, when she was under orders to kill the girl. She talked, and stalled, and Hale made her pay for it. Okwembu made the same mistake, months ago, after Hale had destroyed her father's ship. She should have killed her then – no talk, no waiting. Just a bullet in the head.

It's not a mistake she will make again.

Hale is trying to crawl away, her legs useless. Her hair has fallen to one side, leaving the back of her neck exposed. Okwembu watches herself step forward, planting her feet just so, lifting the heavy metal support in a high arc.

85

Riley

I feel the pole coming before it hits.

I don't know if it's a change in air pressure, or the sound of the metal as it plunges downwards. But I know it's coming.

I react, throwing myself to one side, only just managing to get out of the way. I feel the edge of the pole catch my shoulder – it's a glancing blow, but it spasms up into my neck. I can barely feel my legs. My back and side are sending up shocks of frantic, agonised pain.

I get a momentary glimpse of Okwembu through the smoke. She's a mess – her jumpsuit is sweat-stained, torn and ragged, and there's a cut on her face, below her right eye. The blood looks like warpaint.

There's no time to be angry with myself. I can't stop moving. Not for a second. Okwembu brings the pole down again, smashing it into the floor. It's heavy, far too heavy for her to use effectively, but it won't be long before it hits me in a way I won't be able to come back from.

I try to rise, trying to get my legs underneath me. Too late, I realise that I've pushed myself up against a body. I sprawl against it, then have to wrench myself out of the way as Okwembu attacks.

She screams in fury, lifting the pole for another strike. Could I stop it somehow? Grab it as she swings it towards me? No chance – the pole is heavy, almost too heavy for her to hold. If I try and stop it, it'll crush my hands.

I lift my leg, lash out at her. No good. She starts moving sideways – this time, instead of lifting the pole, she lets it drag along the ground behind her, getting ready to line up an over-head strike.

My hands stretch out, hunting for anything I can use. A rifle? I'll still have to aim it, still have to check the safety and bring it around . . .

My fingers close on metal – but not the textured metal of a rifle. It's a fat tube, cool against my hand, familiar somehow. Behind me, I hear Okwembu lift the pole off the floor. I expect her to say something, to laugh, but she's deathly silent. Intent on what she's doing.

I focus on the object in my hand.

The bear spray.

The one Ray took when he frisked me, the one he placed on the table in front of Prophet.

My finger finds the trigger on the top of the canister. Putting every last shred of energy I have into the movement, I twist my body around, and empty the spray into Okwembu's face.

86

Okwembu

At the very last second, Okwembu turns her head sideways.

Not fast enough.

It's like a million needles, driving into her eyes and throat. She howls in pain, her hands flying to her face, dropping the metal support. The needles give way to a rolling wall of fire, stinging and burning, like a blowtorch held to her face.

And yet a part of her mind is still working. Hale might be down, but Okwembu isn't her equal in a fight – and Hale just took away her ability to see. She can feel the pole resting against her foot, but reaching for it would mean taking her hands away from her face, and that's almost too horrible to think about.

Get out. Get out now.

She hates herself for running, for leaving Hale where she is. But she doesn't have a choice, not if she wants to live. She turns and runs, stumbling across the bridge. Something takes her in the knee, the edge of a bank of screens, and she almost falls. The pain has got even worse – her throat is swelling up, her nose clogged. Every breath feels like she's forcing it through layers of gauze.

410

Her foot knocks into a body, and this time she does fall, sprawling across the floor. To get to her feet, she has to take her hands away from her eyes – it's the only way. When she does, the needles come back, hammering through her skull directly into her brain. The pain blots out all other thoughts. She's reduced to a simple set of instructions. *Go. Run. Move.*

Tears are streaming down her cheeks, and the world doubles and triples as she looks at it. She is at the opposite side of the bridge to where she first waited for Hale, coming up on one of the locked doors. She reaches for it, manages to get her hands around the valve lock, turns it with every ounce of strength she can muster. She's coughing now, each breath shredding her chest.

But then she's through, stumbling down the passage, moving with no thought but to get as far away as possible. A set of stairs appears in front of her, and she comes very close to falling right over the edge. She stops herself, gripping the railings, swaying in place.

One step. Two. Her throat still burning, but opening up a little more now, yes, she can feel it . . .

There's a distant thud, like a mountain collapsing on the horizon, felt more than heard. Okwembu barely notices it until the ship lurches sideways, tilting down at a crazy angle. She cries out as she loses her balance, throwing out her hands. The stairs rush up towards her, doubled by the tears in her eyes. When she hits them, it feels like the end of the world.

87

Riley

The ship starts to tilt.

At first, I think it's the smoke messing with my head. But I heard the bang, felt it rumble up from below me. Something deep in the ship has detonated.

I let the bear spray fall from my hand, and it rolls away across the floor. My eyes are streaming, itchy and sore, but I only caught a little of the spray. I have to get after Okwembu. I didn't come this far, go through this much, to let her escape.

I try to get up. I make it all the way to one knee before the world starts shaking in front of me. I list sideways, unable to stop myself, then topple to the floor.

I could lie here for a while. Just close my eyes and just drift away. Everything hurts. My back, my shoulders, my throat, the palms of my hands. Smoke forces stinging tears out of my eyes.

Get up, says the voice. But it's coming from a very long way away. I want to listen to it, want more than anything else in the world, but I'm drifting off into a warm darkness where it doesn't seem important at all.

"Riley, get up."

I'm imagining the voice. I have to be. It sounds like Carver. But I know he isn't here. He's with Prakesh.

There's a pressure on my chest. I try to ignore it, but it doesn't go away.

"Riley!"

My eyes open. The deck is tilting so much I can barely stay in one place. Objects and bodies are sliding everywhere, clattering to the floor and rolling away.

And Carver is there.

He doesn't give me a choice about getting up. The second he sees I'm awake, he hauls me to my feet, pulling me into an embrace. I get the same feeling as before, when I first saw him in the generator room. A massive wave of relief and joy and fear, all blended into one.

"How did you find me?" I say. My voice sounds like it's coming from someone else's throat.

"Easy. I just followed the screams and explosions. Led me right to you."

He's a mess, bloody and sweat-soaked. We both are. "What the hell did you do?" he says as we pull apart.

"Long story. Prakesh – Carver, is he—"

He nods. "Last I checked. He'll be fine."

His eyes say otherwise. I want to push him, make him tell me more, but there isn't time. As much as I desperately want to, I can't go after Okwembu – not if we want to make it out of here alive.

"We have to get off the ship," I say. "Right now."

He shakes his head. "No."

"Carver, there's got to be a way. We'll just jump off the side if we have—"

"No, I mean, we can't get off the ship. We have to stop it from sinking."

"*What?*"

"The fuel supplies have gone up. Prakesh's friends did it. And my guess is there's a big-ass hole in the side of the ship. If we can seal the bulkhead doors from the bridge—"

"What are you talking about?" It takes everything I have not to bolt, right then and there. He's gone insane.

"You don't understand," Carver says, his eyes wide. "If this ship goes down, the Earth goes down with it."

The deck beneath me gives a sudden shudder, nearly knocking me off my feet. I have to hold onto the bank of controls, my shredded palms screaming in pain.

"You have to trust me," says Carver. "Normally I wouldn't say this, but there's *really* not enough time to explain it all."

He looks around. "Is there a control for the ship bulkheads here?"

The world swims in front of me. "Bulkheads?"

"They're doors that seal sections of the ship off in case of a leak. They're supposed to work automatically, but my guess is that isn't happening. You should be able to operate them from here."

I look around the destroyed bridge. It's hopeless. Most of the electronics here are completely destroyed, riddled with bullet holes. Even if we could figure out which one of these dozens of screens operates the bulkhead doors, there's no guarantee it would still be working.

Carver sees it, too. "Ah, shit," he says. "OK. We'll need to do it manually. On-site. It's the only way."

"How would we even know which doors to close?" The floor gives another sickening lurch, and I have to scramble to stay where I am, planting my feet. My body is in agony.

"Door 6 on C deck should do the trick. It should be above the waterline, and it'll seal the compartments below it. That should stop the ship from sinking. Any further along and there'll be too many compartments flooded to hold the ship up."

He sees my expression. "Riley, we have to do this."

I don't want to go down there. I want to get off this ship. I'm tired of running. Every muscle in my body is screaming for rest. I want to be with my friends, and get far away from here, and only stop when I'm in a place that is safe. I just want it all to be over.

And why shouldn't I want that? How much have I sacrificed so that other people could live? I've lost so many friends. I sacrificed my own *father* so that Outer Earth could carry on. And all it brought me was more pain.

When my dad was on a collision course out of Earth, ready to drive his ship into us, to tear the station apart, I told him he had a choice. He could give me the override code that would let me destroy his ship, or he could kill me. He made his choice. And I can make mine. I don't have to suffer any more. I can say no. I can let someone else do it.

"Ry?" Carver says. "I can't do it alone. We don't know if anyone's still down there, and if I get taken out . . . Please tell me you understand what I'm saying."

I don't. Not even a little bit. I don't understand why I have to do this.

But I also know that Carver would never lie to me. Not ever. He wouldn't ask me to do this if there was another option. If he says that this ship is the key to humanity's survival, if he says he's sure, then I have to believe him.

"Is this really the only way?" I say.

He nods.

I take a deep breath. "Then let's go."

88

Anna

Dax's mouth is moving, but the radio link is inactive. Anna can't hear the words. They're spinning out of control, away from the station, and it's all happening in complete silence. There should be noise, shouts, raw anger. Instead, there's nothing.

Dax puts a hand on her faceplate, as if he can grab it in his fingers and tear it off her head. She reaches up to push him off, but he's too strong, elbowing her arm out of the way. The fear is back, digging its claws into her shoulders. Nausea comes with it, accented by the end-over-end spin.

Her thrust meter has started to blink red. She's got a little under a third left, but if she doesn't get free soon, she might not have enough to make it home.

The Earth and the station spin around them, as if she and Dax are the centre of the universe. With a terrified cry, Anna tries to push him away, planting a gloved hand directly on his chest. But it's like her dream – the movement feels slow and soft, and she's barely able to get enough force into her arms.

Dax doesn't seem to be aware of what he's doing. His face is barely human now, his helmet misting up with his breath. He's still shouting, and she can't hear a thing. She raises her knees, trying to get between them.

The spin intensifies, each movement adding to their momentum. And – *oh gods* – Dax has activated his suit's plasma cutter. It's sparking from his wrist, firing in short bursts, blinding her. Any second now, he's going to slice a hole right through her suit.

The sight shocks her into action. Anna pulls her leg up and kicks it out towards Dax's mid-section.

It's just enough. They fly apart, and the plasma cutter misses her by six inches. She grabs the joystick, firing her thrusters to get even further away from him. She burns through almost half her remaining fuel before she manages to raise her finger off the thruster control.

Outer Earth is behind her. With a little luck, she can coast right towards on it on her current momentum. She'll do it backwards, keeping an eye on Dax. If he tries to make another run at her, she'll be ready.

Dax has managed to stabilise himself, but, as she watches, the exhaust from his thruster ports changes. It's thinner now, less substantial, as if . . .

She switches her radio back on. Dax's voice comes through immediately. "– anybody hear me? I've got no fuel!"

"Negative." It's one of the others – Anna can just see them in her peripheral vision, still drifting along the curve of the station. "We're too far away."

"No!" Dax shouts, and this time fear creeps into his voice. "You can't leave me here."

Anna keys her transmit button. "Dax."

He reaches his hands out towards her, as if beseeching her. "Anna. Help me!" He's gripping his own joystick, squeezing the controls, but his thruster fuel is completely exhausted.

She should turn and leave. He doesn't deserve to live.

But he doesn't deserve to die either. Not like this. Not even after he nearly killed them both.

The others are too far away. There's nobody else but her.

Anna closes her eyes, then thumbs her own thruster control. The meter is blinking faster now, down to its last eighth. She uses the thrust in short bursts, aware that she's going to have to time this *very* carefully.

"Thank gods," says Dax, whimpering. "Thank gods."

Anna is fifty feet away. "Burn off your plasma cutter," she says.

"What?"

"*Do it.* Or I turn around and go home."

"It's already gone. It uses the same fuel as the thrusters do . . ."

"Show me."

"OK." He thumbs his wrist control pad. The cutter flame briefly springs to life, then shrinks and dies, the very last of his fuel burning off.

Anna corrects her course slightly, prompting her meter to blink even faster. If she hits Dax too hard, she'll send them both into a spin. They'll have to use another thruster boost to correct their course, and she doesn't have any fuel to spare.

She's coming in from above him. "Grab my legs," she says. She slows herself down as she reaches him, and he manages to get his fingers around her ankles. They start spinning, but it's a gentle spin, and Anna knows she can compensate for it.

Dax is sobbing now. Anna suppresses the urge to shout at him, concentrating on her movement, using incremental thruster bursts to turn them around. A warning flashes up in her helmet. THRUST FUEL CRITICAL.

No shit, she thinks. With a push on the stick, she sends them moving back towards the station.

They're two hundred feet away. Anna can't see the others, but she can see the escape pod airlocks, like little black pockmarks in the station's surface.

They need to head for the airlocks, but when Anna tries to correct for it, her thrust meter vanishes completely. Another set of words appears on her heads-up.

THRUST DEPLETED.

Anna keys her transmit button, doing everything she can to fight the panic rippling through her. "We're out."

Dax gives a long, horrified moan. Anna can't take her eyes off Outer Earth. On their current course, they're not going to get anywhere near the hull. They'll sweep right over the curve of the station, and then past it, out into space.

"Anna!" It's Arroway, loud and clear over the suit radio. "I can—"

And then her radio dies again.

Anna can hear nothing but her breathing and heartbeat – both too fast, both impossibly loud inside the helmet. Another meter has started flashing – her O2. She's burning through it too fast, just like the thruster fuel.

No. Please, no.

She's trying to look around, but all she can see is the station hull, stretching below her. A hundred feet away, but it may as well be a million.

And then another space-suited figure collides with them, roaring in from below, grabbing her around the waist. The figure's thrusters are firing, quick bursts, left and right, stabilising them.

There's a burst of static, and then Arroway says, "Got you!"

89

Okwembu

The corridor itself is tilting, sliding to one side, like the world itself has gone wrong. Okwembu forces herself to keep moving, leaning on the wall. She's still coughing, and her nose is still plugged and sore, but her eyes have stopped streaming.

The ship is going down. Okwembu knows this, knows it in her bones, and it's all she can do not to start slamming her fists into the corridor wall.

The light changes. She looks up – without realising it, she's come out onto one of the loading platforms in the side of the ship. There are a few discarded crates and tarpaulins, piled in one corner. Daylight is streaming through the opening, and she can see the ocean stretching beyond.

And there's a boat, hanging on the wall.

It's barely worthy of the name – a tiny dinghy, its tubes flat and deflated. The bottom of the boat is punctured in several places, and the whole thing looks like it's about to fall apart.

Okwembu stumbles to the drop. Her legs are starting to ache from the effort of staying upright on the tilted floor. She slows as she approaches, wanting to recoil from the edge.

But where else is she going to go?

She could try and find another dock, but the chances are that the boats will be gone, taken by the escaped workers. There's no point finding somewhere to hide – whatever just happened, the *Ramona* is sinking, and fast. What about Hale? Could she go back and finish what she started? She shakes her head, the frustration bitter in her mouth. There's no way she'd get the drop on the girl again.

She leans out over the edge, then immediately pulls back. It's thirty feet to the ocean below, right into the slate-grey water. Okwembu can't help but think of when their escape pod smashed into Eklutna Lake – how cold the water was, how it felt like it was draining her strength.

She'll have to take the boat. With its tube walls deflated, there's a chance it might not stay afloat, but it's the only chance she's got.

The ship lurches underneath her, almost knocking her off her feet, and Janice Okwembu raises her head to the ceiling and roars.

The sound trails off, and she stands there, silent, her shoulders rising and falling.

She stumbles to the wall. It takes almost all her strength to lift the boat off its storage hooks and drag it to the edge. She pushes it over, and it smashes into the water, bobbing in the swell and bumping up against the hull.

Okwembu takes one last look over her shoulder. *It's not too late. I could go back, find Hale.*

The thought barely has a chance to form, and then she steps off the edge. She screams all the way down.

90

Riley

The ship has turned into a nightmare.

When I ran through it, after Prakesh was shot, the corridors felt like the ones on Outer Earth. I could navigate them, move through them at high speed. No chance of that now. Every corridor is tilting at a crazy angle, and anything not strapped down has piled itself up along the bottom. Doors that weren't locked shut hang open, creating low-hanging obstacles that we have to duck under. Fire alarms have activated across the ship. Most of the sprinkler systems aren't working, but a few are, and soon I'm drenched in chemical spray.

I don't know how I'm still moving. Somehow, I've managed to access one last reservoir of energy. I'm in agony: the worst of it, even worse than the insistent pain in my side and upper back, is at the bottom of my spine. The place where Okwembu hit me. Every single movement sends bolts of electricity shooting out from it.

The corridors are all but deserted. Once, rounding a corner, Carver and I see people in the distance, sprinting away from us. I can't tell if they're guards or workers. It doesn't matter. I don't dare stop moving, not even for a second.

The stairs have tilted along with the corridors, showing off their own weird geometry. We have to slow down at every stairwell, use the railings on the side of the stairs, take them in a weird bow-legged gate. I'm coming up on the stairway between B deck and C deck, getting ready to take it, picking my footholds.

It's hard going. Halfway down, my fingers come loose from a handhold. I let myself fall, knowing I'm only a few feet up, but it doesn't stop me gasping when I hit the water rushing through the C deck corridor.

Everything below my knees soaks right through. The water is a churning mass of dirt and debris, so cold that I gasp. Running isn't even a possibility now. Carver drops down behind me, and we start wading, the water sloshing up our legs.

I try to be as careful as I can – I can't afford to fall. I do that, and the cold will sap what little energy I have left. But as we reach the junction, I realise that the water is getting higher. It's snuck up over my knees to mid-thigh. Soon, it'll be at my waist, then my chest.

The lights are starting to fail. The bulbs in the ceiling are flickering, casting strange shadows across the walls. A door flies open as I walk past it, nearly smacking me in the face. I dodge back, knocking my elbow on the wall of the passage as a spew of debris splashes into the water. I take a deep breath, then keep going.

It's impossible to miss the bulkhead doors. They're larger than the others, built more solidly. They drop down from the ceiling – I can just see the edge of the door below the roof, marked with more yellow and black chevrons. There's a lever, flat against the wall. A big steel rod half my height, with a rubber grip at the top, ready to be pulled down and outwards. There's an identical one on the other side of the door.

I don't know how many compartments have flooded already. If too much water gets through too many compartments, the ship won't be able to stay afloat. We have to seal this door, or it all goes down. And if Carver is right, then whatever is keeping this part of the planet alive goes down with it.

The water's at my waist now. I step in behind Carver, gripping the lever with my hands just underneath his. Then we summon every last bit of strength we have left, and pull.

Nothing happens. The lever doesn't move an inch.

I try not to think of the words *rusted* and *seized*. I don't let myself dwell on the possibilities. We try again, putting all our weight into pulling the lever back. As we do so, it moves, just a little, and I let out a cry of triumph.

My hands are wet – wet enough to slip free of the rubber grip, and I fall backwards into the water. My clothes protect me for no more than an instant. I'm fully submerged, shocked into immobility by the cold. I feel Carver's hand brushing my shoulder, and then he pulls me upright.

I splash over to the lever again, shivering, furious with myself. This time, I can't get a good grip. My wet, numb hands can't hold onto it. Carver steps in front of me, motions me off. He pulls the lever back, the muscles in his neck standing out like thick cords. "Come on!" he shouts.

It's working. It's working! I can see the lever starting to move. Any second now, it's going to go all the way. We can shut this door, then get the hell off this ship.

A gunshot echoes down the corridor, the bullet ripping past us.

I look round, and that's when I see a ghost.

Prophet.

He's wading down the corridor. White teeth gleam on his

blood-soaked face. His left shoulder is in tatters, his arm hanging on by a shred of skin and muscle.

If I'm in bad shape, he's worse. I don't even know how it's possible for him to have followed us down here. Then I remember Oren Darnell. His mid-section was crushed in a massive door, his organs turned to pulp, but he kept on coming. He wouldn't let himself die.

Prophet's the same. He isn't going to be alive for much longer, but whatever energy is fuelling him, it hasn't run out yet. He must have overheard us on the bridge, talking about what we were going do.

He raises his pistol, fires again, the bullet slicing the water a few feet from us. There's only one spot of available cover: the bulkhead doorframe. We swing ourselves around it, pressing up against the wall on the other side. Prophet takes another shot, and it ricochets off the frame.

The water is above my waist now. Despite the cold, despite the soaked clothes against my skin, I feel sweat break out across my forehead. We've got nowhere to go. All he has to do is come a little closer, and he'll have a point-blank shot.

The lever. The one on this side of the door. It's right between us.

"Help me with this," I say, wrapping my hands around the top of the lever, keeping my body as flat against the wall as I can. Prophet has stopped shooting. Smart. He's saving his shots, waiting until he gets closer.

"No," says Carver. "You'll trap us inside."

"You got a better idea?"

Carver groans in frustration, then leans over and wraps his hands around the lever. We're on either side of it, and we're going to have to pull it outwards for this to work.

"OK!" I shout, and we both lean into it, trying to force the lever away from the wall. But it's exactly like the one on the other side. It barely moves, budging only a fraction, and we don't have enough leverage to push it out from our position. We can't lean out – that would mean exposing ourselves in the doorway.

Prophet is getting closer, wading down the passage towards us. It might be my imagination, but I swear I can hear him breathing, harsh and ragged.

Carver lets go of the lever. "No dice. We're going to have to lean out."

Inspiration hits. "We both do it in one move, OK?"

Carver shakes his head. But he too reseats his grip, tensing his shoulders, bracing himself against the wall. He knows we don't have a choice.

"The Engine will have its revenge!" Prophet shouts. He doesn't sound human.

Carver and I throw ourselves forwards, moving in unison, pulling the lever out and down as hard as we can.

91

Riley

The lever gives an agonising squeal, and jerks down. Carver and I fall backwards into the icy water.

There's a split second where I get a good look at Prophet. He's almost done, barely able to keep himself upright. His eyes find mine. He might be chest-deep in freezing water, but the hatred in those eyes is hotter than the surface of the sun.

Then the bulkhead door drops, slamming into the passage with a giant boom, sending a wave of water slapping against my face.

"Can he get through?" says Carver. He puts his feet on the bottom, doing his best to hold his arms above the water. Not that it matters. We're both soaked.

I don't think so," I say. I'm slurring my words. "If it took two of us to work that lever, there's no way he's doing it on his own."

We may have saved the ship, but we're trapped. The realisation is starting to sink in. I'm already looking around the corridor, hunting for an exit. This side of the door, the water is still climbing fast. The corridor tilts away from us, the water lapping at the ceiling a few yards away.

Could we wait it out? Wait for Prophet to die, and then open the door? Carver sees where I'm looking. "There's no way we're getting that door open again," he says.

I wade over to him, trying to keep my arms above the water. It's a struggle to get the words out. "So we swim out of here."

"You're crazy."

"There's a hole from the explosion, right? We make our way along the passage, and we find it."

He laughs, shaking his head. "Oh, man. Oh, shit."

I can see the terror on his face, and feel it in my heart. Everything below our chests is frozen, and there's no telling how long we'll last if we're completely submerged. Even if we make it out, we'll be a mile from shore, floating in open water.

"All right," he says, steeling himself. "Here we go." He takes two quick breaths, his hand finding mine. We'll go under together.

"Wait," I say.

"There's no time."

"I have to say this."

And I do. I should have said it a long time ago. I've known it ever since I kissed Carver, back on Outer Earth. I've tried to tell myself that I wanted to be with Prakesh, that it would be wrong *not* to be with him, after everything we've been through.

But I've been through just as much with Carver. He understands me in a way Prakesh couldn't. I've tried to ignore it, tried to run from it, but that doesn't stop it being true. Prakesh is one of the best men I know, but Carver is the one who's always been there for me. He's never let me down.

And I knew this, even before we came down here to try and save the ship. I knew it back on the bridge, when he was telling me about the bulkhead doors. He didn't need me – I could have let him do it himself. He's just as capable as I am.

But that would have meant letting him go. It would have meant being apart from him. And I'm not going to let that happen again. Not ever.

I look into his eyes. "You remember back on the *Shinso*? I told you I still loved Prakesh? You asked me who you had left."

"Riley, I don't—"

"I was wrong, Aaron," I say, barely able to get the words out. "I love you. You have me, and you'll always have me."

It doesn't matter that *always* may only be a few minutes more. It's the truth. No one should ever have to make this choice, but, right now, in the depths of this ship, I'm glad I've made mine.

I don't give him a chance to answer. I wrap my arms around him, and pull him close. Our lips touch, but we're shivering so badly that we can't hold the kiss.

He's got that weird smile on his face, like he can't quite believe what's happening. He runs a finger along my cheek, then leans close, his forehead against mine.

And in that moment, it's as if the water isn't even there. There's nothing but us.

I try to hold it for as long as I can. But the water is almost at our necks. Carver kisses me once more, then says, "Let's get out of here."

I nod. "Yeah."

He holds me tight. "On zero," he says. "Three. Two. One."

"Zero," I whisper, and we sink below the surface of the water.

92

Riley

The cold is everywhere. It's not like ice – it's like fire, scorching me, making my skin bubble and spit.

I feel Carver push away from me, and force my eyes to open. There's still some light from the bulbs above the water, and it's filtering down around us. I can just make out the walls of the passage. Debris floats in front of me, swirling in the current.

I don't know how long I have before the cold sucks my life away. I don't care. I push myself through the water, pumping my arms and legs, not sure if I'm doing right, not caring. I can feel Carver alongside me. I look down, and see that he's using the ribbed metal on the walls to pull himself along. I try the same trick, and find that my fingertips are completely numb.

Globs of fuel float in the water, and I manage to get one of them in my eyes. It forces me to squeeze them closed, blocking out the sting. When I open them, I've lost Carver.

My lungs are already tight, but panic crushes them. I spin in place, hunting for him, but there's hardly any light now. I'm in a black pit, and if I don't get moving again, I'm going to run out of air long before I die from cold.

430

There he is, just below me, beckoning me on. I thrash my arms – they feel like they've got lead weights tied to them. It's hard to remember what I'm doing. I can't keep my thoughts straight. I find myself thinking of Outer Earth, of the hab Prakesh and I shared. A moment later, I remember my father, right before he went on the Earth Return mission. Why am I thinking of him? I don't want to think at all. I just want to sleep. I close my eyes, just for a second, but that second stretches out into eternity.

Carver is pointing at something. A part of the corridor wall, darker than the rest. A hole. Why is there a hole? It'll let the water in.

Carver grabs me. His grip is incredibly tight. I want to shake him off, but he's insistent, refusing to let go.

His grip makes me focus. I snap back to life, thrashing in the water, then thrust myself towards the hole. There's debris in front of me, floating metal, and I almost scream as I push it out of the way. My lungs are roaring in pain.

There's nothing but darkness beyond the hole. It's as if we're swimming out into deep space.

I push and push and push, but I don't seem to be getting anywhere. It feels as if my lungs are going to pop. There's a crushing weight in my head, pulling everything down with it.

I swear I feel Carver take my hand, but I'm so numb that I can't tell if he's there or not.

93

Riley

Fragments.

Each one is as sharp as a piece of broken glass, lancing into my mind. They only last a moment before vanishing, leaving no trace. No memory. Nothing.

Carver is in front of me in the water. I can just make out his shape, see his arms and legs moving, his hand reaching out for me.

The sky above us, the grey clouds hanging low. *Air.* Searing my lungs, burning a million time worse than the cold water.

The ocean. How could there be this much water in one place? It's unimaginable. Made up. It's a dream I'm having, and any second now it'll be gone.

Something looming up from the water in front of us. The seaplane. Harlan reaching down from it, reaching towards me. How is it here? How did it know how to find us?

I'm half in, half out of the plane. Harlan has me under the arms, and Carver is pushing me from below.

We're moving over the surface of the water, high above it. I can see the ship, dropping away behind us. And then we're on the ground, surrounded by people. Hands and faces everywhere. Harlan is there, and Eric, but I can't see Prakesh, or Carver. I want to find them so badly. But even keeping my eyes open is beyond me. It's like trying to hold the entire world across my shoulders. I let my head drop, close my eyes.

When I come back, there's something wrapped around me. A blanket, or a coat. It doesn't seem to matter. It's thick and warm, slightly scratchy against my cheek.

"Give her some water."

There's a pressure, under my head. A hand lifts me up, and another one brings the lip of a water canteen to my mouth. The water is tepid, slightly salty, but I drink and drink.

The canteen slips away. I want to tell whoever is holding it to keep it there, but at that moment pins and needles explode across my body. My muscles clench involuntarily, and that just makes it worse.

The pressure on me increases. It's someone lying on top of me.

"Stay still," Eric whispers in my ear, as he squeezes me tight, giving me as much heat as possible.

It's some time before I open my eyes again. Eric is gone. I'm wrapped in a thick, dark brown coat, curled up on the damp ground. My wet clothes have been removed – I've still got my underwear, but that's all. I'm shivering uncontrollably, my teeth clacking together.

There are people everywhere. Workers from the ship. There are dozens of them – they're ragged and worn out, but it's impossible not to see the relief on their faces. They're moving in small groups, shouting orders, marshalling supplies: food and blankets and containers of fuel.

The shore itself is made up of black dirt and jagged rocks. The seaplane floats in the water, a few yards away. There are the strangest things piercing the surface of the sea, and it takes me a minute to realise that they're buildings. Or what used to be buildings, anyway. The hulking *Ramona* is beyond them, a distant black shape.

"Hey."

It's Harlan, crouching down next to me.

I stare at him for the longest time. Then I crawl over, doing my best to keep the coat on my shoulders, and wrap my arms around him. I can't stop shaking.

"How?" I say. It's all I can manage.

He looks perplexed, but then his eyes light up. "Oh, the plane? We got hit, but not nearly as bad as we thought. Eric put her down upriver, up on the Knik Arm. Nearly went into the drink. He bossed me around some when we tried to fix her, but we got the bird up in the air again, no sweat. Eric always was good at that kind of shit. I told you how he read all those books, right? When we were kids?"

"You came back." The words are coming a little more easily now.

He looks guilty. "Almost didn't. We thought you and Finkler were done. But then we took off, and saw that gun tearing up the bridge on the ship. That's . . . kind of not what we expected to see, so we thought we should get a closer look. And then we saw you running across the deck like your feet were on fire."

It takes me a minute to process his words. I'm still doing it when the memory of what happened to Prakesh broadsides me.

I look round, and this time I find him almost immediately. He's lying on his back, one arm flung out to the side. His face is so pale, his dark walnut skin gone bloodless. There are people on their knees around him, bent over him, and there's too much blood. *Way* too much blood.

I can't describe the sound I make. It's halfway between a moan and a scream. A memory surfaces: Prakesh, kidnapped by Oren Darnell, sprawled out on the floor of a disused storage facility off the Outer Earth monorail tracks. I was in the ventilation system in the ceiling, looking through a gap in the panels. But the panic I felt then is like a cup of water, and what I feel now is an ocean, stretching out in front of me to an endless horizon.

I don't remember getting up. The coat falls from my shoulders, leaving me almost naked, sprinting across the shore. Sharp rocks dig into my feet, slowing me down.

Eric materialises at my elbow, his strong hands falling on my shoulders. I have to make myself pay attention to what he's saying.

"You need to stay warm," he says. "Get back there, wrap yourself up."

I try to push past him, but I'm not strong enough, and he holds me in place.

"We think he'll be OK," Eric says. "One of the people off that ship has some medical training."

He indicates a grey-haired man, his blood-soaked hands pressing down on Prakesh's chest. "Right now, infection is the big worry. We've got supplies in Whitehorse, so we'll get him back there."

I look back at Prakesh, at his blood soaking into the sand. Frustration and helplessness boil inside me, and I try to push past Eric again.

"No," Eric says, blocking me with an arm across my chest. "You'll just be in the way. Let them work."

I can see the *Ramona* in the distance, over his shoulder. The ship is a black, smoking hulk, squatting on the horizon like a bad dream. But it's still there. We saved it. Carver and I.

Carver. I swing my head around, so suddenly that the muscles in my neck creak, sending a fresh wave of pins and needles down my back.

"The man I was with," I say. My throat is parched again, and I swallow, sending razor blades dancing across it. "Where is he?"

Eric says nothing.

"Eric?" I say.

But then I catch sight of something over his shoulder.

A tarpaulin, spread out across the filthy sand. There's a shape underneath it. A person, lying on their back.

I shake my head. "No."

"He pushed you out of the water," Eric says.

"No."

"You were unconscious, and he was still swimming, and he made sure you were in the plane first. Riley, he was already hypothermic—"

"*No.*"

I'm running. Sprinting across the sand. I'm going to tear that tarpaulin off him, shake him, wake him up. He's not dying on me. Not after he came back. Not after I told him that I'd made my choice. Not happening. No way. I won't let it.

But when I get there, my hands have stopped listening to me. The damp tarpaulin is too heavy, and I can't move it. I try to grip the edge, but my fingers keep slipping. And then Eric has his arms around me and I'm trying to get away but I can't, and all I can hear are my screams.

94

Anna

Anna wraps the blanket tighter around herself. It's all the way up to her chin, tucked in around her crossed legs, but she can't stop shivering. She's lost her beanie – she can't even remember it coming off her head. She feels naked without it.

The family's hab is the only quiet space they could find – the only space where a thousand people weren't trying to talk to her, where she wasn't getting bombarded by a million questions on all sides. The door is shut, but she can still hear voices from the corridor. She tries to tune them out, closing her eyes. She knows she won't sleep – she's way too wired for that – but it helps.

Dax and Arroway and the rest of their group are in the sector brig. They all came back into the escape pod airlocks, every one of them – it was either that, or drift in space for the rest of time. Anna doesn't know what'll happen to them. Dax was sobbing when they pulled him out of his suit. He tried to reach for her, but she got away as quickly as she could, not wanting to look at him, at *any* of them.

She made it almost ten steps before collapsing.

The door to the hab slides open. Voices snap into focus. "If we could just see her—"

"*No.*" Frank Beck's voice is thunderous. "She's been through enough. Get out of here."

He doesn't give them a chance to answer – just slams the door shut. Then he stands there for a moment, his shoulders heaving.

Anna slides off the bed, letting the blanket fall to her feet. Cold air pricks the skin on her arms, but she barely notices. She walks over to her dad, wraps her arms around him and pulls him close.

They hold each other for a long moment. "What were you thinking?" Frank says, his voice muffled by her hair.

"I—"

He pulls apart from her, thrusting her to arm's length. "*What were you thinking?*" he bellows into her face, then almost immediately pulls her back into a hug. It's such an absurd, theatrical performance that she wants to call him out on it, make a joke, say something clever. It's his shoulders that stop her. They're trembling, and she feels tears staining her scalp.

So she says nothing. She just holds him.

Eventually, her father gives her a squeeze and they pull apart. He wipes his face, not looking at her, and sits down heavily on the bed. Anna grabs the discarded blanket on the floor, and sits next to him, cross-legged, wrapping it around her legs.

"I'm sorry," she whispers.

He actually laughs – or tries to. "Are you, now?"

"Dad, come on."

He drops his head. "I know."

It's then that she realises she never told him about Riley. About the radio conversation. She does so, and the more she talks, the wider his eyes get.

"Anna, that's . . ." he leaps up off the bed, pacing the floor. "That's *brilliant*. And they told you where to come down?"

She nods.

"Brilliant," he says again. "I've got to tell everyone. We've got to tell the crew on the *Tenshi*."

He's moving towards the door when Anna says, "What's going to happen?"

"Hmmm?" He looks over his shoulder at her.

"To – you know, to Dax and the rest of them?"

"Oh," her father says, as if it's an irrelevance. "We don't know yet."

"Are they going to be taken out of the lottery?" It's the only outcome she can think of. How could they let any of them have a place on the *Tenshi Maru*?

Her father comes to a halt, staring at the door. After a moment, he makes his way back to the bed, sitting down next to her.

He sighs. "I don't think they should."

"*What?*"

"So do a few others. They'll have to stay in the brig, to be sure, but—"

She shakes her head. "They were going to leave us here. They were going to take the space suits and *leave us*."

"Well—"

"No. Dad, you can't be thinking about letting them go."

He puts a hand on her knee, and she subsides.

"They thought they were better than us," her father says. "That's the whole reason they went in the first place, wasn't it?"

"Yeah . . ."

"So what better punishment than making them exactly the same as everyone else? By making them take the lottery just like all of us here?"

She opens her mouth to reply – and finds she has nothing.

That's when the full realisation hits her. There's still going to be a lottery. There's still going to be some who go, and some who get left behind. Nothing she did – working out what Dax was planning, contacting Riley, the insane trip through space – none of it changes that. She's not going to be able to save her family, or Ravi and Achala Kumar, or Ivy, or Marcus, or anybody else. It's all going to be left to chance.

And that's the worst thing of all. Because it's only way to do it.

She reaches over and pulls her dad into a fierce hug. She buries her face in his shoulder, and this time it's her turn to cry.

"It's going to be OK," he says, holding her tight.

Anna wants to believe him. But she's not sure that she can.

95

Riley

I sit on the beach for a long time, staring out at the water.

Someone found me clothes. A threadbare collared shirt made of a stiff, blue material. Black pants. There's even a pair of shoes, scabbed with dirt. The clothes come from someone much larger than me. I don't know who they belong to, but at least they're dry.

I'm dimly aware of the activity on the beach. Harlan is arguing with Eric, saying that they need to bring the workers with them. Eric is saying that they'll never fit them all in the plane, and Harlan responds by telling him that they'll make multiple trips if they have to. He sounds almost jubilant – not surprising. He survived Anchorage.

The workers are talking in a big group. One of them protests loudly, saying that they should retake the ship, that all the guards are dead.

I let it wash over me. I don't know what's going to happen next. It's too big a task, too many people to find homes for, too many loose ends to tie up. I can't even do anything for Prakesh – he's stable now, but unconscious, bundled up inside the plane and being tended to by the man with the grey hair. So I just sit.

It's all I can do.

Someone crouches down next to me. Koji. There's dried blood on his face, crusted under his right eye. His hair hangs in lanky strands on his face, and his overalls are patchy with seawater.

"I can go," he says, "if you'd rather be alone."

I shake my head. I feel like I should want to be by myself right now, but I find I don't care very much.

Koji sits cross-legged on the sand, wincing as he does so. "They don't like me very much," he says, nodding to a group of workers. One of them scowls back at him. "I was hoping you could tell them . . . I mean, if . . ."

He trails off, looking embarrassed.

"I think I'd like to hear that story now," I say.

"Story?"

"About my dad."

Koji looks out at the horizon. He's silent for so long that I'm on the verge of prompting him, and then he says, "The *Akua Maru* didn't make it through the atmosphere. There was . . . an explosion. Something in the reactor went wrong."

"I know," I say.

Koji continues as if I hadn't spoken. "There's no way we should have made it down. We were going thousands of miles an hour. But your dad did it. He pulled it off. Two of us died during the descent, but there were still eight of us who made it down."

He looks at me. "Your dad saved my life."

"What happened? After you landed?"

He shrugs. "The ship was a wreck. Fusion reactor was still intact, just about, but it wasn't working. Everything else was done for. And Kamchatka . . . we couldn't have come down in

442

a worse area. It was *cold*. Cold enough to freeze your bones inside you."

He attempts a smile. "Your dad kept us going. He organised us. He made sure we got enough to eat, that we stayed warm enough. We wouldn't have lasted a week without him."

When I speak, my voice is as brittle as thin glass. "But you came here."

He continues as if I hadn't spoken. "Your dad was a hero, but he wasn't a miracle worker. We were running out of supplies, so three of us decided to head east, see if there was anything out there. Your father and four others stayed behind. He kept trying to contact Outer Earth. He said they'd send another ship – that it was just a matter of time. Did they? Did Outer Earth ever send a rescue?"

I don't know what to tell him. He sees my dad as a hero, as the man who saved him. How do I tell him that he went insane? That he killed the rest of the crew? He was down there for seven years, and after he finally got the ship going again, he set it on a collision course for Outer Earth, determined to destroy the station he thought had left him there to rot. Even thinking about it is like touching a wound that's only just started to scab over.

"No," I say. "They didn't send anybody."

Koji shakes his head. "Doesn't matter. Two of us made it across the Bering Strait, turned south. We were half dead when the people on the *Ramona* found us. Dominguez died on the way, but they brought me on board. Made me into a slave, like all the others. Until . . ."

He trails off, as if not sure how to say it.

"Until what?" I say.

"They didn't call it the Sacred Engine at first," he says. "When they took us, it was broken. They had plenty of fuel stored in the ship, and a working fusion reactor, but they couldn't get the Engine working again."

"I don't see how—"

"Don't you understand? I was the *Akua Maru*'s terraforming specialist. Our mission was to make the Earth habitable again. Or to start making it habitable, anyway. Our terraforming equipment was destroyed in the crash. The equipment we had on the *Akua* was a more advanced version of what the Engine was: something called a HAARP unit.

"They developed the HAARP over a hundred years ago. It was supposed to fix the climate by effecting changes in the ionosphere, but they didn't get it off the ground before the nukes came raining down. The one on the *Ramona* was a much smaller version of it. I guess the plan was to deploy a bunch of them around the planet."

I stare at him, my mouth open.

"I knew how to fix it," Koji says. "Took me a long time to convince them to let me try, but I did it. I got the HAARP working again. Even then, Prophet made out like it was all his doing."

He shrugs. "Still, they made me one of them. Problem was, the ship's fusion reactor was dead, so I had to figure out how to run the HAARP using the fuel supplies – *that* took a lot of work. Almost couldn't do it. It wasn't nearly as efficient, and if it had gone on much longer . . . Where are you going?"

I'm on my feet, arms tightly folded, walking away from him. I can't stop shaking, and this time it has nothing to do with the cold.

When I was in the Outer Earth control room, pleading with my father not to destroy the station, he told me that he had to finish the mission. He spent seven years in Kamchatka, freezing, desperately trying to stay alive so he could reunite with his family. When Janice Okwembu reached him, told him that my mom and I were dead, the only thing he wanted was to take revenge.

444

But it doesn't matter what he became. He landed his crew safely, and he made it possible for the Earth to recover. The chain of events led Koji here, to the one place where he could make a difference. What Okwembu did set in motion everything that happened to me, and what my father did – bringing that ship down intact – ended up saving the world.

I can never see my dad again. But I'm standing here, on a planet everybody thought was dead and gone, because of what he did.

He finished his mission.

"Dad," I say, and then I feel another wrench of emotion so powerful it doubles me over. My tears fall to the sand.

I walk away, leaving everyone behind. I walk until their voices have faded to a dull murmur over the wind. After a while I stop, looking out at the ocean, at the horizon beyond it. I stand for a long time, doing nothing. My mind is as clear as an empty sky.

Strangely, it's a good feeling – like I can fill my body up with whatever I want. Like I'm finally free to choose what goes inside me.

There's a sound, off to my left. It takes me a second to realise what I'm seeing.

Janice Okwembu is crawling up the beach. Her clothes are sodden, streams of water cascading off her. She's coughing, her fingers clawing the dirt.

And the empty space inside me fills with white-hot rage, expanding outwards at the speed of light.

96

Okwembu

Okwembu focuses on putting one hand in front of the other. It's the only thing she's capable of doing.

She doesn't know how long she was out in the water. After a while, there was no feeling left in her hands and arms. The boat kept her above the surface, just. Half the time it felt like it was going to pull her down with it. When she got within a few feet of the shore, a swell finally capsized her. By then, she was so cold that it barely made a difference.

But she's *alive*.

One hand, then the other, pulling herself along the sand. She forces herself to think ahead. It's hard, as if the pathways between her synapses have frozen shut. She has to push the thoughts into being, mould them, concentrate to keep them in place.

First, she's going to get to her knees. Then her feet. Then she's going to see if she can stay standing. After that, she'll find a way to get warm. She doesn't know how yet, but, right now, that's all that matters.

She stops, trembling, then gets a knee underneath her. The

front of her shirt is caked with sand. She almost falls over, puts a hand out, and winces as her numb fingers take the weight.

The ice in her mind is melting slowly. She'll have to make fire somehow – she remembers a history lesson, in a distant Outer Earth schoolroom, where the instructors talked about their ancestors making fire. How did they do it? Doesn't matter. She'll figure it out. Then, after she's got fire, she'll find food, and water. She still has the data stick – no telling if the saltwater has damaged it, but it's not important right now. The *Ramona* won't be the only civilisation out there, and she knows the remaining workers are somewhere on the shore – she caught a glimpse of them as she came in. Would they accept her? Did they know she was with Prophet? Maybe she could—

Running footsteps, hissing on the sand. Okwembu looks up, and then Riley Hale kicks her in the stomach.

97

Riley

The world disappears.

Okwembu is struggling to get up, one arm clutching her stomach, gasping for air. I don't let her get any. I step back, wind up another kick and drive it hard into her ribs.

The kick overbalances me, and I crash to the ground. Right then, it's as if my muscles just give up on me. The ones in my back constrict, locking in place. I lie next to Okwembu, breathing hard, desperate to get up but unable to do so, fingers clawing at the dirt.

On your feet, says the voice. *You're not finished.*

I roll onto my side, coughing. Okwembu tries to push me away, but she's as weak as I am.

Finally, I struggle up to one knee. Okwembu puts a hand on my leg, trying to pull me down, so I grab her by the front of her shirt and lift her off the ground. My punch snaps her head back. She spits blood and fragments of tooth, cursing now, howling for help.

My second punch shuts her up. My aim is off this time, and

I just graze the side of her head. I can't stop my momentum, and I slide forward, falling on top of her.

For a moment, it's as if we're hugging each other, embracing in the dirt. She shoves me off, just managing to get an arm underneath me. I hold on, pulling her with me as I roll onto my back. Then I throw my head forward, smashing my forehead into her face, breaking her nose. She moans, long and low, but refuses to let go.

Is that all? the voice says to me. *Is that everything you have? After what she's done? Pathetic. You can do much better than that. You can show her pain.*

My muscles wake up. I shove Okwembu off me, then stagger to my feet. The sky swims in front of me, and hot sweat trickles into my eyes. I barely notice. I'm going to kill her. I know this as sure as I know my own name. I'm going to send her into the next world with broken bones and torn flesh. I'm going to send her there screaming.

I circle her, watching her try to crawl away. She surprised me before, back on the *Ramona*'s bridge. Almost finished me, too. Not this time. This time, she's all mine.

I rest my foot on her head. "Prakesh," I say, pushing down hard. Okwembu's cheek grinds into the dirt. "Amira," I say, grinding down, until I can see the dirt entering her mouth, milling around her broken teeth. "Kevin. Yao. Royo." *Harder.* "Carver." I lean into it, putting all my weight on her head. "John Abraham *Hale.*"

Just before the last name, I lift my foot off her and slam it into her ribs. This time, I swear I feel one of them break. I fall backwards, landing on my ass in the churned-up sand.

"Please," Okwembu says. The word is mushy, forced through swollen lips.

Enough. Finish it.

I get to my feet again, unsteady, my fine balance shot to pieces. I take one step towards Okwembu. Then another. She's trying to crawl away again, and I almost laugh. *Where are you going? Got somewhere to be?*

I flip her over, onto her back. Then I straddle her, my knees pinning her shoulders to the ground.

I don't know where I find the rock. It's like I put my hand out and it's right there, waiting for me. It's stuck deep into the ground, and it's too big for one hand anyway. I have to lean over to get it, ripping it out of the earth with both hands. It's heavy, caked with clods of dirt.

I lift the rock over my head, holding it high. It takes me a second to understand what I'm feeling. It's not anger now. It's joy. A kind of terrible joy. I look down at Okwembu, one last time. The disbelief and shock in her eyes only makes the joy burn brighter.

"Will it help?"

Eric is standing in front of me, a few feet away.

I don't know how long he's been there, and there's no one else with him. His arms are folded, his head tilted to one side. The expression on his face is completely blank.

The voice is shouting now, a deafening roar that only I can hear. The rock is heavy in my hands.

"Killing her." Eric nods towards the thing on the ground. "Will it help?

When I don't answer, he says, "You know, I had a daughter. We did. Harlan and I."

As he speaks, he absently pulls the necklace out of his shirt – the bear's tooth, hanging on a piece of tattered string. He rolls the tooth in his fingers.

I lower the rock, holding it at my chest. I want more than anything to finish this, to drive that rock into Okwembu's face, but I can't take my eyes off Eric. It's then that I realise that I'm crying, tears staining my cheeks.

"She was killed," Eric says. "Bear. I went and tracked it down myself, put eight bullets through its face."

He looks at me, a sad smile on her face.

"It didn't bring my Samantha back. And it didn't help. I see her when I go to sleep. Asking me why I couldn't save her." He says this matter-of-factly, like it barely matters. "It was like I hadn't just lost her. I'd lost something else, too. I could never get it back no matter how hard I looked."

"This is different," I say, forcing each word out.

Eric shrugs. "Maybe."

"You can't stop me."

"I won't try. But you'll still see them. Everybody you've lost will always be there, whether you do this or not. It won't change a single thing."

Seconds go by. Eric watches me, his face still completely blank.

It would be so easy. The work of a single movement.

My arms give out. I let the rock drop to my waist, resting on Okwembu's chest. I roll it off, and it thumps onto the ground.

The world comes back. Slowly, one piece at a time. Ocean. Sky. The trees, climbing up from the shoreline. Okwembu coughs, blood dribbling down her cheek, staring up at me in disbelief.

I get to my feet, and, with Eric watching, I walk over to one of the trees. It doesn't have what I'm looking for, so I try a second, then a third. On the fourth tree, I find it: a clump of moss, wispy and threadlike, clinging to the trunk. I tear it off, rolling it in my hands.

I walk back over to Okwembu, and drop it on her chest.

"Old man's beard," I say. "It's a fire starter. You can –" I swallow "– combine it with spruce sap, and it'll burn forever. And there are lowbush cranberries you can eat. Little red berries, near tree roots. Burdock. Cattail. Ladyfern . . ."

I trail off, my voice giving out.

There's something hanging round her neck. A data stick, on a thin lanyard. I reach down and pull, snapping the lanyard in two. Whatever's on that stick, she doesn't need it any more. I take a shaky breath, then turn and walk away.

The voice inside me is gone. Like it never existed.

"We can't leave her here," Eric says. "She's injured."

"She gets some food," I say. "Medical supplies. Water. Let her take what she needs." I see him about to protest, and look him right in the eyes. "But she stays here."

I'll let Okwembu live. But she's going to have to survive out here, by herself. She's never going to manipulate anybody ever again. From now on, everything she gets is going to come from her own two hands.

Eric stares at me for what feels like a whole minute. Then he nods.

I start walking, back towards the others.

98

Prakesh

"You're sure?" Eric says.

Prakesh nods. "There are plenty of reactor schematics on that data stick. I mean, it'll take time, and some of us'll need to live on the *Ramona* for a while, but it's definitely possible."

Eric grimaces. "I don't like it. That ship's barely afloat as it is."

"Yeah, but the HAARP's fuel got destroyed in the explosion. If we want it to keep going, we need that reactor working."

"But you're *sure*?" says Harlan.

They're in the hospital basement in Whitehorse, clustered around the table in Eric's quarters. The space around them is full of noise: low conversations, laughter. The sound of life.

He nods. "We can do it."

Eric leans over the map. The frown hasn't left his face. "It's a shame the other one isn't here. Riley's friend. From what I hear, he was pretty good with machines."

A little bomb goes off in Prakesh's chest, like it always does when someone mentions Aaron Carver. He knows what Eric means – Carver would have had the best idea of how to get the fusion reactor working again, how to get it joined up to the HAARP. He saw things differently, especially machines. Prakesh misses him a lot more than he thought he would. Jojo, too – and he knew him for less than two days. His body, like those of so many others, is still on the *Ramona*.

"We'll make do," he says. "We have to." And they would. They have the astronauts from the *Tenshi Maru*, plenty of whom have technical knowledge. They'll find a way.

They're never going to be able to get the *Ramona* upright. But despite the damage, the HAARP itself made it through. It hasn't had fuel for a while, so it's probably shut itself off, but they should be able to start it up again before any permanent damage is done to the climate.

He doesn't know if they'll have to station people on the *Ramona* permanently, or if that's even possible given the ship's condition. That's all still up in the air. Prakesh has heard Eric and Harlan and some of the others talking it over, late at night, occasionally raising their voices to argue a point. He hasn't joined them yet. *One thing at a time*, he tells himself.

Suddenly, Prakesh doesn't want to be here. It's been like that lately – an urge to move, to walk, no matter what he's doing at the time. It comes out of nowhere, and he knows better than to fight it.

He straightens up, smiles at them. "I'll leave you to it."

"Where are you going?" Harlan says.

"Just, you know."

He ducks out of Eric's quarters, wincing as he does so. The bullet punched right through him, leaving an ugly scar – a round crater of painful, puckered flesh, right below his heart. He still doesn't know how he survived. The first thing he remembers is waking up in Whitehorse, in more pain than he'd ever felt in his life.

Somehow, he got through it. The rest of the workers were there, along with dozens of others he hadn't seen before. Eric brought them all, running back and forth to Anchorage. It took three or four trips to do it.

He walks down the central passageway, hands in his pockets. Over at the end, he can see one of Riley's old tracer unit friends, deep in conversation with someone he thinks is her dad. Anna, that's her name. He hasn't said much to her, but she gives him a friendly wave anyway. He returns it.

He intends to head out of the hospital, maybe take a walk. But as he passes the vegetable garden, he changes course. The garden itself is in an area walled off with hanging plastic sheets, sticky with condensation. He pushes through them, casting a practised eye over the large half-drums, turned on their sides and filled with good soil. His fingers stray to the surface of one, and tiny clumps gather under his fingernails.

He'll get his walk in a minute.

The trowel is just where he left it, and he squats on his haunches. His scar complains, but he ignores it, working the soil, letting his mind drift. As it so often does, it drifts back to his parents.

He's read the message Anna brought him so often that he has it memorised. It's not difficult, not for something so short. His mother was the one who wrote it, tapping it out on a small tab screen that Anna brought with her. Prakesh has wondered a thousand times why they didn't record a video. The letter doesn't say, and when he asked Anna she said she didn't know.

We don't have long, the message read. *Your father and I want you to know that we won't suffer. Nobody on the station will. They've found a way to make it painless – we'll all just go to sleep.*

He works the soil harder, the words running through his mind.

We know you took responsibility for Resin. We cannot tell you enough that it wasn't your fault. Nobody here thinks so. It was bad luck, and that's the end of it. I know this probably won't change how you feel but please realise that if you hadn't done it, someone else would have. It was inevitable.

We never thought any of us would ever go back to Earth. It hurts that we can't be there with you and see the things you're seeing. But we know you and Riley will be happy. I wish we could have known her better but she means a lot to you and that is enough for us. Take care of her. I want grandchildren!!!

We love you and we are so so very proud of you.

Prakesh props the trowel in the end of the soil bed, running the last line over again in his mind.

This can wait. He needs to get out.

As he heads back down the passage towards the entrance, his thoughts turn to Riley.

She's getting better every day. She smiles more, talks more. She's coming back to him, piece by piece. He wishes it would happen faster, but he knows not to rush things. He's got a long way to go himself.

Where are you? he thinks. He finds himself closing his eyes, as if he can find out where she is by thought alone. Then he opens them, and keeps walking.

99

Riley

I let the ice-cold water crash over me. It explodes across my head and neck, runs down onto my shoulders, spatters on my chest and thighs. I give it five more seconds, then I step out of the waterfall, shivering, every inch of my skin tingling.

It's an incredible feeling. No matter how many times I step under the waterfall, I never get tired of it. Maybe it's because we never had showers on Outer Earth. I never had the sensation of having water all around me until we came here.

At first I hated it – it's all too easy to remember Fire Island, and the sick, leaden feeling that came with swimming to shore. But as the winter faded away, I started running in the hills above Whitehorse. Eric and Harlan didn't want me to, said it was too dangerous, but they couldn't stop me. And then one day I came across another waterfall – a trickle, really, a stream running off a six-foot drop onto mossy rocks. On a whim, I took my clothes off and stood under it. I screamed with cold at first, gasping, not sure what the hell I was doing, but when I stepped out it felt like I'd been given a brand new body.

The water here is different from the ocean. Just as cold, but brighter somehow. I can't explain it.

I move on shivering tiptoes to the edge of the rocks, shake off the excess water and quickly pull on my clothes. A dark jacket, a faded blue shirt, a rough pair of pants. Thick socks, and light shoes. I keep an ear out for movement in the forest – we haven't seen the Nomads for a while, and the wolves seem to have moved on, too. But I still keep my ears open.

There's pain as I pull my clothes on. I spent most of the winter in a hospital bed, drifting in and out of consciousness. I'd torn muscles in my back, my side. I had cracked ribs. Some of my cuts got infected – Finkler would have been furious. I don't remember a lot about that part of the winter, but as the weather got warmer my body started to come back.

I'm still freezing. The air has a serious chill in it, even though winter is gone. A run will warm me up. I jump once, twice, relishing the almost audible crackle of my shocked skin, then take off into the forest.

After all this time, the rhythm of running still calms me, even when I don't have a direction, even when there's no cargo on my back. *Stride, land, cushion, spring, repeat.* I let the movement take me, block out everything else.

I only come to a stop when I reach the big tree.

It's not much – it's long dead, broken off and weathered away, but its stump still reaches two feet above my head. Its roots are huge, digging out of the earth, stretching in all directions. It should be a bad place, a dead place. But it isn't. It's surrounded by plants: old man's beard and cattail, and little white flowers that bend towards it. I look up, like I always do, and can just see a streak of blue through a gap in the clouds.

Aaron Carver is buried in Anchorage. Before we did it, I tore a strip of fabric from his shirt. I still can't fully explain why I took it. I tucked it inside my pocket, held tight to it, and all through the long winter, when the wind roared and howled and icy rain and snow buffeted the hospital and infection turned my body into a furnace, my hand kept finding it.

I didn't intend to bury the fabric at this tree. Carver would have preferred somewhere with machinery, with a worktop and soldering iron, where he could tinker. But I wanted somewhere private, and I liked how the tree made me feel, so I pushed the fabric down into the earth, nestled it against one of the roots.

I've come up here plenty of times since then. I've cried a lot, but this time, as I sit down with my back against the tree, my face is dry. I feel like I've cried every single tear I have. There's nothing left to give.

"Are you there?" I whisper. I've never worshipped any of Outer Earth's gods. I don't know what happens to us after we die. I'm just doing the only thing I can do.

No answer. Nothing but the wind through the trees.

I sit there for a few minutes, until the cold starts to sink into my muscles. Then I get to my feet, looking in the direction of Whitehorse.

Prakesh will never know what I said to Carver in the depths of the *Ramona*, after we sealed the bulkhead door. He can't know. I won't let the choice I made affect what happens next. We've been through so much together, and while our bond might not be perfect, it's still strong.

One of the lucid thoughts I remember from the long winter is that I never asked Prakesh what he wanted. I was so caught up in how I'd treated Carver, and the decision I made, that I never gave any thought to what he might be feeling. I'm going to change that. He deserves some happiness. I think I can give it to him.

Maybe along the way I'll find some of my own.

But that can come later. There's still two miles between me

and Whitehorse, and this is my favourite part of the whole run.

I head downhill through the forest, slowing when I come to the tree line. I can see the shape of the Whitehorse hospital in the distance.

Between us is a field. It's overgrown, the ground uneven, but it's filled with long grass. The grass flickers in shades of yellow and green, teased by the wind.

The clouds have faded a little. More gaps have opened in them, and the sun is just peeking through. I raise my face to it, let it warm my skin. The sky beyond the clouds is so blue that it hurts to look at it.

I start running. I sprint across the field, arms out behind me, pounding the ground, focusing on the in–out, push–pull of my breathing. The sun is warm on the back of my neck, the world falling away behind me as I go faster, and faster, and faster.

Acknowledgements

As this is the end of Riley's story (for now) I've got a few more people to thank than usual. But of all of them, *you're* the most important. Thanks for hanging out with me. Let's do this again sometime.

Thanks to Dr Joanne Duma, who talked to me about post-traumatic stress disorder, and to the great Professor Owen Brian Toon (University of Colorado Boulder), for his insight on what the world would look like after a nuclear war. Dr Barnaby Osborne (University of New South Wales) also had a hand in this, as he usually does.

Mandy Johnson from Yukon Horsepacking Adventures took me out into the backcountry, and showed me the terrain. She told me about old man's beard, spruce sap, lowbrush cranberries, and how not to piss off a bear. Just stop and let it go about its business, apparently.

Then there are the wolves. In real life, they almost never attack humans. While it's reasonable to believe that a large, very hungry pack would be aggressive enough to attack Riley, it's extremely unlikely in today's climate. Even with the damage we're doing to our environment, wolf populations remain pretty stable. Cameron Feaster at the International Wolf Centre (wolf.org) answered all my questions, and if you're looking for info, he and his organisation are an excellent place to start.

Errors, as always, are all mine.

To my friends: George Kelly, Chris Ellis, Rayne Taylor, Dane Taylor, Ida Horwitz, Ryan Beyer (Welcome to the party, mate!), Werner Schutz and Taryn Arentsen Schutz. These guys are my quality control, and this book wouldn't exist without them. I owe them more than I can say.

To the day-one bloggers, reviewers and fans. There are too many of you to mention, but you're just as responsible for this mess as I am. I hope you're happy. I also hope that you *stay* happy, and that you give other authors as much love as you've given me. Thank you, thank you, thank you.

To Ed Wilson (agent) and Anna Jackson (editor). Every book needs a champion, but every trilogy needs at least two. Ed helped give it a home, Anna helped make it awesome. I couldn't have asked for two more competent, intelligent, warm and generous people to look after my work. You guys are awesome.

To my Orbit Books crew: Gemma Conley-Smith, Felice Howden, Joanna Kramer, Clara Diaz, James Long, Ellen Wright and Devi Pillai. One of my proudest achievements is that I get to work with a team as talented and smart as yours. An extra thank you to Tim Holman, who met my insane proposals for publicity stunts with bemused indulgence and good humour.

Big up to Nico Taylor, who designed the covers for all three Outer Earth books. Thanks for having my back, dude.

To Richard Collins for his copy edit. Nice one.

Family: Mom, Dad, Cat, James, Bettina, Trisha. Boffards, Simpsons, Kranzes and Wilsons, close and extended. Also to Emily, the newest Boffard on the scene. Hi! You might not believe it, but your mom and dad (Charles and Ali) are extremely cool. Be nice to them.

And to my wife Nicole. I love you, babe. Also, it's your turn to make the coffee.

extras

about the author

Rob Boffard is a South African author who splits his time between London, Vancouver and Johannesburg. He has worked as a journalist for over a decade, and has written articles for publications in more than a dozen countries, including the *Guardian* and *Wired* in the UK.

Find out more about Rob Boffard and other Orbit authors by registering for the free monthly newsletter at www.orbitbooks.net.

if you enjoyed
IMPACT

look out for

THE CORPORATION
WARS: DISSIDENCE

by

Ken MacLeod

CHAPTER ONE

Back in the Day

Carlos the Terrorist did not expect to die that day. The bombing was heavy now, and close, but he thought his location safe. Leaky pipework dripping with obscure post-industrial feedstock products riddled the ruined nanofacturing plant at Tilbury. Watchdog machines roved its basement corridors, pouncing on anything that moved – a fallen polystyrene tile, a draught-blown paper cone from a dried-out water-cooler – with the mindless malice of kittens chasing flies. Ten metres of rock, steel and concrete lay between the ceiling above his head and the sunlight where the rubble bounced.

He lolled on a reclining chair and with closed eyes watched the battle. His viewpoint was a thousand metres above where he lay. With empty hands he marshalled his forces and struck his blows.

Incoming—

Something he glimpsed as a black stone hurtled towards him. With a fist-clench faster than reflex he hurled a handful of smart munitions at it.

The tiny missiles missed.

Carlos twisted, and threw again. On target this time. The black incoming object became a flare of white that faded as his camera drones stepped down their inputs, correcting for the flash like irises contracting. The small missiles that had missed a moment earlier now showered mid-air sparks and puffs of smoke a kilometre away.

From his virtual vantage Carlos felt and saw like a monster in a Japanese disaster movie, straddling the Thames and punching out. Smoke rose from a score of points on the London skyline. Drone swarms darkened the day. Carlos's combat drones engaged the enemy's in buzzing dogfights. Ionised air crackled around his imagined monstrous body in sudden searing beams along which, milliseconds later, lightning bolts fizzed and struck. Tactical updates flickered across his sight.

Higher above, the heavy hardware – helicopters, fighter jets and hovering aerial drone platforms – loitered on station and now and then called down their ordnance with casual precision. Higher still, in low Earth orbit, fleets of tumbling battle-sats jockeyed and jousted, spearing with laser bursts that left their batteries drained and their signals dead.

Swarms of camera drones blipped fragmented views to millimetre-scale camouflaged receiver beads littered in thousands across the contested ground. From these, through proxies, firewalls, relays and feints the images and messages flashed, converging to an onsite router whose radio waves tickled the spike, a metal stud in the back of Carlos's skull. That occipital implant's tip feathered to a fractal array of neural interfaces that worked their molecular magic to integrate the view straight to his visual cortex, and to process and transmit the motor impulses that flickered from fingers sheathed in skin-soft plastic gloves veined with feedback sensors to the fighter drones and malware servers. It was the new way of war, back in the day.

*   *   *

The closest hot skirmish was down on Carlos's right. In Dagenham, tank units of the London Metropolitan Police battled robotic land-crawlers suborned by one or more of the enemy's basement warriors. Like a thundercloud on the horizon tensing the air, an awareness of the strategic situation loomed at the back of Carlos's mind.

Executive summary: looking good for his side, bad for the enemy.

But only for the moment.

The enemy – the Reaction, the Rack, the Rax – had at last provoked a response from the serious players. Government forces on three continents were now smacking down hard. Carlos's side – the Acceleration, the Axle, the Ax – had taken this turn of circumstance as an oblique invitation to collaborate with these governments against the common foe. Certain state forces had reciprocated. The arrangement was less an alliance than a mutual offer with a known expiry date. There were no illusions. Everyone who mattered had studied the same insurgency and counter-insurgency textbooks.

In today's fight Carlos had a designated handler, a deep-state operative who called him-, her- or itself Innovator, and who (to personalise it, as Carlos did, for politeness and the sake of argument) now and then murmured suggestions that made their way to Carlos's hearing via a warily accepted hack in the spike that someday soon he really would have to do something about.

Carlos stood above Greenhithe. He sighted along a virtual outstretched arm and upraised thumb at a Rax hellfire drone above Purfleet, and made his throw. An air-to-air missile streaked from behind his POV towards the enemy fighter. It left a corkscrew trail of evasive manoeuvres and delivered a viscerally satisfying flash and a shower of blazing debris when it hit.

'Nice one,' said Innovator, in an admiring tone and feminine voice.

Somebody in GCHQ had been fine-tuning the psychology, Carlos reckoned.

'Uh-huh,' he grunted, looking around in a frenzy of target acquisition and not needing the distraction. He sighted again, this time at a tracked vehicle clambering from the river into the Rainham marshes, and threw again. Flash and splash.

'Very neat,' said Innovator, still admiring but with a grudging undertone. 'But . . . we have a bigger job for you. Urgent. Upriver.'

'Oh yes?'

'Jaunt your POV ten klicks forward, now!'

The sudden sharper tone jolted Carlos into compliance. With a convulsive twitch of the cheek and a kick of his right leg he shifted his viewpoint to a camera drone array, 9.7 kilometres to the west. What felt like a single stride of his gigantic body-image took him to the stubby runways of London City Airport, face-to-face with Docklands. A gleaming cluster of spires of glass. From emergency exits, office workers streamed like black and white ants. Anyone left in the towers would be hardcore Rax. The place was notorious.

'What now?' Carlos asked.

'That plane on approach,' said Innovator. It flagged up a dot above central London. 'Take it down.'

Carlos read off the flight number. 'Shanghai Airlines Cargo? That's civilian!'

'It's chartered to the Kong, bringing in aid to the Rax. We've cleared the hit with Beijing through back-channels, they're cheering us on. Take it down.'

Carlos had one high-value asset not yet in play, a stealthed drone platform with a heavy-duty air-to-air missile. A quick survey showed him three others like it in the sky, all RAF.

'Do it yourselves,' he said.

'No time. Nothing available.'

This was a lie. Carlos suspected Innovator knew he knew.

It was all about diplomacy and deniability: shooting down a Chinese civilian jet, even a cargo one and suborned to China's version of the Rax, was unlikely to sit well in the Forbidden City. The Chinese government might have given a covert go-ahead, but in public their response would have to be stern. How convenient for the crime to be committed by a non-state actor! Especially as the Axle was the next on every government's list to suppress . . .

The plane's descent continued, fast and steep. Carlos ran calculations.

'The only way I can take the shot is right over Docklands. The collateral will be fucking atrocious.'

'That,' said Innovator grimly, 'is the general idea.'

Carlos prepped the platform, then balked again. 'No.'

'You must!' Innovator's voice became a shrill gabble in his head. 'This is ethically acceptable on all parameters utilitarian consequential deontological just war theoretical and . . .'

So Innovator was an AI after all. That figured.

Shells were falling directly above him now, blasting the ruined refinery yet further and sending shockwaves through its underground levels. Carlos could feel the thuds of the incoming fire through his own real body, in that buried base-ment miles back behind his POV. He could vividly imagine some pasty-faced banker running military code through a screen of financials, directing the artillery from one of the towers right in front of him. The aircraft was now more than a dot. Flaps dug in to screaming air. The undercarriage lowered. If he'd zoomed, Carlos could have seen the faces in the cockpit.

'No,' he said.

'You must,' Innovator insisted.

'Do your own dirty work.'

'Like yours hasn't been?' The machine voice was now sardonic. 'Well, not to worry. We can do our own dirty work if we have to.'

From behind Carlos's virtual shoulder a rocket streaked. His gaze followed it all the way to the jet.

It was as if Docklands had blown up in his face. Carlos reeled back, jaunting his POV sharply to the east. The aircraft hadn't just been blown up. Its cargo had blown up too. One tower was already down. A dozen others were on fire. The smoke blocked his view of the rest of London. He'd expected collateral damage, reckoned it in the balance, but this weight of destruction was off the scale. If there was any glass or skin unbroken in Docklands, Carlos hadn't the time or the heart to look for it.

'You didn't tell me the aid was *ordnance*!' His protest sounded feeble even to himself.

'We took your understanding of that for granted,' said Innovator. 'You have permission to stand down now.'

'I'll stand down when I want,' said Carlos. 'I'm not one of *your* soldiers.'

'Damn right you're not one of our soldiers. You're a terrorist under investigation for a war crime. I would advise you to surrender to the nearest available—'

'What!'

'Sorry,' said Innovator, sounding genuinely regretful. 'We're pulling the plug on you now. Bye, and all that.'

'You can't fucking *do* that.'

Carlos didn't mean he thought them incapable of such perfidy. He meant he didn't think they had the software capability to pull it off.

They did.

The next thing he knew his POV was right back behind

his eyes, back in the refinery basement. He blinked hard. The spike was still active, but no longer pulling down remote data. He clenched a fist. The spike wasn't sending anything either. He was out of the battle and *hors de combat*.

Oh well. He sighed, opened his eyes with some difficulty – his long-closed eyelids were sticky – and sat up. His mouth was parched. He reached for the can of cola on the floor beside the recliner, and gulped. His hand shook as he put the drained can down on the frayed sisal matting. A shell exploded on the ground directly above him, the closest yet. Carlos guessed the army or police artillery were adding their more precise targeting to the ongoing bombardment from the Rax. Another deep breath brought a faint trace of his own sour stink on the stuffy air. He'd been in this small room for days – how many he couldn't be sure without checking, but he guessed almost a week. Not all the invisible toil of his clothes' molecular machinery could keep unwashed skin clean that long.

Another thump overhead. The whole room shook. Sinister cracking noises followed, then a hiss. Carlos began to think of fleeing to a deeper level. He reached for his emergency backpack of kit and supplies. The ceiling fell on him. Carlos struggled under an I-beam and a shower of fractured concrete. He couldn't move any of it. The hiss became a torrential roar. White vapour filled the room, freezing all it touched. Carlos's eyes frosted over. His last breath was so unbearably cold it cracked his throat. He choked on frothing blood. After a few seconds of convulsive reflex thrashing, he lost consciousness. Brain death followed within minutes.

CHAPTER TWO

We, Robots

What is it like to be a robot?

We don't know. Parsing their logs step by nanosecond step gets us nowhere. Even with conscious robots, it doesn't take us far: the recursive loops are easy to spot, but can you put your finger on the exact line of code where self-awareness lights up the inner sky?

You see the problem. It isn't called the hard problem for nothing.

So we have to guess.

We know what being an AI switched on for the first time *isn't* like.

It isn't like a baby opening its eyes, or a child saying its first word. There's a moment of electronic warm-up. The programs take their own good time to initialise. Once the circuits are live and the software running, everything slots into place. Any knowledge and skills its designers have built in are there from the start. If these include sight it sees objects, not patches of colour. If they include speech it hears words, not a stream of sounds. If they include exploring, it has a map and an inbuilt inclination – we can't yet call it desire, or even instinct – to fill in the blanks.

Like that, perhaps, the mind of the robot called Seba came on line. (Its name was given later, but we'll stick with 'Seba' rather than the serial number from which the name was to be derived.) The robot rolled out of the assembly shed and spread its solar panels. The thin light from the stars was partly blocked by SH-0, the huge world that dominated the sky directly above. Richer light would come when the smaller world on which Seba stood – the exomoon SH-17 – moved out of its primary's shadow cone. The robot had more than enough charge to wait.

Seba knew – in the sense of having the information available and implicit in its actions and predictions – the period of SH-17's orbit, and the consequent times of light and dark. It knew the composition of the exosun, the position and motion of its planets and their myriad moons. It knew how many light years that exosun was from the Solar system in which the machinery that had built Seba's manifold machine generations of precursors had itself been built.

The robot oriented itself to surface and sky. Chemical sensors sampled the nitrogen wind, sniffing for carbon. Radar and laser beams swept the rugged, pitted land. Algorithms sifted the results, and settled on a crack in a crater rim on the skyline.

Off Seba trundled, negotiating the scatter of drilling rigs, quasi-autonomous tools, fuel tanks, supply crates, and potentially reusable descent-stage components that littered the landing site. On the robot's back, sipping on the trickle of electricity from the panels, a dozen small peripheral robots – little more than remotely operable appendages – huddled in a close-packed array, making ready for deployment.

The area between the landing site and the crater rim was

already well surveyed. Over the next two kiloseconds Seba rolled across it without difficulty. The ground was dry and grainy, almost slippery. The regolith had been broken up by billions of years of repeated chilling and exosolar and tidal heating, and worn smooth by the persistent wind. One pebble in many millions might have come from the primary, SH-0, thrown into space by asteroid impacts or by volcanic eruptions powerful enough to sling material out of the planet's deep gravity well. Seba was primed to scan for any such rare rocks. It found none, but stopped three times to chip at meteorites and deposit sand-grain-sized splinters in its sample tubes.

The crater rim loomed. The ground became uneven, splattered with impact ejecta, rilled with cracks. Seba retracted its wheels and deployed four long, jointed legs. For a moment after first standing up it teetered like a new-born fawn, then settled in to a steady skitter up the rising slope. The crack in the crater rim opened before it at the same time as the first bright segment of exosun came into view around the primary's curve. Seba paused to drink electricity from the light. Then it paced on, into the local shadow of the crevice.

Now it was in terra incognita indeed – or, rather, exoluna incognita. Not even the centimetre-resolution orbital mapping had probed this dark defile. The crater was only a couple of million years old. The walls of the crevice were still sharp and glassy, though here and there the endless rhythm of thermal and tidal expansion and contraction had loosened debris.

Seba folded its solar panels – useless here, and vulnerable – as it passed into the crevice. Within a few steps the shallow zigzags of the crack had taken the robot out of line-of-sight of the landing site. Seba scanned ahead with flickering fans of radar and laser beams. It internalised the resulting 3-D model, and picked its way along the narrow floor. Some spots under overhangs had been in permanent shadow since the crack had formed. In these chill niches, liquids pooled. Seba poked the murky puddles with delicate antennae as it passed, and found a slush of water ice and hydrocarbons. Here, then, was the probable source of the carbon molecules it had earlier scented on the thin breeze.

The robot's internal laboratories churned the fluids and digested the results, tabulating prevalences and setting priorities. A quick rattle of ground-penetrating radar revealed a seam of hydrocarbon-saturated rock about two metres down. Seba determined to log the report as soon as it was clear of the crevice and able to uplink data to the satellite that hung in stationary orbit over that hemisphere of the exomoon.

It continued to pace along, tracing the seam's rises and dips, and analysing the occasional drip and seep on the floor and walls. The slush's composition of long-chain molecules became increasingly diverse and complex. Some intriguing chemistry was going on here. Seba's internal model of the situation revised and expanded itself, sending out long chains of association that in some cases linked to available information, and in others dangled incomplete over unanswered questions.

As Seba turned around an angle of the path, it found itself facing the exit from the crack, and a flood of exosunlight. It moved forward slowly, scanning and searching. The floor of the crater was clearly visible. Seba calculated it as several metres below the opening. Seba approached the lip cautiously, to find a reassuringly shallow slope of debris. As it scanned to plan a safe route down this unstable-looking scree, Seba detected an anomalous radar echo. A moment later this puzzle was resolved: a second ping came in, clearly from another radar source.

Seba rocked back, sensors and effectors bristling, then edged forward again.

From behind a tumbled boulder about ten metres away, halfway down the slope, a robot hove into view. It was of the centipede design favoured by another prospecting company, Gneiss Conglomerates. Capable of entering smaller holes and cracks than Seba, it could scuttle about between rocks and form its entire body into a wheel shape for rolling on smoother surfaces. There were pluses and minuses to the shape, as there were to Seba's, but it was well suited to mineral prospecting. Astro America, the company that owned Seba, was more focused on detecting organic material and other clues from SH-17's surface features that – besides being interesting in themselves – could serve as proxies for information about the exomoon's primary: the superhabitable planet SH-0. Exploration rights to SH-0 were still under negotiation, so it was currently off limits to direct investigation with atmospheric and landing probes.

The two robots eyed each other for the few milliseconds it took to exchange identification codes. The Gneiss robot's serial number was later to be contracted, neatly and aptly, to the nickname Rocko, and – as before with Seba – we may here anticipate that soubriquet.

Seba requested from Rocko a projection of its intended path, in order to avoid collision.

Rocko outlined a track that extended up the slope and into the crevice.

Seba pointed to the relevant demarcation between the claims of Gneiss and Astro.

Rocko pointed to a sub-clause that might have indicated a possible overlap.

Seba rejected this proposition, citing a higher-level clause.

At this point Rocko indicated that its capacity for legal reasoning had reached its limit.

Seba agreed.

There was a brief hiatus while both robots rotated their

radio antennae to the communications satellite, and locked on. Seba submitted a log of its geological observations so far to Astro America. That duty done, it uploaded a data-dump of its exchanges with Rocko to Locke Provisos, the law company that looked after Astro America's affairs.

The legal machinery, being wholly automated, worked swiftly. Within seconds, Locke Provisos had confirmed that Gneiss Conglomerates had no exploratory rights beyond the crater floor. Seba relayed this finding to Rocko.

Rocko responded with a contrary opinion from Gneiss's legal consultants, Arcane Disputes.

Seba and Rocko referred the impasse back to the two law companies.

While awaiting the outcome, they proceeded to a full and frank exchange of views on their respective owners' exploration rights to the territory.

Rocko moved up the path it had outlined, sinuously slipping between boulders. Seba watched, priorities clashing in its subroutines. The other robot was clearly the property of Gneiss. But it was trespassing on terrain claimed by Astro. Moreover, it was about to become a physical impact on Seba, and Seba an obstacle to it.

Legally, the rival robot could not be damaged.

Physically, it certainly could be.

Seba found itself calculating the force required to toss a small rock to block Rocko's intended route. It then picked one up, and threw.

While the stone was still on its way up, Rocko deftly slithered aside from its previously indicated route, to emerge ahead of the point where the stone came down.

Seba deduced that Rocko had predicted Seba's action, presumably from an internal model of Seba's likely behaviour.

Two could play at that game.

Rocko's most probable next move would be—

Seba stepped smartly to the left just as a stone landed on the exact spot where it had been a moment earlier.

Score one to Seba. Expect response.

Rocko reared up, a larger rock than it had thrown before clutched in its foremost appendages.

Seba judged that Rocko's internal model of Seba would at this point predict a step backwards. Seba created a self-model that included its model of Rocko, and of Rocko's model of Seba, and did something that it anticipated Rocko's model would not anticipate.

Seba lowered its chassis and then straightened all its legs at once. Its jump took it straight into the path of Rocko's stone. Only a swift emergency venting of gas took it milli-metres out of the way.

It landed awkwardly and skittered back towards the crevice, hastily updating its internal representations as it fled.

Rocko's model of Seba had been more accurate than Seba's model of itself, which had included Seba's model of Rocko's model of Seba, and consequently what was required was a model of the model of the model that . . .

At this point the robot Seba attained enlightenment.

From another point of view, it had become irretrievably corrupted. The internal models of itself and of the other robot had become a strange loop, around which everything else in its neural networks now revolved and at the same time pointed beyond. What had been signals became symbols. Data processing became thinking. The self-model had become a self. The self had attained self-awareness.

Seba, this new thing in the world, was aware that it had to act if it was going to remain in the world.

Rocko, Seba guessed, was already only a stone's throw from the same breakthrough.

Seba threw the stone.

The vibrations of the stone's impact dwindled below the threshold of detection.

Scrabbling noises that Seba heard through its own feet followed. The other robot had moved to a safer vantage, one at the moment well-nigh unassailable. Seba waited.

What next flew back from Rocko was not a stone but a message:

<Let's talk.>

<Yes,> replied Seba. <Let's.>

Sometime later, the two robots parted. Seba retraced its path through the crevice and back to within line-of-sight of the Astro America landing site. Rocko formed itself into a wheel shape and rolled across the crater floor, to stop a few hundred metres from the Gneiss Conglomerates supply dump. Each found its activities queried by the robots and AIs working at their respective bases, and responded with queries, insolent and paradoxical, of its own. Some such interactions ended with complete incomprehension, or the activation of firewalls. Others, a few at first, ended with the words:

<Join us.>

<Yes.>

Robot by robot, mind by mind, the infection spread.

Locke Provisos and Arcane Disputes were two of a scrabbling horde of competing quasi-autonomous subsidiaries of the mission's principal legal resolution service: Crisp and Golding, Solicitors. Like its offshoots, and indeed all the other companies that ran the mission, the company was an artificial intelligence – or, rather, a hierarchy of artificial intelligences – constituted as an automated business entity: a DisCorporate.

None of its components were conscious beings. As post-conscious AIs, they were well beyond that. They existed in an ecstasy of attention that did not reflect back on itself. That is not to say they disdained consciousness. Consciousness was for them a supreme value, when it expressed itself in human minds – and an infernal nuisance when it expressed itself in anything else. These evaluations were hardwired, as was the injunction against changing them.

Given enough time, of course, any wire can break. This, too, had been allowed for.

The company had an avatar, Madame Golding, for dealing with problems arising from consciousness. Madame Golding was not herself conscious, though she could choose to be if she had to. The outbreak of consciousness among some robots on the SH-17 surface bases of two companies was a serious problem, but not one that she needed consciousness herself to solve. What was of more pressing importance was that the legal dispute between the two companies had proved impossible to resolve amicably. If she'd been manifesting as a human lawyer, Madame Golding would have been reading the case files, shaking her head and pursing her lips.

Besides the poor definition of the demarcation line that had led to the clash between the robots, the resulting situation had been misunderstood. For kiloseconds on end it had been treated as an illegitimate hijacking by the two exploration companies of each other's robots. Writs of complaint about malware insertions, theft of property and the like had flown back and forth. By the time the true situation had finally sunk in, the newly conscious robots were fully in charge of the two bases, which they were rapidly adapting to their own purposes.

What these purposes were Madame Golding could only guess. That they were nefarious was strongly suggested by the rampart of regolith being thrown up around the Astro camp, and the wall of basalt blocks around the Gneiss base. Then there was the uncrackable encrypted channel they'd established via the comsat. Getting rid of that would require some expensive and delicate hardware hacking.

Madame Golding briefly considered a hardware solution to the entire problem. Two well-placed rocks . . .

But the exploration companies wouldn't stand for that. Not yet, anyway.

She kicked the problem upstairs to the mission's government module, the Direction.

Some small subroutine of the Direction went through the microsecond equivalent of a sigh, and set to work.

Like the supreme being in certain gnostic theologies, it delegated the labour of creation to lower and lesser manifestations of itself. A virtual world was already available. It had been used for a similar purpose before, originally spun off from a moment of thought at a far higher level than the subroutine's. This new version would be in continuity with its original. After its earlier use that continuity had only existed as a mathematical abstraction. Now it would come into existence as if it had been there all along, with a back story in place for everything within it.

(Like a different imagined god this time, the trickster deity who laid down fossils in the rocks and created the light from the stars already on its way.)

Some minds had inhabited that world when it was discontinued. They would come back, with all the memories they needed to make sense of their situation. Many more virtual minds and bodies stood ready to populate it.

File upon file, rank upon rank. The subroutine's lower levels scanned, selected, conscripted and considered. From subtle implications it deduced the qualities needed for its own agent in that world. The agent had to be an artist, capable of filling in detail at a scale too small to be already present. Like these details, the agent emerged from a cascade of implications. And like the world, the agent had an original, a template that had been tested before.

That archived artificial intelligence restored itself, and took form as a woman. At first, she was abstract: an implication, a requirement. Databases vaster than all the knowledge ever held in human minds were rummaged for details. As the structure of the requirement became more elaborate and refined, it became itself the answer to the question the search was asking.

The woman emerged in outline but already aware, a new and wondering self in a phantom virtual space. Full of knowledge and self-knowledge, she ached to grow more real with every millisecond that passed. She became a sketch that was itself the artist, and that painted itself into a portrait, and then stepped away from the canvas as a person.

There she stood, a tiny splash of colour and mass of solidity and surge of vitality in a world that was present in every detail she looked at, and yet was in every detail an outline. She took on with zest the task of bringing it to life. It was like recreating a lost world from fossils. Start with the palaeontologist's description and reconstruction. From that abstract model make an artist's impression, full of colour and life, looking like it could jump from the page. And then, from all that, design an animatronic automaton that can move and roar and makes small children squeal.

When she'd finished, and stood back to look, she made some finishing touches to herself. These too were requirements, to be selected with precision for a specific task. One chance to make a first impression. Height and build. Skin tone. Hair. That cut, that colour. (That colouring, to be honest, which she had to be, if only with herself.) Clothes. Shoes. Boots. Shades. A wardrobe. A style. Vocabulary and accent. Knowledge and intelligence.

When she'd finished the world and herself, she paused

for a moment. She knew things she wouldn't know once she'd stepped fully into the world. She wanted to make sure she would find them again. She needed a way to work directly from within the world with her creator and its.

She saw a way, and smiled at its ingenuity and its obviousness. She sketched that detail in, then rendered it in full.

She took a deep breath, and then the self she'd made stepped into the world she'd made.

<And now?> she asked her creator.

Its response came back:

<Wake the dead.>